Lost

Daughters

Also by J. M. Redmann

The Intersection of Law and Desire: A Mystery

Lost

Daughters

J. M. Redmann

W. W. Norton & Company

New York   London

Copyright © 1999 by J. M. Redmann

First Edition

For information about permission to reproduce selections from this book write
to Permissions, W. W. Norton & Company, Inc. 500 Fifth Avenue,
New York, NY 10110

The text of this book is composed in Fairfield Light
with the display set in Rotis Semi Sans.
Desktop composition by Alice Bennet Dates
Manufacturing by Quebecor Printing, Fairfield, Inc.
Book design by Chris Welch

Library of Congress Cataloging-in-Publication Data
Redmann, J. M. (Jean M.), 1955–
Lost Daughters / J. M. Redmann.
p.   cm.
ISBN 0-393-04028-3
I. Title.
PS3568.E3617L67   1999
813'.54—dc21   99-10422
CIP

W. W. Norton & Company, Inc. 500 Fifth Avenue, New York, N. Y. 10110
http://www.wwnorton.com

W. W. Norton & Company Ltd., 10 Coptic Street, London WC1A 1PU

1 2 3 4 5 6 7 8 9 0

Acknowledgments

Sometimes writing seems to be an activity in which my only human contact is to rather peevishly mutter, "I'm writing, leave me alone." But, were that the case, then my writing would be bound by the deficiencies of my imagination and the gaps in my knowledge. Fortunately for me, I have an almost perfect coterie of friends and associates—honest and warm—who helped with the birthing of this book. Karl Ezkovich, aka Carol Escapade, for his comments and for graciously letting me steal from his real life; Kathryn Kirkhart, for her advice and for catching all those pesky typos; Kathleen M. Adams, for learning to truly understand what I meant by, "I hate titles"; Linnea Due, for being a writing buddy and pointing out that I don't know the days of the week; Lori Morgan, for her thoughtful comments and the still unused invite to Seattle—I'll get there yet.

Many thanks to my editor, Jill Bialosky, for the kind and gentle pushes she gave me in the right writing direction, and also her assistant, Eve Grubin.

And last, and most certainly not least, my fabulous agent, Victoria Sanders.

Lost

Daughters

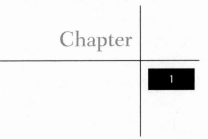

Chapter

1

Where was she? I wondered, as I finished arranging the cheese platter.

The doorbell rang.

It was Joanne Ranson, a longtime friend, briefly lover, and sergeant in the New Orleans Police Department.

Cordelia and I were giving a party tonight. I had just gotten back from some last-minute errands and I was beginning to worry about where she was.

"Believe it or not, Alex is working late and I'm the one on time. She's at some stupid press conference with the mayor and she can't get away." Alex was Joanne's lover. Her day job was being a political flunky, though she wouldn't have described it that way. Her polite terms were liaison for culture and arts for city hall. She was good enough at her job to have survived more than one administration.

As I closed the door behind Joanne, I said, "She's not the only one. Cordelia is working late, too." I hoped it was just working late.

"I'm the first one here? Am I that early? I came here directly from work."

"No, you're just not as fashionably late as everybody else."

"Three years. How does it feel?" Joanne wasn't just asking a throwaway question; she could be far too discerning at probing my soft spots and weak thoughts.

"I don't know. How do you feel about that?" I deflected her.

"Asked you first," she rejoined easily.

"I don't know," I repeated, groping for an answer. "Sometimes it's wonderful and . . . sometimes it's terrifying. I feel I have so much to lose. Is she all right? Does she still love me? What's wrong with her that she loves me?"

Joanne shook her head at that, but said nothing.

"Sometimes . . ." Then I paused, wondering if I could be this honest even with Joanne. She and Alex have had their difficulties, I reminded myself. ". . . I feel caught. Cordelia gets in her let's-clean-the-house-now mode and I'm in my chill-out-and-read-something-mindless state. She goes into the kitchen and bangs pots around just so I'll know she's working and I'm not. And, of course, I don't go help her, just to make the point that we're not going to do everything on her schedule just because she's a big important doctor and I'm a shiftless PI. And at some point, she curses in an un-Cordelia-like way and she mutters something like, 'This would be a hell of a lot easier if I had some help.' And I . . . well, I think I wouldn't have to put up with this shit if I lived alone."

"Last night?" Joanne asked with her usual annoying discernment.

"I told her I'd clean up today and not to worry about it. But . . . oh, hell." I decided that I didn't want to do the blow-by-blow, particularly as it ended with me yelling at her that she could forget about any anniversary party because we'd only make it to two years and three hundred and sixty-three days as far as I was concerned, before I stomped out in righteous indignation. And realized that I had no place to go, so I ended up sitting on the porch in indignation that rapidly became less and less righteous.

"I gather things worked out. Or is this a divorce party?"

"No, we sort of worked things out." At least I thought so, but where was she? I had waited on the porch until the lights went out and Cordelia had gone to bed before I came back in. The kitchen and downstairs bathroom were both clean. She'd left a note on the kitchen counter, asking if I could please do the bathroom upstairs after my morning shower and a list of things that needed to be picked up. The sight of her scribbled handwriting caught me in a flux of emotions: I was both annoyed and relieved that she assumed we were still together and that we would be celebrating our third anniversary tomorrow. I was also abashed at my behavior, though not abashed enough to completely overcome my irritation.

Cordelia had still been awake when I'd come upstairs.

"Do you still love me?" I asked as I slid under the covers.

"Of course I do," Cordelia answered, with just the right amount of vehemence to reassure me. "Do you still love me?" she asked softly.

"Yes, I do," I said realizing that she, too, needed reassurance. "Although there are times . . . times when your . . . work ethic is very much in evidence."

"An interesting way to put it. But it's not my fault. I have a Yankee mother."

"At least you have one."

Cordelia was silent for a moment. "I can't win that competition. I'm sorry your mother left when you were five, but I can't change that." She sighed softly, then said, "I'm too tired for this." She turned on her side, facing away from me.

I lay stiffly on my back, staring at the ceiling, wondering what to do next. I considered getting up and going downstairs and doing something like vacuuming just so she would know what it felt like to be disturbed by someone else's industriousness. Some thinking part of my brain vetoed that. Finally, that pesky thinking part of my brain pointed out that I could either keep this going or I could end it. I decided that all the gossips of New Orleans who predicted that a former bayou slut like me could never stay in a relationship with a nice uptown girl like Cordelia would get too much enjoyment if we broke up on the eve of our third anniversary.

I turned on my side and curled around Cordelia. "I'm sorry," I murmured in her ear.

She responded to my touch and apology, taking my hand in both of hers. "I'm sorry you don't have a mother. But I can't—"

"No, you can't fix that," I had finished for her. "You're not my mother, you can't be."

"But I can be your lover," she had answered.

"Hey, you going to come to your own party?" Joanne broke into my thoughts.

"Yeah, I am," I replied. "I was just thinking . . . thinking that love is wonderful and exasperating."

Joanne gave a short laugh, then said, "Yes, it is. So what is it right now? Wonderful or exasperating?"

"Both." Then I echoed her laugh. "Why is everything so complicated?"

"Because it just is," Joanne answered easily.

The doorbell rang.

"More guests. You won't be the only one," I told Joanne as I went to answer the door.

Danny and Elly entered. Danny and I had been friends for a

long time, meeting in college, though we had actually grown up in the same small town. The same small segregated town. We had briefly been lovers after college. She was now an assistant district attorney for Orleans Parish. Elly was her lover; they had been together over five years. She was a nurse and worked with Cordelia at the clinic.

We did the usual round of hugs and greetings, and Joanne and I launched into explanations of where our lovers were.

The doorbell again sounded and this time I ushered in my cousin Torbin and his lover Andy.

"We've been across the street watching, waiting until a reasonable number of guests arrived. Not too early, nor too late," Torbin said. He and Andy weren't loitering. They lived in the neighborhood.

Torbin and I were first cousins, though, of course, we looked nothing alike since we're not really related. He is the classic tall blond. It had taken us a while to clue in that we were both gay, but once we realized that we shared the common bond of coming from the same family and being queer, we had become close friends and allies. Torbin had many talents, but his most visible one was being a drag star in the Quarter. We both enjoyed immensely how much it annoyed our family, particularly my Aunt Greta. Andy, seemingly Torbin's opposite, was dark, bookish, and a self-described computer nerd.

The phone rang. It was Cordelia. "I'm at the morgue."

"But it's our anniversary," I blurted out, before the thinking part of my brain engaged. "Why are you at the morgue?"

"They want me to ID a body. Her pants pocket had an appointment card with my name on it," Cordelia replied.

"How long will you be?"

"I don't know, not too long, I hope. I don't like to look at dead bodies. Particularly ones . . ." she trailed off.

Masochist that I was, I left an expectant silence for her to fill.

"Particularly ones that haven't been discovered for a week or so. I'll have to shower and change before I can enjoy myself. They're calling me. Got to go." Cordelia hung up.

I put the phone down, wondering why whomever couldn't have found the body a day or so earlier. We would have been happier all around. Cordelia and the morgue people wouldn't have had to deal with such a decomposed body and I wouldn't have had our third anniversary celebration disrupted.

"She's at the morgue," I told the assembled guests.

"Stood up on your third anniversary. How tacky," was Torbin's comment.

"I don't think it was her idea."

"The morgue? I hope not. Unless the fair Cordelia is a good deal kinkier than we ever suspected."

"Torbin . . ." I cautioned, even though Cordelia wasn't around to be embarrassed by his speculation on her sex life.

"As long as she doesn't ask you just to lay there and play dead, you needn't worry," he continued.

I left Torbin to enjoy his wit, while I fulfilled my hostess duties. Just as I had gotten a libation of some sort in everyone's hands and the cheese and veggie trays placed around the room, the doorbell again chimed.

I opened the door to Cordelia's cousin Karen. She was, as usual, impeccably dressed, just casual enough to fit in. Cordelia had never been comfortable coming from an old, moneyed New Orleans family. Karen had no such qualms. She liked money and the things that it could buy. She was still struggling with the things it couldn't buy. Despite both being lesbian, she and Cordelia hadn't been close in the way Torbin and I were. Only in the last few years had they done more than see each other at the obligatory family events. Karen had recently become the chair of the fund development committee for Cordelia's clinic. She was good at being greedy and she had discovered how uplifting it was to be greedy on someone else's behalf.

"Where's Cordelia?" she asked, not seeing her cousin. "Not hiding in the kitchen?"

"No, she got held up with work." I forwent the morgue explanation. Karen had problems with pimples, let alone dead bodies.

She rolled her eyes, not able to understand having the kind of work that required missing a party. Karen took advantage of Cordelia's absence to give me a quick kiss on the lips. When I'd first met Karen several years ago (before I met Cordelia) we'd had a brief—more than brief, one-night—fling. Karen still had a bit of a crush on me.

Cordelia was a great believer in the virtues of monogamy and she didn't like being reminded that I had a past that was anything but.

"She'll be here pretty soon," I told Karen. I didn't return her kiss, particularly when I caught sight of the next guest.

Lindsey McNeil was making her way across the lawn. The cane she had to use was the only evidence of the damage done by a car wreck years ago.

Cordelia had to navigate through the women that I'd slept with. Given the size of the lesbian community in New Orleans and how active I'd been, there was no avoiding it. Lindsey was the only one of Cordelia's ex-lovers that I had to encounter. It didn't help that Lindsey was a strikingly beautiful women, a highly respected psychiatrist, and currently single. It was even less helpful that she and I had had a brief affair. I'd tripped down jealousy lane more than once because of Lindsey. She and Cordelia remained friends. My jealousy journey wasn't helped any by Lindsey working one afternoon a week at the clinic. I had made it a point to start showing up on that day to meet Cordelia after work, until I realized how ridiculous I looked. Then I purposely stayed away, until I hit the ridiculous mark in the other direction.

"Hello, Micky," she said. "Congratulations on three years. Hi, Karen." She nodded in her direction.

Karen took a moment before recognizing her. "Lindsey? I thought you'd gone to Europe."

"I did. I came back." Lindsey leaned in to kiss my cheek, her hand on my shoulder to steady herself.

"Come on in," I said, wanting to get back into the living room with other guests to serve as chaperones. I ushered them in with a quick, "What would you like to drink?" That gave me an excuse to busy myself at the bar.

Then the doorbell rang again and I let in Hutch and Millie. Good, a safe straight couple. Hutch Mackenzie was Joanne's partner. He was Saint-sized—the football sinners, not the canonized variety. He and Millie Donalto had been living together for a number of years and had always put off marriage for "just a few more years of sin," as Millie put it. She was a nurse and also worked at the clinic with Cordelia and Elly.

Their arrival required another round of explanations for Cordelia's absence.

"I'd die if I went to the morgue," was Karen's comment.

"That's one sure way to get there," Lindsey added.

Cordelia's presence at the morgue prompted Danny, Joanne, and Hutch to reminisce on their many trips there. With their medical backgrounds, Elly, Millie, and Lindsey found nothing remiss in descriptions of dead bodies and lost brains. However, Karen looked like the wine (fairly good wine, I might add) she was drinking was rancid vinegar.

"Good thing you're not serving steak tartar," Torbin commented.

Hutch didn't notice the underlying suggestion in Torbin's comment and continued, "It had been over three weeks before they found that body. Let me tell you, three weeks off in the swamps of New Orleans East isn't a pretty sight. And a water moccasin was curled up on his chest, cozy as could be, like a boy and his puppy. It wasn't the body that was the problem, it was that damn snake."

"A live snake can do more harm than a dead body," Joanne pointed out.

"Yeah, so there's this putrid, stinking, rotting corpse"—that sent Karen to the kitchen—"with one huge snake coiled on top of it and four big policemen and the hunter that found him, and we're all just looking at each other."

"Vegetables. We're going to eat vegetables for the next week. Nothing resembling meat," Torbin muttered.

"No tomatoes or red peppers," I whispered back at him.

"Perhaps we should suspend the gross body competition until later. It seems not all of us are enjoying these tales," Lindsey said, earning a few points in the sensitive shrink department.

The door opened and Cordelia entered. It was an understatement to say she didn't look like she'd had a good time at the morgue. I was glad that she had just missed walking into a discussion about dead, putrid, rotting bodies.

"Hi, sorry I'm late," she said. Her face was tired and haggard-looking, as if it had already been a long day before viewing a dead body was added to it. She put up her hands to forestall the chorus of greetings and questions. "I'll be social in a bit. Right now I've got to change." She headed upstairs to our bedroom.

I started to follow her, but the doorbell rang again and I was the only host in the vicinity. I let in Alex, Joanne's lover.

"You know it's a sad day when doctors, lawyers, cops, and drag queens can get to a party on time, but political flunkies can't," Alex said as she entered. She sighed and put her briefcase down next to the door. "Where's your better half?" she asked me.

"Changing. She just got here."

"Good, so I'm not so late."

"No, you're late. She was just late, too. Your much better half is trading dead body stories with Danny and Hutch."

"Why I love her—tales of dead bodies and always hugging around the gun."

"Not to mention the handcuffs."

"Micky, I'm not that kind of girl." Alex pretended to be shocked.

I heard the shower upstairs come on. I didn't think Cordelia needed me checking on her there. "So can I borrow them sometime?" I bantered.

"Cordelia's not that kind of girl, either," Alex returned in kind. She and Cordelia had been friends for a long time. Alex claimed that they were born in the same hospital, but Cordelia amended it to meeting in junior high.

"How do you know? Ever try to cuff her?" Alex had slotted Cordelia into the "nice" girl category a long time ago and left her there. I tried not to let her assumptions lie peacefully.

"No, I haven't. But I do know Cordelia fairly well and I doubt that she's chained up every night."

"Naw, it gets boring after awhile," I told Alex.

"What are you two going on about?" Joanne asked as she joined us.

"Your handcuffs and what you do with them off-duty," I answered.

"Flirting again?" Joanne asked Alex.

"No," Alex replied. "Micky's just trying to convince me that she plays with handcuffs in the boudoir."

"I'm sure Micky has," Joanne said. Her slight emphasis on my name was enough to let me know that she didn't like the length of time Alex was spending with me.

"That's right, Micky's done anything and everything," I retorted. "Let me go see how Cordelia is." I turned away from them.

I heard Alex's "Joanne!" but nothing after that.

Alex and I had been bantering, Joanne read it as flirting, and she didn't want to watch her lover flirt with another woman. But I didn't like being reminded that three years with one woman was a major distinction for me.

Cordelia was just coming out of the shower when I got upstairs. She still had a bit of a tired and distracted look, as if caught in the past events of the day.

"Hi," she said. "Thanks for keeping things going."

"No problem. Alex just got here, so you're not even the latest one."

She gave a slight smile, letting the evening slowly replace the day. "That's good to hear. I'd hate to be the last one to arrive at a party I'm giving."

"We're giving."

Clad only in a towel, her hair still wet and tousled, she turned to me as if I had said something that needed to be paid attention to. And she smiled, not a half-smile, but a full, open smile. "Yes, we are. Thank you for the last three years, Micky. Can I have thirty more?"

"Only thirty?"

"It's a start."

With the ease of those who have touched often, we were in each other's arms. It changes so quickly, I thought. Whatever annoyance I'd felt with Joanne had disappeared, chased away by Cordelia's smile and the comforting warmth of her arms around me.

Then we kissed, a deep kiss that turned from comfort and closeness to passion.

"Think our guests will notice if we don't appear for a couple of hours?" I said when we finally broke off.

"We could just tell them to go home."

We kissed again, lingering together before finally bowing to the demands of the evening.

I knew I should have gone downstairs to be with our guests, but I wanted to hold on to this moment of closeness. I watched her dress. She didn't even have to ask if I would hook her bra; a slight turn in my direction was a perfect and complete communication.

"How do I look?" she asked.

"Gorgeous. No one will wonder why we've been together for three years. They'll wonder what took me so long to find you."

"Thanks. My ego needed that." With that, she took my hand and we went downstairs.

"Well, if you two were virile men, we'd know what you were up there doing," Torbin heralded our entrance. "But I've heard from good sources that two women can't do it in less than half an hour."

"Torbin, I hate to disillusion you, but your fellow drag queens are not the best source of what two real women can or can't do."

"Oh, so you were doing it?" he shot back.

"I took a quick shower and changed my clothes," Cordelia prosaically answered.

I shook my head at Torbin to indicate that this topic was closed.

"Sorry to be so late coming to my own party," Cordelia apologized. "But I'm sure most of you know about these last-minute things."

"I vaguely remember them," Danny said. "This last month has been mercifully slow."

"Yeah, I know," Hutch seconded her. "A few barroom brawls, the usual drug shootings. We could use a juicy serial killer to enliven our days."

He had spoken jokingly, but Cordelia's hand suddenly tensed. That gesture told me that the body she'd identified hadn't died of natural causes.

"Be careful of what you ask for," Joanne cautioned her partner. As a harsh punctuation, her beeper went off. Then another beeper sounded. It was Danny's. A moment later, Hutch's pager added its note to the cacophony.

Joanne clicked hers off and turned to Cordelia. "Just a hunch, but could this have anything to do with your reason for being late?"

Cordelia's grip on my hand again tightened. "It may." Her voice was strained. "The woman was . . . she was . . . murdered."

"How? Can you give me any details?" Joanne had left the party and was at work.

"Wait," Alex cut in. "There are civilians here. I want to be able to sleep tonight. If you must discuss this, can you LEOs at least go out back?"

"Leos?" Karen puzzled. "Are we doing astrology here?"

"Law Enforcement Officers," I supplied.

Danny had gone into the kitchen to make the required phone call. Hutch was trying to decide whether to head in her direction or to stay with Joanne.

"You're right," Joanne relented. "Sorry. Let me call in and see what's up." She headed for the kitchen phone, saw Danny was on it, paused for just a beat, then went to listen in on Danny's conversation. Hutch followed Joanne into the kitchen.

I glanced at Cordelia. Her face had regained its haggard look.

Danny finished her phone conversation and, after a moment of talking with Joanne, came back to the living room. "So much for not working overtime. Sorry, Mick and Cordelia," she said.

"Will you be late?" Elly asked her.

"Don't know. I hope not."

"Oh, no, you don't," Millie said to Hutch, digging in his pockets for the car keys. "The boys in blue can drive you home. I'm not going to be stuck trying to get a cab to the Westbank."

After a bit more sorting out on the car front, the three of them were gone.

"Isn't it the PI who always solves the murder cases?" Torbin kidded me.

"Only in books and on bad TV shows. No, I'm perfectly content to let other people go after murderers and rapists. Give me a missing poodle any day to a serial killer."

"What kind of things do real PIs do?" Lindsey asked.

"Boring, mundane stuff, for the most part. We sit at our computers, we make phone calls, we wait for our calls to be returned.

I do a lot of missing person stuff. Other PIs specialize in things like white-collar crime, or work for defense attorneys. Some do only divorces, but I hate that kind of stuff, so I avoid it."

"How do you actually find a lost poodle?" Torbin quizzed me.

"It's my specialty—Lost Poodles-R-Us. The reality is that you put up flyers, go to the pound, call the roadkill folks, stand on street corners and call, 'Here, Precious,' and make a fool of your-self. I did once help a guy get his stolen snake back."

"What kind of snake?" Lindsey asked.

"I didn't ask. My task was to canvass all the local pet stores and see if any of them had been selling more than their usual load of live mice to his brother or his cousin, the suspects. The brother appeared, bought his more-than-enough mice, and I asked him some putatively innocent questions about what he was going to do with the mice—you know, subtle things like, 'Are you going to feed those to an anaconda?' He claimed to be a mouse lover, but his garbage gave him away. I never actually saw the snake, which made me happy."

"His garbage?"

"Glamorous PI work—we sometimes go through people's gar-bage. His had a very incriminating snakeskin in it."

"How do you find missing people?" Torbin asked.

"Depends on why they're missing. Is it an army buddy you're looking for or a deadbeat dad skipping out on support payments?"

"There's a kid in the show who's making noises about finding his real parents. How hard is it to find a parent who gave up a child for adoption?"

"That depends on whether they want to be found or not. Some parents want to know what happened to the kid they gave up. They're willing to be found. Was it a formal adoption? Are the records sealed?"

"I have no idea. But if he keeps whining about it, I'll send him your way."

"Sometimes I think you made the better choice," Alex said to Cordelia. "A lover who has enough sense to choose lost poodles over chasing murderers."

"I'm very happy with the choice I made." Though the reply was to Alex, Cordelia looked at me as she said it, with a smile that was both soft and radiant.

I couldn't help but smile back at her, although I tend to avoid the mushy stuff in public.

"You did make a good choice," Alex said.

Then I did a round of hostess duties, filling wine glasses and the like, redistributing crackers so the plate didn't look so one-sided.

While I was busy with my duties, the party sorted itself into two groups. Cordelia, Elly, Millie, and Lindsey were in the living room discussing fun and exciting things from the world of medicine.

Torbin, Alex, Andy, and Karen were in the kitchen, pursuing the topic of the differences between gay men and lesbians.

"It's not just the cat thing. Gay men have cats, too," Torbin said, defending his ownership of two of the beasts.

"And I don't know a single lesbian who eats tofu, so it can't be that," Karen said.

"Maybe it's the penis thing," Alex commented. "If it doesn't come off, you're a gay man."

That conversation sounded much more interesting than winding my way through medical jargon, but I edged myself onto the couch next to Cordelia. Somehow it was important to be close to her, to just feel the warmth of her leg against mine. I remained close to her for most of the evening, except when hosting demands pulled me elsewhere.

Despite the party not breaking up until almost one o'clock, Joanne, Danny, and Hutch didn't return.

After everyone had left, I poured Cordelia another glass of

wine and told her to sit while I did the cleaning and putting away that had to be done tonight. She didn't argue; she just gratefully sat down on the couch.

"Thank you, Micky," she said as I came by to pick up some glasses in her vicinity. "I feel like our three years was properly celebrated."

"Good, that's how you're supposed to feel," I answered as I headed back to the kitchen.

When I came back into the living room a few minutes later, Cordelia didn't notice me at first. She was staring into her wine glass, her face somber.

"You okay?" I asked as I sat down beside her.

"Yeah . . . yeah," she said, looking up at me. "I'm just . . . that woman upset me."

"Want to talk about it?"

"No, not really. I want to get her out of my mind." Cordelia took my hand in hers. She was quiet for a moment before continuing. "She didn't die an easy death. I know enough about forensics to know that not all her wounds were postmortem."

"How was she killed?" Despite her protest, talking about it seemed to be what she needed to do.

"I'm not sure. She could have bled to death. I only saw her face and torso. No marks of strangulation."

"Was she battered?"

She didn't reply immediately. "No, not really. At least as far as I could tell. No bruises. But . . ." Again she paused. "But she . . . was mutilated. She was . . . I don't want to talk about this. I'm sorry . . . I just can't. Hold me. Just hold me."

I put my arms around her. "Did you know her?"

"Not really. She came in once several months ago. I only saw her long enough to refer her to Jane, our gynecologist. She had another appointment for sometime next week."

"You think this might have anything to do with you or the clinic?"

"No, that's very unlikely. Just bizarre luck that she happened to be one of our patients. But . . . what disturbs me is that . . . I think she was a lesbian. I don't know for sure, I'll have to look at her chart, but . . ." She trailed off.

"Could that have had anything to do with her being killed?" I asked.

"I don't know. I . . . hope not." She downed the last of her wine, then put her head on my shoulder.

"Do I need to do anything more in the kitchen?" Cordelia asked, although she didn't stir.

"Nope, all taken care of," I assured her.

We sat still for a few minutes more, then she took my hand and we went upstairs. But Cordelia couldn't suppress several yawns as we undressed.

"No wild sex tonight?" I said after her fourth one.

"Probably not. I'm sorry. I really wanted you earlier. Now I'm just tired.

With that, we got into bed.

"Curl around me, at least until I fall asleep?" Cordelia asked.

I didn't reply, I simply did as she asked, molding myself into her, wrapping an arm around her waist.

It seemed not to be thought out, but Cordelia took my hand in hers, pulling our arms tightly together, then she moved my arm and hers over her chest and breasts, as if wanting the protection of bone over flesh.

We fell asleep that way.

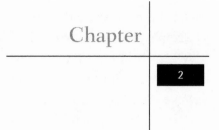

Chapter

2

"Oh, Mick, I'm sorry. I didn't mean to really do it. I was just joking at the party. But I do promise not to do it again."

Torbin's voice caught me with my head in the trunk, stretching for the grocery bag that had shifted out of easy grasp. I let the cat food go for the moment and looked at my cousin.

"What are you sorry about?" I asked.

"It was late at night, the show was over, and a snifter of decent cognac loosened my tongue and the thought processes that control it."

"Yes?" Nothing would speed up Torbin's storytelling, but he did require a few prompts and nods from me to prove that I was giving it the attention it deserved.

"I don't think you've met him. He goes by Bourbon St. Ann.

Not very original, using Quarter street names." Torbin's current name was Lola Nola.

"I've got ice cream." I pointed to the grocery bags still in the trunk.

"Ice cream? Must be nice to be a lesbian. You don't need to watch your girlish figure."

"Torbin!" I responded to his implied insult.

"Men are such beasts. All they ever think about is the physical. But women can see the inner light of the soul. That's what I meant."

"Of course. I never doubted it. But can we get back to what it is you're sorry for?"

"Oh, that. The scene is set. Late night, my fingers entwined about a snifter of cognac, and Bourbon St. Ann still in costume plops himself down next to me. He's one of those needy fellows. His life story if you so much as ask him the way to the john. He's young, twenty at most. Bit of a drifter. Came here last Mardi Gras and hasn't left."

I gave Torbin his well-deserved nod of encouragement.

"His parents threw him out when they found out he was gay. His adopted parents," Torbin emphasized. "He wants to find his real mother."

I couldn't stop myself from groaning. "And you gave him my name?"

"And I gave him your name," Torbin confirmed.

"Why do people think that someone who rejected them as a cute little baby is going to love them as an adult?"

"I think B. St. Ann is in that obsession stage, seeing Mom, apple pie, and the American flag all rolled into some long-lost maternal parent."

"You did give him my office number and not my home number?"

"I wasn't that big a fool. Is Cordelia home?" Torbin was standing on the porch, waiting for me with my grocery bags. "It's past the time most normal people sit down to dine."

"If only sick people would observe the dining hour . . ." I let us into the kitchen.

"Surely you don't want to sup alone?" Torbin began putting away the groceries. He had been here enough times that he knew where things went.

"Sorry, tonight is microwave night in this house."

That was enough to persuade Torbin to saunter across the street to his house.

There were definite advantages to living across the street from Torbin and Andy—cat-sitting, company, sharing things from drills to spices needed at the last minute. (Contrary to conventional wisdom, they had the drill and we had the spices—Andy likes to do carpentry and I enjoy cooking.) Support whenever one of us needed to deal with the family "out there," as Torbin referred to them. We were the lavender sheep and not always welcome at family gatherings.

And there were a few disadvantages to having Torbin so close. Like the tacky comments when we didn't retrieve our paper until the afternoon. Or when I did something foolish like storming out after an argument, Torbin was there to witness it.

I ran back the day's accumulation of phone messages. The first was Danny wanting my recipe for oyster dressing. Then Alan from FM Books to say that my order had arrived. Then the machine clicked off. No call from Cordelia saying she had to work late. Or identify dead bodies in the morgue.

Last week, she had worked late every night. Being a doctor's wife has, as far as I'm concerned, more minuses than pluses. A lot of suppers alone, everything from sleep to sex interruptible, and sometimes I had to ask Cordelia to tell me about her day in a language that resembled English. If there was a benefit, it was that being a doctor was what she wanted to do and she was good at it. Better a happy, absent doctor than a grumpy, present executive.

I finished putting away the groceries, then started a load of laundry. I knew better than to start supper until she actually came through the door, but I could throw together a salad while waiting for her. I had just finished cutting up the carrots when the phone rang. So much for dinner, I thought as I picked it up.

But it wasn't Cordelia.

"Micky," Torbin said.

I started to ask him what he was sorry for now, but something in his voice stopped me.

"Charlie's dead," he said quietly.

"What?" was my first reaction, then, "Oh, Torbin, I'm sorry."

Uncle Charlie was Torbin's father. Charlie had not been pleased when his only son had turned out not just gay, but flamboyantly gay. He and Torbin had a relationship that seesawed from love and affection to estrangement. After the third threat of being disowned, Torbin had taken to calling his father by his given name. Charlie never objected, as if he preferred to be less of a father to Torbin, less connected to the changeling his son had become.

"Heart attack. Right in the middle of dinner," Torbin continued as if trying to make sense of it. "Alice just called. She said it was quick—that Charlie didn't suffer. She said . . . Oh, hell." Torbin was silent. I could hear him fighting against tears.

"I'm coming over," I said.

It was a moment before he replied. "No, no, don't. I've got to go. I'm going to meet them at the hospital, then go back to . . . Mom's." It had been Mom and Charlie's.

"Do you want me to go with you?"

I heard the door open, then Cordelia called out a hello to me. Torbin started talking again. I didn't answer Cordelia.

"No, maybe not just yet," he said.

"Micky?" Cordelia came into the room. I waved her silent with my hand. She merely nodded and went back into the kitchen, not sure what she was interrupting.

"Alice says Mom is just staring at the wall, she hasn't even mentioned that there's a half-eaten roast sitting on the table. I think it needs to be just us kids tonight. Mom would be mortified if it got out she left a pot roast on the table for hours."

"All right. Call if you need to. Late's okay."

I went to the kitchen. Cordelia was looking through the mail on the counter.

"Uncle Charlie's dead. That was Torbin on the phone."

"Oh, Micky . . ." She put the mail down and wrapped her arms around me. "How's Torbin taking it?"

"Shock. Grief. He and Charlie needed another fifteen years to work things out. Now he'll never get it."

Cordelia didn't say anything. She didn't point out that I, too, needed years to work out my relationship with my father—and my mother—and I hadn't gotten them, either. I rested my head on her shoulder, unable to stop the rush of memories.

My father, Lee, officially Lemoyne Robedeaux, was the oldest of three brothers. He wasn't my real father, but marriage to my mother had given him the legal status. She had been sixteen and pregnant enough to have been thrown out of her house. My father had taken her in, then married her. When I was five, she left. The memories of a young child, a few very old pictures, and some letters were all I had left of her.

My father was killed in a car wreck when I was ten years old. Aunt Greta and Uncle Claude had taken me in. Uncle Claude, the youngest brother, had deferred to his wife in anything that concerned the children: their three—Bayard, Mary Theresa, Augustine—and then me. Aunt Greta thought that the solution to my crying and sleepless nights was discipline. If she punished me enough, my terror would go away. Of course, it hadn't, it had changed into hatred and then bitterness. At midnight on my eighteenth birthday, I had left that house.

Uncle Claude was the most successful in the material sense. His was white-collar, middle management in a company that sold marine paint.

Uncle Charlie had been the middle brother. Never as financially successful as his younger brother, he never had the blank, disappointed look of a man trapped in a dry marriage like Uncle Claude did. Uncle Charlie and Aunt Lottie enjoyed each other's company. He would follow her around in the kitchen as she cooked dinner. Sometimes in the evening they would sit on the back porch, Uncle Charlie smoking his cigar, Aunt Lottie sometimes knitting, shelling peas, her hands always busy.

I was always welcome there. But Uncle Claude, with his white-collar success, had moved us to the suburb of Metairie, with its tidy houses, neat lawns, and servants of a different color who came only by day. Charlie and Lottie remained in their Irish Channel home even as the neighborhood changed. It was the life they knew, near the docks where Charlie worked. Aunt Greta, and thus us children, didn't visit that neighborhood very often.

Now Uncle Charlie was gone, only Uncle Claude left of the Robedeaux brothers.

Chapter

3

Torbin called in the morning. Cordelia had already left for work. We didn't talk long; he was exhausted and had been up most of the night. He gave me the details of the visitation and funeral. There would be a big family gathering after it.

Torbin passed the phone to Aunt Lottie. I murmured a few words of sympathy that she barely heard. She wasn't ready to let go of Charlie. Then the phone was passed to Alice, Torbin's oldest sister. She and I weren't close, but we'd always gotten along. She was a nurse and had seen enough real tragedies not to worry about who a few of her relatives chose to love. Torbin had two other sisters. Mary Maria Grace, whom we referred to as Mary Mary, was a paralegal at a snobby corporate law firm and she thought that having a brother who did drag was the worst thing that could happen to her. I heard her voice in the background, but we didn't talk. She usually avoided me as if afraid that because I was attracted to women, I would have to make a pass at her if she got too close. I occasionally considered doing it because it would probably turn her hair all gray, a tragedy comparable to having a drag queen brother. Torbin's other sister, Francine, had gone to college in Oregon and stayed in the Northwest. She was flying in from Seattle, her latest perch, that evening.

After Alice and I hung up and I performed the necessary cat feeding, I headed downtown to my office.

It used to be both office and apartment until Cordelia and I had moved in together three years ago. First in her apartment in the French Quarter, and the past year in the Faubourg Marigny, a gay neighborhood just downtown from the Quarter. I'd had a good year and earned enough to put up half of the down payment. Cordelia, who knew how important it was to me to have that kind of equality, had made no comment, simply let me pay my share. It had been a struggle, but I was slowly beginning to accept Cordelia carrying more of the financial burden, letting her get the check when we went out to eat, even paying the mortgage when I had a slow month. (Even getting a mortgage was a concession to my foolish pride—she could easily afford to buy our house outright.) Not only was she a doctor, but she was the granddaughter of Ignatius Holloway. She'd had several generations of money passed down to her when he had died.

Gradually, I began to accept that, for Cordelia, money was not power. At least, not with me. What she had, I had, and the choices we made were equal. That she paid for the couch didn't mean that I couldn't veto her color choice (and I had; color and design aren't Cordelia's forte).

One of the great luxuries her money had given me was the freedom to choose which cases I took. I kept my downtown office because I wanted to be that kind of detective. No uptown divorces for me. I still occasionally accepted the kid-with-a-lost-cat case.

I got to my office a little after ten. I started to do paperwork, that ubiquitous accompaniment to daily life, but Uncle Charlie's death kept tugging at the edges of my concentration. His heart had beat only sixty years before giving out.

A knock on the door interrupted my thoughts. There was a time when I could have kept it unlocked, but that time was past. I crossed to the door, glanced through the crack in the less than perfect fitting frame, then opened the door.

I didn't recognize the woman who entered. She was in her late fifties, maybe early sixties, wore a frumpy flowered dress and a cloth coat that fit better ten pounds and a few years ago. But the clothes were clean, the dress with pleats that had been perfectly ironed when she left the house this morning.

"Micky Knight?" was her first question.

I affirmed that I was and ushered her to a chair.

I waited, offering her the respect of silence.

She finished arranging herself, looked at me, and said, "I need to find my daughter. I haven't much left anymore and I need to hold what I can."

"Tell me about your daughter."

Her eyes clouded for a moment, not tears but the weight of memory. "Oh, she was the prettiest baby, cooed and gurgled from the day she was born . . . but I guess that's not what you need to know." She pushed the memory away.

"How old is she now?" I asked.

"Twenty-eight years and six months. I haven't seen her in ten years."

"She left ten years ago, when she was eighteen?"

For a moment, the woman didn't reply. I realized that I didn't even know her name yet. "She didn't leave, Lord help me. My husband was a good man. Thought he did the right thing."

"Was she pregnant?" I gently probed. My mother's story.

"No, no," she said slowly. "Worse than that—at least we thought so at the time. My husband—God rest him, he only passed a year ago and already I'm going around him—my husband, he said he didn't sit at that counter and he didn't go to Selma to have his daughter turn into that kind of unspeakable trash. He told her to get, get out. We lived in a small world. Talk got back to me. Enough for me to know where she was, some idea of what she was doing. Went to stay with her friend. A white girl, had her own car, new car, did well, I guess." She couldn't bring herself to say 'lover,' to admit that her daughter was a lesbian. "Then she and her friend stopped getting along. And Lorraine wasn't around to be talked about anymore. Like life swallowed her up." The woman was silent.

I had listened to her without taking any notes. Now I opened a notebook. I knew life couldn't just swallow you up, not even death could, we all leave trails of paper and numbers, a life reduced to the coldness of type on paper.

"Let me get your name," I said.

"Mrs. Joseph Drummond," she answered, still tied to the husband who had banished her daughter. It was, I realized, a powerful combination of courage and need that had compelled her to search for her daughter. "I'm Mazzie, Mazzie Drummond." She handed me her voter registration card. I copied the spelling of her name, then her address from it.

Mrs. Drummond had come prepared. She brought Lorraine's birth certificate, high school transcripts, baptismal record, vaccination charts, all the pieces of her daughter's life that she still could touch.

"You're very thorough, Mrs. Drummond," I told her as I took them all and made copies, even the ones I saw no use for. They were pieces of her daughter's life and I treated them as such. I handed her back the originals. She seemed relieved that they had come back so quickly to her.

"Do you know the name of your daughter's . . . friend?"

Mrs. Drummond replied slowly, her face carefully masked. "Suzanna Forquet."

As she had, I kept my face neutral. Suzanna Forquet would

not like me asking about a long-ago black woman lover—oh, no, not at all. That I would enjoy her discomfort immensely I counted as one of the perks of the job. Suzanna Forquet was married to Henri Forquet IV.

Karen, Cordelia's cousin, had her faults, but being an inaccurate gossip was not one of them. She had told me that Suzanna Forquet had refused to make a donation to Cordelia's clinic (Cordelia never referred to it as her clinic, but I always thought of it that way) because "Cordelia is being a little too open about the way she is. I can't be associated with that." Karen, as the chair of the fund development committee, had taken great offense at Suzanna's refusal. After some debate, we decided not to tell Cordelia. Oh, yes, I would enjoy questioning Suzanna Forquet.

Mrs. Drummond was fumbling with a frayed cloth coin purse. From it, she pulled a wad of bills. "I want you to look for my daughter for a hundred dollars' worth." Her face was proud. She had worked hard for this money. "It's all I can afford right now. If a hundred dollars won't do it . . ."

I took the proffered bills. Mrs. Drummond would not accept charity. "You've given me a lot of information, made it as easy as possible. I'll do my best to find your daughter." The hundred wouldn't cover anything like my usual expenses and fees. But this was one of the cases that Cordelia's money would allow me to take. Mrs. Drummond was a mother who had bothered to look for her daughter. Mine never had.

I used the computer to print a contract.

After she signed it, she asked, "Do you think you can find her?"

I replied with a question. "Do you think your daughter wants to be found?"

It was only then that she considered that her daughter might not want to be reunited with her. "Oh, good Lord, yes. I hope so." And that was when she broke down.

I handed her a tissue, but didn't interrupt with words.

"I'm sorry," she said as she wiped the wet streaks. "Don't know what came over me."

"You love your daughter."

"I do love my daughter," she quietly affirmed.

"I'll do my best to find her."

After she left, I sorted out the copies I had made, creating a biography of Lorraine Harper Drummond from scattered pieces of paper.

She was five feet four inches tall and weighed one hundred and twenty-one pounds. Her hair was straightened, paying obeisance to the fashions of the time, but it wasn't an elaborate style. Lorraine Drummond was not a woman who paid great attention to her looks. She did what she had to do to get along, but that was all she did.

In Lorraine's high cheekbones and direct eyes, I could see what had attracted Suzanna Forquet. She was a handsome woman, with an air of independence about her that even a standard high school picture couldn't hide. That she had never contacted her mother after being thrown out meant that her independence went deep.

I hoped that it was her stubborn independent streak that kept Lorraine Drummond away. That finding her wouldn't lead me to one of the common tragedies of life: the teeth of an unnamed corpse finally matched to dental records. Or that Lorraine had moved far away a long time ago, making her trail difficult to follow.

I again glanced through the material Mrs. Drummond had given me. Lorraine was a good student, mostly A's and B's, taking college prep courses, biology instead of home economics. Mrs. Drummond had included letters of acceptance from Tulane, LSU, and UNO, as if saying, "I may clean peoples' houses, but my daughter is smart enough to go to college." Mrs. Drummond probably was, too, but people of her skin color hadn't been welcomed into either LSU or Tulane when she was a young woman.

Mrs. Drummond had given me everything but Lorraine's Social

Security number. But given what I had, that would be easy to get. I probably didn't need to question Suzanna Forquet. I made a deal with myself: I would call up a friend who worked in the alumni office at Tulane. If she gave me Lorraine's current address, I would skip Suzanna. She had a one-phone-call reprieve. But more than one call and she and I were going to have a little chat.

A mother looking for her daughter. For a moment an image of another mother intruded. But my mother had left when I was five. Sporadic letters and postcards arrived until I was around ten. Then nothing. I had kept writing to the last address I had for her, but my letters always came back. The first few times, I hoped it was just some bizarre mistake—I hadn't written the address neatly enough or something like that. I laboriously printed out the address, then tried typing it, going through four envelopes before I was satisfied. But they still came back. I kept writing for the next year or so. That address was the only connection I had to her. It was so hard to give it up, admit there was no way I could reach her. Somehow, I'd felt certain that when she found out my father was dead and that I was living with Aunt Greta and Uncle Claude, she would come to rescue me.

I rescued myself, I thought bitterly, left when I was eighteen.

The past was gone. I found a manila folder and labeled it LORRAINE DRUMMOND. I put my notes and the copies into it.

Then I hauled out the New Orleans phone book. Always try the simple and easy first. It usually doesn't work, but if it does, you feel like an utter fool if you've spent several hours trying the difficult and complicated. No Lorraine Drummond, L. Drummond, or any likely variation listed. Last chance, Miss Suzanna. I dialed my friend at Tulane. Lorraine Drummond had not gone to Tulane.

Well, I thought with the satisfaction of those forced to do what they wanted to do all along, Suzanna Forquet could give me some idea of whether or not Lorraine had gone to college.

Who knows her? I ruminated as I flipped through my address book. The three names that seemed most likely were Karen; Alexandra Sayers, Joanne's lover; and Lindsey McNeil. I looked at that short list. Sometimes it seems like there are only fifty lesbians in the world.

Alex seemed like the safest bet. I dialed her work number. Her secretary informed me that Alex was in Baton Rouge and was expected to be there for several days.

I tried Karen next.

"Suzanna Forquet? Oh, dear," was her response. "You haven't heard?"

"Heard what?"

"I ran into her and Henri at one of those boring art openings. American champagne, that kind of affair."

I resisted debating Karen about her snobbishness. It was an ongoing battle and one that would only waste time now.

Karen continued, "I was with a woman, so she was avoiding me like I was a poor relation. Anyway, Henri had to tell this horrible AIDS joke—did you know I just went through the NO/AIDS Task Force training to become a buddy?"

NO/AIDS was the local AIDS service organization. "You did? Good for you." I didn't rush Karen; this was the way her thought patterns worked. I would get the story eventually.

"Can you believe that? I haven't been matched yet. Sometimes I think I'm crazy. What the hell do I have to offer someone dying?"

"You're not crazy. And you can certainly offer good gossip and a great video collection."

"Yeah, I guess. Doesn't seem like much."

"Nothing seems like much when someone is dying."

"As I was saying, Henri made this stupid joke about AIDS and fags. So I decided to put a stake in his little upwardly mobile heart by inquiring if he was descended from the Forquet that was a corrupt carpetbagger who was killed in a brawl in a whorehouse with his pants down. He, of course, denied it. I, of course, in my most innocent voice then asked, "Oh, so when did your family arrive? Couldn't have been earlier than the turn of the century, then, unless you're related to that Yankee carpetbagger and his bastard children."

"Karen, you are evil." New Orleans is a class-conscious town. Being a descendant of one of the original French settlers is a thing much desired.

"Miss Suzanna got huffy, she didn't want anyone to think she'd married a mere descendant of a carpetbagger. She told me how much I'd upset her husband with my inaccuracies. So I, of course, after all that American champagne, had to reply, 'But dear, the rumor mill says that Henri is more upset by the sight of a vagina than anything I might have said.'

"I have seen nothing of Miss Suzanna or Mr. Henri since that fateful evening. Of course, their circle is a bit more nouveau than mine."

"No great loss there."

"No loss at all. Are you being sarcastic?"

"Me? Am I ever sarcastic about the movers and shakers of New Orleans?"

"You're being sarcastic," Karen decided.

"Any idea of how Suzanna and Henri arrange their trysts?"

"Henri travels a lot. He's too paranoid to do anything suspect within a one-hundred-mile radius of the greater New Orleans area.

"Suzanna . . . well . . . Suzanna is going to take a hard fall someday soon."

"Why's that?"

"She slums."

"Slums? Perhaps you mean sleeps with people not in her upwardly mobile snobbish class?" Karen wouldn't have to ask if I was being sarcastic this time.

"No. Well . . . no. She favors young black women. Has affairs that last a few months, then boom, they're over. Suzanna gets bored. That's a good way to create enemies. So far, nothing's blown up on her, but it's probably just a matter of time. Talk is getting around. People who aren't gossip mavens have repeated these stories to me."

"Any useful details? Names, dates, that sort of stuff?"

"No, usually just along the lines of, 'We saw her with another one.'"

"Another one?"

"A young black woman."

"Oh, that's right, slumming."

"Look, Micky, you know what I mean. White women like Miss Suzanna do not, in polite society, make a habit of sleeping with black women."

"I'm half-black," I baited her. "What does that make your cousin Cordelia?"

"I thought you were Greek!" Karen said, clearly taken aback. I couldn't tell whether it was at her faux pas or that I might be telling the truth.

"My mother was Greek. But my father? Who knows? Olive skin, black curly hair. Could be."

"You've made your point. I'll try and toe a more PC line," Karen offered as a hasty defense.

"Just because you were brought up a racist doesn't give you an excuse to remain one," I shot back, annoyed at her dismissing me with the PC cliché.

"Remember, Micky, it's not my PC-ness that gets me invited to the kind of parties that gives you this information. Besides that, I like your friend Danny and her lover Elly."

"Karen!"

"What?"

"Some of my best friends are bubble-headed blonds. Get it?"

Karen was silent for a moment. I don't know whether she got it or if she decided retreat was her best option. "All right, all right.

I'll see if I can get any more dirt on Miss Suzanna. Talk to you. My call waiting is calling."

It's not my job to educate the Karen Holloways of the world, I thought as I put the phone down. To her a racist was someone who burned crosses if he could get away with it. Since she didn't do that, she couldn't possibly be a racist.

I debated for a moment letting go of Suzanna Forquet. Talking to her wasn't necessary, I wasn't kidding myself about that. But my aggravation with Karen goaded me. I looked up Lindsey McNeil's number. I called her at work, giving my inquiry a patina of professionalism, and left a message. A psychiatrist, she was with a patient.

While waiting for her to call back, I focused on the routine of finding a missing person. The first thing was to make sure that Lorraine Drummond was still alive. I filled out the paperwork to see if the Social Security Administration had notice of her death.

As I finished up, I heard footsteps on the stairs. There was a knock on my door.

Opening it, I ushered in a young man who had to be Bourbon St. Ann. He was skinny—effete, even. His hair was a slicked-back brown with too-obvious blond highlights in it, and hadn't been recently cut. His face had the raw, naked look of makeup hastily washed off, the pale skin seeming to need the rouge and grease paint to come alive.

"You Micky Knight? Torbin sent me," he said in a mumble that was both hasty and defiant.

"Why don't you tell me what's going on?" I asked as we seated ourselves.

"Torbin didn't tell you?"

The slight hint of a whine in his voice annoyed me. "I'd like to hear it from you," I replied neutrally.

"I can't pay a lot. But I'd like to find my mother. My real mother." He didn't elaborate.

I guess that for him not giving much money and not giving much information went hand in hand. "You were adopted?"

His "Well, yeah," indicated that I'd asked a painfully obvious question.

"Adoption records are sealed."

He stared at me. He had a problem. I should solve it. It should be that simple. I wasn't meeting his expectations.

"I guess you can't help me, then," he finally said, his whining turning into truculence. "Torbin said you could. Guess he was wrong." He pushed himself out of the chair, ready for his dramatic exit.

I should have let him just walk out the door. But his last shot rankled me. I took the challenge.

"Sit down. I can help you. Get rid of your TV detective notions. I'm not going to solve this in an hour with commercial breaks. You have a part to play here, too. I need to know everything you know about your adoption. I can't just pull your mother out of thin air."

"If you think you can help," he sighed as he sat back down. The Queen had granted me an audience.

"Do you know where you were born?"

"Here."

"Here?"

"Somewhere around here."

"New Orleans? Louisiana? The South?"

"Around here. New Orleans, I think."

"The more you can narrow it down, the less work I'll have to do."

"Isn't that what I'm paying you for? To do the work?"

"'Can't pay much' is what I recall you said. How would you like that money spent? On me finding out things you already know? Or on things you don't know?"

"Somewhere in the greater New Orleans area. That's the best I can do."

"How did you get that information?"

"My adopted mother blurted it out. Said I was the bastard of a New Orleans whore."

"Do you think it's true?"

"Only info I've got."

"Have you registered with any of the agencies that try to reunite adopted children with their biological parents?"

"Uh . . . well, not yet," he slowly acknowledged, sheepish at admitting that his desire to find his mother hadn't been strong enough to take the first easy step. "But I don't know how to do that."

I went to one of my file cabinets and pulled out how-to-do-that and made copies for him. Finding people is the bulk of what I do. "Here's how. Go do it."

He reluctantly took the paper. "I'm not real good at this."

"Do you want to find your birth mother or was that just a drunken whim?"

"Well, yeah, I'd like to find her, but . . ." He trailed off into boyishness. His shy smile probably worked on straight women and gay men.

"But you want it handed to you in a neat package, without spending much of your time or money on it."

"Well, no, that's not . . . I'm just . . . paperwork flusters me." He cocked his head and lowered his eyes. In a dim bar after a few drinks, he was probably cute.

"I'm a queer girl, it won't work," I told him bluntly. "These are the easy hurdles. You can jump them yourself. Right now what I've given you is free. Next time it costs. Save your money and do it yourself."

"I'm eighteen years old and I'm dying," he blurted out.

"You have AIDS?"

"HIV positive," he corrected shortly. Bourbon St. Ann was manipulating me. This was probably his trump card. If cute boyishness didn't work, then it was time to pull out the deathbed routine.

I didn't doubt that it was true (if I were a true cynic, I'd decide he was lying about being infected). But I resented the way he was using it to try to bully me into doing his bidding.

"If those don't work, call me and we'll take it from there."

"Thanks for all your help," he said sarcastically. He tromped out the door, leaving it open just to be extra annoying.

I started to refile the papers I had copied for him. What if my mother was looking for me? What if her name was in one of those files, hoping someday I'd come searching? No, I told myself, hastily shoving the file back in the drawer. I wasn't adopted, my mother lad left me. But she'd occasionally written until I was ten. It was only after I'd moved in with Aunt Greta and Uncle Claude that her letters stopped. Could she have lost track of me then?

I pulled the file back out and looked at the instructions I'd given to so many others. It was very unlikely.

I made another copy of the form and filled in the information. I did it quickly, as if speed wouldn't give hope time to build.

I glanced at my watch. Uncle Charlie's visitation was tonight. I had to go home and get ready. I locked up hurriedly, casually tossing the envelope in my to-be-mailed box, as if it were routine.

Chapter

4

Cordelia and I dressed for the funeral, her in a sober navy suit and me in my basic black dress, one of the few dresses I owned (I didn't feel right about calling up Torbin to borrow one of his, given the circumstances).

I said little as we drove uptown. I thought of Torbin confronting the family bigots and ignoramuses through the grief of his father's death. I wasn't really a Robedeaux; no one had expectations for me to dash. Torbin was Uncle Charlie's only son. I may have violated major taboos, but he had crashed through sacred ones when he came out.

"You're pensive," Cordelia said as she turned into the parking lot for the funeral home.

"Thinking," I answered slowly. "Ready to go in?"

Cordelia followed me into the funeral parlor. Charlie and Lottie had a lot of friends; they were active in the church and other organizations, and were always surrounded by people. Even in death Uncle Charlie was surrounded by people. The room was full of people.

Of course, my Aunt Greta would be the first gauntlet we'd have to face. She was standing in the widow-guard position, the place where everyone who wanted to speak to Aunt Lottie would have to pass by. I glanced around the room, looking for Torbin and an excuse to bypass Aunt Greta.

"Michele, darlin'. Glad to see you managed a dress."

I turned to the voice. I knew it well.

Five years older than me, my cousin Bayard was not aging gracefully. His paunch had spread, pulling his suit jacket to a tight sheen. His dark brown hair was too uniform in color, he had to be retouching it, and it was plastered across his head in an attempt to hide how thin it was.

"Hello, Bayard," I replied as neutrally as I could. "Too bad that suit's so tight on you. Been a few years?"

"Now, Michele, it's Uncle Charlie's funeral. You be nice," he chided me. "This your latest gal pal?"

The five years he had on me—that and being the legitimate older son—had given him tremendous power over me when I had lived in that house out in Metairie. He had used that power in ways I didn't care to remember. He still liked to play at the memories of those days, by being just a little too pushy, until he got a reaction from me.

The press of the crowd was too close to easily brush by him. I determined that I was not going to cause a scene at Uncle Charlie's visitation.

"Ain't gonna introduce me?" Bayard prompted me.

"This is my cousin, Bayard Robedeaux." I paused for a moment before allowing him access to her name. "My lover, Cordelia James. Dr. Cordelia James," I added.

"A doc, huh?" Bayard put his hand out. "It's gettin' to be time for my physical exam."

I didn't know what Cordelia would do. I clenched my fist, fingernails into palm, to keep from losing my temper. I wanted to get her away from his leer.

Cordelia gave his hand a brief glance, but pointedly didn't take it.

"Aren't gonna shake my hand?" Bayard baited her.

But Cordelia didn't have years of stored anger and powerlessness inside her ready to explode. She merely replied, "No, I think not."

Bayard, taken aback by her cool refusal, tried again, "No? Why not?"

"I'd prefer not to." Cordelia took my arm and pulled me through a gap in the crowd.

"Goddamned dyke," Bayard said, causing several heads to turn.

"You're magnificent," I told her.

"My mother always told me that a lady was someone who never did anything unintentionally rude. And trust me, my rudeness to him was intentional."

"There's Torbin," I said, spotting him beyond a column.

"He's a very handsome man," Cordelia remarked. "Reminds me of you."

"Torbin's blue-eyed, blond, and not a blood relation, remember?" I watched him as we approached. He was in a black suit that fit perfectly, a plain crisp white shirt, and a tie that was just a cobalt blue. His stark simplicity bespoke an elegant eloquence. Torbin always dresses well, I thought wryly, even for his father's funeral.

"Maybe it's your sensibility," Cordelia murmured.

"Micky!" Torbin called when he spotted me.

I was warmed by the genuine smile that crossed his face. The bonds that hold us to life and love are as fragile as a smile, the warmth of a hand in yours. Uncle Charlie's sudden death was a reminder of how quickly these bonds could be taken from you.

I wrapped my arms around him.

"Thanks," he finally whispered as we disengaged

We stayed with Torbin and Andy until it was time to leave.

As I hugged Torbin good-bye, he asked, "You'll come to the family thing tomorrow after the funeral? Both of you?"

"Yes, we'll be there," I assured him as Cordelia nodded her assent.

With that, she and I threaded our way through the people still left, carefully avoiding both Bayard and Aunt Greta.

"Thank you," I told Cordelia as we unlocked the car door. She looked tired. "You must love me a lot to put up with my family today and tomorrow, through all this."

"Micky, I'd do it just for you even if I didn't know Torbin. And I do love you a lot."

With that we drove home.

I had to wear the same black dress to the funeral. Dressy clothes aren't the mainstay of my wardrobe and Cordelia and I are too different in size for me to pilfer anything from her. She did lend me a string of pearls to add some variation to last night's basic black.

I tuned out the service, turned away from memories of a childhood spent in churches like this one. No, not quite. Only after I moved in with Aunt Greta did church become a twice-weekly obeisance. My father's attitude toward church was that God shouldn't have made the fish jump so high on Sunday if He had wanted him to go to church. Or as he said, "You find God in your everyday or you don't find Him at all."

The service was over, people stood up. The pallbearers brought Uncle Charlie's casket down the aisle.

Cordelia and I made our way out of the church. "You'll have to give me directions," Cordelia said as we got in the car. "I don't know my way around Metairie very well."

I told Cordelia the way to the house I had run away from on my eighteenth birthday.

It seemed unchanged. For as long as I had been away, there should have been some mark, some sea change to note the absence of over fifteen years. Still pale yellow brick, the lawn losing its summer luster of green, the shrubs surrounding the house the three feet tall they had always been. Only the car in the driveway was different, a late-model Cadillac.

The door was ajar, not a wide-open welcome, but just enough room to say, come in only if you belong here. Cordelia followed me in.

The front living room, the formal room that we kids were rarely allowed in, was filled with people.

"Michele! Little Micky!" We were waylaid by Great-Aunt Eunice, in her late eighties or early nineties, whose head barely made it past my waist. "Lordy, how you're grown. I keep asking Greta when you're going to come visit. Rosemary, look who's here, Little Micky Robedeaux."

"Hello, darlin'," Cousin Rosemary drawled. "It's so good to see you. Oh. Except at an occasion like this," she said, suddenly remembering we were at a funeral gathering. "I mean, it's good to see you, even at this occasion, but this isn't a good occasion, if you know what I mean."

Great-Aunt Eunice called out, "Hello, Billie Ray. Look who's here. Little Micky Robedeaux, Lee's daughter, all grown up."

Billie Ray was another of the myriad cousins. He looked somewhat familiar, but I couldn't claim to really remember him.

"Hey, ya, Little Mick. I shoulda known you were Lee's daughter. You look just like him." Billie Ray gave me a hearty handshake.

"Most people say I look like my mother," was the only reply I could come up with to his obvious lie.

"There's that. Now, you ain't got his coloring," Billie Ray went on. "But you've got his chin. All three Robedeaux brothers had it, though Claude's is gettin' a little lost these days. Lee's forehead, too."

I nodded, unable to avoid stealing a glance at Cordelia. Her face was carefully neutral, giving no sign of how fanciful she knew Cousin Billie Ray's claim of family resemblance to be.

"That may be," Great-Aunt Eunice cut in, evidently a bit more up on family gossip than Cousin Billie Ray was. "So, Little Micky, you living here in the city? You married yet?"

"I live down in the Marigny."

"Oooh, that's dangerous," Rosemary interjected. "So close to the French Quarters."

"I'm sure she lives in a safe block," Great-Aunt Eunice cut in. "You married yet?" She wanted her question answered.

"Um . . . no, I'm not. Not the marrying kind, I guess," I fumbled out. "Cordelia and I are roommates." There, that should be obvious without being obvious.

"Oh, that's nice," Cousin Rosemary put in. "Good to have someone to talk girl talk to until the right man comes along."

"Well, you must of got it from your mother," Great-Aunt Eunice said dryly. "She wasn't the marrying kind, either."

Another swarm of cousins descended and Cordelia and I extricated ourselves during the chorus of hellos. I didn't feel like being introduced over and over again as Little Micky.

We found Aunt Lottie back in the den. She had never been comfortable in the formal front room. She gave both me and Cordelia a hug. I caught a glimpse of Aunt Greta in the kitchen. She was not going to let anyone outdo her in the food department.

This place where I hadn't been for so many years, the faces I hadn't seen—only together for a death. I found Torbin. He looked tired and drawn.

"Half of them talk to me to offer sympathies. The other half are curiosity-seekers. Have to have a good look at the queer son," he muttered to me. Then he was claimed by another horde of the sympathetic and the curious.

"Keep Andy company," I told Cordelia. "I'm going to do my distasteful duty and offer to help in the kitchen."

"You're a brave heart."

I nodded and headed for the kitchen. All the counter space, the breakfast nook table, everything was covered with food. I saw at least two hams and a large turkey. People always brought food for funerals.

Aunt Greta was in the midst of this, an ironed apron on over her proper black funeral dress. Uncle Claude was with her.

"I don't know why you can't put it on the grocery list when you use something up," she was saying to him. "Now how am I going to make cocktail sauce for the shrimp with no horseradish?"

"I'm sorry, Greta. Guess I forgot," he mumbled a hasty apology. He wasn't looking at her, instead glancing around the kitchen seeking escape. He saw me. "Hey, Mick, how are ya?"

"Michele?" Aunt Greta turned around to face me.

"Hi. Uh . . . I thought I'd see if you needed help." I suddenly wondered why I had come in here. Was it habit? Old places bringing back old patterns? When I had lived here, it was understood that I would always help in the kitchen.

Aunt Greta looked from me to Uncle Claude, obviously caught between the fact that she did need help and not wanting to accept it from the bastard child.

"Hey, Greta, better get some food out or your kitchen'll be invaded." Cousin Rosemary poked her head in. "You need a hand?"

"Yes, please, Rosemary, dear. If you could put things on the serving platters. I don't need your help, Michele." She turned from me to point Rosemary to the stack of platters.

"Come on with me and let's get some horseradish," Uncle Claude said. "We'll be right back, Greta," he added as he made his exit. I followed him out through the front room.

"Looks like we'd better walk," he said once we were outside. He nodded at the cars blocking the driveway.

"That little store still down the block?"

"Still a store there. One of them chain places now."

I considered congratulating Uncle Claude on the used-up

horseradish. It was certainly a convenient excuse to get out of the house and away from Aunt Greta. But that would be acknowledging what everyone knew, but no one spoke about—that Claude and Greta were not the happiest of married couples.

"Nice of you to offer to help out. Mary Theresa ain't stuck her head in yet," he said.

"Or Gus or Bayard. Sons can help out in the kitchen, too."

"Well, not Greta's sons. She don't think a man's place is in the kitchen. Unless it's to fix something."

We walked on for a bit in silence. I noticed that Uncle Claude was moving slowly. Beads of sweat were on his brow.

He is getting old, I thought. His hair was starting to go from gray to a lighter white-gray. There was a puffiness to his face, as if the beating of his heart were too sluggish to pump all the fluid away. Maybe he felt old because his brother, with only two years between them, had just died. Claude was the only brother left.

"I know I gotta stop this," he said as he took out a cigarette. "Doc's been after me. So I don't smoke in the house anymore. It's a start."

"Got to start somewhere."

"Yeah. Somewhere." He loosened his tie, then unbuttoned the collar. "Been a while since I've done much walking. Too many years behind a desk."

"I can run on to the store, if you'd like," I offered.

"Naw, that's okay. Nice to be out of the house for a while. It's Greta's show, anyway."

"Okay, we'll take it slow. It's hard for me to walk in heels," I said as I slowed my steps even further.

"Sure is humid. Don't feel much like fall," he commented as he wiped his brow. "Mind if we sit a bit on this bench?"

"Good idea. No sense in hurrying back," I agreed as we sat on a bus stop bench.

"Your business going okay?" Uncle Claude asked.

"Fair enough. I like the hours. How's yours?"

"Pretty good. Nice thing about seawater and salt air, makes boats need to be painted every so often."

For some reason, he wanted to talk to me. I didn't know if it was to get away from Greta, and I was a convenient excuse, or because he was clumsily trying to make up for all those years of neglect. I let the silence be. He could fill it if he wanted.

A bus came by. I waved it on.

"I was just talkin' to Charlie a few hours before. Then gone, just like that. But when your brother goes . . . makes you realize how quick that grim reaper can come for you. I guess I'm old enough I got to think about things like that."

"No one gets out of life alive. We've all got to think about it sometime or another," I said.

"I've got some regrets." He took a puff on his cigarette. "Figure if I get to heaven Lee's gonna kick my butt for the way I let Greta treat you."

It's too goddamned late, I almost retorted. Don't apologize now that it doesn't matter. But it mattered to him, I realized. With death hovering so close, he needed to make some atonement for what he had done. I didn't say anything because I knew I couldn't keep the bitterness out of my voice.

"There were rules back then. Home, kitchen, kids, those all belonged to the woman. Men went out and worked, took care of cars, that sort of stuff. And you know how Greta is about rules."

"Yeah, I know."

"Husbands and kids gotta obey the rules."

"Or at least not get caught disobeying them," I amended, remembering the things Bayard had done to me.

"Yeah, old Greta had a third eye about that."

"Not with her own kids," I retorted.

"She was strict with everyone, but I guess stricter with you. Felt you had been raised out in the bayous with no mama, that Lee had been too loose with you. She felt girls had to be brought up right."

"And boys were to be brought up wrong?"

"Well"—Uncle Claude shrugged—"boys will be boys."

"And what will girls be? Victims?" I shot back. I knew how this script was supposed to go: Uncle Claude would get this off his chest, I would be a nice girl and forgive him, and everything would be okay. But life takes things from you. I lived part of my childhood in terror, stalked by my cousin. There could be no recompense that would wipe that away.

Uncle Claude was silent. I wondered if he was going to pretend that he didn't know what I meant, or just ignore what I'd said. But finally he replied, "Did Bayard or Gus mess with you?"

"Gus was glad that there was someone else to blame, but that was all he did."

"Bayard?" he asked softly.

"Bayard," was all I replied.

Uncle Claude rubbed both his hands across his face as if trying to wipe some stain away. "How long?" he asked from between his hands.

"It started a few months after I came here. It ended two days before I left."

"Oh, Jesus," he muttered. "Why didn't you say something?"

"Because he would have said I was lying and Aunt Greta would have believed him. What other outcome could there have been?"

"Oh, Jesus," he repeated, rubbing his face. Then suddenly he sat up straight, his face turning an angry red. "That slimy son-of-a-bitch. He's my son and I call him that. Goddamn him!"

His anger left me strangely unmoved. Like the apology, it was far too late.

"He shouldn't of taken advantage of you like that!"

"No, he shouldn't have. He shouldn't have been able to." I shifted my gaze from him, not wanting to see how my words had affected him.

"Oh, Jesus, oh, God," I heard him say. "I hoped it wasn't that bad, but hope don't make things go away." He was silent for a moment. "I don't suppose it'd help much if I went back to the house and whupped his ass. I'm like-minded to do it."

"No, it wouldn't help much," I said gently. "And Aunt Greta would be screeching at us both for ruining all her hard work."

"Yeah, she sure would. Gotta pick your battles with Greta. The day she's trying to outdo Lottie's potato salad ain't the day to do it."

I looked at him, the red in his face subsiding back into the worn and aged gray. We're all so frail, I thought. One misstep, one blind eye and damage that you never wanted and that can never be undone.

"Never should have married her. But by the time I knew that, we had two kids and one more on the way. Too late to change. You got one life and I make a stupid mistake like this. Don't you do it. Don't do like I did. Boy or girl. I used to think it mattered. Just find someone to really love you. If I failed in anything in life, that's what I failed at. And I was stupid enough to think it hurt mostly me." He looked at me. This time we met each other's gaze.

That simple statement would do. You have been hurt and I am sorry. Sometimes that is the only recompense that you can hope for.

"Guess we should be headin' back."

"Guess we should get the horseradish first."

"Guess you're right." Uncle Claude grinned at me, the smile that reminded me of my father so much, that as a kid I would do anything to get from him.

"Why don't you stay here and let me run my younger legs down to the store? Can't have Aunt Greta upset 'cause you're sweating and huffing and puffing."

"You go ahead. I'll just sit and watch the buses go by." He gave me another smile, then handed me five dollars to go to the store with.

Uncle Claude had already started back to the house when I caught up with him, horseradish in hand.

I gave him his change.

"Thanks," he said. "You know, sometimes I think, of all my kids, you turned out the best."

"Don't tell Aunt Greta that," I answered, but I was surprised that he had referred to me as one of his kids.

"Well, not today. But maybe . . ." He trailed off.

We walked in silence until we were almost to the house. Uncle Claude spoke, as if he had to get something in before we entered. "Now's not the right time, but there are some things you should know. Things we kept from you as a kid. You're not a kid now. Got the right to know your past. Maybe next week, you and me can get together, when we get through this funeral stuff. I got some things to give you. From your dad . . . and mom. Also, you should know . . . hell, it's complicated, I'll tell you then."

Part of me wanted to take Uncle Claude's arm, stop him there on the lawn, and demand some answers, at least a bare outline. But it was the day of his brother's funeral. Guests—and his wife—were waiting for him.

"Next week sounds good. There are things I'd like to know." It had waited this long, another week or so wouldn't matter.

We entered the house. Uncle Claude took the horseradish to Aunt Greta in the kitchen. I went to find Cordelia, wondering how she was faring in the midst of all my relatives. Fine, it seemed, as I caught sight of her, sitting with Andy and Torbin and Alice, Torbin's oldest sister.

As I joined them, Torbin said, "Oh, dear, it looks like we're about to endure the ritual of the sit-down family funeral dinner."

I glanced in the direction of what had caught his attention. Aunt Greta, assisted by Rosemary and a few other cousins, was bringing out several laden platters from the kitchen. Aunt Greta was going all-out, as if this were some sort of competition. Her cooking had never compared to Aunt Lottie's, although all of us had enough sense not to say that to her. But she knew, the second helpings not taken, the leftovers from family gatherings always hers. Today was her day; what better triumph than to cook for the widow who had always been the better cook? I counted two hams, a turkey, several kinds of bread, and two large bowls of the potato salad that had always been Aunt Greta's cooking Waterloo.

There were three tables set up. The corner one that Torbin and I claimed with Cordelia and Andy seated six. Then there was Aunt Greta's formal dining table, a showy Queen Anne with all the leaves and extensions stretching it to fit ten. Then there were two shoved-together card tables with a fancy tablecloth thrown over them to disguise the summers that they had spent in the backyard.

The last two chairs at our table were claimed by my cousin Gus and his girlfriend (wife? I didn't know).

Now in his late twenties, Gus still had the little-boy hangdog look that he'd always had when we were growing up. He'd never been as clever, or as devious, as his older brother Bayard. His girl-friend had high, teased blond hair and too much makeup for any viewing closer than ten feet.

Gus, as usual, didn't talk much. He had never gone out of his way to be mean to me the way Bayard and Mary Theresa had, but he had never stood up for me, either. Given that Bayard was seven years older and Mary Theresa five, that was probably a pragmatic stance. His girlfriend Ronnie ("Hi, I'm Veronica, but call me Ronnie") did most of the talking for them. To her credit, she was unfazed when Andy was introduced as Torbin's lover and Cordelia as mine.

"Oh, I love those shows down in the Quarter! We'll have to come see you sometime," she told Torbin when she found out what he did.

She and Gus were running a video rental shop on Old Metairie Road, so most of the talk was about movies.

My attention wandered as they chatted about a movie I hadn't seen. I watched Uncle Claude, carving first a ham, then the turkey, Aunt Greta helping him with her instructions. "Not so big a piece, Claude." "That knife's not good for cutting through bone, use the other one." He looked tired and constrained, dutifully changing knives or cutting smaller pieces as Aunt Greta requested.

How do you resign yourself to this kind of life? I wondered. Pass your days in small bits with TV or sports magazines, like he had when I was here as a child? What happens when you realize that you only have one life and that it will never be what you wanted it to be? Surely Uncle Claude had dreams beyond a stale wife and a middle-of-the-pack suburban house? Was this why he wanted to talk to me? Was forgiveness and recompense what he had to hope for?

I had a vision of shaking him and saying, "It's not too late. Divorce Aunt Greta. Find some cute bimbo. Sail to the Bahamas like you always said you wanted to." Maybe next week, when we talked, I would say it. I didn't know.

Plates of turkey and ham made their way to our table. Ronnie told a funny story about her and Gus's "Aunt Greta Warning system," that they always had to cover up the porno videos ("We rent more of those than Cinderella, you betcha") with drop cloths and claim that they were doing renovation. Aunt Greta never questioned that the renovations had been going on over a year. Ronnie opined that Aunt Greta didn't want to know what was under those drop cloths. "Though I'm tempted to stick one of those tapes in their VCR just to see if it would spice up Claude and Greta's sex life." Gus blushed slightly at Ronnie's suggestion that his mother and father still had sex. I had been so unconvinced that someone like Aunt Greta could have a sex life that I was beginning to suspect that it took a triad of virgin births to produce her three children. But maybe, like Uncle Claude, she was trapped by what life expected of her; unlike his slide into the oblivion of hours of TV, she had settled for trying to control life's details.

"You look preoccupied," Cordelia said to me in a soft voice.

"Oh . . . family." I shrugged.

"Ah, yes . . . family."

I watched them. Torbin and Andy discussing Bette Davis movies with Ronnie, Gus looking on. Who they were, and who they had been, came to me as a kaleidoscope of images: Gus, once beckoning "this way" to get me out of the path of an oncoming Aunt Greta; Torbin as a young skinny cousin I talked to at family gatherings, some sense of connection between us before we realized what that connection was.

I glanced over at the main table. Uncle Claude, finally relieved of his carving duties, was sitting still, as if needing to rest from slicing through a ham. Aunt Greta was beside him, but with no connection beyond that proximity. Two strangers with three children between them. Next to Aunt Greta was her daughter, Mary Theresa. Years of smoking and suntans had taken their toll on her skin. I remembered her teenage phone conversations and being referred to as the "brat from the bayou." Bayard sat at the end of the table, as if no one should question his deserving the extra space, the cousin who had taken me with him when he got a puppy and let me pick it. And who had used that kindness against me.

"Oh, Claude, is that all the potato salad you're going to have?" I heard Aunt Greta say.

I looked back at them. Uncle Claude was passing the potato salad down the table. I couldn't see the amount on his plate, but obviously it didn't meet Aunt Greta's expectations.

"Can't eat it all. Gotta leave some for other folks," he said with a sheepish grin at her hectoring.

"Don't worry. I made plenty."

Cousin Rosemary passed the potato salad back to Uncle Claude, his fate sealed. He smiled weakly at her.

Abruptly, he set the bowl down on the table with a clatter. He can't hold it, I thought. Uncle Claude, the always-obedient man, wouldn't choose this time to rebel. His hand wavered, then clutched at his chest.

Death took him utterly by surprise. Somehow I knew that that was what it was, that contained explosion inside him. He sat like a man whose legs would never again support him. His clutching hand fell limply into his lap. And, as a macabre and absurd finale, his head rolled forward into the potato salad, splattering it across the table.

They're all dead. All the Robedeaux brothers are dead.

Cordelia was the first to move. She knew too well what had happened.

"Help me," she said to me as she headed for him.

Aunt Greta let out a high-pitched wail, though it was hard to tell if it was because of her husband or the glob of potato salad that was dripping down her face.

I followed Cordelia. She lifted Uncle Claude by his shoulders, pulling him out of the potato salad. Grabbing his napkin, she wiped his face off.

"Help me put him on the floor," she instructed me. Together, we lifted him from his chair and laid him on the floor. His face was ashen and gray.

Alice, who was a nurse, joined us. Cordelia was kneeling beside him, her face close to his.

"He's not breathing," she told Alice.

"Claude," I heard Aunt Greta wail, "Claude, you've made a mess."

Shut up, silly woman, I wanted to say. Then I realized she was in shock. She had to know something was terribly, terribly wrong.

"Call nine-one-one," Cordelia instructed.

I was kneeling next to her and started to get up, but Cousin Rosemary jumped up from the table to do it.

Cordelia started giving him artificial respiration.

"What are you doing to my dad?" Bayard bellowed.

Also in shock, so I wrote it off.

"Saving his life, you asshole," someone answered. It sounded like Torbin.

Cordelia paused in her breathing to feel for a pulse. "No heartbeat," she told Alice.

"Oh, God," Alice responded. "I've got a bad shoulder. Can you . . . ?"

"Yes," Cordelia answered. She moved away from his head, then locked her hands together and placed them over his breastbone.

"Oh, good Lord, what's the address here?" Rosemary called from the kitchen, flustered at the 911 operator's request. "I don't live here, you see, and . . ." Someone called out the street and number, but Rosemary was too busy explaining to the 911 operator why she didn't know the address to listen to the address. "What was that? What?" she called.

Cordelia began forcing Uncle Claude's heart to beat, counting five, then pausing to let Alice breath for him.

"What's wrong?" I heard Rosemary from the kitchen. "He was eating potato salad, well, he wasn't actually eating it, but . . ."

"Myocardial infarction," Cordelia called out to her, obviously not thinking about the level of her audience.

"What?" Rosemary said.

"Heart attack," Alice answered as Cordelia was counting the number of heartbeats she was trying to push through his chest.

"Heart attack," I repeated for Rosemary. Alice was again breathing for him.

"Heart attack. Heart attack. That's what they're saying. Heart attack," came Rosemary's flustered voice from the next room.

Can they do it? Can they pull him back from death? I watched

Alice and Cordelia working, intense concentration on their faces. How we push limits, refuse to accept them, forcing a heart to beat and lungs to breath to hold death at bay.

"What's happening? What's wrong with Claude?" Aunt Greta wailed.

"Come, Greta. Don't watch this," Aunt Lottie said. She led Aunt Greta away from the table, the widow leading the almost widow. Aunt Lottie carefully wiped potato salad off Aunt Greta's face. She seemed not even to notice.

"I'll wait out front for the ambulance," Torbin said, walking past us.

Other conversations swirled for a moment around me, then stilled into a chasm of expectation. But his heart did not start beating, Cordelia was still pushing on his chest, and the hushed whispers began again.

Bring him back. It's not time for his life to be over, I silently pleaded.

The wail of the ambulance approached, drowning the hushed whispers as it drew closer.

There was a brief moment of silence, then the sound of voices. I could make out Torbin's "This way," and the clatter of the EMTs as they came into the living room. I stood up and backed away to give them room.

Suddenly Uncle Claude was surrounded by men and women. The reverent hushed whispers replaced by the purposeful cacophony of those to whom this was another day and another stranger.

I didn't want to watch anymore. My witnessing would not influence this dance on the edge of death. I didn't want the memory of the ways they would probe and pry at him, as if his body could be shoved back into life.

I turned and went into the kitchen. Rosemary was there, covering and wrapping food, as if a perfectly preserved ham would make a difference.

"Oh, is he going to be okay?" she said when she saw me.

"They're doing all they can," I answered.

She nodded and went back to her plastic wrap and tinfoil. And maybe it does matter. She couldn't stop him from dying, but she could prevent the food from spoiling.

I walked through the kitchen to the backyard. It was still as small as I had remembered it, but someone had planted flowers, yellow and white roses against the back fence. This flowered backyard seemed so foreign. I couldn't imagine Uncle Claude back here with the pansies and roses. Aunt Greta? Did she have a soul that included flowers? But could even the most perfect flower garden balance out the dryness of her heart?

The screen door slammed.

"So you had to get away from that mess in there, too?" It was Bayard.

I didn't answer him.

"Daddy sure found a new way to get out of eating Mama's potato salad."

"Shouldn't you be in there with her?"

"What's the matter, don't like my company?"

"Not especially."

"You used to." His leer bordered on sadistic.

I just stared at him. Could he really be doing this? Clinging so ferociously to the old patterns of power that he was blind to everything from the intervening years to his father's dying inside the house? "Shut up, Bayard," I retorted harshly. "I'll let it pass that this is some bizarre way of dealing with what's going on inside, if you shut up now."

He took a step toward me. "C'mon, Mick, you don't mean that." He took another step.

I moved back. He's too blind to see how things have irrevocably changed. The same house, the same backyard, the same people, but things have changed.

"We had some good times together," he continued.

"*We* didn't," I shot back. "Maybe you did and you were too selfish to see how much I hated it."

"You didn't hate it." He reached for me.

"Don't touch me."

"You didn't hate it. Don't pretend you did." He put his hand on my shoulder.

But things had changed. I slapped him as hard as I could. I wanted there to be no mistake in this message.

Bayard's head snapped back with the force of my hand against his cheek.

"You bitch," he sputtered. "Hitting me while my father is in there dying."

I didn't even stop to consider it. I spit in his face. With that I shoved past him and reentered the house.

Evil has a beer belly and a receding hairline.

Cousin Rosemary was now doing dishes. Bayard didn't follow me back in, the only glimmer of an intelligent thing he'd done yet.

I remained in the kitchen with Rosemary as a chaperone. Framed in the doorway, I had a partial view of Uncle Claude surrounded by EMTs. His shirt had been cut open. Off to one side, Cordelia and Alice stood, not saying anything, just watching the men and women around Uncle Claude, as if their vigilance would help keep his heart beating. In unison, they backed up, heralding the approach of a stretcher.

Was his heart beating? Had they brought him back? For a moment I hoped, then I saw the grim expressions of the EMTs. They were rushing him to the hospital, still pushing for a miracle.

Aunt Lottie came into the kitchen. "Where's Bayard?" she asked.

"Uh . . . I think out back," I muttered.

She gave her head an angry shake. "Well, he needs to act a bit like a man and take his mother to the hospital."

Her evident disapproval of him took me by surprise. I had

always thought that Bayard put up the perfect facade of a paragon of virtue.

"He just needs to settle down," Rosemary said to mollify things.

"He's about forty. I suspect he's settled as far as he's going to settle," Aunt Lottie dryly replied. She went into the backyard to find him.

I went back to the living room. I wanted to be near Cordelia when Bayard reappeared.

Gus and Ronnie were supporting Aunt Greta between them. She looked scared and confused, an expression I had never seen on her face before.

"I'm sorry, Aunt Greta," I murmured as they passed me. She didn't answer or even look in my direction.

She stopped to look at Cordelia. "What happened? What did you do to him?"

At times, you know people and how they will act, where they will stumble and fall, because they've tripped on the same place so many other times. I wanted to stop what I knew was about to happen, but as Cassandra had learned, knowing the future doesn't mean you can change it.

"I'm sorry, Mrs. Robedeaux," Cordelia said. Her voice, low and compassionate, was a contrast to Aunt Greta's harsh whine.

"If he dies, it'll be your fault," she retorted.

"That's not—" I started, but Cordelia put her hand on my wrist to silence me.

"We did all we could, Mrs. Robedeaux," she replied, her voice still soft and gentle. "He's getting the best medical care possible."

Aunt Greta turned from her, almost by instinct realizing that attacking Cordelia would be fruitless.

"Where's my son?" she wailed.

"I'm here, Mama," Gus, still awkwardly supporting her arm, answered.

Again, I knew what would happen, actions and reactions written on the wall as if we can never change.

"Bayard. Where's Bayard?" Aunt Greta dismissed Gus.

"Here, Mama," he answered, Aunt Lottie having found him and made him do his duty. "Don't you worry, I'm right here." He smoothly edged Gus away. Gus's face had that defeated look that I had seen so many times when we were growing up together. Ronnie started to let go of Aunt Greta's arm to remain with Gus.

But Bayard said, "C'mon, Ronnie, you come with me. I need you to help with Mama. Gus, someone needs to stay here and hold the fort."

Cousin Rosemary, in her innocent bumbling way, came to Gus's rescue. "Oh, no, Gus, you go on. I'll clean up everything here."

Seeing a crack in Bayard's maneuver, Ronnie reached out with her free hand to Gus. "Gus, honey, you need to be with us."

"Don't worry, I'll lock up," I volunteered. "I still remember how."

Bayard glanced at me with a sour look before herding them out. His voice trailed back, "Gus, you might better take your car, don't know how long it'll be. Might be better to have two cars."

"Bad times don't make bad people nice," Aunt Lottie commented. "Thanks for helping out. I guess we should go to the hospital." She sighed, then asked Cordelia, "You think he's gonna make it?"

Cordelia slowly shrugged. "I don't know. Maybe, if there's not too much damage to the heart."

"Lord, it seems like Claude couldn't bear to be left here all alone." With that, Aunt Lottie squeezed Cordelia's hand, gave me a hug, and headed for another hospital ordeal.

Torbin reappeared. "Are you going?" he asked us.

"No," I answered. "I'll stay here and clean up. I imagine that the cleaning supplies are still in the same place. Are you?"

"Mom is. I'll go with her. She's still reeling from Dad's death."

"We'll be home. Call if . . . just call."

"Of course." Torbin gave me a big hug.

"Anytime," I added.

Then he and Andy were gone.

"We can go to the hospital if you want," Cordelia said.

"No, I think not." We were silent for a moment, then I asked, "What are his chances? Will he make it?"

For me, Cordelia shook her head. "He might. But . . . we never got his heart beating. That's not a good sign."

Suddenly I wanted her to hold me. "Let's clean up and get out of here," I said, turning from her and the temptation to put my arms around her.

Potato salad was still spewed across the table and on the floor where Uncle Claude had lain.

The cleaning supplies were where they had always been, even the same brands, in their new and improved states.

Only Cordelia, Cousin Rosemary (I wasn't sure what degree of cousin she was, and now didn't seem like the time to ask), and I were left. Cordelia and I tackled the living room, the tables with half-eaten food still spread over them. Cordelia took it upon herself to clean up after the EMTs, knowing that the detritus of the medical world was familier to her, but for us would carry resonances of a man dying. I mopped up the potato salad, even running the mop over the table. Aunt Greta wasn't here to see it and she would never know. We kept Rosemary supplied with dirty dishes as we cleared off the tables, so she remained at the sink.

"I hope the spare key's still in its usual place," I said after a final inspection to make sure everything was clean and that there weren't any drips of potato salad hidden anywhere.

The key was. After locking up and getting Cousin Rosemary's extended good-bye ("Oh, you live in the same place. How nice. It's nice to have someone to have girl chat right there. Yes, that's nice"), Cordelia and I headed home.

"It shouldn't be too long," Cordelia said as she unlocked our door. "Myocardial infarction—heart attack," she translated for me, "you either know one way or another."

It wasn't long. Cordelia and I both exchanged a glance before I reached for the phone.

"Mick?" Torbin was on the other end.

"Yes, it's me."

"Uncle Claude didn't make it."

I repeated his words to Cordelia, then said to Torbin, "Guess he didn't want to be the only Robedeaux brother left here. Should I have gone to the hospital?"

"Wait, let me check for listeners." There was a moment's pause. "Only Andy around. Yes, you should have come to the hospital. You could have watched Bayard see how many times he could get away with letting his hands rove in Ronnie's direction before Gus did something very un-Gus-like. Mary Theresa's two brats gave a demonstration of how juvenile delinquents behave when they're five and six years old. You know what one of them said when Mary Theresa ever-so-gently informed them of Uncle Claude's death— 'Shut up, your grandpawpaw's dead'? The child replied, 'So? I want french fries and a Coke and I want them now.' My mother was about to pack that child over her knee and give it six years of discipline in one fell swoop, except that Aunt Greta began a keening wail that the highest-priced professional mourner would have envied, so Mom got distracted by her. Then Aunt Greta started on a diatribe about lesbian doctors and how her husband would still be alive, et cetera, et cetera. Bayard joined in, amending 'lesbian' to 'dyke.' The two of them were railing high style until Alice, my fair-minded, even-tempered sister, had enough and reminded them that it was both she and Cordelia who were giving Uncle Claude CPR and that they're doing so gave him the only chance he had. I could see the nurses behind the nursing station silently cheering her on, because they were heartily weary of the Robedeaux clown show. So, yes, you should have been at the hospital for all that."

"How are you?"

"Ready to get the hell out of here." His voice had a ragged, tired edge. "But I thought you should know."

"Yeah, thanks for calling. It's not likely anyone else would."

We said our good-byes and I slowly hung up the phone.

"Oh, Micky, I'm sorry." Cordelia reached out for me and I moved into her arms. I surprised myself by bursting into tears. The closest Uncle Claude and I had ever been was in the conversation from this afternoon. Was I crying because there still had been possibilities for him and they were now gone? Or, more selfishly, was I really crying for myself? That a man who had always been in my life was gone?

Cordelia held me, saying nothing.

I finally composed myself and broke our embrace to find some tissues. I needed to wash my face.

That taken care of, I took her hand and led her into the bedroom. I suddenly wanted a deeper touch than just a fully clothed embrace.

We stood at the foot of the bed, our arms loosely around each other. I felt awkward, unsure of how to make the transition out of these funeral clothes, hose, slips, their clumsy removal, to laying across the bed with her. Cordelia was waiting expectantly for a cue from me.

"Hold me," I mumbled, to hide the overwhelming uncertainty that had caught me. Her arms tightened around me. I rested my head in the crook of her neck, feeling the warmth of her bare skin against my forehead. I knew I wanted her to make love to me, to keep at bay the looming sense of my mortality, to scream into some void, "Yes, I know someday you'll take me, but now I'm alive."

Cordelia gently kissed my forehead. I lifted my face to her, offering my lips.

In the three years we had been together, we had learned each other's signals, nuances; we could be both more subtle and more bold in asking for and receiving touch.

Her kiss was soft, restrained.

I returned her kiss, but mine wasn't soft and restrained. She hesitated for a moment as my tongue entered her mouth, then responded with the same intensity. I had trusted that she would, I realized; three years together had given me that much trust.

We didn't speak, except for Cordelia's murmured offer of "Let me do that," as she reached to help my fumbling hands unhook my bra.

It wasn't smooth and perfect, our undressing and climbing into bed. For a brief moment, I wondered when that had happened, when comfort and closeness had replaced the need to be perfect for the new lover. When we realized that neither of us was faultless, yet love still held. That's the miracle of love, that someone knows us well enough to know the ways we fail and are weak, and yet loves us still.

Cordelia took the lead, somehow knowing that I wanted this physicalness, but was too spun by the day's events to do anything but follow.

Afterward, when I lay in her arms, I knew that that was what I had really wanted, the special moment of closeness after we've made love, our arms around each other, my face against her breast without the insistent tug of sexual desire. It was a moment that said to the void, "I am alive and well and at peace."

Chapter

5

I woke up with a groggy feeling, as if time were moving in lurches and fits and I had no idea where it had landed, what the time was or even the day. I vaguely remembered Cordelia's clock going off at a too-early hour. That gave me a clue that it was still a weekday.

Uncle Claude's dead. Remembering that didn't clear up my grogginess; instead it added a layer of grief to the muddle. Then a skein of anxiety trickled in. Would anyone call to tell me about the funeral arrangements? Or would I be left to read about it in the paper a day late?

I sat upright and started to throw myself out of bed. Torbin would tell me. Or Aunt Lottie. Or I could probably even call Cousin Rosemary. I lay back down, but couldn't shake the feeling that I needed to be doing something. I just had no idea what that something was.

I finally got up, deciding that no matter which something I ended up doing, a shower would be an appropriate prelude. After I was properly cleaned and coifed (a comb through my hair), I decided to pay obeisance to my anxiety and make a few phone calls.

Torbin, being the easiest, was first. I got his answering machine. He did keep drag queen hours. I left a message asking him to call me.

I sat drinking coffee, which was doing little to calm my agitation, when another course of action presented itself. I grabbed the phone book. What was the name of Ronnie and Gus's video store? I skimmed the list of video rental places, hoping I'd recognize the name if I saw it. Rescue by Video. That was it.

"Video Rescue." I recognized Ronnie's voice.

"Hi, Ronnie. This is Micky. Micky Knight, Gus's cousin," I identified myself.

"Oh, hey, darlin'. How ya holdin' up?"

"Fair to middling. How's Gus doing?"

"He's off being the good son, takin' care of his mama. It's a dirty job, but someone's got to do it."

"I'm trying to find out if there've been any funeral arrangements made yet."

"You'd think the Pope died, the way Greta's demanding and fussing. Aunt Lottie and Gus are doin' most of it, so ya called the right person. It's tomorrow, prime time, Saturday at one P.M. It'll be the high and holy type service, so wear your most comfy girdle. Lottie talked Greta out of tryin' to do another funeral feast. Said people'd be worn out by it. My guess is that no one would show up unless they could certify that the potato salad wasn't left over."

"Well, it would have been a way to get rid of the leftovers. Thanks for the info, Ronnie."

"Hey, no problem. Just stay between me and that lecherous cousin of yours."

"Bayard? Sorry, not me—I stay as far from him as I can."

"You're his cousin, almost a kid sister. He doesn't try shit with you, does he?" Ronnie sounded properly outraged.

"I'm adopted, not really related, so I guess he thinks it's okay."

"That's gross. He's just a gross shithead. Well, then, we'll have to stick together and protect each other. I'm of a mind to bring some of Grandma Fenella's special hot sauce—makes Tabasco look like a drink of cool water—and squirt some on a delicate place."

"Your aim's that good?"

Ronnie let out a snort that turned into a cackle. "Ya got a point. Might need a magnifying glass to see the target. No, he sure ain't porn star material." She let out another loud snort. "But Greta's got his chain jerked real short. She alternates between wailing, 'Why? Why'd Claude have to pass so soon?' and, 'Where's my son? Where's Bayard?' Havin' a grievin' mama cramps his skirt-chasing."

"Too bad it's only temporary."

"I don't know about that. I think Greta's gonna play the widow card as long as she can. I don't mean to be disrespectful, but I think the woman spent too many years on her knees in church, messed up the blood flow to her brain."

"Bastard children like me don't dare say such things. But I think you've got the picture."

"Customer's comin' in. I gotta make a livin'. See ya tomorrow."

I had my information. And the comfort of confirmation that I wasn't the weird, crazy one, they were.

Since it was still in the vicinity of morning and I had a good chunk of usable day before me, I decided that it was time to make my way to my office. I did have a few cases pending and I didn't want anyone, particularly myself, to think I was living off my rich girlfriend.

I fed the cats before I left, doing my best to keep them from expecting to be fed on Cordelia's schedule. That was way too early in the morning for me to be opening sharp metal things.

Then I headed downtown to my office. Both yesterday's and today's mail was waiting for me. Junk and bills, two days with nothing thrilling. The answering machine blinked accusingly at me, its winking light a sign of messages unanswered.

I ran it back to listen to two hang-ups, a clearly wrong number ("Yo, Spider, you there? You owe me, man"), then a message from Lindsey McNeil returning my call, another hang-up, and last and least, a message from Bourbon St. Ann: "Um, hi. I thought of a few more things. I sent that stuff off. How long do I wait? Can you give me a call?" And with that, the accusing red light changed to a mollified green.

Since I had called her, Lindsey deserved the first call back. However, she was still with a client, presumably not the same one, though I could name a few people who would benefit from twenty-four-hour-a-day therapy.

Bourbon St. Ann wasn't a paying client. I would call him back when and if I felt like it.

Next I checked my computer to see if I had any interesting E-mail. I did need to make sure that Lorraine Drummond's address wasn't waiting for me in cyberspace before I pestered Suzanna Forquet.

It was. She lived three blocks from where I now sat.

Computers and the Internet have turned what used to be leg-work into chair work. Sara Clavish, located in the office next door to mine, used to have a Cajun cookbook business, until, as she said, "Sixty-nine is too old to be hauling around heavy books." She met a computer and had a harmonic convergence—she could sit comfortably, listen to music, and search the world. I now farm out a lot of what I consider boring, tedious computer searches to her. Even though we're a door apart, we communicate more by E-mail.

Well, maybe I could do my good deed for the day and make someone's mother happy. I turned off the computer.

She may be at work, I thought as I locked up my office, but three blocks wasn't very far out of my way. It was a nice day for a walk. In New Orleans, that means it's not raining and you're not drenched in sweat by the bottom step.

I rang the buzzer at the address my computer had given me. A young white man opened the door. He didn't look like someone my version of Lorraine Drummond would have as a roommate.

"Hi, I'm looking for Lorraine Drummond," I said, forging ahead.

He blinked uncomprehendingly at me. He blinked again, though this time with a hint of comprehension. "Uh . . . I'm Steve and my lov . . . roommate is Vaughn. We just moved in."

"I see. Do you have any idea what happened to the woman who used to live here?"

He just shook his head, the uncomprehending blink returning.

The woman from the house next door decided, like all good New Orleanians, that her input was required. "You lookin' for Lorraine?"

I admitted that I was.

"She moved away last month. Why you lookin' for her?"

I gave my standard lie. "I'm a private investigator" (that's not the lie part) "and Lorraine's due an inheritance. I'm trying to find her so she can get it." I flashed my PI license. Good thing Louisiana finally started licensing us so I had something official to display. Most people are willing to help find someone who is due money.

"Sorry, can't help you. I don't know where she went."

"Did you get the impression that she was making a local move? Or to somewhere out of state?"

The next-door neighbor pondered this for a moment. "It was a little truck from that place up on St. Claude. Now that I think about it, I recall she made a couple of trips."

"Is there anyone around here who might know where she went?"

"Well, let me think on that for a bit." She thought on it for a bit. "Nope."

"Do you have any idea where she works?"

"Well, give me a minute." I gave her a minute and a half. "No, not really. She was usually dressed and out by eight-thirty, so maybe someplace in the CBD."

The CBD, or Central Business District, is the area of town that gives New Orleans its skyline, with a number of tall office buildings. It wasn't the narrowest of search fields.

"Thanks for all your help," I said to the neighbor. To Steve, I added, "Sorry to have bothered you and your . . . roommate." I winked to let him know I had a roommate, too.

With that, I headed back to my office.

So much for quick and easy. Lorraine Drummond had moved, and her new address hadn't yet filtered into the easy-to-find places. I hoped she wasn't as bad as I was about those things. I didn't bother changing address the last time I moved until I'd gone through two boxes of checks that still had my old address on them.

I would find Lorraine Drummond. This is just the way life is: Nothing is ever as simple and easy as you hope it will be.

But, I thought as I headed up the stairs to my office, now I had an excuse to hunt down Suzanna Forquet. However tarnished, every cloud has a silver lining.

As I unlocked the door, the phone rang. I got to it by the third ring.

"M. Knight Detective Agency," I answered.

"Hi, Micky, this is Lindsey."

"Hi, thanks for calling back. Do you know a Suzanna Forquet?"

"Why do you ask?"

Damn shrinks, they always answer your perfectly good question with a question. "I'm trying to find someone and she's a possible link."

"A possible link? How?"

"I'll answer that question if you answer mine. Do you know her?"

"Yes, I do. Now you can answer my question."

"An ex-lover of hers."

"Woman?"

"Yes."

"Oh, boy, Suzanna's going to love to chat with you about that."

"So I've heard. She's not a client of yours, is she?"

"I do mostly kids and adolescents, remember?" Lindsey answered without answering.

"There are a lot of adults that still qualify as kids and adolescents. I'm trying to get someone to introduce me to her. Can you do that?"

"What are you doing tomorrow night?"

"Tomorrow? Saturday?" The gears in my brain were grinding. Uncle Claude's funeral was at one.

"Do you have to check with Cordelia?" Lindsey asked.

"I have a funeral in the afternoon. My uncle died."

"Didn't you go to his funeral yesterday?"

"No . . . well, yes. How did you know that?"

"I was at the clinic. Cordelia wasn't there and Millie told me she was with you going to your uncle's funeral."

"Different uncle. That was Uncle Charlie, Torbin's Dad. This is Uncle Claude. He died of a heart attack right after his brother's funeral."

"The uncle who raised you?"

"If sitting in front of the TV can be called raising me."

"So you weren't very close to him."

"I lived in that house for eight years. Is that close or not? You're the expert, you tell me."

"I'm not the expert on your life. It's up to you to call your relationship close or not."

"No, we weren't close. Are you satisfied?"

"So why are you so angry that he died?"

I hate it when people, particularly shrink types, name an emotion that I didn't even know I was having until they point it out. Naturally, I wasn't about to admit that to her. "Why do you think I'm angry?" I replied, as calmly as I could.

"Grief often has anger mixed with it. Especially if a relationship is unresolved. An uncle that you lived with after your father died, who was nothing more than a channel-changer, has the possibility of being an unresolved relationship. Besides that, you sound angry."

"I do not," I said angrily. "Okay, yes, I do. But you're not my therapist."

"No, I'm not. But many people aren't comfortable talking about grief and death. Losing two uncles in the last week is a pretty good reason to be angry."

"I didn't lose them. I know exactly where they are."

"So, where are you?"

Lindsey had a way of asking questions that made you feel you needed the answer more than she did. Where was I? I did need to know the answer to that question. "I guess . . . maybe I am angry. We talked, Uncle Claude and I, for a little bit after Uncle Charlie's funeral. It was . . . not much, but a bit of a connection. He apologized for the way I had been treated. And . . . he seemed ready to make a change. Maybe even leave Aunt Greta."

Lindsey merely made one of those affirmative sounds.

"But I guess he did that, didn't he? He died and left Aunt Greta here alive. I guess I'm angry that he was just starting to take those first steps, realizing that he could have had a different life when . . ." I trailed off.

"When he died," Lindsey finished for me.

"Not fair. Not fair at all."

"No, it's not," she agreed.

We were silent for a moment. Then Lindsey asked, "How old were you when you went to live with them?"

"Ten. Just turned ten."

"That's when your father died?"

"Yes. Wouldn't have lived with them if he hadn't."

"What happened to your mother?"

"She left when I was five. Didn't want to be stuck in the bayous raising a kid, I guess."

"Did you ever see her again?"

"No, no, I didn't. She wrote for a while, postcards, letters, drawing—she always drew me pictures. She went to live in New York. Then . . ."

"Then?"

"Then they just stopped. Nothing. I kept writing to the last address I had for her, but . . . my letters came back."

"Ever wonder what happened to her?"

"Sometimes. But mostly I wonder how she could have just left me like that. Left me with . . . could you just abandon a child to the care of someone like Aunt Greta?"

"Is that what you think she did?"

"What else?"

"Maybe something happened to her? Do you even know if she's still alive? Maybe your aunt and uncle didn't tell her what happened?"

"That's possible. But why stop writing? If she sent the letters to Bayou St. Jack's and they came back, it's hard to believe she wouldn't contact Uncle Claude or Uncle Charlie to find out what happened."

"Maybe she wrote and your aunt intercepted the letters."

"Maybe. But usually one of us kids got to the mail first. She would have had to be awfully lucky to get every letter."

"Have you ever considered looking for her?"

"I've *considered* it. But . . . if she didn't want me, why should I want her?"

"Curiosity. Just to find out what happened to her."

"Do you think I should hunt down my mother? Confront her? Demand to know where she's been all these years? Are you imagining a happy reunion?"

"No, nothing like that. Those kinds of reunions often aren't happy. You're a big girl, you wouldn't even need to hire a private investigator to do it. Maybe she didn't abandon you, maybe she died. What's easier for you to carry? Not knowing, assuming she abandoned you? Or perhaps knowing she's no longer alive?"

I didn't answer. I didn't have an answer. What *had* happened to my mother? What did I really know? She had left when I was five, and moved to New York City. From there she had sent me cards and letters, sketches of where she lived, her cat, other city scenes she thought I might like. But I had never gotten anything from her after I had moved in with Uncle Claude and Aunt Greta. I had gone to college in New York hoping to find her, that somehow fate would bring us back together again. When it hadn't, I cursed fate and lived my life without her. Did I want to know, to have the final knowing of either her death or that she had left her daughter behind, her only looking back a few postcards and letters? What did Uncle Claude want to give me? Could it answer any of my questions?

I finally replied to Lindsey, "I don't know. I'll keep considering it. Now, can we get back to the original reason for my phone call?"

"Ah, Suzanna Forquet."

"You said something about tomorrow night."

"Yes, I did. A party uptown. To celebrate the publication, by one of my fellow shrink types, of a book entitled *Happy Marriages: The Experts' Guide to Keeping the Flame Alive*.

"Suzanna Forquet is going to be there?"

"It's at her place. She and Henri are close, personal friends of the Happy Marriage couple."

"I can't wait."

"Of course, Suzanna won't like me showing up with a woman. On the other hand . . . you're her type."

"I thought she liked them darker than me."

"She likes the Creole look, so I've heard. But she may be too busy being part of a perfectly happy couple to flirt with women."

"I'd hate to miss such a gala affair."

"More closet cases per square foot than anywhere else in the continental United States."

"Let me say yes, unless something comes up at Uncle Claude's funeral."

"You sure you want to cram both of these in one day?"

"It will probably make it the most interesting day of the year. But, yeah, I'll be okay. I'll call you after I get back, to set the details."

"Page me. Let me give you the number."

She did, I wrote it down, and that settled how I was going to meet Miss Suzanna.

I started to read, but Lindsey's probing had riled my subconscious. I couldn't stop thinking about Uncle Claude. Once he took me to the doctor, I had a bad earache. I couldn't recall why Aunt Greta hadn't taken me, but she wasn't around, so Uncle Claude had. No eleven-year-old enjoys going to the doctor. Instead of taking me straight home, as I'm sure Aunt Greta had instructed, we played hooky and went to the special snow cone place across town. I don't remember us talking more than Uncle Claude asking what flavor I wanted. And, after we'd thrown our used napkins and paper cups away, saying not to tell Aunt Greta.

But even the nostalgia that surrounds death couldn't blur other memories: Uncle Claude sitting only a few feet away, staring resolutely at the television as if nothing else mattered, while

Aunt Greta first berated me, then took a belt to me, for taking the stamps to write my mother. He never looked in our direction.

That was what I was left with, the memory of a complicated man, mixed kindness and neglect. His death had closed away the possibility of change and recompense.

But would Uncle Claude really have broken away from Aunt Greta after all those years of custom and compromise? Or would he have just, as he did with the snow cone, only rebelled if he thought there would be no consequences? Much as I wanted the perfect ending, it was hard to imagine him openly defying Aunt Greta or standing up to his middle-aged son.

What did he want to tell me about my past? What part of his conscience did he want to assuage?

The phone rang. I didn't want to think about these things anymore, so I picked it up. "Knight Detective Agency."

"Uh . . . hi, Micky. This is Bourbon St. Ann. I did all that stuff you suggested. But I haven't heard anything."

"It may take awhile. The wheels of bureaucracy grind slowly."

"I guess. I don't feel like I have time. I know I'm being pushy, but I want to get settled before . . ." He trailed off. In his voice was a scared young boy who knew he was sick and knew he would die young.

"All right," I said. "I'm going to ask you a lot of questions. Just answer them as best you can. Don't editorialize. Let's start with your real name."

"You won't like it."

"Don't editorialize. Just answer."

"Stone Hudson. My mother wanted to name me after a movie star without naming me after a movie star."

He was right, I didn't like it—what a name to be stuck with—but I wasn't going to tell him that. "Middle name?"

"Zachary. She thought it sounded classy. You see why I had to become a drag queen, just to get away from that name."

"It's not that hard to change your name," I said, violating my rule about editorializing. "Any chance your parents will talk to me?"

"Well, maybe. My mother hasn't ever been known to stop talking. Where do you think I got this from? But I don't think the best approach would be to be up-front and honest. Of course, that never was the best approach in my family."

"How can I contact your mother?"

"Astral projection might be safest."

"Answers, not editorials."

"They live over on the Gulf Coast, in Ocean Springs. Try as hard as I can, I've never been able to forget either that address or the phone number." And that was all the preamble it took to get him to give me the information.

"Do you know your real birth date?"

"We always celebrated my birthday on August tenth. But I got the impression that that was the adoption date, not my actual plop-out-of-the-womb date."

"Year?"

"Nineteen seventy-five."

I was, I realized, (just barely) old enough to be his mother. "When did you find out you were adopted?"

"When did I figure it out? In high school biology class. That genetic shit. You know, two blue-eyed parents can't have a brown-eyed child. I came home and asked my mother what color the TV repairman's eyes were. After her usual moaning, she finally admitted that I was adopted. Which I was relieved to hear, because it meant that I was right about my parents never having sex. If they'd actually had me, they'd have had to done it at least once. Frightening thought, my parents having sex, but not as scary as my mother cheating on my father."

"Did she say anything about the adoption? Any idea how it was arranged?"

"Just because my mother talks a lot doesn't mean she says much. She just muttered something about telling me someday and that I came from the Lord and did it matter which way He delivered me?"

"When did you know you were gay?"

"Around when I was four and I felt an irresistible pull to the Barbie shelf in the toy store. GI Joe did nothing for me until the day the neighborhood juvenile-delinquent-in-training took his sister's Ken doll, bent him over, and had old Soldier Joe assume the position behind him."

"How did your parents find out you were gay?"

"The usual shitty way. The football coach caught me sucking his son's dick. Sonny boy acted like the most virginal thing on the planet, blubbering to Daddy that he'd never done anything like it before. He'd only been nailing me for the last few months. So football Daddy calls my mother, tells her I've corrupted his son and he's going to have me kicked out of school.

"Honey, let me tell you, I didn't wait for that story to make the locker room rounds. I hitched a ride out of that hellhole into this one."

"You just ran away? How old were you?"

"Sixteen. Ran like a nun in a whorehouse. Or should that be a whore in a nunnery?"

"How'd you survive?"

"Three guesses. The first two don't count."

"Hustling?"

"Right-o. It wasn't that hard. I just started charging for what I'd given out for free."

"You've had no contact with your parents since then?"

"Right, no contact. Unless you want to call two hang-ups as contact. Yeah, that's right, little baby boy got scared out on the road all by himself, so he called his mama. She hung up on him. He was so pathetic, he called again a few weeks later. She hung up again."

"You never tried again?" I asked gently.

"No, little baby boy was out all on his own." He was silent for a moment. "You know, you'd think that with two mothers, at least one . . . oh, hell. You got any more questions?"

"Not at the moment. I'll try to contact your mother, but don't get your hopes up. Remember to be careful about what you ask for. You may get it."

"When do you think you might hear something?"

"Call me in about a week. We'll take it from there."

"Okay . . . look, uh, thanks. I'll pay you a little bit when I can. Hey, if you ever want to come see the show, I'll get you in for free."

I thought about pointing out that Torbin could just as easily get me in free, but I didn't. Bourbon St. Ann was young enough to think that there would be a time when he would have some money and that he would pay me. "Thanks, I'll think about it," I responded to his offer. It was a genuine offer, as genuine as air and hope and the optimism that tomorrow would be better.

I wasn't sure why I had agreed to take the case. Even if he found his biological mother, it wasn't likely that she would turn into the mother of his dreams. Was I, as the shrinks would have it, identifying with someone who had also been left motherless? Bourbon St. Ann wasn't exactly a model citizen. The streets had taught him the hard lessons of survival, the kind you learn when the only person who cares whether you live or die is you. But underneath that hardness and manipulation, the scrappy me-first attitude, was a scared eighteen-year-old boy. Maybe that was why I had taken the case. How do you say no to a scared and lost little boy?

I prepared a case file, listing all the information he had given me. I even made up a billing sheet. Maybe I could write it off at tax time. Though it was only midafternoon, I decided to call it a done day.

As I locked the door, I felt a little guilty about not doing more to find Lorraine Drummond. I reminded myself that I would be meeting Suzanna Forquet tomorrow. The virtuous side of my nature pointed out that that had less to do with finding Lorraine than sating my desire to bedevil Suzanna Forquet.

I headed down the stairs with the thought that I had just been to a funeral and was going to another one. That should give me an excuse to do what I wanted. At least it shut up my virtuous side.

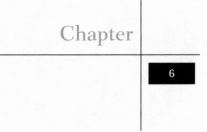

Chapter

6

I wasn't well stocked in funeral clothes. It wasn't often that my wardrobe was called on to provide three suitably somber ensembles in one week. Cordelia did suggest that I was dithering about clothes to, as she delicately put it, "avoid other issues."

"I'm sorry, I'm flustered. I guess this is disturbing me more than I'm admitting. Like the perfect dress can make everything okay."

"If only it could."

"But I guess a perfect dress won't bring Uncle Claude back and it won't make Aunt Greta like me."

"So you might as well wear the black one."

That finally settled, I applied myself to the task of putting on and cursing panty hose. In my experience the two are always linked. Then we were dressed and ready to go, me in my twice-worn black dress and Cordelia in a deep maroon one. She had to

dress for work more often than I did and consequently her wardrobe was more varied.

"You must love me a lot," I said as we got in the car. "To go to
two lugubrious family funerals in less than a week with me."

"It's not like you can control when people die." Then she
added, "It's not like anyone can."

The church parking lot was already crowded when we got
there. Another man taken quickly, another crowded funeral.

As we edged through the church door, I suddenly realized that
I had to make a decision when we entered the church. Was I family? Did I sit up front? Aunt Greta and her children had always
treated me like an interloper. They would resent my sitting with
them as one final intrusion into their lives, particularly having
Cordelia with me.

"Where do we sit?" I whispered to Cordelia. She looked at me
with a sad smile that said that I was the only one who could
decide. It wasn't for her to choose if I belonged to this family or
not.

"Come with me, honey." Aunt Lottie came up beside me and
took my hand. As she led us up the aisle, I noticed that she had
also taken Cordelia's hand. She brought us to sit with her and her
family. I gratefully slid in next to Torbin. We were in the second
pew, part of the family, but not intruding on Aunt Greta.

Aunt Greta glanced back. Our eyes caught for just a moment;
I gave her a brief nod of acknowledgment. An odd look of triumph
and relief passed over her face. I had come to the funeral. I had
lived in her house for eight years and to have not come would
have been an indictment and an insult. She quickly turned away
and did not again look back.

At first, I paid attention to the service, the ritual of the words.
That thin skein of protection against mortality, the generation I
was born of, was gone. Ashes to ashes. They were gone.

Torbin put his arm around my shoulders. Tears glistened on
his cheeks, too. Somehow, I knew his tears fell for the same rea-

sons mine did. Not for the loss of a good life gone, but for the holes and gapes, the rough spots that would retain their sharp edges through memory. Torbin was left with a father who had always been ambivalent about him. And I was left with an uncle who should have taken the place of my father, but who hadn't, save for that small abortive gesture on the day of Uncle Charlie's funeral.

Suddenly I wanted to know if my mother was dead or alive. I wanted to know who she was, what had happened to her. Was she still living flesh or had she, too, gone to ashes?

The service ended. We didn't linger. The people that were here were not really part of my life anymore.

As Cordelia drove away, I turned to her and stated, "I want to find my mother."

She looked at me, clearly surprised. For a moment, she said nothing, concentrating on driving. Finally she replied, "If that's what you want, you should do it. But Micky . . . be realistic about it. It's not likely that, even if you find her, there'll be some grand reunion."

"I just want to find her. Know she's dead or alive. I don't plan to actually make contact. I have no illusions. She knew where to find me if she wanted to."

Cordelia took my hand, but made no reply.

When we got back home, Joanne's car was parked out front. She was just coming down the steps as we pulled in.

"I was hoping to catch you in. I just wanted to talk to Cordelia for a few minutes," she said.

"About?" I nosily asked, as if I had a right to question anyone questioning my lover.

"Let's go inside," was her answer.

"We just came from the funeral of Micky's uncle," Cordelia said, a subtle apology for my churlishness.

"I can come back if this is a bad time, but I only have a few questions."

"It's okay. Come in," Cordelia answered.

As I closed the door, I said, "Can we at least take off our panty hose, or do we have to suffer through your inquisition with them on?" I wanted my home sanctuary undisturbed and I admitted, somewhat childishly, that I wanted Cordelia to be paying attention to me, not answering Joanne's questions.

"Get comfortable, but I will be quick," she answered.

Not bothering to retreat to the bedroom, I kicked off my shoes, reached under my dress, and pulled down the offending panty hose. I might prefer not to have Joanne here, but I did want to hear what she wanted to talk to Cordelia about.

"Does the name Yvonne Jackson sound familiar to you?" Joanne asked her.

Cordelia thought for a moment, then shook her head. "Should it?" she asked.

"Not necessarily," Joanne answered. "She was murdered . . . the same way the first woman was."

Cordelia shuddered in response.

Joanne continued, "We're pursuing all leads. Were these just random victims or is there a link between them?"

"You think she could have been a patient of Cordelia's?" I interjected.

"We have to check it out."

"I can't place the name," Cordelia replied.

"I have a picture with me." Joanne hesitated for a moment. "But it's an autopsy photo."

"Then I guess I have to look at an autopsy photo," Cordelia said with a grimace.

Joanne took a folder out of her briefcase. Cordelia looked at the photo, although she didn't reach over and take it from Joanne, as if not wanting to touch even a photo of a dead woman.

I glanced at the picture, looking over Cordelia's shoulder. It showed only her head, hiding the carnage done to the rest of her body. Even with her eyes mercifully closed, hers was clearly a face not in sleep, but in death. The muscles completely slack, blood no longer pumping, gave her face a hollow, deserted look.

I quickly turned away. I didn't need the faces of dead women to haunt my dreams.

Cordelia stared at it for a moment more before saying, "I don't recognize her. I'd have to check the files at the clinic just to be sure, but she's not familiar."

"I'd appreciate it if you would. Call me with your results," Joanne said.

"Should I go in today? Or can it wait until Monday?"

"If you can do it Monday, that'll be okay."

"It'll be easier then, when our office manager is in. She knows the files much better than I do."

"Even if you don't find anything, call me and let me know."

"Of course," Cordelia responded.

"That's all I needed. Thanks for your time," Joanne said, then she added to me, "Sorry about your uncle. Was it expected?"

"Heart attack. Right after his brother's funeral."

"That's rough. How are you?"

"I'm okay. It's not like I've had much to do with this family since I was eighteen."

Joanne glanced at Cordelia to see if I really meant what I said.

She was smart enough to not directly contradict me. "She'll be okay," Cordelia told Joanne.

Joanne nodded, and with that, she was gone.

Cordelia suddenly looked tired. The brief act of looking at that photo seemed to have drained her.

"My turn to get out of these damn panty hose." She pulled them off just as unceremoniously as I had, in the middle of the living room.

"I'm sorry," I said.

"For what?"

"Too many funerals. That picture."

"I'll admit that none of this is a lot of fun. But you can't control the funerals that enter your life. Or pictures of . . " She didn't finish the sentence.

"The woman from the clinic? Was she . . . a lesbian?" I asked, remembering Cordelia's earlier suspicions.

"I don't know. I keep meaning to look at her chart, but I haven't yet."

"You are very busy," I excused her. "And it's probably not that relevant." With that we went to the bedroom to finish taking off our funeral clothes.

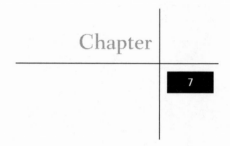

Chapter

7

I realized that I had already made the decision to go with Lindsey to Suzanna Forquet's party. The quickness of death gave an added urgency to finding Lorraine Drummond for her mother. The woman whose photo both Cordelia and I stared at this afternoon was about her age.

I wasn't quite sure how to tell Cordelia what I was up to. ("I'm going to a party of a bunch of uptown mega-closet cases with your ex-lover" didn't seem the best opener, though it was the most honest.)

But fate, or at least the cycles for grant applications, was on my side. Cordelia informed me that she had to spend most of the evening working on one.

"We're trying to get prenatal and parenting classes going and we want to hire a health educator and outreach worker," she explained.

"That's okay. Actually, I have some detecting work to do."

"Oh?" she said, paying more attention to the stack of papers in her hand than to me.

"Yeah, going to an uptown hoity-toity party."

"That is work for you."

"I hope you don't mind, but Lindsey is my entrée into this circle."

"Why should I mind?" Then she looked at me. "Unless you're doing something more than just meeting at a party."

"No, she's just taking me to this party so I can . . . find out a few things. Besides, I probably have more to worry about concerning you and Lindsey than you have to worry about me and Lindsey."

"Then I have nothing to worry about," Cordelia reassured me.

"Then we both have nothing to worry about. Except me surviving this swanky event."

"And me surviving grant-writing hell."

Cordelia headed to her study and I called Lindsey to tell her our date was on.

As usual, my wardrobe was a problem, but this time I wasn't confined by the somber demands of a funeral. I finally settled on a sweater of raw silk and a suede pair of pants.

After calling out a good-bye to Cordelia and getting a muffled reply from beyond the study door, I went out on the porch to wait for Lindsey.

The night had just the barest touch of chill. I was fine in my sweater as long as I didn't get too adventurous and outdoorsy.

Lindsey was right on time, her red Jaguar easy to spot as it turned onto my block.

"You sure you want to do this?" she asked as I slid in.

"A mother is looking for her lost daughter. That seems important to me. Yes, I want to do this." Partly true, though I knew that Suzanna Forquet was not my most direct path to Lorraine Drummond. I also wanted action to fill the empty spaces that grief and regret were threatening to fill.

We made small talk, the weather, the Saints' latest losing streak, as we drove together.

Suzanna and Henri lived in one of those opulent St. Charles Avenue mansions, the kind of home that tourists always ask if it's a museum.

Valets awaited to take Lindsey's car.

"Do you suppose this is just for the evening, or is this how they usually park the family vehicle?" I commented after Lindsey had relinquished her keys.

"It is hard to imagine Miss Suzanna parking her own car. Are you a date or just a friend?" she asked, taking my arm as we made our way up the massive front steps.

"Which is safer?"

"I'll introduce you as 'my friend' and make it fraught with meaning. Suzanna prefers a challenge. Let her think that flirting with you is an annoyance to me."

"What if she out-and-out makes a play for me?"

"I won't tell Cordelia."

"That's not what I meant. How do I gracefully extricate myself?"

"Well, I don't think anyone would believe my throwing a jealous fit and demanding you come with me. I could do a pretty good 'And how do you feel about it?'—nothing like psychoanalyzing to slow things down."

"I'm on my own, I guess."

"Not quite that bad. I'll come find you and say my leg hurts too much to drive and you'll have to take me home."

With that, we had ascended the stairs and were before the massive oak door. It opened without us having to knock. Another well-trained servant.

The inside of the house well matched its outside facade.

Suzanna (or her interior designer) had talent and taste. The entrance hall was painted a pale golden yellow, making it warm and welcoming. There were a few pieces of art on the walls, an eclectic yet harmonious mix of paintings and photos. The focal point of the room was an antique side table with an arrangement of winter flowers and grasses that complemented the colors of the room.

"Impressive," I commented in an undertone to Lindsey.

"Very. It's a gorgeous house."

My next comment was cut off by a call of, "Lindsey! How good to see you!"

I knew it was Suzanna Forquet, although she didn't look like I had imagined her. Her hair was dark, probably her natural color or close to it. I had pictured something like Karen's perfect blond looks. She wore little obvious makeup. Her high cheekbones and perfect skin seemed to need none. She gave Lindsey a welcoming hug. As my arm was still linked with Lindsey's, I was close enough to get a waft of Suzanna's subtle perfume. Her hair, long and curly, held none of the forced stiffness of hair bent to fashion's whim. So, both her hairdresser and interior designer are good, I thought to myself.

"Suzanna," Lindsey said as they drew apart, "I'd like you to meet my friend"—and she did put just the right amount of emphasis on it—"Michele Knight."

"How do you do?" Suzanna replied, turning to shake my hand. And giving me a look that was very direct. But she was very gracious about it.

"Michele," Lindsey continued, "this is my friend"—very different emphasis—"Suzanna Forquet."

"I'm pleased to meet you," I said.

Her hand lingered in mine just a moment more, then she let go and took Lindsey's other arm.

"Come this way. I need to introduce you to our honored guests, Betty and Benjamin. Plus the food and drink are this way."

"How did you meet Betty and Benjamin?" Lindsey asked as Suzanna led us into another perfectly appointed room, this one in muted blues, with its artwork and flower arrangements perfectly echoing the colors of the wall and trim.

"Some charity thing a few years ago. Henri"—she pronounced it sans the American *H*—"and I ended up sitting with them at the same table. Betty and Benjamin are both psychologists—they met over the white mice and mazes—and they told us about their idea for a book, they were tired of reading about dysfunctional people, they wanted one about functional people. And from that idle talk, here we are now."

She nodded at the illustrious Betty and Benjamin. They were surrounded by all the other people that Suzanna had introduced them to.

"Oh, Suzanna," someone called.

I quelled my impulse to sing, "Don't you cry for me."

She gave a quick shake of her perfectly coifed head. "I'll catch you later, Lindsey. It was wonderful to meet you, Michele. I hope we get a chance to chat before the evening's over"—she didn't obviously direct that at me—"and be sure you get some of the lobster before it's all gone." With that, she headed toward the person who had been hailing her. A perfect hostess, she met him with a radiant smile (good dentist, too) but her parting words to us left the impression she'd prefer to spend the evening in our company.

"So that's Miss Suzanna," I commented. "Where's Henri?"

"I don't see him at the moment, but I'll point him out when I do."

"She isn't what I expected."

"It's hard not to like Suzanna," Lindsey replied, understanding what I meant.

"Uh-oh. We're in trouble," I said as a clump of people moved, giving me a better view of Betty and Benjamin.

"What?"

"I know Betty."

"That's not illegal, last I heard."

"It's still a felony here."

"Ah. Pre-Cordelia, I assume."

"Way pre. She picked me up in a bar and I spent the weekend with her at her place across the lake." I added, "I was a drunk and a slut in my twenties."

"That's a harsh assessment."

"I spent the weekend with her *and* her lover," I said, to prove the slut part.

"I hope you had a good time," Lindsey said.

"The perfect nonjudgmental shrink."

"Not quite, but from your brief version, it sounds like you were all consenting adults. No kids or dogs, I assume?"

"No, nothing like that. A pretty extensive assortment of toys. So you think it's a good idea to get drunk, let strange women pick you up in a bar, and go with them to a place where you can't call a cab to get home?"

"I didn't say it was a great idea. But you seem to have survived and made it to a healthy, loving relationship. Betty's doing fine; she's in a perfect marriage."

"Aren't you supposed to ask me how I feel about it?" I said sarcastically.

"Only if you were lying on a couch and I was being paid money to do so." Her voice was still calm and steady, not at all affected by my attack.

"Maybe this wasn't such a good idea," I muttered. "I mean, I expect to run into my ex-tricks in the downtown dives, but not here in uptown opulence."

"If you're not comfortable, we can leave. But I'd hate to miss seeing the expression on Betty's face when you say hi and remind her of your tryst."

Get over it, Micky, I told myself. Getting angry at Lindsey wasn't going to change my past. "The person you should be watching is Benjamin. Yeah, let's stay. Keep a scorecard, see how many of my one-night stands we can run into here."

"Sometimes you have to go into the lion's den, even if it is a ritzy uptown one. You sure?" Lindsey asked gently.

"I'm sure. I've got to make peace with my past sometime. Let's go find the lobster before it's all gone."

"Ever been in therapy?" Lindsey asked as we made our way to the food table.

"Why? You need business?"

"Don't worry, I'm not soliciting for myself. Just curious. Sometimes it does help."

"And sometimes it doesn't," I rejoined before letting down my defenses long enough to admit, "Yes, I've been in therapy. Cordelia . . . well, she didn't make it a condition of our living together, but she strongly recommended it."

"Did it help?"

"Yeah, it did. It didn't make me perfect, though."

"Nothing makes any of us perfect. Except perhaps death."

Then we had to plunge into the mob surrounding the lobster and shrimp and that ended all talk of therapy.

Lindsey ran into several people she knew. I kept getting introduced as her friend. Suzanna breezed by a few times, consumed as she was by her hosting duties. She once clasped my hand as she passed, murmuring, "I'm glad you're still here." It was subtle, but obvious; Lindsey certainly divined Suzanna's intent. Good thing we weren't really lovers.

"There he is," Lindsey said, as we disengaged from a clump of her fellow pysch types. She nodded in the direction of a man who was making his way to the bar.

Henri was also not what I expected. He was spectacularly nondescript. His hair was brown, really just brown, to classify it further would be to call it dishwater brown, but that's as far as it could be described. He wore gold-rimmed glasses that made his eyes seem small and lost in his face. His cheeks and nose had none of the fine, chiseled structure of Suzanna's. They were softly rounded as if his were a generic face. Nothing was unpleasant about his appearance, but nothing stood out, either.

"He needs to take up dueling. A scar on his cheek would give him some character," I whispered to Lindsey.

"You're right," she whispered back. "The doughboy needs a scar."

"What does he do?"

"Protects his family money. Tries to keep Miss Suzanna from spending it all."

I glanced around the perfectly decorated room. "How does he do that?"

"Probably the same way she gets him to spend it. Mutual black-mail. They know too much about the skeletons in each other's closets."

"How do you know all this?"

"Rumor, innuendo," was Lindsey's evasive reply.

"One of Suzanna's ex's is a client of yours," I said, suddenly having a good idea where her information was coming from.

"You know better than to ask that. Even if it was true, I couldn't tell you."

"I won't ask. But if your source is confidential, that pretty much leaves your clients."

"Careful, I'll tell Cordelia about the weekend with the toys," Lindsey cautioned me. Her tone was bantering, but underneath there was a clear signal that this was not a subject to pursue.

I didn't. "Hey, I think it's time to go say hi to Betty and Benjamin, that perfect couple."

"Let's," Lindsey agreed.

They had a few copies of their book spread tastefully around them, with a blown-up copy of the cover on a table behind them. This was the excuse for this party. Nothing so tacky as actually selling the book, of course.

I had even decided on my approach to meeting Betty. After the introductions, I narrowed my eyes slightly and said, "Haven't we met . . . ." and left a pause just long enough for her to remember where we had met, before I said, "Oh, no, I'm mistaken . . . you look like someone . . . I met once. But it was at a place across the lake. And it was several years ago."

Betty was cursed with fair skin, and the blush that spread across her face was spectacular.

It didn't help that Lindsey was introduced as, "Of course, you know Dr. McNeil. She was the keynote speaker at the sexual abuse conference in New York City."

Betty barely met Lindsey's eyes, no doubt afraid that Lindsey was well acquainted with her sex life or, worse, that she would appear in some future article as B. with her collection of corsets and silk stockings. ("B. was know to lure young women across the lake and entice them to wear . . . One has to speculate on the method and manner in which B's mother introduced her to the standard female undergarments to imprint on her their use as fetish objects.")

We didn't dally with Betty and Benjamin. Poor Betty might have spent the entire night blushing.

After that, Lindsey's legs were starting to tire, so we found a place for her to sit down. I left her there to wander a bit, also to get her another glass of wine.

I lingered for a while at the food table, not very crowded now because the lobster was gone. I guess Betty and Benjamin weren't important enough to warrant extra servings of lobster. It wasn't that I was enticed by the now-picked-over platters of hors d'oeuvres, but Henri was only a few feet away, the center of attention in a group of two men and two women, so I stayed by the food. It wasn't necessary to watch him, he could have little bearing on the case of Lorraine Drummond, but it was interesting.

Henri did most of the talking. I couldn't overhear the conversation, but rhythm and flow and body language told me more than just the words would. Henri was turned ever so slightly away from the woman standing next to him. Some of that was because the man on his other side was doing more talking than anyone else, except for Henri. If one of the other people said something, Henri would turn toward that person. However, after watching them for a bit, I realized that his default position was turned slightly toward the two men and away from the two women. Also, if either of the women said something, his reply to them was shorter than his replies to the men. If one of the women said something that the others laughed at, sometimes he didn't laugh, or only briefly. But he would laugh, often louder than the others, when one of the men said something funny. The more perceptive of the two women quickly found someplace else to be.

Henri was one of those men who doesn't like women. That, by itself, wouldn't have told me whether he was gay or straight. There are straight men who don't really like women, can't see them as people with ideas and independence.

But I did get all the proof I needed that Henri was indeed gay. The party swirled about them and his little group broke up. When he thought that no one was looking, he let his eyes follow the retreating back of the man he had been talking to the most. It was a blatantly, even arrogantly sexual look. It was a look that told me that Henri was assured that, despite his bland looks, he could want strikingly handsome men (as this one was) and get them. There was no longing in his glance, only desire.

I suddenly had a glimpse of understanding as to why Suzanna pursued her relentless liaisons. She was a commodity to Henri. They may both have chosen to hide their sexualities, but there was no equal partnership in their subterfuge.

I went to get Lindsey her wine. Suzanna caught up with me at the bar.

"I've been wondering all evening. Can I ask your background?"

"Mongrel," I replied. "Isn't that obvious?"

"You're not drinking?" she asked as she saw the bartender hand me a club soda.

"I did enough drinking in my twenties to last a lifetime." I wondered what Miss Suzanna would make of that. Party girls usually like other girls who party.

"Just as long as it's not my choice in wines that's driving you away," she replied easily. Lindsey was right, it was hard not to like Suzanna. "So, what kind of mongrel are you?"

"Why do you want to know?" I bantered.

"I must confess, idle curiosity."

"It's not pretty."

"But you are," she said, escalating the flirting.

"Thank you," I said. "I'm a bastard. My mother was Greek." (Was? Is? I felt a pang at not knowing.) "I don't know who my father was. A mongrel bastard."

"In your brief telling, it sounds almost romantic. Though I'm sure you didn't feel that way growing up."

"No, I didn't."

"Suzanna." Our tête-à-tête was interrupted. "A call for you. She says it's important."

"Thank you, Bror," she said to the man who was standing beside her with a phone. She gave me a sorry-this'll-be-just-a-minute look before picking up the phone.

I took a step away to give her a bit of privacy. I ostensibly was looking at a collection of photos on the wall, but had gotten enough of an angle so that I could watch Suzanna and the man still beside her.

Bror was tall, with pale, white-blond hair. His face was open and smiling, the look of a man who knew that he was not only very good-looking, but at ease and comfortable in his surroundings. He was a servant, but a servant with the privilege of overhearing his mistress's phone conversations. For he was still holding the base of it while she talked.

He radiated a hypermasculinity, hypersexuality. I wondered how he liked being a lesbian's lapdog. Then I wondered if he and Henri weren't an item and working for the wife was just a cover.

Bror was a very handsome, sensual man, he wouldn't come cheap, but Henri's money might be enough to buy him.

He glanced at me, then gave me a smile and a wink to let me know that he knew I was listening to the conversation. His easy inclusion of me gave me a hint of why Suzanna let him into her life. He had the warmth that Henri lacked.

"I can't today," I overheard part of Suzanna's conversation. "I'll see you Monday. I've already told you that."

If I were to guess (and I certainly was in a guessing mood) I'd say that the current girlfriend was making demands that Suzanna wasn't prepared to meet. And I found it very interesting that Bror was privy to those kinds of conversations.

"We'll talk then. I've got to go." With that, she hung up the phone, not even waiting for a reply from whomever was on the other end. "Thank you, Bror," she said, handing him the receiver. He put it back in the cradle for her. Unless she needed the security of a corded phone—as in arranging trysts with lovers—there seemed little reason to go through the bother of having a servant to track her down with one. He disappeared through the door from which he'd entered, trailing the secure wire with him.

"Who did these photos?" I asked, to make it appear that I had been intently studying them and not observing her.

"I did. Believe it or not."

"They're very good." Not a complete lie. Some of them were reasonably decent.

"Thank you. It's a hobby of mine. Do you like photography?"

"I like looking at pictures."

"I've got tons of them. I'd love to show them to you. If I could take time out from my hostessing duties, I'd do it tonight." Her voice was low and intimate, as if there was nothing she'd rather do than get rid of all her guests and spend time with me looking at her photos.

"We can't deprive the guests of your company."

"Sometime this week? What are your working hours?"

"I make my own hours." I didn't add that the hours I'd be with her would be working hours.

"I'm tied up on Monday. How about Tuesday? Come by for lunch and we can spend the afternoon looking at photos until you're bored witless?"

"Tuesday sounds fine. Will it be you, me, and Henri?"

"Henri? Oh, no, he'll be out of town. He doesn't like looking at my pictures. It'll just be the two of us. You don't mind, do you?"

"No, I don't mind at all." It suited me perfectly. Here, at this party, surrounded by guests and her husband, Suzanna could be an elusive target, but an afternoon with just the two of us would give me a much better chance to get my questions answered.

"Good. I'll see you around one."

"One it is. I'd better bring Lindsey her glass of wine before she comes in search of me." I picked up her glass from where I'd set it.

"Get her a fresh one. That wine's best well chilled. And blame any delay on me."

Lindsey was also right about Suzanna liking challenges, I thought as I exchanged the slightly warm wine for a perfectly chilled glass. She clearly thought she'd just made a date with Lindsey's date and she wasn't averse to letting Lindsey in on it.

"Mission accomplished," I told Lindsey as I handed her the wine.

"Yes?"

"I'm to view Miss Suzanna's photo collection on Tuesday afternoon."

"And you'll use your time alone to ask her a few questions?"

"Who says shrinks aren't perceptive?"

"Only other shrinks. Are you ready to get out of here?"

"After you finish your wine."

"Don't worry, I have no compunctions about wasting Suzanna's wine. And I am driving." She put the glass down. "Give me a hand getting up."

I did and she took my arm, using both me and her cane to steady her tired legs.

We said a thank-you and good-bye to Henri, who was standing near the door. His only notice of us was to narrow his eyes slightly when he caught sight of Lindsey's hand tucked in my elbow. Henri clearly didn't like two women touching on his property.

Notice her cane, fool, I felt like saying. She's holding on to my arm because her battered legs can't easily navigate your massive stairs. But Henri's obsession was that someone might find out he's gay, so he saw only what threatened him.

Lindsey was tired. We didn't talk much as she drove me home. I wanted to ask her what she knew about Suzanna Forquet, but the questions would only be to sate my curiosity. I didn't need the answers to find Lorraine Drummond.

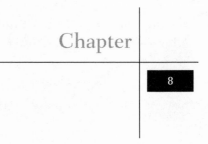

Chapter

8

Sunday, I proved I loved Cordelia, even going so far as to help rewrite a section of her grant when she was crashing and I was (relatively) perky. She keeps doctor's hours, and nine P.M. at night was not the time for her to be sitting behind a keyboard doing things like mistyping "count." My butch side hates to admit it, but I am a much better typist than she is. Sometime around eleven, I sent her off to bed with promises of one final proofread and a printout of a clean copy. What I do for love.

Monday was a perfect fall day, clear, enough dryness in the air to evaporate the usual hazy humidity, and enough of a chill to promise jackets by evening.

I headed to my office without a clear purpose and wishing the demands of the day would take me into the sunshine.

There were no messages on my machine, nor did the mail

require more than to be removed from my mailbox and put into my trash can. The silent phone seemed to have little need of my company.

I considered heading over to the Gulf Coast to talk to Bourbon St. Ann's mother, but I hadn't come up with an approach that would get the information I wanted without too much fuss. Plus it was about a three-hour drive there and back and I wanted an earlier start for that than I had gotten today.

I was talking to Suzanna Forquet tomorrow. However, I was not so foolish as to depend on her alone to bring me to Lorraine Drummond. I had also sent a letter to Lorraine's old address with an address correction request on it. The post office should send it back to me with her current address. People can dither and dally about changing addresses for voting and at banks, but they usually let the post office know where to send the mail. However, that letter wasn't going to come back in today's mail.

You can't do what you can't do, I told myself, to quiet my sense that I should be doing something to reunite these mothers with their children.

It took a few moments before it filtered into my brain that I had taken on a third case of a daughter finding her mother. It was my face in the mirror. With that realization, I closed up the office and knew where this day with its perfect sunshine would take me.

If the traffic was light, it was a ride of forty-five minutes, and, no matter what the traffic, twenty-some years.

I drove across the Crescent City Connection, the bridge that would take me over the Mississippi, then headed south. I was going to Bayou St. Jack's, the small town where I'd spent my first ten years. It was in the bayous below New Orleans, a place that changed slowly, if at all.

My father had owned a shipyard there, taking care of the fishing boats that trawled from the bayous to the waters of the Gulf of Mexico. I still owned it. Aunt Greta had tried to make me sell, but I had refused. I wasn't sure how I had managed to do that. As my legal guardian, she should have been able to sell it if she wanted. Uncle Claude? Was he responsible? That was the only thing that made sense. He and Uncle Charlie had sold their shares of the property to my dad, but that didn't mean he would want to see his boyhood home sold into the hands of strangers. She may have needed his signature to sell. I felt a catch in my breath as I suddenly wanted him here to ask about it.

Too late. Too damn late. Maybe I wasn't only coming out here to look for echoes and traces of my mother, but to make sure the ghosts of the three Robedeaux brothers would see that their shipyard was taken care of.

I followed the familiar winding road, its curves dictated by the meandering of the bayou. The trees wore their winter green, muted, mixed with the browns of leaves that would not see another fall, and a few spots of color, anomalies against our ever-green pines and oaks.

The turnoff to the shipyard had no markings. If there ever had been a sign, I couldn't remember it. People knew where Lee Robedeaux's shipyard was. After he was gone, there was no reason for people to know that an old shipyard was here. The weeds and the rain kept trying to reclaim this narrow track, a relentless battle that found me every few years filling ruts with oyster shells and hacking bushes to keep the road passable.

It had been a few months since I had been out here. I drove slowly, wanting to have any new holes or fallen tree limbs announce themselves gently. I now used the place as a retreat from the city. Cordelia and I often came out here when the chaos of events, like the Sugar Bowl or Mardi Gras, threatened our sanity. As I lived more and more of my present out here; the past had retreated in its claims on the place.

But today I was here to find that past.

My car, spared any rough jars or broken limbs, pulled into the clearing. For a moment, I remembered the way it had been a long time ago. My father's big red truck, usually parked halfway between the house and the docks, his assistant Ben's smaller white truck parked near my father's, following it as Ben followed my father around. Usually there would be at least three or four other cars there, men working on their boats, men waiting for their boats to be worked on, or men who just liked to watch boats being worked on. There would be a boat or two tied up to the dock, and, near the dock at the far end of the clearing, several more held gently in cradles, their ungainly hulls hoisted in air to be painted and repaired.

Then the ephemeral memory was replaced by the present. My lone car, the clearing encroached upon by the overgrowth of the surrounding woods, no boats at the dock, and the once mighty sling used for hoisting the tonnage of shrimp boats now rusted and rotted into uselessness, like a once powerful man in advanced age, still the voice and shape of who he was, but the power and glory long gone.

The house was a long rectangle of boards surrounded on three sides by a porch. It had been built off the clearing, set in the woods so the leaves could provide shade in the scorching summers and protection from the cold, wet winds of winter.

I got out of my car, then held still for a moment, trying to peer through my memories to find those of my mother. But the recall of a child of five was small beside the memories that crowded in from between ages five and ten. I could recollect only brief images, her face in the sun, but that was it, no hint of where we were or why we were there or why I remembered this image of her.

Slowly, a few other memories seeped in. Running to her after being frightened by a big dog, and the way she enfolded me in her arms and kept me safe. Being read a bedtime story. I couldn't remember the story, what it was about. I just had that image of being tucked in bed, a dim light on, my mother sitting next to me on the bed, and the comforting sound of her voice.

What did these few fragmented memories tell me? I wondered as I went up the steps onto the porch. I stood there, turning away from the house, surveying the clearing and the bayou beyond it.

These scant and scattered memories told me that my mother loved me. I felt safe and secure with her. I hadn't known that for sure until now. Even prying at the doors of my memory gave me no harsh recollections. I realized that it wasn't so much the acts and the events, but that I did feel loved and cared for in those years when she was here. Living in Aunt Greta's house had given me many lessons in what it felt like to be an unwanted child.

I knew I carried an intense anger at my mother for leaving me when I was five, then disappearing after my father's death.

"You could have at least written and said you were sorry, god-damn it!" I yelled into the empty clearing.

But the ghosts here were quiet and didn't reply.

I tried to separate my anger at her desertion of me from the kind of mother she had been when she was here. Then I realized that I didn't have to. The abandonment by a weak and indifferent mother would not have given me this howling sense of betrayal that my mother's leaving had.

How could she have loved me and cared for me, tucked me in at night and read me stories, only to walk so completely out of my life?

"You'd better be dead, that's the only goddamned excuse you've got."

I turned back to the house, unlocked the door, and went in.

The door opened onto a large room. At the end of the house nearest the bayou, there were two bedrooms off this room. At the other end was a kitchen and a bathroom. For a long time I hadn't bothered with electricity, until Cordelia pointed out, "You only pay for what you use. You don't have to leave the refrigerator running when you're not here."

But I didn't immediately turn on the lights; the sunlight filled the room. I knew what I wanted and where it was, but I didn't go there. Instead I went into the kitchen. It was the same, the old porcelain sink with stains that would never wash out, the old-fashioned refrigerator with its rounded edges that Cordelia always hinted she'd be glad to replace. But I'd grown up with the refrigerator and it was hard to let it go.

Then, as if it were important that I check each room, search for memories in the walls and floors, I went to the bathroom. Nestled on the woods side, we had never bothered to screen the windows with curtains. The leafy cover prevented any accidental viewings and it was an innocent time when men looking in bathroom windows wasn't thought of. But one of the first things Cordelia and I did was put up curtains to cover these windows. The uncovered windows might have sufficed for a quick trip to the toilet, but clear windows didn't lend themselves to long playful showers. We had also redone the plumbing; the rusty pipes had had little life in them. The old clawfooted tub was a keeper, but the sink and all were recent. Their gleam seemed too new, a direct displacement of my memories of the old.

From the bathroom, I returned to the main room, pausing at each window as I headed to the bedrooms. First I went to the one I now thought of as the guest bedroom. It had been my father's. And my mother's? I knew I had always thought of the other bedroom as mine, so I assumed that they had shared this one. But I couldn't be certain.

What had their marriage been like? Certainly, it had been one of convenience. A thirty-four-year-old man marrying a pregnant sixteen-year-old who had been thrown out by her family wasn't a relationship built on a slow foundation of love and trust. But had it come, at least something resembling affection?

It was bitter to admit that it probably had not. As a child, I had loved my father. He had always treated me not just with kindness and fairness, but as if I really were his flesh-and-blood daughter. In the intervening years I had thought little about what kind of marriage he and my mother had had. I had loved my father and didn't want to confront the idea that my mother had not. If there was an answer, perhaps that was it—she had not abandoned the child, but instead had run from the man. But even if she felt trapped and hated him enough to run away, why not contact me after he died?

The bedroom where they had lain so many years ago revealed nothing.

Hatred should leave a stain, I thought. If she hated him enough to have abandoned a child, some mark should be left. How can so much passion leave nothing behind?

I left that room and went into what had been my room. It was the one that had changed the most. The twin bed I had slept in as a child was gone. The mattress was frayed and lumpy and the bed frame rusty from too many years of neglect. Plus Cordelia, at six feet tall, is not terribly comfortable in anything as cramped as a bed that small. There was also an armoire that we had picked up at an antique sale to replace the flimsy and small chest of drawers that had held my childhood clothes.

There were a couple of throw rugs to cover the bare wooden floors that I had grown up with. Just their color and shape changed the room so much.

But what remained was an old beat-up wooden desk. It wasn't built for a child; I had had to prop myself up with pillows and a thick book under my feet until I was about eight or nine. I had always been tall for my age and by then I was close enough to adult height to use the desk without help.

I sat at that desk now, with its scarred top and the place in the corner where I had carved my initials. I ran my fingers over the MAR. Michele Antigone Robedeaux. It wasn't until I had escaped Aunt Greta's home that I had wanted to get away from the Robedeaux family enough to change my last name to Knight. I had taken Knight from the name of my grandfather's boat, *Knight of Tides*. I never knew him, but my father had kept that brass plate taken from the boat and hung it over the fireplace in the big room. It was still there.

I opened the bottom drawer of the desk. In it was a box containing the scraps of paper, letters, drawings, photos, everything that I had left from my mother.

I put the box on the desk. It was an old tin cookie box, the paint and letters worn into hieroglyphics.

I opened the box, surprised at how full it was. My relationship with my mother seemed so fragile and small, that I would have thought only a few scraps of paper remained to mark it.

The letters were jumbled, no order to them, intermixed with pictures and other memorabilia of a child's life—report cards, class photos, the years mixed, myself at six next to myself at nine.

I started by sorting the contents into different piles, my mother's letters and postcards in one pile, any pictures of her into another, the rest in a third pile.

As I sorted the letters, I realized that she usually sent me something every week. For a child, five to seven days can seem like an eternity of waiting. But as an adult I saw the accumulation of all those weeks of writing, the stuffed box and the piles of letters. I ended up making two piles of what she sent me. Sometimes it was just a quick note or a postcard with a few lines scribbled on it. I separated those out from the real letters.

I tried not to look at the pictures, to keep myself to the mechanical task of sorting. But one picture arrested my hand. At first I thought somehow a picture of me as an adult had gotten mixed in with the others. I looked at it, a woman holding a child of around four or five. The picture was of me, but I was the child, not the woman. It was my mother holding me.

As I stared at the picture, I could discern a few subtle differences between us. She had a bit of a hook in her nose where mine is straight. There was just the slightest hint of a cleft in her chin, which I didn't have. But the hair, the mass of black curls we both shared, forehead, eyes, cheeks, lips, mine stared back at me from the photo of her.

I sat for several minutes staring at that picture, then several minutes without seeing it. I felt an aching sense of connection with her. I had to know who she was and what had happened to her. For the first time, I considered actually meeting her. I had thought that I only wanted to find out where she was, to trace the story of her life from a safe offstage position. But now, if she was alive and could be found, I wanted to find her, to walk up to her and again see the face so close to mine, and say, "I'm your daughter." I knew to do that would give her one more chance to abandon me. But I also knew I had to meet her.

I finally put the photo down, shuffling it under some others to keep that haunting face from pulling my attention to it.

Once I had completed my piles, I took the letters and put them in order by date. I was hoping that the chronology of them would give me some clue I might miss if I just read the letters out of sequence.

I wasn't sure when my mother had stopped writing. In that horrible disarray after my father's death and moving in with Aunt Greta and Uncle Claude, it seemed that I had lost her letters, too. But perhaps she had been writing less and less frequently and had stopped altogether some time before he had been killed.

But that wasn't the case. Her last letter to me was mailed four days before he died. I had gotten it that day. Looking at the faded envelope, I remembered giving it a hurried reading as he called for me to get ready to go with him into the city. But I was the only one who had returned from that trip.

Two days earlier, she had sent me a postcard, a plain white blank one on which she had sketched the door to her apartment building with its quirky gargoyle on the lintel. I had a whole stack of them, brief little thumbnail sketches, bits and pieces of her everyday life that she wanted to share with me. I guessed that she wasn't able to afford a camera and the cost of taking pictures, but she did have pen and paper and enough drawing ability to give me the places and people as she saw them.

No, the letters had not tapered off, just abruptly stopped.

I reread the last letter. It revealed only the ordinary details of her life: There had been a snowfall the day before, but it had warmed up too much for the snow to remain. She had been taking classes, trying to get her degree, so she mentioned how glad she was going to be when it was all over in a few months. But she had been writing to a ten-year-old and had included few of the details that I was interested in now, like what she was studying and where she was going to school. My guess was that she had been finishing her BA, but New York City wasn't exactly a one-college town.

Of course, she had been kicked out of high school once the pregnancy became obvious. They were still doing that when I was going to high school, so I knew that pregnant girls wouldn't be welcome during my mother's school days.

I knew the return address on that last letter by heart. I had sent—I don't know how many—letters there, hoping she would come for me. It had been a struggle; Aunt Greta had been parsimonious with stamps and envelopes. I remember her point-blank saying little girls like me had no business writing pretend grown-up letters. Uncle Claude had finally relented, giving me an envelope and stamp and taking my letter to the post office.

But she never wrote back. I had written another letter, and another. After that, Uncle Claude had shaken his head and said, "Honey, she's not writing back. Don't waste your time." He spoke with a kind sadness, but I couldn't let it go.

Late at night I snuck out of my room, finding the place where I'd seen him take the stamps and envelopes from. I'd stolen a couple of each, then quietly left the house, walking the ten blocks to a postbox in the middle of the night.

About two weeks later that letter came back (and I was the first to check the mail, so I didn't get scolded by Aunt Greta) with

No Forwarding Address written on it. I knew it must have been a mistake, sent to the wrong place, or maybe I hadn't written the address clearly enough. I sent another letter, but it also came back.

I tried again, laboring over every letter in her name and address, as if making them perfect would get the letter to her.

But this time Aunt Greta saw the letter when it came back. She took Uncle Claude's belt after me for that one, alternately screaming at me for stealing stamps and envelopes and for disobeying her. As I found out, disobeying Aunt Greta was a capital crime in that household. I had been there about six months at that point, and had long since figured out that Aunt Greta was not a kind, loving person, but this was my first offense (out of many) where she'd hit me with a leather belt.

When she was finished—twenty hits, I counted—she told me that I would have to get used to discipline, I couldn't run wild like I had in the bayous, and that it had hurt her more than it had hurt me. I considered saying that next time I would use the belt on her so I could truly be punished, but I was only rebellious, not stupid.

I had tried again writing my mother, using a friend's return address, but the letters still came back.

It took me over a year of writing and getting letters back to finally give up.

I had gone to college in New York City. A part of its pull was the hope that I could find my mother. I just knew, with the surety and naïveté of an eighteen-year-old, that somehow, in that big teeming city, we would find each other. After a few weeks of learning my way around, I had gone to that address that I knew by heart. The gargoyle was still there, guarding the door, but my mother was long gone, not even a memory to the tenants I talked to. I hadn't expected to find her there, but I had hoped to uncover some trace, a resonance of her in the building where she had lived. The door with its lurking figurine matched the sketch she had sent me, but that was all.

I had not found her in New York. Beyond that old address, I had not really known how to look for her. At times, I disconcerted myself with wondering if I had just missed her, that she had been walking down the same street just minutes earlier or was coming into the subway station just as I was getting on a train.

I shook my head to clear the haunting thought. She had probably left New York long before I even got there, I told myself now.

Besides that, I had spent a fair amount of time in New York's lesbian bars, not the best places to be looking for lost mothers.

Not finding her during my years of college had added another layer to my simmering rage, as if she knew I was looking and had deliberately refused to be found. The rational adult knew that this was foolish—my mother had no way of knowing I was there—but that abandoned child had felt abandoned once again.

It was getting late, I realized. I hadn't finished reading the letters. You can take them with you, I told myself, they don't live here. But it seemed a dividing line would be crossed if I took these letters and pictures from their place in the past and brought them where I lived my present life.

I looked again at the picture of her holding me. I wanted to find this woman. I carefully replaced everything in the box, keeping them as much as possible in my sorted piles. I left the picture on top.

I knew I would be stuck in rush-hour traffic going back to the city. I considered going into Bayou St. Jack's to find a phone. Cordelia would still be at work, but I could leave a message warning her that she might get home before I did. Since that rarely happened, I wanted her to be prepared.

But unless there were major problems on both bridges and the ferry wasn't running (and only hurricanes or a quarter inch of snow were likely to accomplish those things), I shouldn't be too late. I was going into the city while others were going out.

The parents that had thrown out their pregnant daughter had left Bayou St. Jack's many years ago. I knew this, not because I had looked for them, but because Bayou St. Jack's is a small town and people talk and they remember in small towns. Danny's parents still lived out here, and it was much too small a town for gossip not to slip over the color barrier. My mother's family had moved a few years after they had thrown her out. With the blurring of hindsight and changing mores, it seems everybody thought them kicking her out for being pregnant was a horrible thing to do: "They weren't really a nice family anyway, why that man was always yelling at his wife and kids, knew he couldn't be trusted, your mom was probably lucky to be kicked out." Some even hinted darkly that perhaps he had something to do with her being pregnant. Foreigners were capable of anything. Someone thought they moved to the Midwest, "Ohio, Omaha, one of them places," others California: "No, Bordeaux, I tell you, it was Los Angeles. They sure belong in a city of lost angels." I had gotten all this in only two trips to the store. If I went into town to use the store phone I would probably find out that they had gone back to Greece or been abducted by aliens.

As out of date as it was, the address I had for my mother was a good seven or eight years more recent than the one I had for her family. Besides, tracking them down was not a guarantee that I would find her. I would look for them only if nothing else worked.

People going to the Westbank weren't going to get there anytime soon, but going my direction I only had to deal with the usual rush-hour madness.

My phone impulse turned out to be unwarranted. I got home before Cordelia did. She had left two messages on the machine. One telling me that she would be late, the other telling me that she would be later.

I quickly threw together a salad and took some chicken breasts out of the freezer. When Cordelia got here, I would throw them in the microwave to defrost, then grill them, put some rice on, and that would be dinner. I usually cooked and she usually cleaned up because I liked cooking and she liked the mindlessness of cleaning up.

Since I couldn't do most of that until she did arrive, I took out the box with its letters and photos.

Cordelia came in about a half hour later. I was sitting on the couch with the contents of the box spread over the coffee table.

She didn't interrupt my reading, but bent over to kiss me on the cheek.

"Tell me who this is," I said, putting down the letter I had been reading to hand her the photograph.

Cordelia glanced at it for a moment. "It's you." She looked at it again. "Holding a child? Taken, what, ten years ago? You look . . . different."

"It is me," I told her. "Taken when I was about three or four years old."

She looked again at the picture. "It's your mother. My God, she looks like you."

"Actually, I probably look like her."

"Whatever. It's astonishing. Where'd you get this?"

I told Cordelia about going out to the shipyard as I went to the kitchen to prepare dinner.

As we sat down to eat, Cordelia asked, "Do the letters tell you anything about how to find her?"

"No, not really. The most concrete piece of information is the return address, and that's pretty old at this point."

"So nothing really useful?"

"Well . . ." What was useful? What did I call the emotion I had felt when I first looked at that picture? "The letters didn't fade away, they just stopped. I got the last one the day my father was killed."

"Why do you suppose the letters stopped?"

"I don't know. It just doesn't make sense. She wrote me at least once or twice a week . . . then nothing."

"Do you think something happened to her?"

"What do you mean?"

Cordelia was too accustomed to death and dying not to bring it up. "What if she got killed? Would there have been any way for you to have found out if something like that occurred?"

"You'd think someone would have known she had a daughter . . ." I trailed off, speculating about possibilities.

"But if it happened around the same time, it's possible that the only contact was your father—"

"And," I cut in, "if he was dead and I had been hijacked to that Metairie hellhole, there would have been no one to call, a phone never answered." We were silent for a moment before another possibility occurred to me. "Or maybe Aunt Greta and Uncle Claude did know, but decided not to tell me."

"That would make sense. A child who's just lost her father doesn't need to learn that her mother is also dead."

"Then, sure. But . . . to never tell me? Or maybe . . . maybe that's what Uncle Claude wanted to talk about."

"Twenty-three years is a rather long time to delay telling someone her mother is dead."

"I guess that's were I begin, to find out whether she's dead or alive."

"Do you really want to know?" Cordelia asked gently.

"Yes, I do. If . . . if she is dead, at least I'll know she didn't abandon me."

"She did when you were five," Cordelia pointed out.

"She left me with my dad. She knew he would take care of me. As a kid I was very angry at her for it. But as an adult . . . I can understand. It was a rational compromise between sacrificing herself for me and living her life. Maybe she'd only agreed to stay until I was old enough to go to school. I loved my Dad, but that doesn't mean she did. There are so many things I don't know. She never even visited. When I'd ask my Dad, he always said she lived far away and couldn't afford it. But . . . never in five years? As a kid I accepted that, but now . . ."

"I don't want you to get hurt, Micky," Cordelia said softly.

"I have to know what happened."

Cordelia took my hand and held it for a moment.

Then we continued eating our dinner and talked of the other details of our lives.

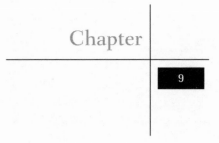

Chapter

9

What do you wear to lunch with someone who wants to seduce you, but from whom you want sensitive information?

I stood pondering the contents of my closet. I could wear the black dress just for consistency's sake. Also because it had one more wearing in it before a trip to the cleaners was a requirement. Even the two-birds-with-one-stone benefits didn't quite convince me that I should wear a black dress to luncheon with Miss Suzanna.

Instead I put on a pair of jeans that Cordelia said showed off my ass to good advantage. That was as sexy as I was going to get. I topped that with a black cotton sweater. It did not show off my breasts to good advantage, but having a "boyish" figure, I didn't have much breast to show off. However, the sweater was warm and, given the chilly temperature that had arrived in the night, that counted.

I considered taking my beat-up old Datsun (I know it's Nissan now, but it was Datsun back when this car was made) just to see its sun-bleached, lime-green, scratched, and dented body parked in front of Suzanna Forquet's mansion.

About a year ago, Cordelia had insisted on two "real" cars in the family. She hated driving mine, always afraid that something like the transmission would break and she'd get stuck driving on the interstate with no gear above second (it had only happened once). She had gone out and bought herself a new car (while I was getting the transmission fixed on mine) and encouraged me to drive her old one. She still putatively owned both cars, but the second one had become so much mine that she had to ask me when she wanted to use it. I must admit, it is nice to drive a car in which both the radio and the air conditioner work. I still keep my old car and use it for things like surveillance, so I could be in two different cars, or for hauling messy things like Christmas trees or sacks of live crawfish.

I decided that, much as I might enjoy the sight of my dismal Datsun on Suzanna Forquet's pristine driveway, the purpose of my mission would be better served by the sedate Honda.

I headed uptown just before one, guessing that about ten minutes would be an acceptable fashionably late arrival.

The door opened almost instantly after I hit the brass knocker. It was Bror who let me in. I surmised that his presence was a caution for any of Suzanna Forquet's tricks lest they expect too much. I must admit I would have preferred a tête-à-tête with just Miss Suzanna. When the interview was over, I didn't think I'd be a welcome guest and I didn't want to find out how Bror handled guests who weren't wanted.

"This way," Bror led me. "It's good of you to come visit Suzanna. She enjoys showing off her photos." He was open and welcoming, making me feel like I was really doing Suzanna a wonderful favor by coming here. And he gave no hint that I was here for anything other than photo-looking. Discreet and charming.

He led me beyond the rooms I had seen at the party, up to the second floor. A long hallway took us to the back of the house, and off it was a bright, sunny room, all windows and skylights, perfect for leisurely breakfasts or intimate lunches.

"Suzanna will be here in a moment," Bror informed me before withdrawing. "Enjoy your lunch."

The table was set and awaiting us. An assortment of fruits—kiwi, strawberry, several melons—smoked salmon, various cheeses, shrimp, and other temptations covered the table.

Off to the side, a small bar was set up. With, I noticed, only nonalcoholic drinks. It is hard not to like Suzanna, I thought wryly. I poured myself a glass of designer water.

Suzanna entered, carrying a tray laden with two bowls of steaming soup. "Something for today's chill. The damn humidity of this city can make it feel so much colder than it is," she said as she set the soup bowls on the table. "Henri says I have to feed my guests before I subject them to my photos."

"The food is welcome, but Henri exaggerates its importance."

She smiled at my gallantry as she poured herself a glass of expensive water. "I often do appetizer lunches, I hope you don't mind." She sat down and I followed her lead.

"Not at all. This looks wonderful."

It was. The soup was a butternut squash which Suzanna implied she had made herself. To test her, I asked for the recipe (I also wanted the recipe, as it was very good soup).

"I'll admit I don't cook all the time, but I do enjoy fooling around in the kitchen and making a mess. I threw together this soup last night."

So she might actually do some cooking, but I doubted she did any cleaning up. She also gave me the recipe. We spent most of lunch talking about food and cooking, innocuous and innocent subjects. I wanted to get her comfortable and relaxed with me before I started questioning her. Besides, the food was good and I was hungry. I didn't have to clean up her kitchen, either.

After lunch, Suzanna led me to a small (compared to the rest of the house) study off the sunroom. The sure hand of her interior designer was evident, but this room had a more used and lived-in feeling. The walls were covered with photographs, presumably Suzanna's. There was a large desk in one corner with papers, contact sheets, and other paraphernalia spread across it to indicate that this wasn't just a gorgeous antique, but a gorgeous antique that was used.

On the opposite wall from the desk was a long and deep couch. It looked very comfortable, and, I noted, was easily large enough to accommodate a wide variety of activities beyond just sitting and looking at portfolios.

"Would you like coffee, tea, anything?" she asked, adding, "There's a bathroom down the hall."

"No, thanks, I'm fine," I replied to both offers.

She sat on the couch. Since my choice was between that or across the room in the desk chair, I joined her.

For a moment, neither of us said anything. We were probably formulating how to bring up our very different agendas.

"All these yours?" I said, indicating the photos on the wall. My thought was to find a picture that could in some way bring the conversation around to Lorraine Drummond. Since Suzanna didn't seem to be in a hurry to show the pictures, I thought I'd better push it along.

"Those on the far wall are all mine," she said. "The ones over our heads are other photographers'." She had a slight smile on her face, as if she was pleased with herself. Maybe she thinks my seduction is fait accompli, I thought.

I was just far enough away from her that she would have to

give me a clear warning of movement if she wanted to get physical. But she didn't make any move. Instead she gave me a long, appraising look.

"Did you really come here to look at pictures, Michele Knight?"

"That's what you invited me here for." Parry and thrust.

"Are you and Lindsey having an affair?" she asked, abruptly changing the subject. She seemed to want to catch me off guard.

"What do you think?" I decided the less information I gave, the better. I wasn't going to out-and-out lie, but I was willing to let her assumptions lead her astray.

"I think it very unlikely that a woman living at the same address as Cordelia James would be having an affair with Lindsey McNeil." She dropped her bombshell with great aplomb, her smile still staying small, even though the look on my face gave it reason to spread into a triumphant one. "I'm not a fool, I do my research," she added.

It may be hard not to like Suzanna Forquet, but it is easy to underestimate her.

"So why are you here?" she continued as I remained silent. "You don't want me as an enemy. Cordelia's money can buy you a lot of protection, but I'm a betting woman and I wouldn't bet it would be enough." The smile was gone, her mouth turning into a hard line. "You won't be the first person who's tried to blackmail me."

"That's why you think I'm here?"

"What else makes sense?" she shot back. "Sex? A quick romp with me could permanently sever you with Cordelia's fortune. For that kind of money, even I could be monogamous. You're a private detective, not a gallery owner, so I doubt your only purpose for being here is to look at my dilettantish photos."

"So, you could blackmail me. Just tell Cordelia I'm here with you," I pointed out.

"I'm sure she knows. What's she want, a donation for her clinic? Not willing to spend her own money?"

I started to jump to Cordelia's defense, but I realized that Suzanna had taken control of this exchange and I had to get it back. Being defensive and reacting to her accusations wasn't the way to do it.

"If I can get so much money from her, why would I want to blackmail you?" I asked in the most reasonable voice I could.

"Money isn't the only thing people want. Power, favors, control." Suzanna spoke as if she knew these things well and what the lust for them could drive people to.

I laughed. The seriousness of her obsession was almost comical. I let myself laugh because I thought it would set her off balance. "I'll be glad to tell you why I'm here, but you'll be disappointed," I said. I wondered if I could make her understand why a mother looking for a daughter was so important. I wondered if her world had room for any such values. I had just seen the hard and cold side of Suzanna Forquet, the part of her that decided it was acceptable to marry Henri and lead this life of deceit for the money and power it gave her.

"Disappointed? How?" Her eyes flicked across my face, trying to see what I was up to now.

"Sorry, no blackmail, no extortion, nothing that romantic. I just want some information. You can say no and I'll leave."

Now it was Suzanna's turn to be on unsure footing. "What do you want to know?" she asked warily, but her lips had relaxed slightly from their former hard, rigid line.

"I'm trying to find someone. A mother hired me to search for her daughter. The mother hasn't seen her daughter in over ten years. It seems you know the daughter."

"Who is it?" Suzanna demanded.

But I wasn't quite ready to tell her that yet. "When I was a young girl, around five, my mother left." I might as well tell her this; her private investigators had probably already informed her of it. "To this day, I don't know why or what happened to her. I'd give anything . . ." I stopped, the catch in my voice real. It can be treacherous to use real emotions; they aren't so easily confined as false ones. I just wanted Suzanna to believe me; I didn't want to break down in front of her. I coughed to clear my throat. "So it matters to me when a mother goes to look for her daughter."

"Who is it?" she asked again, her voice no longer demanding.

"Lorraine Drummond." I hoped she would remember.

"Lorraine? God, that was a long time ago." Clearly she had decided I wasn't a blackmail threat if she admitted to knowing Lorraine. "I don't know that I can help you. I don't know where she is or how to contact her."

"Any information you can give me would be useful. Old addresses, phone numbers, the names of friends . . ."

"Wait. I can give you a name. A friend of hers, but I can't promise that either the address or phone number is still the same."

"Like I said, anything would help."

She got up and went to her desk and opened the center drawer. From it, she took out an address book. If I ever did want to blackmail her, I'd know where to look. She flipped through it until she found the entry she wanted. She sat back beside me on the couch, just a bit closer, as she copied it down on a piece of paper. I glanced at the page she was copying. There were a number of names scribbled on the two pages I could see. I read a few of the names, but didn't recognize any of the women. She finished, then got up and replaced her address book in its safe place.

Suzanna again sat beside me on the couch, started to hand me the paper, but held it back instead. "They kicked Lorraine out. Why does her mother want to find her now?"

"Mr. Drummond died recently. I guess her mother decided life was too short and she wanted to find her daughter."

"I rather liked Lorraine. I hope it works out."

"If you liked her, why'd you break up with her?" It wasn't a necessary question, but I wanted to push a bit to see how far I could go.

"I didn't break up with her. She left me." Seeing my somewhat skeptical look, she continued, "Lorraine didn't want to be an 'other woman' and I wasn't about to give up this." She indicated with her hands the room and the rooms beyond it. "Not for anybody."

"I understand," I said. I didn't add that what I understood was why Lorraine would break up with her given those conditions.

"Do you despise me?" she suddenly asked, catching a nuance in my voice. I had underestimated her again.

"I don't think I would have made the choices you have," I said carefully.

"You're with Cordelia because you love her?" she challenged.

"Yes, I am. You might not believe this, but sometimes I wish she didn't have the money."

She looked at me for a moment. "I believe you. I don't know that I understand you, but I believe you." She stared at the paper in her hand, then turned back to me and said, "Don't worry, I'll give this to you. But first I'm going to tell you a story. One that I don't want repeated." For a second the hardness returned to her lips.

I nodded to indicate that I would honor her request.

"I grew up trailer trash out in St. Bernard Parish. Adopted trailer trash; I guess my real mother was even more trash than the people who took me in. From when I was around six to ten, we had a house, a shack that let in every cold wind. There were seven of us kids. We'd fight over who had to sleep closest to the window when it was cold. Then my Dad got into a brawl and broke his back. His disability check didn't go much further than the beer he drank. We ended up back in a trailer. Ever eaten turnips for four days in a row?"

"No, I haven't. My father wasn't a rich man, but we were never that poor."

"We were. Poor and stupid. All three of my brothers spent time in jail. My two older sisters were pregnant by the time they were sixteen. I felt like I lived in some horrible trap. My father snoring and stinking in the cramped living room. Sometimes he was too drunk and lazy to roll himself to the bathroom and hoist himself onto the toilet, so he'd just piss on the floor. Leave it for one of his daughters to clean up."

"I'm sorry," I said.

"I did what I had to do to get out of that trap. I gladly took Henri's name when I married him. I made up a past for myself, something far more acceptable than white trash. I'm not in contact with those people I grew up with. It may sound brutal and harsh, but I want nothing to do with them. Sometimes I pretend it was just a bad dream. You may not make the choices I've made, but you didn't have to escape the kind of trap I've had to escape."

I thought about pointing out that hell comes in all shapes and income levels. I had never gone hungry when I lived with Aunt Greta and Uncle Claude. Not for food, just love.

"Do you think your parents loved you?" I asked without thinking.

"At best, it was love divided by seven. My maw"—Suzanna lapsed into the drawl, then caught herself—"cleaned people's houses and did sewing at night. I guess she loved us, but she was usually too tired to do more than yell at us not to play in the road or stick our fingers in the heater. Is that love? Does it matter?"

I wanted to say, yes, it does matter, it matters more than anything. But I had never known the brutality of want, cold and hunger eating into my days. Suzanna and I stared at each other across the chasms of what we did not have. It is what we do not have that we want so desperately. That which we can never have, a childhood made whole, is perhaps what we want most desperately of all.

She handed me the piece of paper. The story was over.

"I would prefer my name not be mentioned," she requested.

"There's no need. I've had a few other lines of inquiry going."

"So why did you even bother to come looking for me?" she asked easily, a touch of flirtatiousness back in her voice.

"You were the most . . . fascinating." (But it doesn't take much to be more fascinating than an envelope with a yellow address correction sticker on it.) "And the most challenging," I added because it was true and Suzanna would be flattered by it.

"Good. I like being a challenge. I also like challenges." She shifted, reaching to put her hand on the back of my neck. "What would it take to get you to spend the afternoon with me?" Her hand made it clear that she wasn't asking me to look at her photographs.

"I love Cordelia," I answered.

"A love that doesn't allow any detours, I take it." Her hand continued rubbing the back of my neck and playing with my hair. "What do you see in her?"

"For one thing, she's not married to a man."

That stopped her hand. "You're one of those puritans," she scoffed at me.

"Just because there's money and opulence doesn't mean it's not a trap," I retorted.

"A puritan all around, aren't you? I've done my research. You weren't always so sexually pure," she shot back.

"No, I wasn't," I admitted. "But it's not the sex I object to, it's the buying and selling of it."

"Is that what you think I'm doing? Have I offered you any money?"

"Some offers are implied. A sumptuous lunch in your mansion. It may be just for an afternoon, but you offer access to your wealth."

"Why is that such a horrible thing to offer? You know, I helped Lorraine through college after we broke up. So Cordelia inherited her money from her grandfather, a racist, anti-Semitic bastard. I get mine from my husband who is none of those things. Why is hers so pure and mine so contaminated? You'll find my name and Henri's at the top of a good number of charity lists."

"Not Cordelia's clinic, because she's too far out of the closet," I returned. "Besides, I doubt that you forget your generosity at tax time."

"That was Henri's decision, not mine."

"You think you're not bought?"

For an answer she strode to her desk, took out a checkbook, and hastily wrote out a check. She handed it to me.

"It's not necessary."

"It is for me. I'm sure you'd approve if I divorced Henri, got my social work degree from Tulane, earned twenty-four thousand a year, and bought a run-down house in the Bywater that my true love and I would slowly fix up."

"Is that such a bad life?"

"No, not for other people. I wanted too many things for too long. Come with me some day, Micky. We'll go visit the trailer I grew up in. I could even take you to the place I went to when I was twenty-three and young enough to hope for . . ."

"For?"

She shook her head, as if clearing away false hopes. "Henri and I had been married for two years and I decided to go back—nostalgia made my roots look less tawdry—and to find the mother who gave me up. I had hopes . . . wishes, that she would turn out to be someone I could gladly call mother." Again, she shook her head. "So I paid the money to the right people and they told me where to find her. It wasn't far from where I grew up. I traveled down that old cracked road that turned into a dirt road that became a rutted dusty track. I stood in front of the house that was hers. Two mangy dogs were under the porch with its rotted steps. In the middle of the overgrown yard was a couch. Just sitting there in the open. Off to the side of the house was a pile of old tires beside a cheap baby crib.

"I turned around and left. I'll never go back. I'll never go back to that," she said, finishing in an intense whisper that told me she wasn't talking about just the physical location. "Until you've been down that road, you can't tell me I've made the wrong choices."

"No," I admitted, "I can't."

"I don't mislead my lovers. They know who I am and what they'll get. No lies about love and forever like so many women bandy about, so don't judge me there. You weren't doing any better when you were my age."

"How old are you?"

"Twenty-eight. Remember, I did my research. I know what you were doing at twenty-eight."

I made no reply. I knew what I had been doing when I was twenty-eight. Time might take Suzanna to a place where she would want more than just the material things to balance out the privations of her childhood. Or the wants might be too deep to ever assuage. But there was nothing I could say today that would change anything. Just as there had been nothing anyone could have said to me when I was twenty-eight and drinking and sleeping around and thought that those things solved my problems.

"Don't judge me," she said again.

"I won't judge you, Suzanna. You're right. I haven't lived your life. Thank you for helping me find Lorraine Drummond. I should be going."

"You know you're leaving as a challenge that I've yet to overcome."

"Life would be boring if we overcame all challenges," I said as I stood up. "And on behalf of Cordelia and the clinic, thanks for the check."

"You're welcome. I'm not going to confront Henri on this one—he's too paranoid about anything gay linked to the Forquet name—but I can throw in a check every now and then. Keep it anonymous," she added.

I nodded agreement, then folded the check and put it in my pocket.

"I'll see you out," she said as she led me back into the sunroom where we'd had lunch.

As I followed her through the rooms, I was again struck with their tasteful elegance. If it was a trap, it was a very comfortable one. Suzanna had what she wanted, and perhaps the freedom to find what she needed. She had her photography, her tasteful lunches that made four days of eating turnips a bad memory from a long time ago. Who was I to judge?

We were back in the foyer.

"Thank you for an interesting afternoon. Of a very different kind," Suzanna said.

"You're welcome. I'm relieved you found it interesting."

"Very interesting," she flirted. "So, unmet challenge of mine, will I see you again?"

"Perhaps; the fates are capricious."

"You'll just leave it to fate?"

"It's safer that way."

"I don't know that I believe in safety." She took my face between her hands and kissed me.

I didn't kiss back, but I didn't break away, either. Suzanna had given me help when she didn't need to and had nothing to gain from it. I didn't blatantly need to push her away. She was intelligent enough to understand subtle hints.

She held the kiss for a long moment, probing for a response from me before finally breaking it off. "Still an unmet challenge, I see," she said softly, her face very close to mine, her hands on my cheeks.

"Still," I answered.

"Suzanna," came a voice from the other end of the foyer.

"A moment, Bror," she answered. Suzanna made no move to break the intimacy of her touch. Bror was clearly allowed into the innermost sanctum.

"Henri is on the phone. He instructed me to find you." Bror made it clear he was instructed to find her wherever she was. I wondered if he invaded her studio or merely knocked on the door in a way that couldn't be ignored.

"I've got to go," she said to me. "I can only hope that fate is kind to me." With that, she let go of me and turned to where Bror was waiting with the telephone.

I let myself out. Suzanna might be able to handle his presence with complete poise, but knowing that he had watched our kiss disconcerted me. Though it seemed to not have bothered him, he betrayed nothing other than his easy acceptance of spying us.

I hurried to my car and quickly drove off, not quite trusting in fate to get me far enough away.

Part of my discomfort was that I did like Suzanna and found her attractive. Her kiss hadn't been unpleasant. Once we've found our true love, we're not supposed to find anyone else's kisses pleasant. Perhaps that was only for perfect people, and I certainly wasn't perfect.

But I had what I wanted, the name and address of someone who could help me find Lorraine Drummond. Certainly that was worth one not-so-unpleasant kiss.

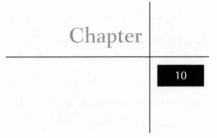

Chapter

10

Cordelia's alarm clock woke me up. Our hours are varied and, much as I love her, I don't pay obeisance to either rising or going to bed in lock-step with her needs.

This is your own fault, I thought, listening to the uninterrupted whine of her alarm. I wondered if it was guilt or a need to prove something to myself that made me start what I knew wouldn't be finished by Cordelia's bedtime. Well, not entirely my fault; Cordelia hadn't exactly said, "No, not tonight, I've got to get some sleep."

It had been a slow, subtle seduction. I had cooked one of her favorite meals, grilled salmon steaks, placed a glass of wine by her plate.

When she said, "It's my bedtime," I had not been so blatant as to say, "I'll join you." Instead I had offered to come up with her to tuck her in and kiss her good night.

Tucking her in had turned into a back rub.

It was long beyond Cordelia's usual going-to-sleep hour before we finally rolled away from each other.

Cordelia, beside me, was still in that deep part of sleep that could ignore even shrilling alarm clocks.

"Cordelia, honey, time to wake up." I hate being awake enough to wake someone else up.

"I'm tired," she mumbled as she groggily sat up. She rubbed sleep away from her face, then got out of bed and trudged to the bathroom.

I felt guilty enough to get up and put on the coffee while she was in the shower.

I heard her footsteps travel from the bathroom to the bedroom to get dressed. A few minutes later, she came down the stairs.

"Smells like coffee," she said at the foot of them.

"I'm trying to make up for keeping you up so late last night." I handed her the cup of coffee I had already poured.

I sat with her while she ate, wanting to keep the tendrils of last night's closeness still around us. Cordelia was polite enough to tell me that I didn't need to be up just because she was. But she seemed glad that I chose to stay with her. We talked little, a brief discussion on what to have for dinner, a comment or two about the weather, nothing profound. Intimacy comes from such moments as these, I thought as I watched the morning light touch her hair.

Those moments pass quickly. Cordelia finished her breakfast, put the dishes in the sink, and with one hasty morning kiss was out the door.

I sat in the kitchen, lingering over a cup of coffee, trying to decide the basic question of whether or not to go back to bed and the secondary question of what I was going to do if I stayed up.

I opted for staying up. I also decided that with an early morning start like this, a trip to Ocean Springs and talking to Bourbon St. Ann's mother was in the offing. That decided, it was my turn for a shower.

There are two routes from New Orleans to the Mississippi Gulf Coast, the prosaic but speedy interstate and the more scenic but slower Highway 90. I-10 is a long stretch of pine tree forests occasionally bisected by exits with gaudy gas stations. Ninety cuts through rustic fishing camps, then hugs the beach all the way to Ocean Springs.

It was a perfect day for a drive and I was tempted by the more scenic way, but decided that if my interview with Bourbon St. Ann's mother went nowhere, I would console myself with a pretty drive home.

My ruse was fairly simple. I had a clipboard with a nicely printed list of questions that I hoped would pass me off as an opinion-poll taker. I had formulated a number of questions about abortion (that usually gets people going—one way or another), adoption, and homosexuality.

The hour-plus interstate drive was as boring as I predicted it would be.

After I turned off at the Ocean Springs exit, I stopped at one of those gaudy gas stations. Nice girl poll takers in small Southern towns should not be dressed in faded jeans and old sweatshirts as I was. After gasing up my car, I went to the restroom, one of those old-fashioned little room ones. In there, I changed into a navy suit, a light gray shirt (pink would have been better, but I don't own a pink shirt), the odious panty hose, and low-heeled dress shoes; I was tall enough as it was. I even put on dangling earrings for the extra touch of femininity—can't be too feminine in a small Southern town. I amended that snobbishness to add, when going to visit mothers who have cast out their gay sons.

My mufti complete, I went in search of Lancelot Lane, off

Camelot Circle. Those street names strongly hinted of subdivision, unimaginative subdivision at that.

The house was one of those look-alike houses built probably in the sixties or seventies, the kind that, instead of going from new to old, went from new to tacky. It was mottled brick, the mixed hues striving to look old, but the heavy-handedness of the grays and sands added to the red had little chance against the modern ranch-style architecture and the windows framed in silver aluminum. The yard was fairly large and well kept. Bright red gingham curtains were visible at the front windows. If you liked subdivision living, it probably wasn't bad.

I glanced at my watch. It was just a little after nine-thirty. I would probably snarl at any stranger who came tapping on my door at that hour. But I was guessing that people who hated homosexuals wouldn't be sinful enough to sleep late.

I suddenly had a moment of panic when I wondered if I should be wearing some makeup. Don't all "real" Southern women wear makeup? But it was too late to worry about it. Even if I hurried back to the highway with its plethora of fast-food restaurants, oil lube places, and drugstore chains, I knew that confronting the aisles and aisles of lipsticks (could there really be that many shades of red or do they just rename them year after year?), blushes, and eye shadow would so confound me that I'd just walk back out of the store.

As a teenager, I'd worn the stuff, but more to fit in than because I wanted to. After high school, I had left my mascara behind with nary a regret.

Maybe I'd get Torbin to give me a few lessons and help me pick out a couple of those shades of red that wouldn't look too terrible on my olive-complected skin. I wanted to be prepared the next time I had to play nice Southern girl again. Quelling my panic attack, I decided that I was an opinion-poll taker from New Orleans and was too sophisticated to wear makeup.

My persona again firmly in place, I got out of my car (Cordelia's, of course—my lime-green Datsun, besides being unlikely to make the trip, would have clashed with my navy suit).

I walked up the perfect subdivision flagstone path and rang the bell.

An "Oh, just a minute," came from somewhere back in the house.

It was just a minute before I heard footsteps crossing to the door. It quickly opened, a testament to how few locks a small Southern town used.

The woman who opened the door was clearly more of a morning person than I was. Her makeup already was on. Her hair color was the obligatory dyed blond that women clinging to their youth always go for. She looked nothing like Bourbon St. Ann, their lack of blood tie clearly written in their features. Her face had a heart-shaped roundness that middle age was beginning to pull down. When she was young, she had probably been called pretty or cute, never beautiful or striking. I wondered if she had ever resented her chiseled, good-looking son, so unlike her.

"How do you do?" I said, shifting my clipboard from one hand to the other so she would be sure to notice that essential prop. "My name is Michele King. I'm with a group called Mainstream Opinions. We're located in New Orleans," (and too chi-chi to wear makeup) "actually in Metairie, if you're familiar with the New Orleans area." Metairie being the white-bread area and probably more reassuring to her than sin city New Orleans. I handed her a fake business card with the name Michele King on it and a made-up address on I-10 Service Road. I had made them up yesterday. Have computer, will print fake business cards.

She took the card and smiled at me. That Metairie address was probably a good idea.

"I'm taking a survey," I continued, "on how people feel about many of the important issues facing us today."

"Why don't you come on in and I'll get us a cup of coffee?" Mrs. Hudson offered.

"Thank you. I'd appreciate that." I was relieved to find she was enough of a sinner to drink coffee.

I followed her into the house. The living room was neat and clean, the furniture colonial stuff, like the house too shiny and new to pretend to be antique. Mrs. Hudson led me back to the kitchen.

It was a bright yellow done to death in a duck motif. Duck pot holders, duck hand towels, a duck teakettle, duck refrigerator magnets. I half-expected to see a rubber ducky in the sink.

"Oh, this is so cute. I love your ducks." Falsehoods when using a false name don't count, I told myself.

"I think they make the place much more cheerful. Don't you think?"

"Oh, absolutely. Very cheerful. Such a pretty yellow."

"How do you like your coffee?"

"Just a little bit of milk." The coffee was already made. Mrs. Hudson had obviously gotten up early enough to make coffee, clear up the breakfast dishes, and put on her makeup.

To duck out (pun intended) of any more lies about her kitchen decor, I continued my spiel. "Our polls are anonymous, so I won't be taking down your name or address. If you have the time, I'd like to ask you the questions from our in-depth survey. It'll take about an hour and I'd be glad to come back if now isn't a convenient time."

"Oh, no, now's fine. I've got the husband off to work, the dishes done, and my favorite program doesn't come on until one."

"Thank you. It would be a great help to us."

"But are you sure you want to ask lil' old me this stuff? Nobody's ever asked my opinion before." The hint of coyness behind her comment was the first sign that she was Bourbon St. Ann's mother. He had used a similar tone at times with me.

"You're exactly who we want. The forgotten, hardworking American. The kind of person who offers coffee to strangers and who has a cheerful kitchen."

Mrs. Hudson smiled again at me. "You're right, we're the type of people whose opinions should be heard," she said, letting me know that I was going to hear hers.

"Thank you, ma'am. As I said, your name will never be attached to this, so it's very important that you give honest answers."

"Don't you worry, I'm a very honest woman." She set our coffee cups down on the table of a built-in breakfast nook. The table had its very own duck salt and pepper shakers.

I did a rundown of the usuals. Her husband was an accountant. She admitted to being forty-five. They had lived in this house for the last twenty-two years. Her husband's income was a little over fifty thousand dollars. ("He's been with the firm a long time and he's a very hard worker," she let me know.) They went to church every Sunday. And, according to her, they had not been blessed with children.

"Have you ever or would you ever consider having an abortion?" I asked.

"Absolutely not. I think abortion's a crime."

"Are there any circumstances in which you think a woman should be able to terminate a pregnancy?"

"Now, I don't think those welfare queens should be popping out a baby every time some man gives them a piece of fried chicken, but they should be sterilized, not making us taxpayers pay for their sins."

"Abortions aren't funded under Medicaid," I said, before thinking better of it. Mrs. Hudson didn't seem like the kind of woman who wanted facts to interfere with her opinion.

She looked blankly at me for a moment, then said, "And they shouldn't be," as if I had agreed with her. "Anyone on welfare ought to have her tubes tied. That's the kind of welfare reform I'd like to see."

I made no reply, scribbling down the gist of her answer like a dutiful poll taker. "What if the child were deformed?"

"God wants us to love all the children. He has a reason for giving them to us."

"What if you knew the child was going to be homosexual?"

She again gave me her blank look. It lasted longer this time. "Well, if you knew he was going to be homosexual, you'd just whup him enough as a kid to make him normal."

"How do you feel about adoption?"

"I'm in favor of it, of course. If more girls had their babies and gave them up, we'd have more good babies for adoption. Who wants to adopt a crack baby or an AIDS baby? Those middle-class girls need to put their babies up for adoption instead of taking the easy way out."

"Have you ever adopted or would you consider adopting a child?"

This time her look wasn't blank but instead confused, her eyes avoiding mine, clearly groping for a lie to go with her earlier claim of having no children. "Well, of course I would consider it. I mean, I have, but . . . circumstances weren't right, I mean, my husband and I weren't always so well off as we are now. . . ."

"Can you pinpoint the main reason you decided not to adopt?"

"Well, not really. Not a main reason. A lot of little . . . not so little . . . important reasons, you know, but not a big reason."

I wondered if she knew how much her voice had changed from its defiantly stated opinions on welfare queens to the tentative hedging she was now displaying. "I'm sorry, ma'am. These questions seem to be upsetting you. Have you had a bad experience with adoptions? Are you adopted?"

"On, no, I'm not adopted. I know who my parents are."

"Were you turned down as an adoptive parent?"

"No, we weren't turned down. We—" She abruptly stopped. "Would you like that coffee refilled?"

"I've still got half a cup, but thank you. Let's go on to some other questions," I said, leaving myself room to go back to these if I needed to. "Do you think homosexuals are born the way they are, or do you think they become gay because of the way they're brought up?"

"I'm sure they're born that way," she snapped out.

"Why do you think that?"

Her mouth opened to answer, then closed. I didn't raise my son to be gay so I know he was born that way, was clearly the reply she wanted to make. Her mouth again opened and she said, "Because good, God-fearing people who've raised their children right have had the children turn their backs on everything they've learned and become homosexual sinners."

"People in this neighborhood?"

"Believe it or not, people in this very neighborhood. There was no good reason for their children to turn out that way, so they must have been born sinners."

"Sometimes it's hard to know what goes on behind closed doors."

"I know these people. Nothing like that went on. There was absolutely no reason for that boy to turn out the way he did. We . . . they brought him to church every Sunday, paid thousands of dollars to have his teeth fixed, the husband made him play Little League football, did everything right."

I didn't point out that Little League played baseball. Or perhaps that explained some of Bourbon St. Ann's confusion.

Mrs. Hudson continued, "No one made him wash dishes or learn to cook or any girly stuff. No son of . . . theirs was going to learn women's work. The husband taught him to shoot and hunt when he was nine years old, made him clean and skin the squirrels, spanked him good for crying at killing those 'cute' creatures. Varmints, that's all they are.

"But no, this boy didn't want to play football, didn't like to go hunting, didn't tease the girls with spiders and snakes. Liked to stay with me in the kitchen."

"With you?" I interjected.

"I mean, with his mother."

I was disappointed that she didn't admit to being the mother in question.

"Even as a young kid, he was different," she continued. "I caught him on more than one occasion playing dress-up with his mother's clothes. Even borrowed her lipstick and put it on. Can you imagine a young boy, should be out getting dirty and playing cops and robbers—prancing around in his mother's old house-coat, his lips painted a bright red? That's sick, it's just sick, and he didn't get that from his parents."

"You seem to know quite a lot about this situation. Is this a relative of yours?"

"No, not anymore," she retorted.

"Not anymore? How do you unrelate yourself to someone? I didn't know it was possible to divorce children."

"He's not my child," she snapped back, as if I had accused her of that. "He's not related to me because . . . because . . ." Her mouth stayed open, but nothing followed.

Finally, unable to leave her in her confounded silence, I said, "I'd be very interested in surveying this family. They seem to have the real-life experience that we're looking for. Could you possibly give me their address? You don't need to give me a name if you prefer not to."

Her mouth, which had finally shut, again opened, and again nothing came out.

Suddenly, huge mascara-laced tears rolled down her cheeks. I handed her some duck-patterned paper towels. She crumpled them in her fist, wailing for a few minutes more before finally realizing that she could use them to blot her tears. She clumsily scrubbed the paper towels across her cheeks, catching her lipstick and smearing it to make its red meet the black of her mascara in a smeary S on her cheek.

She took a gulping breath, then sobbed out, "I'm so ashamed.

My son was gay! My husband will kill me if he finds out I told you!" Another wail followed that statement.

"He won't find out. I certainly won't tell him. And if you don't, no one else will."

"But if he reads this, he'll know. . . ."

"Don't worry, he won't read it. This is for social science research and will only be published in academic journals. It'll be so full of statistics and dry academic language that not even the people who are interested in this kind of stuff will read it."

That seemed to reassure her. "I can't believe I'm telling you this. I'm so ashamed that my son turned out to be a pervert. I do want you to know we adopted. The good Lord was trying to tell me something when He didn't bless me with a child. But I was one of six children and all of them had children and I thought I should have children.

"Lordy, we tried for years and years. My husband even complained about having too much sex. Never heard a man complain about that before. Not that I was the kind of girl to do that kind of stuff. Not like today. I was a virgin when I was married. No, I didn't let men have their way with me. They liked me and all, and I had plenty of dates, but I insisted on saving my most precious asset until I was married."

Mrs. Hudson's ardent defense of her virtue gave me a clear picture of just how close she'd gotten to the virgin line without actually stepping over. I guessed she was one of those people who believed that if the penis wasn't actually in the vagina, it wasn't really sex. Maybe I should tell her that, by those standards, I was a virgin, too.

"Not until Elwood and I were almost, actually married did I go all the way. I don't know why God punished me by not giving me children, I was a good girl.

"So, there I was at the ripe old age of thirty-three and no children and a husband who really wanted a son and who felt if I was going to be a wife and stay home all day, I should at least be raising his kids."

Once started, it didn't look like Mrs. Hudson was going to stop. I did some quick addition, thirty-three plus Bourbon St. Ann's stated age of eighteen, equals fifty-one. So either Bourbon St. Ann was actually twelve or she had lied about her age.

"But the problem was," she continued, "this was a year or two after that awful Roe thing and there just weren't any nice babies around. Here we were, a loving family who wanted to raise a son, and we couldn't find any healthy new blond-haired boys around. All the good girls were being selfish and getting rid of their babies."

"Then we got smart. If you ever want to adopt, don't go to those public agencies. Do it private. That's where the good babies are."

This is what I wanted to know.

"Since we paid so much for him, I thought we were getting a perfect baby. Then he plays with my makeup, prances around the house in my heels, asking if he could wear my girdle. Elwood gave him a good whipping for that one, then whipped him again for crying so much about being whipped."

"What happened to your son?"

"What happened to him?" she repeated, slowly, as if she never thought about what might have happened to him. "Well, of course, we couldn't have that kind of . . . in our house. He had been caught fooling around with one of the other boys. Not just any other boy, but the son of a very prominent citizen. I've never been so embarrassed in my life. It was all over town like nobody's business. My pastor told us it was a good idea not to show our face in church for a while, until things died down. The other boy was lying through his teeth, saying he'd never done anything like that before, but he was two years older so I bet he led Stony boy on. But his father owns some businesses and lives out in Gulf Hills and his son played football, so he had to make my boy the villain."

"Did you talk to your son about it? Did he tell you what happened?"

"Just something about it not being the first time they'd fooled around and that it was the other boy who'd asked him over. I don't really remember, I was so upset. I know he was trying to tell me his story, but my nerves were too far gone to make sense of what he was trying to say. Besides, if it was a . . . sex thing"—she lowered her voice for the S word—"that was his father's business and I was going to let him deal with it. A mother shouldn't have to fool about anything like that with her son. I knew I should have had a daughter. Girls don't do things like that. I mean, I know they get p.g., but they don't do that kind of stuff."

I repeated my question. "What happened to your son?"

"This was the worst thing that's ever happened to me. What would you do if your own minister told you not to come to church? I had never told anyone that we adopted Stony boy, but after that I had to let everyone know. I couldn't let people think he was really my son."

I looked down at my bogus clipboard so she wouldn't see my expression. I again asked, "What happened to your son?"

"My husband told him to leave. That until he straightened up and acted like a man, he wasn't welcome here." She quickly justified it by saying, "It was for his own good. We thought if he quit getting three squares a day and having a roof over his head, he might figure out that a normal family wasn't such a bad thing. We were really thinking more of him than us. Elwood put him on a bus to New Orleans and told him to only come back when he could be a normal boy and like girls."

"Did he come back?"

"We couldn't keep him here, you have to understand. Our church only took us back after he left. But we really did it for him. He needed to know that life wasn't going to be easy if he wanted to live a perverted life. We had to try and save his soul."

I looked back at my clipboard, as if searching for the next question. I told myself it would do no good to point out to Mrs. Hudson that there's not much a sixteen-year-old boy on the streets can do to survive except sell his body. Putting Stony boy on a bus to New Orleans was the least likely way to straighten him out. It was, however, a quick solution to their public relations problem. With this for a mother, I could see why Bourbon St. Ann was looking for his biological one. I finally found enough composure to say, "I'm sure you did what you had to do. It must have been hard."

"Oh, it was, it was. It was a month before we could go back to church and even then the people kept looking at us. It was terribly hard.

"Can we go back to your son's adoption? Can you explain how you arranged it?" I ruffled through a few pages in my clipboard as if this were an important area that we had missed and I had to go back to it.

"It's been so long ago," she said slowly.

"You said you did it privately. How did you manage that?" Mrs. Hudson didn't seem to notice that my questions had little resemblance to anything one was likely to find on an opinion poll.

"My husband did a lot of it. Now, let me try to remember . . . we didn't do it here, of course. We went over to New Orleans. Just outside New Orleans, really. There was a lawyer there who did this kind of thing. I don't know how my husband found him, but he did. So he, that lawyer, made all the arrangements. I remember going to his office once or twice and then meeting him at the hospital to take the baby. He showed us a picture of the mother. We wanted to see it to make sure she was healthy and not retarded-looking or crazy, but we never met the mother. We probably should have. That slick lawyer probably showed us a fake picture and the real mother was a walleyed loon."

"Outside of New Orleans? Do you remember where?"

"Oh . . . something with an S, I don't really remember."

"Slidell?"

"No, that's not it."

"St. Rose?"

"No, nothing with a saint in it. Oh, wait, wait, that place with a battlefield."

"A battlefield?"

"My husband pointed it out, wanted to stop there. He likes wars and stuff, but it was rainy and I wasn't slogging around on wet grass."

New Orleans has managed to preserve its architecture of yore due to the lack of battles fought there. In fact, my imperfect historical knowledge recalls only one battle of New Orleans. "You mean Chalmette?" I ventured. Chalmette is a town just downriver from New Orleans where the famed Battle of New Orleans in the War of 1812 was actually fought.

"Yes, that's it. Chalmette."

I imagined her saying it as Shalmette. "Do you remember the lawyer's name?"

She gave me a sharp look. "Why do you want to know? What's that got to do with anything?"

"Nothing, really," I prevaricated. "I just have an uncle who's a lawyer in Chalmette and I was wondering if it was him."

"What's his name?" she asked, her suspicion slowly, but not completely, ebbing.

"Thurgood Marshall." It was the only name of a lawyer that floated across my brain. I hoped Mrs. Hudson wasn't a Supreme Court buff.

"Nope, wasn't him. This guy's name was Chester Prejean. I always thought that was a funny name. Little guy, no chest at all, and they called him Chester."

I scribbled *Eureka* on my clipboard. I had what I needed. "That's all my questions. You've been more than generous with your time." I got up.

"Wouldn't you like another cup of coffee?"

"No, thank you. I've got to be going, but I do very much appreciate you taking your time to answer our questions." I continued mumbling what I imagined opinion-poll taker inanities to be as I made my way across the living room to the door. I didn't want to give Mrs. Hudson a chance to get a long-winded diatribe going.

I kept up the polite chatter as I hurried to my car. I didn't even bother to fasten my seatbelt before taking off.

After her husband died, when she was alone, would Mrs. Hudson come looking for her son? Was it possible this selfish woman could realize how short life was? And even if she did, I thought bitterly, the detective hired would probably trace her son to a death certificate. Would she feel any regret then that she had thrown her sixteen-year-old son out to survive in the streets during a plague? And my bitterest thought was that if she did read his brief story—died of AIDS—she would probably only blame him for what he did to her.

I took the scenic drive home. I needed it.

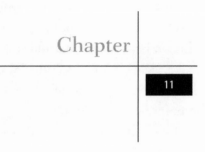

Chapter

11

I got back in the city a little after two and went to my office. Because it was on my mind and I had worked so hard to get it, I looked up Chester Prejean, Esquire, in the phone book. Eighteen years had passed, but it was possible that he was still practicing law in Chalmette.

There it was! How many Chester P.'s could there be? I got an answering machine that squawked a garbled message at me, then cut off before allowing me to leave a message. Obviously, Chester had squandered everything the Hudsons had paid him for their "imperfect" baby instead of investing it in working office equipment.

I didn't call Bourbon St. Ann to update him. After having met his mother, I could understand how he had turned into a whiny, self-centered person. Add to his upbringing the savagery of surviving on the streets, where too often kindness and compassion are for fools, and I began to understand the feralness that lurked behind his young features.

I didn't call him for the selfish reason that a dose of both mother and son in one day was more than I wanted. I briefly considered driving out to Chalmette and knocking on Mr. Chester's door, but Bourbon St. Ann wasn't paying me enough for that kind of alacrity. Hell, he wasn't even paying me enough to go traipsing out to Chalmette.

I also called the number Suzanna had given me, but only got an answering machine. I didn't want to leave a message, so I didn't.

I made notes from my interview with Mrs. Hudson, keeping the editorializing to a minimum, then put them in the Bourbon St. Ann case file. I puttered around for a bit with other paperwork, then gave up and went into what I call a semi-work mode. I pulled up a game on my computer.

Just as I was about to annihilate the bad guy and win the princess's heart (this was a tolerant computer game; even though I had made my character female, it hadn't forced me to choose a prince to rescue) the phone rang.

It was Cordelia.

"Please come by the clinic," she said. Her voice was agitated.

"What's wrong?"

"Nothing, I hope, but . . . Just come—if you can. I'll explain—" She was interrupted by voices in the background.

"I'm on my way," I told her.

It wasn't a long drive, but I still found myself cursing at no less than four stupid drivers—no one here seems to possess the brains or ability to use a turn signal.

There was a police car in the parking lot.

I hurried into the building. The first person I saw was Joanne.

We both looked at each other and said, at the same time, "What are you doing here?"

"Cordelia called me," I explained first. "What's wrong?"

Joanne answered slowly, considering her words. I was, after all, a civilian. "A missing woman. The last place she was definitely seen was here."

"You think it's related to the other cases?" I asked, since she wasn't volunteering the information.

"We have to consider it, given that one patient from here has been murdered." Joanne offered nothing more.

"How long has she been missing?"

Joanne sighed, as if deciding to go ahead and answer my questions. "Since yesterday evening. She should have been home no later than six P.M. last night. It was her mother's birthday and the family was taking her out to dinner. This woman, twenty-two, straight A's at Delgado, has no record, no drug history, nothing in her background that might make her be the kind to just disappear for a few days without notice." She paused for a moment, then said softly, "Sometimes you know. Something happened to Tasha Billings. Something that shouldn't have happened. The best we can hope for is that whoever kidnapped her is still raping her and hasn't killed her yet." Then she was silent, looking in my direction, but not seeing me.

"I hope . . . that she's still alive."

"Yeah, me, too." One of the uniformed policemen called to Joanne.

"Let me find Cordelia," I said.

No one was at the reception desk. I headed down the hallway to Cordelia's office.

She was sitting at her desk, her eyes cast downward as if focusing on the paperwork piled on her desk. But there was no movement, no pen in her hand, nothing to indicate any connection to the piled papers. She was waiting, the impatient, impotent wait of one desperate to change what will be, but with no power at all.

She started when she saw me. "Micky. You came."

"Of course," I answered.

"One of my patients is missing. She was last seen here."

"I know. I ran into Joanne in the hall." I circled behind her to rub her neck, the tension almost palpably rising off her shoulders. Cordelia didn't much like public displays of affection when she was at work or I would have put my arms around her. But her office door was open, as if the openness could bring good news, and the staff and police were running about.

"What did she tell you?"

"Just that. A woman is missing and she was last seen here."

"A woman . . . Tasha came here the first week the clinic was open. One of my first patients. She was seventeen then. I don't know . . . some people get into your life. We'd talk about things, what she was doing in school, she'd ask me questions about sex that she couldn't ask her parents. One day she asked me what a penis looked like, so I got one of my anatomy books and showed her, and we had a talk about anatomy versus personality."

I didn't interrupt, just kept slowly massaging the tightness in her muscles.

"I was the first person she came out to. She came in—for a cold, she said—and when I took the thermometer out of her mouth she said maybe it was her head that needed fixing. I asked her why and she said she liked women better than men. I asked what was wrong with that and she gave me a look and said she preferred women *that way*. She tensed up as she said it, as if expecting me to pull away; I was putting a blood pressure cuff on her.

"She said, 'I guess I'm not going to be the first black woman president.' I replied, 'No, but you can be the first gay black woman president.'

"She told me she knew I was trying to be liberal and tolerant, but you can't be important if you're queer. In fact, it was illegal in this state.

"I remember telling myself to take her seriously, although I wanted to just laugh and say, don't worry, this is just coming out.

J. M. Redmann

But I remembered when I was eighteen and nineteen and I was just as earnest and tortured about it as she was.

"I gave her an earnest and serious answer, told her that gay men and women were doctors, lawyers, owned businesses, taught at universities—you know, the whole list. Then I came out to her. I think she's the first patient that I ever came out to. I mean, there are patients that know, that come to me because they want to see a lesbian doctor. Mostly it never comes up. But I told her. I think I literally opened a door for her. I know she would have found it eventually, but I think I saved her a few months, maybe years, of self-doubt and self-hatred.

"After she left, I felt like I had done something important, a moment of clear and palpable healing.

"She came in every six months or so, a cold, a sprained ankle, time for a pap smear. She'd ask me about colleges, tell me about girlfriends.

"I once pointed you out to her. She was my last patient. I told her on her way out to check out the tall, curly-haired woman in the waiting room. That she was my lover. Next time she came in, the first thing she said was you were really hot-looking and if you weren't nice to me, she'd come after you. Don't worry, I told her you were very nice to me. I'm proud of you and I guess I wanted to show you off. A role model should have a lover."

"I'm glad I made the nice cut-off. After some of my . . ." I said.

"You are nice, Micky," Cordelia interjected. "I asked you to come and you came." She reached up and covered one of my hands with hers and held it. "I needed you and you came."

She sighed and let her head rest against my chest. I said nothing, let our touching speak for me.

Several minutes later Joanne knocked on the doorframe. Though the door was open, she sensed that Cordelia and I would need an announcement of her presence.

"You can go if you want," Joanne said. "We've talked to everyone here."

Cordelia slowly nodded. "I'll tell everyone else to go home, then." She paused for a moment, then asked, "Will you call me if . . . if you find out anything?"

"Yes, I'll call you."

"Thanks, Joanne."

Joanne gave a nod as acknowledgment and good-bye, then turned and left. Cordelia gave my hand a final squeeze before letting go. She stood up and gave me a wan smile, then went into the hallway to tell the rest of the staff that the police had asked all the questions they could think to ask.

I listened as her voice drifted down the hall. Some familiar ones answered her: Elly, Millie, and others I couldn't recognize.

I turned and stared out the window. I lost track of Cordelia's voice as I stared at the sky, white with clouds that allowed neither rain nor sun, a diffuse light that gave no clue to time or the height of the sun. It was a day with no answers.

"Cordelia . . . Oh, hi, Micky."

I turned to face Lindsey. "What are you doing here?" I asked, surprised at her presence.

"I'm here one afternoon a week. This is the one."

"Oh, that's right. I had forgotten."

"I just got out from seeing a client. Is something wrong?"

It's what makes her good, I thought, how quickly she knew to ask if something was awry.

"A patient is missing," I said. And because her look said she had questions and was listening, I told her the rest, a bright, promising girl who shouldn't be lost.

"That is disturbing," Lindsey said when I'd finished.

"Did you know her?" I asked.

"No," she replied, shaking her head. "Cordelia mentioned her to me once or twice, if it's the same woman, but I never met her. I think I gave her a list of coming-out groups to pass on to her." She paused for a moment, then asked, "Are you going to look into this?"

It was my turn to shake my head no. "The police have the resources to do this kind of search. I really don't. I can find people . . . when there's time to find them."

"I guess that's true. Has Cordelia told you about her stalker?"

"Her what?" I demanded, turning to face Lindsey directly.

"It's not like that," Cordelia said over Lindsey's shoulder.

"A stalker?" I asked, looking from Lindsey to Cordelia.

"It only took one pelvic exam for her to fall in love with Dr. James," Lindsey said.

"She's basically harmless," Cordelia quickly put in. "She came in as a patient, said she wanted a lesbian doctor. That's okay, I have several patients who see me for that reason. She sends me flowers and sometimes waits for me after work. That's all."

"How long has this been going on?" I asked.

"About a month or so," Cordelia replied.

"Do you think she's harmless?" I asked Lindsey.

"Hard to say. She's certainly harming herself, living in a fantasy world, unable to connect in any authentic way to people, plus spending a lot of money on flowers. Harmful to others? Who knows? I've never had enough interaction with her to attempt a diagnosis, and even if I spent several hours probing her thought processes, I still wouldn't know for sure."

"Look, I think she's a bit off, but basically harmless. She's maybe five-five and slightly built."

"Did you tell Joanne about her?" I cut in.

Cordelia looked from me to Lindsey, then shook her head. "No, I didn't. Why? I can't imagine a link between this woman and . . . what's happened."

"Suppose she got jealous of your other patients—found out that Tasha was a lesbian and decided that your pelvic exams are for her only," I said.

"Tasha's a jock. Runs track. There's no way this woman could have abducted her."

"With a gun? Hitting her over the head with a baseball bat?

There are a lot of ways for a weaker person to overpower a stronger one."

"I've never felt threatened by her," Cordelia defended.

"She's in love with you," Lindsey commented.

"You need to call Joanne," I told Cordelia. "One good way to predict violence is if someone has done it before. Joanne can see if she's got a record. What if she just got out of St. Gabrielle for assault and battery?"

"All right, I'll call her," Cordelia said, as she edged past Lindsey through the doorway.

Cordelia picked up the phone, then looked at me and said, "Joanne's in her car right now. Why don't we go home and I'll call from there?" She had a tired, resigned look on her face.

Cordelia doesn't make decisions quickly. And sometimes when she does decide, she can be slow and deliberate about acting on it. I knew she would call Joanne when we got home; she wasn't just trying to delay and get out of it.

But I took the phone from her hand. At times I pushed very hard against her methodicalness. It was both a source of conflict and balance for us. At times I needed her to make me pause and think and she needed me to break her out of her deliberate pace.

"I know Joanne's beeper number," I said as I punched it in. A woman's life was at stake.

It took only a minute or so for Joanne to call back. She was on her car phone.

I picked up the phone because I was still moving at a faster pace than Cordelia.

"Joanne, this is Micky. Cordelia didn't mention this because she thinks the woman's harmless. But a patient of hers has been sending her flowers and hanging around in the evening when they get out of work." I was looking at Cordelia, checking my words with her as I said them. "It's been going on about a month. Cordelia thinks she's harmless, but Lindsey and I both feel it can't hurt to check her out."

"What's her name?" Joanne asked.

"Name?" I said to Cordelia.

She didn't answer immediately, the conflict clearly written on her face. This woman was (had been?) a patient and Cordelia was a stickler about confidentiality. I started to hand the phone to her, but she shook her head—it made no difference whether I overheard her tell Joanne or if she told me the name to pass on.

Finally, she said, "Frances Gilmore."

I repeated the name to Joanne. I had an image of her driving her car, talking on the phone, and writing all this down. I hoped she was at a red light.

"Description?" was her next question.

"What's she look like?" I asked Cordelia.

"Five-five, weight around one hundred and fifteen. Twenty-four years old. Not very muscular, no regular exercise, brown hair with obviously dyed blond streaks in it, shoulder-length, green eyes, gold wire-frame glasses, regular features, no visible scars. . . ."

"Thin lips, teeth that haven't seen a dentist in awhile," Lindsey added.

Cordelia shrugged, indicating that she had run out of physical things to describe.

I repeated these to Joanne.

"Job?" Joanne asked.

"Any idea where she works?" I paraphrased.

Cordelia shook her head. "She paid in cash, no record of insurance."

"Someplace where she makes enough money to spend about fifty to eighty dollars a week on flowers," Lindsey commented.

Joanne just sighed at that last piece of imprecise information. "We'll check it out."

"Thanks, Joanne." Then because she was too much of a cop to volunteer information but she might tell me if I asked, I did. "Could this be the killer?"

"Could be. No proof that the killer's male." The static overtook the conversation and she was gone.

I shrugged for an answer to Cordelia and Lindsey.

"I'm exhausted," Cordelia said as I replaced the receiver.

"You did the right thing," Lindsey assured her. Cordelia had a habit of saying she was tired when she was upset. Lindsey probably knew her well enough to know that.

"I hope so. What if siccing the police on Frances doesn't bring Tasha back and only shatters a fragile person?"

"The fragile people get shattered all the time," Lindsey replied gently. "Sometimes they put themselves back together, stronger than when they were broken. Sometimes nothing repairs the damage. If they're going to break, it doesn't really matter which blow does the damage, yours or somebody else's, but something will break them."

Cordelia didn't reply, her gaze again lost in the papers on her desk.

"Let's go home," I said.

She nodded and stood up, closed the blinds, put away her pens in a drawer, the usual routine of leave-taking.

"I know you did . . . what we had to do," Cordelia said as she picked up her briefcase. "I'm not . . . angry, just . . . it seemed both answers were wrong and we had to pick one."

We walked out, keeping with Lindsey's slowed steps, then parted in the parking lot, making quick good-byes as if the words had little meaning.

That night the phone never rang. Joanne didn't call.

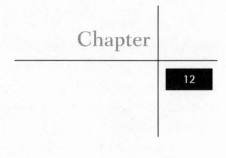

Chapter

12

The morning brought no news, no phone calls, no word from Joanne.

It could be days, I told myself. Or years. Or never. Whether it was only hours or not at all, the details of my life still remained for me to do.

The first thing I did when I got to the office was again call the number I'd gotten from Suzanna Forquet. Still an answering machine. She was probably at work. I decided against leaving a message.

Next I called the lawyer in Chalmette. I also got an answering machine, but this time his worked. "This is Chester," it told me. "If you want to catch me, I'll be in the office from three to five, if not, toots sweet."

I didn't leave a message there, either. I would just go visit Chester in Chalmette between three and five P.M.

So I sat at my desk, staring at the wall. It was Thursday morning at ten A.M.

Thursday at ten o'clock, Aunt Greta would be out of the house. Every Thursday at ten, she volunteered at the church. She always had when I was growing up. Did she still?

What had Uncle Claude wanted to give me?

Someday soon, she would sort through his things, and I might lose forever my chance to have what he wanted me to have.

Could I risk it? It wouldn't make Aunt Greta like me any more if she discovered that I'd broken into her house. Of course, there wasn't much that would cause Aunt Greta to like me any more.

Thievery and going to Chalmette, all in one day. Maybe next time I should listen when Danny tried to talk me into going to law school.

But I had to know what it was that Uncle Claude wanted me to have.

I hurriedly locked my office. I was glad to be driving Cordelia's nondescript maroon car—even Aunt Greta couldn't miss my lime-green Datsun if she happened to come back early.

It took me about twenty minutes to get there. The streets were quiet, only a few cars parked in driveways.

I drove around for a bit, checking out the neighborhood in case Aunt Greta was only running a quick errand, or had stepped over for coffee with a neighbor and was only a few blocks away. But I didn't see her car anywhere, only those houses, built in the same year by the same developer, all of a yellow brick sameness.

Coming from the bayous, with our houses built by different generations, some rough-hewn shacks, others elaborate structures with ornate columns and long verandas, this neighborhood had seemed so sterile and confined.

I parked in front of the next house over, but stayed in my car for several minutes, watching the house for any sign of twitching curtains or shadowed movements. Nothing stirred.

Finally leaving my car, I walked to the door and rang the bell. If Aunt Greta did answer it, I would tell her I had lost an earring and wanted to look for it. A flimsy excuse, but it would suffice should I come face-to-face with her. It was possible that Bayard or Mary Theresa had borrowed her car.

But no one came to the door, nothing moved inside. I rang the doorbell twice more to make sure.

Then, with a quick glance over my shoulder to make sure no one was watching me, I went through the gate to the backyard. I wondered if any of the neighbors might remember me—if they were watching at their windows, would they think I belonged here?

The girl their children had called "nigger" because my skin was the olive of my mother's background, not the freckled white of the other children. For a moment, the memory stopped me and I wanted to just leave this place, leave it as completely behind me as I could.

But I heard a car on the street, so I went on, slipping behind the house, out of sight. I listened as it continued on down the street.

If you don't do it, you'll always wonder, I told myself. With that, I retrieved the key from under the edging stone where it had been hidden for several decades now. I had used it many times, sneaking home late during my high school years, when I had hung out in bars to stay away from this place.

I let myself in, calling out a "Hello?" as I entered the kitchen. If anyone was here or if the neighbors were listening, I wanted to be acting like someone looking for a lost earring, not breaking and entering.

But the house was quiet, a stillness that told me it was empty.

Who was Uncle Claude and where were his secret places? I knew him as a silent man sitting in front of the TV. I thought for a moment, picturing the places that were his, where Aunt Greta didn't interfere. Of course, the red chair in front of the TV. Also, behind the bar in the far corner of the den. He was always the one to fix the drinks when company came over.

I left the kitchen for the den. It wasn't likely, but I lifted the pillow on the red chair, checking under it, but found only crumbs and a penny. I put the seat cushion back, its shape marking the many years he had sat there.

Then I looked behind the bar, but found only what one would expect to find behind a bar, half-full bottles of the usual liquors, piles of tacky cocktail napkins, some from Mardi Gras, others St. Patrick's Day. I ran my hands along the lower shelf, but found only a few sticky spots and a lot of dust.

What if I'm too late? What if she's already found it and thrown it away? I thought. Suddenly I could easily see her, as her memorial to her husband, going through his things in a frenzy, obliterating everything that threatened the memory she wanted to have of him.

Keep searching, don't give up, I admonished myself. Where else? I thought, glancing around the room. No, not here, it was too common a space, no privacy was possible with its doors to the bedroom hallway, kitchen, and living room allowing anyone to enter at any time.

I had briefly shared a room with Mary Theresa when I'd first come here, but she had never forgiven me for usurping her private space, so after the appropriate amount of nagging, Uncle Claude and Uncle Charlie had built a room under the eaves in the garage. It was hot in the summer, cold in the winter, and, after I hit my teenage growth spurt, I couldn't stand up straight, but at least it was only mine.

I went back through the kitchen to the garage. But a quick look around told me my guess was probably wrong. The ladder, made of boards nailed to the wall studs, was almost hidden by junk piled against the wall. Rakes, boards, something that looked like part of a garden fountain, were all stacked in that corner. One of the rungs had come off, leaving a gap between the steps.

I had never been back to that room, not since the stroke of midnight on my eighteenth birthday when I'd left this place.

I gingerly moved the most obstructive of the things away until I could get a foothold on one of the lower rungs. The dust told me that no one had been here in a long time. Perhaps my midnight climb had been the last time anyone had touched these boards.

The little door, cut down to fit into this space, creaked as I opened it, as if complaining of its long neglect.

The bed—cot, really; nothing else would fit—was still there. The chest of drawers that had always wobbled, no matter how often I tried to right it, remained. The lampshade I had bought to cover that naked bulb still hung there, no longer the crisp white that I remembered, now a dusty gray. With no animus of a daily life touching this room—socks on the floor, pictures and a few postcards hung on the wall, a clutter of pennies and dimes on the chest of drawers, an ever-changing stack of library books beside the bed—it looked cramped and pathetic. Suddenly I was swept with a wave of self-pity for the young girl I had been, growing up in this small, airless space. The pity quickly gave way to anger.

I had a vision of finding my mother and showing her this room. Telling her, this is where I lived from when I was ten to eighteen, growing up here until the ceiling bent me over.

Then a mote of sunlight, reflecting off something in the garage, caught an edge of paper that had fallen into one of the cracks in the floorboards. I got down on my knees to reach for it, gently taking the protruding edge between my fingers, lest it fall through the crack.

It was a card, one from my mother. I glanced at the date. It was the card she had sent me for my tenth birthday, the last birthday card I'd ever gotten from her. For a moment, I felt the pang of exhilaration that I'd always felt when one of her cards or letters arrived, as if this found missive had been just sent to me.

She had made the card herself, a heavy cream paper stock. The ink drawing on the front was a curled-up kitten, sleeping peacefully on the porch of my bayou home. The marsh stretched off in the distance, its calm line broken only by the skeleton tree off in the far distance.

My mother and I had once taken the skiff down the bayou in search of that tree. It was a large tree, probably hit by a lightning strike that tore its leaves from it. But its stark limbs had not fallen, the lifeless roots kept it upright, dominating the far horizon, its branches always bare even in the lush green of summer. We had gotten closer to it, but never near it. The bayou curved away from the direction that would have led us to it, and rather than risk the shifting channels of the marsh, we had turned back. But before we had turned homeward, she had sketched that tree, then given the drawing to me, a token of our adventure.

Recall is both fragile and tenacious. It took this card to bring that memory back to me.

She often put the tree in sketches that she sent to me, almost like a signature or a secret code between us.

Inside, the card read, "This is a picture of my cat, Mona Lisa. I call her that because she has a hint of a smile, but won't tell me what it's hinting at. I found her or I should say, she found me, a few weeks ago. She was hiding behind a garbage can, letting people pass her by until I came along, then she stepped out and meowed at me, as if demanding my attention. And I knew it was time for me to have a cat. I thought I'd let her visit you for a bit, let her curl up on the porch for a nap. Someday the two of you will have to visit in person, for she is a discerning cat and would love to meet a smart and wonderful child like you.

"All my love, Mom."

For years, I had kept that card on the dresser. But one day it had fallen off and I had left it, tired of it reminding me that I had gotten no more cards.

My anger ebbed away. What had happened to her, this woman

who wanted me to meet her cat? All her love had been too fragile to keep me from this room. I carefully put the card in my shirt
pocket, not wanting to bend it any more than it already had been
bent by its years caught in the floor.

I glanced at my watch. It was a little past noon. It was time to
leave the bitter memories of this room and continue my search.

After climbing back down the ladder, I carefully rearranged
the detritus that surrounded it, wanting to leave no trace of my
visit, except in my reawakened memory.

I went back into the house and headed for the bedrooms. Perhaps Uncle Claude had converted one of them for his use. I
checked Bayard's first, to get the worst part over with.

The dirty laundry piled under the front window told me that
this wasn't an unused room. Torbin told me that he often dropped
by when he wanted a dinner cooked for him or his clothes washed.
I had a brief malicious idea of finding some of the porno that I
suspected would be hidden—he liked the kink of leaving it at her
house—and leaving it under the laundry he had left for Aunt
Greta, but a shred of conscience stopped me. The recent widow
didn't need to find her son's pornography. Also, the thought of
touching any of his things made me a bit queasy.

Mary Theresa's room was clearly the baby-sitting room. It had
children's toys scattered about and two little kids' beds stuffed in
a corner. Obviously, when she brought her children, this is where
they stayed.

Gus's old bedroom had become a storage room. Bayard and
Mary Theresa still had a place here, but he didn't. Two bikes were
there, a baby crib, boxes pilled against one wall, the bed itself hidden under piles of old clothing. I glanced in the closet. It was
stuffed with piled-up shoes, as if Aunt Greta couldn't throw out
even the most worn of them, and clothes, old-style coats and
dresses, suits that Uncle Claude hadn't been able to fit into in
years.

Even as illicit as this visit was, I was still reluctant to breach the sanctum of Aunt Greta and Uncle Claude's bedroom. We children weren't allowed back there, at least not very often. Bayard had once taken me to their room and said, "You know Mama and Dad do it. They do it right here in this bed. I heard them one night."

I had not replied to him, merely backed out of the room, knowing that neither of us should be here, but that my transgression would cost more than his.

The room was neat, the bed perfectly made, no hint that even sleep took place here, let alone the coupling of sex. The bedspread, a pale green, matched the walls, the curtains, a frilly green gauze, covered the protectiveness of a blind. There was one big dresser that Uncle Claude and Aunt Greta shared. I doubted he would leave anything there, but I quickly opened the drawers and looked through them. Nothing, save for the obsessively neat rows of folded clothes.

Though Uncle Claude lived and slept here, this room was clearly Aunt Greta's. The furniture was her dark, somber style, the muted colors were hers; the only bright color in the house was Uncle Claude's red TV chair.

Then I remembered the little room off back. There was a bathroom behind the bedroom, and tucked next to it was a small room, perhaps intended as a large walk-in closet or changing room. Uncle Claude had occasionally referred to it as his study.

The door was closed. At first I thought it was locked, but it was only the shifting humidity that had caused the door to stick.

This was Uncle Claude's room, the obsessive neatness of the bedroom banished. It was a small room, barely able to hold the cluttered desk, chair, and battered file cabinet that it contained.

The walls were covered with pictures of boats, yellowing cartoons, several pictures of the much younger Robedeaux brothers, including one of my father in his Army uniform, standing next to his young brothers. He was the only one old enough to have fought in World War II. I stared at the picture for a moment, considered taking it—it's my father, it belongs to me—but decided against it. Aunt Greta would know I took it. Better to get Aunt Lottie to intercede for me. She could walk in here, take it off the wall, and tell Aunt Greta, "It's for Micky. It's her father," and Aunt Greta wouldn't stop her.

I began looking through the desk, its cluttered drawers filled with swatch books and samples of the marine paint Uncle Claude sold for a living. There were order forms and invoices, all the piles of paperwork that a middle management position required.

Other drawers held old boating magazines, and one had piles of check stubs and banking statements.

I glanced at my watch: almost one o'clock. Only an hour before Aunt Greta came back.

I paused in my search. The packed desk alone could take several hours to search, particularly if I wanted to do it neatly.

Uncle Claude was not a devious man, but he wasn't a stupid man, either. I was assuming that whatever he wanted to give to me was paper, maybe letters or documents. I was also assuming that he hadn't told Aunt Greta and probably didn't want her to know what he was up to. Either or both of these assumptions could be wrong, but I had to do some triage on my search.

The checks in his desk were something she would probably have access to. It was a joint account with both their names on it. That made the file cabinet a more likely hiding place than the desk.

I turned away from the desk to the file cabinet. The bottom drawer. It was the most awkward to reach and it had a couple of phone books shoved against it, as if it were rarely opened. But the handle was shiny and without dust.

That's when I heard the closing of the front door, then voices. They were in the den, heading this way.

I started to close the door, but had to leave it ajar; the swollen wood stuck and I couldn't force it closed quietly.

I was standing behind the door, out of sight, but anyone looking down the hallway had a view of the door. I recognized one of the voices as Bayard's. What the hell is he doing here in the middle of the day? I thought.

The other voice answered him and answered my question. I couldn't hear what she said, but it didn't matter; her voice was that of a young female, and her tone was giggly flirtation. Bayard was having a quick one in the old homestead. My only hope was that he wouldn't go for the added kink of doing it on Aunt Greta's bed.

And I had thought that the worst thing that could happen would be for Aunt Greta to find me here.

Through the crack in the doorframe, I could see them as they came into the hallway and, mercifully, turned toward Bayard's room.

She was a teased-hair blond, looking barely over the age of consent. Well, of course he would have to go after women that young; women his age know better.

I glanced at my watch again. Bayard knew Aunt Greta's routines as well as, if not better than, I did. He knew she would be back home in forty-five minutes or less. That was probably part of the thrill, also a nod to expediency—forty-five minutes from fully dressed to fully dressed again and out the door, didn't leave much time for foreplay or any of the mushy stuff.

Bayard—or whoever she was—shut the door to his room. I was somewhat relieved to hear a radio turned on. I didn't want to hear them and I didn't want them to hear me as I made my escape.

As much as I just wanted to get out, it seemed prudent to give them a few minutes to get undressed and entwined. They would be less likely to hear me and, if they did, less likely to give chase.

With one quick glance at his closed door, I again turned to the bottom drawer of the file cabinet. I would give myself five minutes to glance through it, then get out of here.

I carefully moved the phone books aside, taking extra care to be quiet. I slowly slid the drawer open, afraid of squeaks or rattles. But it was a quality file cabinet and Uncle Claude had obviously occasionally oiled the rollers. I took its silence as a sign that I should be here.

It was full of files, manila folders stuffed with paper, old folded newspapers, heavy envelopes.

I made a guess and pulled out the first file. Opening it, I saw nautical charts, then a sheet of paper in Uncle Claude's handwriting, notes for a journey he never took. He had wanted to cruise the Gulf of Mexico, down to the Caribbean, on to South America. His notes were careful and precise. There were articles on trips others had taken, places to seek harbor; some of these he had outlined in red ink, marking the places he had wanted to stop. The file was thick with the paper he'd held this dream together with. Some of the articles were twenty years old. He had dreamed it for that long.

I put the folder back. Other folders were for other trips, other oceans he'd dreamed of crossing. I skipped by them, my uncle's deferred and, finally, denied dreams.

Then there were files containing folders on boats, all the specs that a buyer would want to know, glossy brochures on ketches and yawls, the sailing ships that might have taken him on the trips he had planned.

Then I found it. It was a large manila envelope. On it was scrawled, *Lee Robedeaux*. Underneath that, written in a newer ink, was *For Micky*.

I carefully removed it from its resting place between my uncle's dreams, then I closed the drawer and replaced the sentinel phone books.

Bayard's door was still closed, the radio still playing, the disc jockey's voice braying, "And the fifth caller will win two tickets to the Monster Truck show in the Superdome." How romantic.

There was nothing to do but go back through the house. Quickly and quietly, I told myself. Running out of here, as I wanted to do, would probably only cause me to trip and fall. That conjured up an even worse image than Bayard finding me here—sprawled in the middle of the den with a broken leg and both Bayard and Aunt Greta looming over me and the envelope lying beside me for them to take away forever.

I gently closed the door to Uncle Claude's study, trying to leave it as closed as I had found it. With a little discreet tugging, I got it most of the way. Good enough, I told myself. It wouldn't visibly disturb the immaculate lines of Aunt Greta's bedroom. Maybe that was why she kept it so orderly, so that any transgressions would be easily apparent. Maybe Bayard used only his room for his trysts because he couldn't be bothered to clean up and neaten Aunt Greta's.

I tried to slow myself down, keep my footsteps soft and sure. The distance from Aunt Greta's bedroom, down the hallway to the door that led to the den—only twenty feet at most—was the most dangerous.

A quick trip to the bathroom for either Bayard or his bimbo would catch me in a place I had no right to be.

Suddenly the radio was silent, then it picked up again before I began running. The weather announcement and a promise of more great hits from the seventies covered my steps.

Then I was in the den. Should I head directly to the front door? I still had the back door key in my pocket. To put it back, I had to go out the back door. I crossed the den to the kitchen. I wanted to leave no trace that I had been here. And I could still claim that I was here looking for a lost earring. If they didn't notice the fat envelope I was carrying with Uncle Claude's handwriting on it.

I hurried through the kitchen and out the back door. The key in the lock made a harsh click as the bolts slid into place. You're too aware, I told myself, it's not that loud. I again had to quell my desire to run. All I needed was some neighbor to see a less than perfectly white woman running out of the backyard.

I quickly put the key under the hiding rock, then admonished myself to walk out of here like I had been visiting my aunt in search of a lost earring.

Oh, hell, I suddenly realized, I have to walk by his side window. There was a walkway only on one side of the house; the garage, on the other side, was built to the fence.

He might be stupid enough to leave the curtains open, but I doubted, even as young as she was, that she was that stupid. And even if he did see me, what could he really do? There was a good chance that, rather than admit he'd come home for some unexplained reason in the middle of the day, he'd not mention anything to Aunt Greta.

And I didn't have any choice at this point anyway. I crossed the backyard, then turned toward the street. Walk slowly, I reminded myself. Fast movement is more noticeable.

I slowly walked by the bedroom windows, first Aunt Greta's—how quickly it became hers alone—Gus's old room, no longer his, Mary Theresa's. The radio got louder. I was at Bayard's window.

Then I was past it.

They didn't hear me, but I heard them. Again, the words weren't clear, but the meaning was. His tone was cajoling, on the edge of bullying, her answers wavering, unsure.

I quickly crossed the front lawn to the street. It would probably be a long time before she did anything during her lunch hour other than eat lunch.

I unlocked my car and tossed the envelope in.

Bayard, the eldest son, had the front corner bedroom. The window facing the street was heavily curtained, showing a blank face to the world. I stared at it for a minute. He could no longer catch me. That bland window had hidden so many sins. Even this minor one gnawed at me.

I could go ring the doorbell, though Bayard would probably just ignore it.

But sometimes fate offers other alternatives. A brick was lying beside the curb. It had probably fallen off a passing truck. I took a quick look up and down the street—no cars, no people visible—then I picked up the brick.

I slipped back around my car, getting just close enough that I couldn't miss that blank front window. It would land in his dirty laundry. The bed was away from the window, in the far corner.

I heaved the brick through it.

I didn't even wait to watch for the shatter of glass, though I heard it as I jumped back into my car. For one final time, I heard the voices, again no words, but a growling grunt from Bayard and a surprised gasp from the woman.

I turned the ignition and headed down the street. "Someday you'll thank me for this," I said out loud to the girl who couldn't possibly hear me.

I drove to the end of the block, then stopped at the stop sign and held there, watching in my rearview mirror. I glanced at my watch. It was almost two o'clock.

A block farther on, I saw a car turn onto the street. It was a pale green Cadillac, the same color and shape of the one I had seen parked in the driveway.

I gave one last glance in the mirror, but the street was still quiet, all the movement and consternation taking place indoors.

I turned, so the Cadillac wouldn't pass me, and then drove away from that neighborhood.

Chapter

13

Traffic was not kind to me on the way back to my office. Old Metairie Road, my chosen route, was clogged with afternoon shoppers and the convoys of children leaving school. Its two narrow lanes handled the driving insanity at a leisurely pace. What was the most frustrating was that the traffic poked along just enough to make it impossible for me to open the envelope. Every time I'd shift into neutral, traffic would inch forward again.

It was almost three o'clock before I made it back to my office. I tossed the envelope on my desk and made a decision.

Chester Prejean said he'd be in his office from three to five P.M. Between getting there and finding the place, it was at least a half hour from here to there. I had no idea how busy he was, or how many people might be waiting to see him. It wouldn't help my cause if I showed up with a request that would take half an hour and he wanted to be gone in fifteen minutes.

With a sigh, I left the envelope on my desk.

I started to head out, then stopped. I moved the envelope into a drawer, then locked it.

I knew I was being paranoid. Even if Bayard somehow had managed, in the brief seconds it took me to drive away, to get my license plate number—and that was very unlikely—the car was registered to Cordelia.

Still, I felt more secure with the envelope out of sight.

Chalmette is not a far drive from my house, as I live in the downtown part of New Orleans and Chalmette is just down from New Orleans.

It was only a little past three-thirty when I arrived at Chester Prejean's office. The office was a compact frame house, its white paint just old enough to look homey, not shabby. In front was a carved wooden sign, a homemade job without the precision that a professional would give to it. It hinted of barter, a client who paid his legal bill by carving a sign for Chester. The door was open, letting in the sunshine and proving that Chester was indeed here, as his answering machine had promised.

I got out of my car and went up the steps to the porch. There was even an old wooden rocker here; Chester was a good old boy country lawyer or did a good job of pretending to be.

I stuck my head in the open door. It was a wide-open office, with a large desk and a comfortable-looking leather chair behind it. Most of the walls were lined with bookcases. The one nearest the door had the shelves stocked with matched lawyerly tomes, but most of the other bookcases were a hodgepodge of law books. One bookcase even had a few rows of paperbacks, an open admission that sometimes things were slow and that Chester Prejean would sit around reading detective novels.

"Hello?" I called.

One of the far doors opened. "C'mon back to the master conference room and have some iced tea," a voice answered.

I followed the voice back to the master conference room, which turned out to be a kitchen. It was an old-style kitchen, slope-shouldered refrigerator, porcelain sink, a long generous table scarred with mug rings and imperfect chopping.

Chester was standing at a counter, stirring a large pitcher of iced tea.

"Howdy, young lady," he greeted me, finishing his stirring. "You got your choice, Mardi Gras cups or politics?"

"Mardi Gras," I answered. "Politics can leave a bad taste in the mouth." Go cups, which he was pouring our tea into, are the ubiquitous plastic glasses thrown off Mardi Gras floats or given out at political rallies.

"Durn right. 'Specially Louisiana politics," Chester said. "We'll go high-class, with some Rex cups."

Chester poured our tea and brought it over to the table. He motioned me to sit and was enough of a gentleman to wait until I'd seated myself before taking his chair.

I guessed him to be in his mid- to late sixties, but he was probably one of those men who could boast that he could still wear his old Army uniform or college clothes. He was a compact man, some might say slight, but there was a bubbling energy about him that made that description inaccurate. His hair was a steel-gray, only barely thinning at the temples and crown of his head. His teeth were even and white. He smiled a lot and knew the value of a smile. His face had the weathered look of someone who sees the sun regularly, yard work on the weekends, frequent fishing trips.

"Here you go," he said, setting a sugar bowl and plate of lemon slices between us. "I hope you're not looking for a lawyer, because in about an hour I'm going to be retired. And in about a day I'm going to be headed down to the Virgin Islands for a nice long summer vacation."

"Actually, I'm looking for information," I said, and put my PI license on the table.

Chester picked it up to look at it. "Oh, how interesting. I always thought that women detectives existed mostly in books and movies."

It was then that I decided I liked Chester Prejean, because he really did sound interested, not annoyed or threatened.

"Well, Ms. Michele Knight, I'm pleased to make your acquaintance. What kind of information can an old lawyer like me pass on to you?"

"I'm helping a young man search for his birth mother. I managed to get out of the adopted mother that a lawyer in Chalmette named Chester Prejean arranged the adoption privately."

"Well, that'd be me. How long ago are we talking about?"

"The boy's around eighteen or nineteen."

"Twenty years back, huh? Sometimes my memory doesn't go much further than yesterday. Do you think it's a good thing for this boy to find his mama?"

It was a thoughtful question and I decided to give it an honest answer. "I don't know. I think he has expectations that probably won't be met."

"How so?"

"His adoptive parents threw him out when he was sixteen. When I talked with his mother, she didn't strike me as the most maternal and loving mother on the earth."

"Threw him out when he was sixteen? What on earth for?"

"He was gay. Got caught fooling around with another boy."

"Oh, good Lord, that's no excuse to throw a child out. I can't imagine throwing a child out. I've got four of them. Maybe take him to a shrink to get his head on right or pray over him or something. But I truly do not understand how a parent can just throw a child out of his or her life."

"He's had two mothers throw him out of their lives. I guess he'd like to see if he can get at least one back."

"What happened to the boy?" Chester asked.

"His father put him on a bus for New Orleans when he was sixteen. I gather he survived the way most kids on the streets survive."

"Well, that's a rough life."

"Did you ever follow any of the kids you set up for adoption? Check up on them?" I asked.

"Not really. Now, I know what you're thinking, I dumped this poor kid into the kind of family that'd throw him out. Well, maybe I did. Since it was private and all, no social worker to check up on the kids or anything like that. But I purely do believe that I never sent a kid to a worse place than he came from. I think your boy's going to be disappointed. Lot of the girls were real poor, real . . . not another word for it . . . stupid."

"How'd you get involved?"

"Didn't intend to. A second cousin of a second cousin had a friend who was in trouble, as they said back then. I wasn't going to arrange an abortion; wasn't legal back then anyway. I knew a couple that wanted a kid and hadn't been lucky in that respect, so I figured I had a problem and a solution and all I needed to do was some paperwork to put 'em together. So one thing leads to another and another girl ends up on my doorstep. It was always informal, just somebody told somebody. Did it a couple of times a year."

"Do you think you could remember one of them? A couple from over in Mississippi?"

Chester shook his head. "Oh, I might remember this and that, but I'd have to look at the record to be sure."

"Would you be willing to do that?"

Chester chuckled softly, then said, "Follow me, young lady."

He led me out the back door and across the lawn to a garage that had been converted for storage. It was filled with boxes and boxes of files.

I looked around the room at the overflowing boxes stacked up almost to the rafters. Then I looked at Chester. "Somewhere in here, right?"

"Most probably. Now, I have to admit that these files aren't in perfect order. Had one of my teenage grandsons and some of his friends cart this stuff out here. And they paid about as much attention to order and dates and things like that as most fifteen-year-olds would—1960 wills might be next to 1980 real estate."

"No way you can dig it out before your summer vacation," I said glumly.

"I'm retired. If you want to, you're welcome to try. Don't make a mess, put everything back as neatly as you found it."

I looked at him. "You'd let me go through your files?"

"Hell, honey, if there was blackmail stuff in there I'd have retired a long time ago. Lawyers charge so much money for this 'cause it's boring with a capital B. This is all old stuff. Five years back at least. All the stuff less than five years old or still active isn't here. No fishing. I'll be suing you if I find out you told old Mrs. Boudreaux that her husband left his second-best fishing rod to his girlfriend or anything like that."

"No, I won't. Doesn't seem like there'd be much money in a second-best fishing rod."

"Nope, not much. Two of my kids became lawyers. My two daughters." Chester caught himself. "Nothing wrong with that. But . . ."

But he had gone to law school at a time when women didn't become lawyers and he'd imagined his sons as lawyers, but not his daughters. His voice had a mixture of pride and ambivalence. The speed of the world had overtaken him.

"In other words, you can sue me very cheaply, if need be."

"Don't make a mess in the boy's life or the mother's. You're going to have to be the judge of that. Don't just out of the blue dump them together—but you probably know better than that anyway."

"What I'd probably do is see the mother myself, tell her her son is looking for her, and only if she agrees, introduce them."

Chester nodded, as if listening not only to my plan, but checking that I had enough sense to come up with a reasonable approach and that I seemed to have some experience in this.

"Also . . . after you've seen the mother, you might think about whether the boy should meet her. Might be better to have an ideal mother off in your dreams than nowhere at all."

"Maybe. And maybe it's better not to waste your life chasing an ideal you'll never find."

"You get to be the one to decide." He paused for a moment, then continued, "I'll give you a copy of the key—do lock it when you're not here—gotta keep the neighborhood punks out. When you're done with it, just drop it back through the mail slot on the front door. Let's go back to the master conference room and finish our tea."

Chester closed the storage room door and we went back to the kitchen. He gave me a copy of the key and a signed piece of paper authorizing me to hunt through his old files. One of his daughters had taken over his practice, so all the active files had been transferred to her office. He gave me her phone number, in case anything went wrong. With that, I wished him a very happy summer vacation, while the rest of us faced the wet and chilly New Orleans winter.

I retrieved a notebook and pen from my car and went back to the storage garage. I jotted down in the notebook the location of boxes that were clearly labeled. I was looking for files from the seventies. Bourbon St. Ann wasn't sure enough of his age (and I wasn't sure enough of what his claimed age was) to narrow it down to just one year.

I sneezed and decided that I would come back on another day, with old clothes and perhaps a face mask.

I waved at Chester through the window to let him know I was leaving; he waved back but was on the phone.

I could just tell Bourbon St. Ann I'd run into a dead end and save myself rummaging through dusty old files. (I'd have to ask Cordelia if I could get tetanus from paper cuts from those dirty edges.)

I rejected that option. I knew how much I wanted to find my mother. As annoying and imperfect as I found him, it would be very hard to take this from him unless I felt I had no choice—if the files couldn't be found or if his mother refused to see him. But until I ran into those roadblocks, I would keep searching.

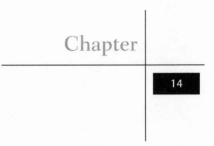

Chapter

14

I went back to my office even though it was a little after five by the time I got there.

It was now my turn to search for my mother. I wanted to look through the envelope that Uncle Claude had made for me.

But a sense of duty to a mother looking for her daughter made me pick up the phone first, to dial the number I had gotten from Suzanna Forquet.

"Hello?" the phone was answered.

"Is this Georgia Sherman?" I asked.

"Who's calling?" she asked. I couldn't tell if she was naturally wary or just had too many telemarketers hassling her lately.

"My name's Michele Knight." To quickly answer her questions before she could ask them, I continued, "No, you don't know me, but I'm not trying to sell you anything. I'm a private detective and I'm looking for someone. I was given your name as a possible source."

"Now, wait a minute. I'm supposed to believe that out of the blue some lady private eye is calling me up and I'm going to tell you where the Maltese falcon is?"

"No, no falcons. Just a person. Her mother hired me to find her."

"Look, sorry I sound cranky, but I'm about to go to work for sixteen hours. I'm not saying I won't help you, but I'd like to have more than just a voice on the telephone. Okay?"

"Sure. I'd be glad to meet if you want. I can show you my license, my listing in the yellow pages, whatever you like."

"Yeah, bring that license. Who are you looking for?"

"Lorraine Drummond."

There was a moment's pause that told me she knew who Lorraine Drummond was, then she asked, "And her mother is looking for her?"

"Yes, Mr. Drummond passed away and now Mrs. Drummond wants to find her daughter."

"I did see the notice about Mr. Drummond's passing," she said.

Georgia Sherman may have been a bit wary, and prudent enough not to directly give information out over the phone, but she wasn't either paranoid enough or guarded enough not to give out information indirectly. Her last comment told me that she knew Lorraine well enough to have noted her estranged father's obituary.

"When do you want to meet?" I asked her.

"How about around noon tomorrow? I get off at eleven. That'll give me an hour to get home and shower off the hospital smells."

"Would you like to meet at my office?"

"Where's your office?"

"Downtown. In the Bywater area."

"Umm. That's way out of my way. I live Uptown off Carrollton. Would you meet me here?"

"Of course. You're helping me. I should make this as easy as possible."

"I live on Cohn Street, by the cemetery." She gave me the address.

"Thanks. I'll see you tomorrow at noon."

It's odd how we're sometimes more protective of others than ourselves. Georgia's willingness to give me her address (of course, she might have known that if I had her phone number I could get it) confirmed my impression of her as someone who didn't have layers of wariness for me to wade through.

My hand was still resting on the phone when it rang. I picked it up.

"Micky, this is Joanne. I'm on my way to see Cordelia. I think you should meet me there." Her voice had the cool, professional edge that she used to hide emotions.

"Bad news?" It was barely a question.

"I think you should meet me there," was her answer.

"I'm on my way."

I quickly locked my office. The envelope had waited all these years; it could wait a little longer.

Joanne's car pulled into the clinic lot just in front of mine. We both got out at the same time. Joanne said nothing, just a nod to acknowledge I was here. Her mouth was a hard line, as if she wanted to keep the words in and never say them.

I followed her into the clinic. The waiting room was empty and no one was in the office area of the clinic. Millie was coming down the hall carrying her purse and with her jacket on. She was looking in her large bag, fumbling for car keys, and she didn't see us.

When she looked up, she abruptly stopped—stopped walking,

stopped feeling for her keys. The tension in her stillness meant she knew why Joanne was here.

"Where's Hutch?" she said softly.

At first I thought it was an odd question, then I realized that our first concern is what's closest to us. It was possible that Joanne was here to tell Millie that Hutch was hurt.

Joanne understood the question and quickly answered, "He's at the scene."

Millie closed her eyes and just barely nodded her head, the relief on her face strongly etched by the sadness of knowing that someone somewhere would get the news she had been dreading. She let out a breath, then said, "Cordelia's in her office. Would it help if I stayed?"

This time I answered, "No, unless you want to." Millie was wise enough to know that grief didn't always need onlookers.

She nodded again and said, "I assume Hutch will be late."

"Probably," Joanne answered.

"Find who did it," she said softly as she passed us.

The door to Cordelia's office was open. I heard voices, hers and Lindsey's.

Cordelia broke off what she was saying in midsentence. "Joanne," she said, suddenly seeing her framed in the doorway. She was sitting at her desk. Lindsey was standing beside her.

I was behind Joanne.

"Micky?" Cordelia questioned when she sighted me.

"I'm afraid I have some bad news," Joanne said.

"Tasha is dead?"

"Yes, I'm sorry," Joanne confirmed.

Cordelia closed her eyes, then quickly opened them as if she couldn't bear the image her mind conjured up. Lindsey put a comforting hand on her shoulder.

"Was . . . was she murdered?" Cordelia asked slowly, almost struggling to get the words out.

"Probably. No autopsy report yet, but . . ." Joanne trailed off, not wanting to give the details of why she thought Tasha was murdered.

"Has anyone told her family yet?"

"I was just there," Joanne replied.

"How . . . how are they?" Cordelia asked.

"Shattered. It's hard for them to go through this."

"Goddamn it! Goddamn it!" Cordelia cried out. "Why? Why her? Why someone . . . someone as bright . . ."

"I don't know why. I may never know why. But I will find out who," Joanne answered.

"Was she . . . like the . . . others?" she asked very quietly.

"I'm sorry, but yes, I think so."

"Oh, God, oh, God, no!" Cordelia let out a ragged breath and said, "Thank you for coming by, Joanne. I know this isn't easy for you I know . . . I hate bringing bad news. This has to be the . . . worst."

"It's going to be a long night for me. I may have to talk to you tomorrow, probably look at her medical record. What will you need from me for that? A warrant?"

Cordelia shook her head. "Permission from the family will do."

Joanne nodded, then said a quick good-bye and she was gone.

Cordelia turned to me and said, "I guess we should lock up and go home. I think I want to get out of here."

In the parking lot, Cordelia asked Lindsey, "Are you going to be all right?"

"I'll be fine," Lindsey reassured her. "I didn't really know Tasha. It hasn't hit me the way it's hit you. Will you be okay?"

Cordelia paused. "Eventually. Tasha should be alive. And she's not."

Lindsey didn't answer. She hugged Cordelia, then got in her car.

When we got home, I offered to fix some dinner.

"Thanks," she said, accepting my offer that tonight I would take care of her.

Cordelia sat in the kitchen while I threw together a salad and heated up some soup. We didn't talk much. Cordelia was tired and worn by the day's events.

After eating, we settled into our usual evening routine, both of us sitting in comfortable chairs reading. But Cordelia was restless, reading for a bit, then getting up to play with the cats or get another book or magazine.

As it was getting close to her bedtime, she said, "Would you be upset . . . if I have a drink before going to bed?"

"No," I replied. "Would you like me to fix it for you?"

"That's not necessary," she said quickly.

"It's not a problem. The liquor bottles are there; I could take a drink anytime I wanted to," I pointed out.

"It just doesn't seem fair. . . ."

"It doesn't bother me when people drink and can control their drinking. It bothers me when people can't control their drinking. Particularly me. I'm going to make myself some ever so genteel herbal tea and I'll be glad to fix you whatever you want."

"Just something with vodka in it. I don't really want to taste the liquor, I just want to fall asleep."

"One something with vodka coming up."

I went to the kitchen and put the water on for my tea and decided on a cranberry juice/orange juice/vodka concoction for Cordelia. That way she would get her vitamin C, prevent urinary tract infections, and knock herself out at the same time.

She took a sip and said, "Are you sure this has any vodka in it?"

Ten minutes later, when she got up to go to bed, she answered her own question. "I think I will be able to fall asleep tonight," she said, steadying herself on the arm of the sofa.

"Looks that way," I said as I put an arm around her waist. "Let's go to bed."

Oftentimes she will be asleep before I'm finished in the bath-room—Cordelia usually sleeps easily—but tonight's agitation lingered on. She was awake when I came to join her.

"I need to sleep. I'm really tired."

"Lie down and let me curl around you," I offered.

Though we said nothing, I could feel her wakefulness as we lay in the dark. We remained that way for several minutes.

Then she took my arm, moved it from around her stomach up to her breasts. She tightly twined her arms with mine, creating a barrier of flesh and bone against her chest.

Only then did she slowly relax, her breathing shifting into the regular rhythms of sleep.

As I was falling asleep, her hand jerked and I felt her body tense. I tightened my arms around her and murmured, "It's all right, you're safe here with me." She stirred slightly at my voice, but didn't really wake up.

"It's okay, you're safe at home," I repeated softly, until the nightmares of her sleep let her go.

But I could not take away the nightmare that had invaded her waking hours.

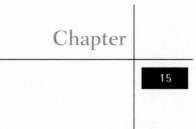

Chapter

15

The next morning, it wasn't until I was under the shower that the events of the day coalesced for me—the envelope from Uncle Claude and my appointment with Georgia Sherman. That hurried me through my wake-up routine. I wanted to see what was in the envelope before I had to leave to see Georgia.

Still, between my sleeping late, feeding the cats, and the rest of life, it was a little before ten when I got to my office.

First, I made coffee before I settled myself at my desk.

Then I took the envelope from the drawer where I'd hidden it yesterday.

It was an old envelope, its paper edges soft and blunted. I carefully opened the clasp, somehow feeling it important not to rip or tear this envelope that held the only legacy I would get from my parents.

I gently emptied it onto my desk, catching the contents with my hand so that nothing tumbled out. It seemed to be mostly papers, some pictures, then something fell onto the palm of my hand. I put the papers and pictures down to examine it. It was a ring, a simple gold band.

A wedding band? I held it up to catch the sunlight. Inside was a worn inscription: "Love Eternal. MAR 1921."

I recognized the ring. It was the one my father had worn. I hadn't known that he had taken it from his father. Maurice Augustine Robedeaux. I had never known him. He had died before any of his sons bore him grandchildren. A seaman from a long family of seamen, too old to fight in the war that left his oldest son with a limp, he had joined the Coast Guard. He had the weak heart that his sons inherited. One night he had gone to the lonely watchtower, and before the morning came, his heart had stopped beating.

Maurice and his Charlotte. She had outlived him, long enough to see her sons beget their sons and daughters. Her picture was here, her face lined and wrinkled by the years of work and weather. In the faded photograph, she was holding a baby, the deep furrows in her brow pressed against the smooth skin of the baby's forehead. Then I knew who the child was. I turned the picture over to read the inscription on the back of it: "Mama with Michele—six weeks old." The faded ink was in my father's hand. It was a picture of my grandmother holding me. I knew she had died before I was two, the engraving on her tombstone told me that. Of course, I didn't remember her, and because my memory held no place for her, she had never been real to me.

But here she was, my grandmother holding me. In the short time that our lives had intersected, my grandmother had loved me.

Then another picture caught my attention. Her face was there, Charlotte, my grandmother, but she was in the background. It was my mother and father. They were both dressed up, my father in a suit I can only remember him wearing for funerals. My mother had on a dress I'd seen only once, packed away in a trunk. I glanced at the back of the photo for an inscription, but there was none. Whoever had taken this picture thought it was too obvious to need a description. It was my parents' wedding day, that was clear to me even at the distance of over thirty years. My mother held a large bouquet of flowers, clutching it across her stomach. But even the roses and the loose-fitting dress couldn't disguise the swelling of her stomach. They both had put on smiles for the camera. My father's grin held a genuine happiness in it—he had wanted a wife and child and if fate had blown them to him from an unexpected direction, he had still gotten what his heart wanted. My mother's smile was tenuous and ambivalent, an odd mixture of relief and resignation. She had been rescued from the shame and struggle of being an unmarried mother, but she was also trapped in a marriage and a life that she would never have willingly chosen.

As even the still, posed photograph couldn't hide the curve of the child inside her, it was not possible that my grandmother, the Charlotte who had borne five children, buried two of them, and raised three, did not know that the baby she held in the other picture was a bastard. And still she held me and loved me.

What had she thought of my mother? Had they gotten along? Fought? Maintained a wary distance with my father caught in between? I realized that that piece of history was lost to me, my only clue to it still photographs. But no matter how I looked at them, they would reveal nothing beyond the scant second caught by the shutter of the camera.

It was hard to read the expression on Charlotte's face. To me, it seemed to hold that same mix of resignation and relief that played across my mother's features. This pregnant sixteen-year-old girl was not the wife she would have chosen for her son, but this day held in it a chance for happiness. A woman who had buried two children and a husband had to know how cruel the world could be.

There was a picture of my father in uniform. He was a young man, his hands on his hips, standing in front of an Army jeep. How long did that young man have before the shrapnel would change him into a man who could only walk with a limp and would never run again?

There was another of him, holding me as a young baby. He looked both proud and perplexed, as if unsure of what to do with that living thing in his arms. His cane, like a third leg, rested beside him in the chair.

Then there was a picture of my mother holding my hand. I was a toddler. We were standing in the main clearing of the shipyard. The sky was gray, threatening, the surroundings were disheveled and chaotic, trees uprooted and a boat half on and half off the dock. I glanced at the back of the picture: "The day after Hurricane Betsy," it said. I would have been around four.

The shipyard had survived the wind and the water, the docks intact save for a few loose boards. Some of the younger trees would not see spring again.

Amid the destruction stood my mother and I, standing tall, her hair blown by the lingering wind, my hand securely in hers, the sky vast with the loss of the damaged trees, the distant marsh broken only by the skeleton tree. It had survived.

"But you let go of me, didn't you?" I said to the picture. Soon after that she would leave.

I put the pictures aside.

There were several letters from my father to Uncle Claude, written when he was stationed in the South Pacific. I only glanced at them; they could be read later. Written long before they met, they would give me no information about my mother.

Another ring slipped out of one of the envelopes. A woman's wedding band, a thin gold one. The light at my desk was inadequate to read the tiny inscription in it. I went to the window with its direct sunlight. It was only a date—"November 2, 1959"—the same date as was on their marriage license. It was my mother's wedding band.

She had given it up. Or had my father asked for its return? I sat back down at my desk and quickly glanced through the remaining papers. My birth certificate, my father's discharge papers, his Social Security card, his death certificate, but no divorce papers. No will, either. I wondered if he had died intestate. I was his only heir and I knew Louisiana had a forced heirship. But I was unclear on the ramifications of it. I'd have to ask Danny to see if it meant anything.

I again examined the wedding ring. It was a plain gold band. I slipped it on my finger. It fit perfectly. I quickly took it off, this solid ring worn by the chimera that my mother had become. It burned a place in my heart to have her memory encircle my finger.

I put the ring on the desk, then placed it back in the random envelope that it had slipped into. I realized that it wasn't one of my father's old World War II letters. The handwriting on the envelope was mine. It was that long-ago letter that I had given to Uncle Claude to mail to my mother. He had never sent it.

It made no sense. Why pretend to mail it? Unless it had something to do with my father not leaving a will. If he hadn't divorced my mother, maybe she still had rights to the property? Did Uncle Claude want to keep control of the land through me? I would have to ask Danny a few legal questions.

I glanced at my watch. I needed to head out for my appointment.

I needed to painstakingly go through everything in here, I thought as I carefully put the papers and pictures back into their envelope home. There were some records from the shipyard that I had barely glanced at, an old address book, some newspaper clippings, and more pictures of the destruction from Betsy. I dropped the clippings to pick up the address book. I quickly searched for my mother's name. It was there, but it was the same one I had sent my returned letter to.

I put the address book back in the large envelope. One of the clippings slipped to the floor. I reached to pick it up and noticed that it was a much newer newspaper clipping than the others. It was a recipe for crawfish bread. On the reverse side was a short blurb about an unidentified body found in the Mississippi and a small ad for an art opening at the LA Gallery. I hurriedly scanned the article about the body—it was a young male. Then I glanced at the art ad. The artist's name was lost in the torn-off edge of the paper. I put it back with the rest. The recipe looked good. I wondered why Uncle Claude had put it in with my father's stuff.

I again hid the manila envelope in a desk drawer. It was past time to be going.

The traffic lights became my nemesis, all of them turning red and blocking my path. As the fifth light in a row winked from yellow to red, I knew I was going to be late. When I saw the eighteen-wheeler spread across two lanes of traffic and not moving, I knew I was going to be later.

I was fifteen minutes late when I finally found Cohn Street and the cemetery. A car was parked in front of Georgia's address. There weren't many other cars around; people were at work and children were in school. I saw no one else as I got out, the slamming of my car door sounded very loud in the quiet street.

That alone probably announced my arrival to Georgia, I thought as I climbed the stairs to her porch. But just in case my slamming door and stomping feet weren't enough to let her know that I was finally here, I rang her doorbell.

I heard no movement from inside the house. I waited for about a minute before pushing the buzzer a second time. Again I waited. Somewhere, a street or two over, I heard a car door slam and then its engine growl to life.

There were still no sounds from inside the house. Maybe she

got tired of waiting and left, though the car parked directly in front of her place argued against that. Maybe I caught her in the bathroom. She was a nurse; she might eat one of those healthy high-fiber diets. I irrelevantly wondered whether the New Orleans sewer system could handle everyone changing to a healthy diet with lots of fruits and vegetables.

After another moment or so of no sounds from within, I called out, "Hello? Georgia?" Then I rapped on the frame of the screen door. Maybe her buzzer was broken.

But still the only response was silence. An uneasy prickle started at the back of my neck. She'd had to work longer hours, or she got tired of waiting for me and took a walk somewhere, or she forgot about the appointment and was off doing other things.

I looked at the house next door. Today's mail was sticking out of the mailbox. I flipped open the lid of Georgia's mailbox. Nothing was there. Someone had taken the mail in. Or else she hadn't gotten any, I reminded myself.

Maybe she'd fallen asleep. I opened the screen door and knocked loudly on the wooden door. "Hello? Georgia?" I called again.

No answer.

I banged again on the door. Now I not only wanted to find Lorraine Drummond, but to make sure that Georgia Sherman was all right.

The door shifted slightly as I struck it. The prickle on my neck traveled down my spine.

I took the doorknob in hand and turned it. The door opened. I pushed it wide, but didn't enter.

"Georgia? Hello? Anyone here?"

I was still for a long moment, listening for any soft breathing, the hint of a floorboard creaking, any sign that someone was here who didn't want to be found.

But the silence held.

I stepped through the door. The first room, dim after the light of the noon sun, was empty. It was a typical shotgun house, one room leading into another.

"Georgia? Are you here?" I called. "It's Micky Knight. Your door was unlocked, so I . . ." I stopped. I was using my voice to fill the silence. I needed to listen for sounds, not make them.

The next room was the second half of the double parlors. It held the stereo and TV, but, like the first room, was empty.

Behind it was the kitchen. I glanced around it quickly, then stopped. On the counter was a bowl of cereal; next to it stood a carton of milk. I touched the milk. It was still cold. Why had Georgia Sherman started to make herself a bowl of cereal, but not finished? The left-out milk nagged me. If she'd made a quick run to the corner store for bananas, it didn't make sense that she'd not put the milk back in the refrigerator.

I almost started to put it away for her, but caught myself and realized that I needed to treat her apartment like a crime scene. Don't move anything, don't touch it unless you have to.

I tried to reassure myself. Georgia could be scatterbrained enough to leave her milk out, but the woman I'd talked to on the phone hadn't given me that impression.

"Georgia?" I called again, not because I thought she might answer, but because the silence had become dense and threatening and I had to break it.

But this time there was an answer. Somewhere from the back of the house came a noise that was between a wheeze and a sigh, ending on an odd strangled gurgle.

"Georgia?" I yelled, wanting a response that said someone was here and alive.

There was a short hallway, built so the bathroom wouldn't have to be walked through to get from the kitchen to the bedroom.

I quickly pushed open its door. Seeing no one, I threw back the shower curtain, but nothing save a clean bathtub was there.

A woman who scrubbed the bathtub like that wouldn't leave a gallon of milk sitting on the kitchen counter.

Only the bedroom was left. Its door was closed.

I pulled out my shirt, using the tail of it to turn the doorknob.

As the door swung open, I heard the strangled gurgle again. For the last time.

There was blood everywhere. How can a human body contain that much blood? was my first thought. Then the heavy, iron smell of it assaulted my senses.

Georgia Sherman had just died.

For a moment, thought of first aid jumbled through my head. Stop the bleeding.

But save for a slight ooze from the wounds on her chest, there was no bleeding. Her blood had left her body and I couldn't put it back in.

I turned and ran out of the house. If Georgia could be helped, it would require everything medicine could offer. I didn't know where her phone was, or if I might not be masking the track of a killer if I picked it up. And I wanted out of that blood-soaked house.

I grabbed my car phone and punched in 911.

"An ambulance and the police. I think a woman's been murdered," I told the operator.

It was a brief conversation, then I was standing by myself on this empty street.

I dialed Joanne's number.

"Joanne Ranson," she answered in her professional tone.

"Joanne, it's Micky." I couldn't stop my voice from shaking.

"What's wrong?" she immediately asked.

"I think this is going to be one of yours."

"Where are you?"

"Uh . . . Cohn. Cohn and, I think, Adams. The cemetery."

"I'm on my way."

"Joanne!" I stopped her, not wanting to lose this connection and the sound of her voice, to find myself alone on the street again.

"Are you okay?" she asked.

"Yeah . . . yeah, I am. I'm on my car phone. Call me when . . . you have a mobile phone, right? Call me and let me know you're on your way."

"I will," she reassured me. "If you're not comfortable, get out of there. No dead heroes."

"Not on my list of things to do today. I've called nine-one-one, so they should be here any minute. I'm going to get in my car and turn on the ignition and if anything threatening comes down the street, like a poodle or a kid on a tricycle, I'm out of here."

"Good, you do that. I've got my portable here. I'm going to hang up and call you right back. Okay?"

"Okay."

"Get in your car." With that Joanne was gone.

I obeyed her, got in my car and put the key in the ignition.

My phone rang. I jerked at the sound, yanking the key out and dropping it on the floor.

"Joanne?" I said, answering the phone as I fumbled for the keys.

"Yeah, it's me," her voice reassured me. "I'm heading out now." She moved away from the phone just enough to let me know she wasn't talking to me. "Anyone seen Hutch? . . . Get him out of the bathroom now."

We didn't have much of a conversation. I basically got to listen to Joanne's progress as she left the station to head my way.

I glanced at my watch. It was only twelve-thirty. Fifteen minutes ago, I had been knocking on Georgia's door.

I thought about going back in to see if there was anything I could do for her. Two things stopped me: the possibility that her murderer could still be hidden somewhere in the house, and the reality that nothing I could do would help Georgia Sherman.

Instead I sat in my car, scanning the street, listening to Joanne's conversations. In the background now I could hear Hutch. I guess they got him out of the bathroom. Every once in a while Joanne would check in on me. "Are you still okay?" or "You with us?" or "Hold on, we're on our way." I would mumble out some appropriate affirmation. The comfort of those mundane words was what I needed.

Then they were in a car (with presumably Hutch driving) and Joanne turned her attention back to me.

"Why do you think this might be one of our cases?" she asked.

I let out a long ragged sigh, reluctant to put the brutal picture into words. "There was . . . a lot of blood. But it . . . it didn't hide all the wounds. She was . . . her breasts were cut open. Carved . . . like X's . . ." I tried to shove the picture out of my mind, staring at the dazzle of sun on my car hood.

"What else did you notice?"

"Blood. Blood everywhere." The image wouldn't leave. "Her hands were tied, something white, underwear, maybe."

"A bra?"

"Maybe. I didn't look closely, but I think some type of undergarment."

"That's his MO. One of the details we've kept quiet about."

"He ties them with their underwear? Humiliate and murder."

"This is a sick character. Why were you there?"

"A case. I'm looking for someone. Georgia is . . . was a friend of hers. We had a noon appointment."

"Did you get there at noon?"

"No, I was fifteen minutes late. I heard a car." I suddenly remembered that car door closing and engine starting. "When I was knocking on her door, I heard a car driving away. Her milk was cold . . . and I heard her die." I was starting to lose control.

"We're on our way, Micky," Joanne responded to the panic in my voice. "Another five minutes or so and we'll be there."

"I hear a siren."

"You'll be okay," Joanne again assured me.

"If I'd gotten here on time, I would have walked into a murder."

"It didn't happen. We have to live with what really took place, not what might have been."

"Is it related? Two patients of Cordelia's murdered? Then a woman I'm supposed to meet?"

"I don't know. It could be coincidence, but . . . I have to investigate the possibility."

The siren wailed closer. I could see the flashing lights of the ambulance.

I felt a hard tenseness let loose at the sight of those lights and realized what a tenuous connection Joanne's distant voice was. If the murderer was still around, her voice couldn't save me. Those lights meant that there was someone besides me, a murdered woman, and possibly her killer on this empty block.

The ambulance was first, but a patrol car came right behind it. They pulled in beside my car. I got out.

I didn't say much, just that there was a probably dead woman in there and though I hadn't seen anyone, I couldn't be sure her murderer was gone.

The cops, two young men, went in first. The EMTs gave them about a one-room lead, then followed.

The sirens had brought out a few onlookers. Several people stood on their porches or yards to catch a glimpse of the tragedy unfolding. Another car came down the street and stopped behind the police car. Joanne and Hutch.

I realized that I was still holding the phone in my hand.

"You can probably hang up now," Hutch greeted me.

I tossed it back into my car.

"They're inside?" Joanne asked.

"Yeah. Two cops, two EMTs."

Another patrol car turned onto the street, going the wrong way for the half-block it took to get to us.

A young woman was driving it. She got out, as did an older man, a detective, I surmised, as he wasn't wearing a uniform.

"Ranson, Mackenzie. How'd you beat me here? Don't tell me this is one of your messy ones?"

"Maybe, Edmunds," Joanne answered his second question. I knew she was in the closet professionally, and didn't know how close a connection she wanted to admit to an out dyke PI like myself.

"So how'd you get word on this?" Edmunds persisted.

The woman with him, deciding that dead bodies were better than detective politics, went to join the other uniforms inside.

"This is Michele Knight," Hutch answered. "She's a friend of mine and she called us."

"You found the body?" Edmunds asked, looking at me for the first time.

I just nodded.

"You know her long?" As he asked the question, he flipped open a small notepad.

"This is the first time. . . . I guess I never met her," I fumbled.

"Why were you here if you didn't know her?"

"I'm a private detective. I had some questions for her to answer."

"Questions? About what?" Edmunds gave me a sharp look. If I wasn't just a private citizen, the rules changed.

Client confidentiality wouldn't hold in an official murder investigation. If he wanted it, he could subpoena me and that would only waste his and my time.

"A mother hired me to look for her estranged daughter. Georgia Sherman is a friend of the daughter. She wasn't willing to tell me where the woman was over the phone, so we arranged to meet."

"What's the name of the woman you're looking for?"

"Lorraine Drummond."

He put it in his notebook. Hutch and Joanne were neither helping or hindering. They would let Edmunds do his routine. I gathered Joanne was going to remain silent on the connection of the two other victims to Cordelia's clinic.

"You've never met her before. How'd you get inside the house?"

"I knocked on the door and it opened."

"Open sesame, huh?"

"It felt wrong. We were supposed to meet and she didn't answer and her door wasn't locked."

"Breaking and entering, huh?"

He was skeptical of my answer and was pushing, but I doubted that he would really arrest me for breaking and entering. Not with Hutch and Joanne here. He stared at me. I stared back.

Our contest was shattered by the screams of a woman from the far end of the block. She was running toward us.

"My baby! What's wrong? Where's Georgia? My baby!"

"We can't let her go in there," Joanne said. She and Hutch ran to intercept the woman before she got to the house.

I guessed it was Georgia's mother. Someone had probably told her that there was a police car and ambulance in front of her daughter's house.

Hutch caught her and literally embraced her in a bear hug to stop her.

I didn't move. I wouldn't lie to her, but I didn't want to tell her what I had seen. As I looked at her, I wondered, is it even possible that a heart could recover from this kind of break?

Joanne was talking to her as Hutch held her.

The EMTs came out of the house, empty-handed. More cars, a crime scene truck, even a camera crew arrived.

Somehow in the building cacophony I heard Joanne's voice. "I'm terribly sorry. It might be your daughter."

"Who else would be in there? In her house? Who else?" the woman wailed.

"I'm sorry," was Joanne's answer. Without a positive ID, Joanne couldn't tell the woman it was her daughter. But who else could it be?

The woman sagged, slipping out of Hutch's grip almost as if melting.

I turned away from Edmunds. "I'm going to move my car down the block, out of your way."

He just shrugged.

I couldn't bear to watch the scene around the house, the mother collapsed on the ground, the empty ambulance driving off.

Halfway down the block, with the house behind me, I only caught occasional glimpses of the rushing men and women in my rearview mirror. It was neither my personal tragedy nor my routine job. I had too many horrific memories for today. I didn't want to add any more.

I could probably leave. Joanne does know how to get in touch with me, I told myself, but still I stayed. I guess I wanted that final confirmation, that it was Georgia Sherman in there and that I had missed walking in on a murder by only bare minutes. But could I have saved her or would I, too, have been killed?

Joanne came and found me about an hour later.

"You still here?" she asked through the car window.

"If I'm not, we're both delusional." I paused, then asked, "Is it her? Georgia?"

"Yes."

"She was murdered the same way the others were."

"It appears."

"She was being killed at about the time we were to meet, wasn't she?"

"She seems to have died very recently."

"What if Georgia Sherman turns out to be a patient of Cordelia's? You think maybe her stalker decided to kill two birds with one stone? Only New Orleans' insane traffic saved me."

"I don't have any answers, Micky. But Cordelia, the clinic, and now you, seem to be a link between these women."

"What have you found out about the stalker?" I demanded.

"When did you join the police force?" was Joanne's reminder

that there were rules here and sharing information with civilians was breaking a lot of them.

"If this woman's obsessed with Cordelia, she could murder anyone at the clinic—Millie, Elly, Lindsey, any of the patients, or even Cordelia. Do you want to play by the rules or save lives?"

Joanne leaned down to the window. "I don't have much. No record on the woman. Comes from a rich family. She does appear to have been institutionalized once or twice. She got hauled into the Charity ER on a psych once, but disappeared into the expensive places, and they don't talk."

"So she is crazy."

"We knew that," Joanne said. "Normal people don't act the way she is. But we don't know if she's harmful or not. She has some kind of juvenile record, but it's sealed and it'll take a bit to get it."

"So she does have a criminal record," I stated.

"Yes, but it could be that she had sex with another girl. Or ran away from home or smoked dope. I'm not saying don't watch out for her, but don't make assumptions. She may not be the killer."

"I know, you're right. I just want some . . . answer."

"We all do. I'm going to need to talk to you later, but there's really no reason for you to stay here."

"In other words, get out of here, you're setting off too many people's dyke detectors."

"Something like that. I'm worried about Hutch's reputation."

I gave her the ghost of a smile. It was all I could manage. "Joanne? It's a favor, but if you find an address for Lorraine Drummond among Georgia's belongings, could you pass it my way?"

"No promises."

"A mother's looking for her daughter. It'd be nice if they found each other."

Joanne just nodded and backed away from the car. A mother who found her daughter wouldn't make up for the mother who had lost her daughter.

I turned the ignition, gave her a brief wave of farewell, then pulled away.

I was halfway back downtown before I decided where I was going. It was a little past two. Cordelia might be having a late lunch. Or at least a few minutes between patients, so I could tell her what had happened. I also wanted to be near her, to have her, if only for a minute, take care of me.

But Cordelia was with a patient. Taking care of someone else, I groused in a childish way. Then told myself that that person would only get fifteen minutes of her time and would have to pay for it. I went into her office to wait.

"Hey, I thought I saw you duck into here," Lindsey said as she stuck her head in the door. "My two o'clock appointment appears unlikely to show, so I'm wandering around looking for amusement."

"Oh. Hi, Lindsey."

"You look like you've seen a ghost," she said as she came into the office.

"I've seen one in the making," I answered softly.

"Seen what in the making?" Lindsey asked, her voice losing entirely its bantering.

"A ghost."

She let my words hang in the air, perhaps hoping for more of an explanation. When none came, she asked, "An accident? Did you see someone killed in a car wreck?"

"No, no it wasn't an accident. I . . . almost saw someone being murdered."

"Murdered?" she said, startled, then the control of her profession reasserted itself. "Why don't you tell me what happened?"

"I don't know if I can to talk about it."

"Then you don't have to talk about it," she replied calmly.

"I guess . . . I guess I do want to talk about it, but I don't want to tell you, then Cordelia, then Elly and Millie, then talk to Joanne again. . . ."

"Joanne? Was it coincidence that she got involved or did you call her?"

"I called her." Suddenly I knew what I wanted to talk to Lindsey about. "There may be a link to Cordelia and the clinic. I was supposed to meet a woman, I got stuck in traffic, was late, and walked in on her just as she was dying. She may have . . . been killed the same way the other two patients of Cordelia's were."

"Two of Cordelia's patients, then a woman murdered where you're supposed to be. Did you ask Joanne if she found out anything about the stalker?" Lindsey saw where I was going with this.

"Yes, but she didn't have much. From a well-to-do family. . . ."

"That explains the flowers."

"Got taken to Charity psych once, but was quickly transferred to one of the posh places. Sealed record as a juvenile."

"Which could be anything, particularly for a girl. Often it's the double standard at work. A girl who smokes dope, stays out late, and cusses like a sailor may get in trouble, where a boy gets a wink and a boys-will-be-boys nod."

"True. But it's hard to believe that two patients here and now this are just random."

"However, we have no real evidence that you were the intended victim."

"No, we don't. We can't be sure that the stalker is the killer and that if she gets locked away in her fancy loony bin for the rest of her life, we'll be safe." Suddenly I felt a flash of hatred for this woman. It seemed likely that she killed Georgia, and if so, she was crazy and she was deadly. I wanted her stopped.

"Also, one woman wasn't a patient here," Lindsey reasonably pointed out, trying to rein in the emotions that were threatening to run away with me.

"No, she wasn't. But there could be some other link. Some other way they knew each other."

"The woman you were to meet? Was she just in the wrong place at the wrong time? If the killer was out to get you, why not go for you at your office or your home? Seems like a more reasonable approach to me."

"This woman's crazy, she's not reasonable," I retorted, chilled and angry that I had lost the safety of my home, with a brief horrific image of Cordelia coming home to what I had witnessed today.

"People can do crazy things in reasonable ways. Even the most insane of criminals rarely go out of their way to get caught."

"What if the woman murdered today was also a patient at the clinic? We might have a lean, mean, efficient killing machine here," I acerbically returned. "Wouldn't it be reasonable for the stalker to save time and effort and kill two at the same time?"

"We can find that out pretty quickly," Lindsey replied, calmly ignoring my sarcasm.

"What is this, therapy one-oh-one? Calm down a client by being extra calm and reasonable yourself?"

"I can understand that you're very upset. Coming upon a murder victim is a scary and unsettling thing. I'm just trying to make sure that the anger and fear you're feeling don't skew your vision."

"Skew you." I said halfheartedly. I was angry and upset and I didn't want to be told to calm down.

"So tell me the name of the woman. Let's see if she was a patient here." Lindsey sat at Cordelia's desk, then turned from me to rummage for a pen and paper in one of the desk drawers.

"Georgia Sherman," I said.

Lindsey jerked back to look at me. All her professional training couldn't hide the shock on her face.

"She's your patient," I stated the obvious.

"Oh, my God. Georgia," she said, then slumped back in the chair.

"I'm sorry."

"She was my two o'clock client. . . ."

Cordelia appeared in the door. She took a look at the two of us, then said, "I guess it's bad news."

"Another woman was murdered," I answered.

"My two o'clock. . . ." Lindsey added softly.

"Your two o'clock? What . . . you mean your two o'clock patient was murdered?"

Lindsey gave a bare nod of her head.

"Oh, no, Lindsey! That's horrible!" Cordelia went to Lindsey and put her hand on her shoulder.

She rubbed Lindsey's shoulder for a moment, then looked at me as if suddenly remembering I was in the room. "You're here because you talked to Joanne and she told you?"

"Well, no . . ." I started.

"Micky found the body," Lindsey answered.

"What?" Cordelia's hand jerked away from Lindsey's shoulder and she started toward me. She hesitated for a moment, as if undecided who needed comforting more. But it was only a brief hesitation, and she came to me.

I stood to meet her and let her put her arms around me.

"Are you all right?" Cordelia asked.

"Yeah, considering."

She held me tightly for a moment, then loosened her embrace.

"What happened?" Cordelia asked me.

I didn't describe Georgia's body, her mutilated breasts, or that I thought I heard her dying gasp. Lindsey didn't need to imagine her patient that way and Cordelia didn't need to know how close I'd come to crossing paths with a murderer. Nor did I tell them that Suzanna Forquet had given me Georgia's name or the name of the woman I was looking for. Lindsey, when she came out of her shock, would probably guess that Suzanna had led me to Georgia, but I felt I needed to pay some obeisance to client confidentiality. Suzanna had asked me not to reveal her name.

"So," I concluded, "another woman associated with the clinic has been murdered. I'm worried that it's your stalker."

"But it makes no sense," Cordelia said with a puzzled shake of her head. "One of the murdered women wasn't even a patient here."

"There may be another link. Maybe they lived next door to each other and your stalker got tired of her music."

"And Georgia Sherman wasn't even a patient of mine. I never saw her."

"We did discuss her once," Lindsey said. "She was the woman having real problems coming out to her family."

"I remember, but that was, what? A five-minute conversation? If, as you suspect"—she looked at me—"this revolves around the woman sending me flowers. . . ."

"The woman stalking you," I interjected.

"Whatever. Why these women? They're not in the center of my life. Why not the people I work with? Or my friends? Or my lover?"

"An irrational mind is a terrible thing to decipher," Lindsey said. "She may be escalating, starting out with people on the border of your life and moving in."

"Yes, save the best for last," I added. "I wish we had a wonderful perfect answer, but we don't. We have to go with what we know. And we know that three out of four of the women killed have a link with this clinic."

"Micky does have a point," Lindsey said.

"But we know one other thing. They're all lesbians," Cordelia stated.

"Wait. How do you know they're lesbian?" Lindsey asked.

"I finally looked up the records for the woman who had the gynecological visit with Jane. There was a note in her chart about no birth control needed. That's Jane's code for this woman doesn't need the birth control spiel again, because she's gay. The woman who wasn't a patient here—I remember reading her obituary and just assuming she was. Thirty-two, never married. You might have to check with Joanne, but I'd bet money on it."

"And Georgia and Tasha we know about," Lindsey finished up.

I looked at my lover for a moment, then said, "I feel stupid, I should have thought of it."

"Do you think Joanne's figured it out yet?" Cordelia asked.

"I don't know. I'll call her and see."

"And . . . if it's gay women being attacked, it may have nothing to do with the clinic. Not in any important sense. This is a small community. A lot of women don't go to see a doctor because they don't want to have to listen to irrelevant birth control lectures or come out and face bigotry."

"And word has gotten through the grapevine that this is a gay-friendly place," Lindsey said.

"Probably every one of those women has been to Charlene's bar, too. It is a small community and we would get that kind of overlap," Cordelia added.

We just looked at each other.

Finally, Cordelia said, "I've got patients waiting. Are you going to be okay?" She directed the question at both of us.

"I'm going to drive around for a bit, that's how I clear my head. Then I have a four o'clock appointment."

"You can cancel if you want," Cordelia told her.

"I know. But I find work a useful crutch at a time like this."

"I've got to get ahold of Joanne," I said.

"You can call from here," Cordelia suggested.

"True, but there are a few other things I need to run around and do." I wanted to see Suzanna Forquet, so she wouldn't hear of Georgia's death on the news.

"Okay. Be careful. Will you come back around closing time? I think I'd like an escort home."

"I shall return," I promised.

With that, we each headed off on our separate ways.

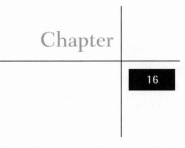

Chapter

16

I went to my office to call Joanne from there. But I wasn't able to reach her. I had to settle for leaving a message.

Before Cordelia and I had started living together, my office had doubled as my living space. So, unlike most mere office spaces, it had a full bath.

I didn't care about being clean for Suzanna Forquet, but I did want to wash away the taint of that blood-soaked air and the fear it had sweated out of me.

After my shower, I had to put my clothes back on. There was a washer and dryer in a shed out back, but it wasn't the kind of place one could wash clothes without wearing any.

As I headed uptown to Suzanna's, I decided that my mission would consist of more than just giving her the news of Georgia's death. Suzanna knew Georgia. If what linked those women was their lesbianism, Suzanna might know something that would be useful. It was very possible that the police would never discover that she and Georgia had once had an affair. Money could buy well-covered tracks. And even if they did, I was willing to bet that Suzanna would answer my questions better than she would those from the police.

It wasn't Bror who opened the door this time. Instead it was a young woman in a uniform that clearly labeled her maid.

"Is Suzanna in?" I asked. "She's not expecting me, but it's very important I speak to her."

The woman took my name, invited me into the foyer, and then disappeared. She gave no hint as to whether Suzanna was in or not.

I was left to wait for ten minutes before the maid reappeared.

"This way," she said.

I gathered that Miss Suzanna was in. She didn't take me upstairs to where I'd met Suzanna before, but instead to a small back parlor.

It took only another five minutes for Suzanna to appear from a patio door.

"Micky, this is an unexpected surprise," she said as she breezed into the room.

"I'm afraid I have some bad news."

"Oh?" Her face showed only a moderate concern, as if she couldn't imagine that any bad news I had would really affect her.

"Georgia Sherman is dead. I thought it might be better to hear it from me than the nightly news."

"Dead? Georgia? But she's young." Suzanna was certainly surprised, but I couldn't tell how much of it was that she didn't expect this news and how much that she was upset at hearing of Georgia's death.

"She was murdered."

"Murdered? That's horrible! Was it one of those stupid robberies? Kill you for five dollars in your wallet?"

"It wasn't a robbery. Whoever did it wanted to kill Georgia."

"Why? Why would anyone want to kill Georgia?"

"How well did you know her?"

"It was a couple of years ago . . . that we were together."

"But you kept up?"

"Yes, kind of. Georgia was pretty closeted. Turns out I was her first. So . . . so, she wanted to keep in contact. Mostly coffee every few months."

"When was the last time you saw her?"

"It's been awhile. A few months at least. We talked a little bit on the phone a week or so ago."

"What did you talk about?"

"Oh, the usual stuff. I think she saw me as a kind of solution to her problem. Her family was giving her a lot of pressure to get married. I don't know, we could just sort of blow off at each other about appearances and passing and that sort of stuff."

My instincts had been right. Suzanna was answering emotionally and giving away far more than she would have if it was Joanne or Hutch doing the questioning. I wasn't easy with using her like this, but Suzanna might know more about the details of Georgia's lesbian existence than anybody else. Somewhere in those details might be a clue to a killer.

"Who else knew that Georgia was a lesbian?"

"Lorraine Drummond did. But only because they'd gone to high school together and Georgia and I ran into her one night when we were out dancing. Since it was a lesbian bar, it was kind of obvious they were both in the life."

"Were they lovers?"

"No. No chemistry, they'd known each other back in those awkward school days. I don't think Lorraine had much patience with Georgia's closeted life."

"But they kept in contact?"

"Georgia was like that. She keeps up with people, doesn't just let them drift away. Christmas cards, a phone call every so often."

217

"Do you think someone got tired of Georgia's keeping in contact with them? Or threatened by it?"

"Oh, no, nothing like that. Georgia wasn't persistent or obnoxious, what I call one of those 'claw' ladies, who dig in and hold on no matter what."

From the vehemence in her voice, I gathered Suzanna had tripped over a few 'claw' ladies.

"Georgia was perceptive," she continued. "If I'd blown her off or been cold, she wouldn't have called back."

"Can you think of anyone who might have wanted to hurt her?"

"Georgia? It's hard to think of wanting to harm her. But . . . she did have a fire-and-brimstone uncle. I remembered she called me up, very upset, because he'd come over for the family Sunday dinner and said if any of his sons turned out gay, he'd shoot them. That they'd be better dead than leading that kind of life."

"Did he have any idea that she was gay?"

"She would never tell him . . . but he might have found out somehow."

"Did she have a girlfriend? Was she dating anyone?"

"Not recently. She wasn't very comfortable going to gay places, so she didn't meet many women. Her last girlfriend was in the military and got transferred to someplace like Alaska a year or so ago."

"So she didn't mention to you if she was seeing someone currently?"

"Actually, she mentioned to me that she wasn't seeing anyone currently. The last time we talked, she was complaining about how hard it was to meet women here and that she was beginning to think she might never have a girlfriend again in her life. But wait, she did say something about running into an ex-patient of hers. The woman thanked her for all of her help and a few days later sent her flowers. But Georgia got a weird feeling from the woman."

"What kind of work did Georgia do?"

"She was a nurse."

"Did she mention the woman's name?"

"No, just that she was weird." Suzanna had been looking out through a window. Suddenly she turned back to me and said, "You're interrogating me, aren't you?"

"Georgia's lesbianism may have had something to do with her murder. It's not likely that her family would know any of this."

"No, they probably wouldn't. But I don't want my name brought into it."

"This is a murder investigation, Suzanna. I'm not going to withhold information from the police that may stop a killer."

"Do you want another donation for Cordelia's clinic?"

"This killer has murdered four women so far. They're all lesbian. You could be next. You may not like having the police ask you embarrassing questions, but it's a hell of a lot less inconvenient than being murdered."

"All right, I see your point. I'm sorry. I just don't think my being involved could help Georgia. But . . . if I can help, of course I will." She looked directly at me, her expression contrite.

It was hard not to like Suzanna, though I suspected her change of heart had more to do with her perception that cooperating would get more for her than fighting. And it would. "I have a friend on the police force. I'll ask her to use as much discretion as possible with this information."

"Thank you. I'll have to trust your judgment."

I bet you say that to all the women you want to get in bed. But cynical as I was, I was also a bit flattered. She did it very well. "No problem," I replied.

"I've got to go. I've got some friends of Henri's I'm entertaining. They'll be wondering about my absence."

"Sorry to have interrupted. Will you be okay?"

"Me? Yes, these aren't people I'm close to. They wouldn't notice that I'm upset."

I almost asked if Henri would, but decided not to. "I can find my way out."

"Will I see you this Friday?"

"Friday?"

"Art Against AIDS. I finally convinced Henri to go this year, since some major hetero TV star is supposed to be there."

"Probably. Cordelia usually gets hit up for these things, then drags me along."

"Micky, thank you for coming by. I appreciate your letting me find this out from you and in private rather than from some impersonal news story." She put her hand on my arm, leaned in and kissed me on the cheek, then turned and went through a door to the patio.

I found my way to the front door. Just as I was opening it, Bror appeared.

"Ms. Knight, I didn't know you were here." I assumed that Suzanna had told him my full name. Or perhaps he had been the one to find it out for her.

"I was . . ." I started to come up with some innocuous excuse, then thought he might be able to talk some sense into Suzanna. Or at least watch out for her. "I just told Suzanna that someone she used to . . . see was murdered."

"Poor Suzanna," he said. "She may pretend to be tough, but she's not, not really. How did you find out about the murder?"

"Uh . . . from the police," I prevaricated. I wanted Bror to look after Suzanna; I didn't want to get into a therapy session with him.

"Interesting. You must have better police sources than I do, because I haven't heard anything yet. And I consider it part of my job to know things like this."

To know before anyone else and in time to control any damage, he left unsaid. "It was more than sources, it was being . . . in the wrong place at the wrong time," I admitted. "Why are you here, Bror?" I asked to skim over the wrong place I had been.

"Henri's second man? You're obviously very smart. Why be a servant?"

He looked at me for a moment, as if calculating whether or not I deserved an answer. I took it as a compliment that he didn't immediately blow me off. "Why? A myriad of reasons. I like the hours, don't have to wear a suit unless I want to. Henri needs me. I like being needed. I like the power it gives me."

"But the power comes from him. You don't own it. What if Henri decides he doesn't need you anymore?"

"Henri will always need me. And if he's foolish enough to think otherwise—well, he won't like the repercussions."

"What would you do?"

"If I go, I take Suzanna, and all the security that Henri has. He'd suffer the consequences of his actions and little Henri wouldn't much like that."

"You don't like Henri?" I asked.

"I like the power I get from him. And he pays well," Bror said with a laugh that answered my question.

"Would Suzanna go with you?"

"Of course she would. She wouldn't stay with Henri without me here."

"Do you like her?"

"Ah, Suzanna . . ." he answered slowly. "I protect Suzanna. She needs someone like me watching out for her. Like my mother did."

"Protect her from what?"

"From Henri . . . from life . . . from herself."

Henri, as if hearing his name, called for Bror, his voice echoing down the long hallway.

"Time to go," I said.

"You can help me. Help me protect Suzanna," Bror said in a soft voice that wouldn't carry to Henri. "If your sources tell you anything, please let me know. It's important I take care of her."

"I'll do my best. I don't want to see Suzanna hurt," I answered.

Then I let myself out the door and Bror went to see what Henri needed.

I glanced at my watch as I drove away. I wanted to call Joanne, and decided to do it from the clinic. I didn't want Cordelia wondering where I was.

Joanne needed to know about a woman who had sent her nurse flowers.

Rush-hour traffic and a few drops of rain stretched a ten-minute drive into almost a half-hour.

Of course, Cordelia was still with a patient when I arrived. She wasn't really good about saying, "Too bad you're sick. We're closed. Come back tomorrow."

I took over her office to call Joanne. This time I got through to her.

"I was just about to call you," Joanne greeted me.

"Great minds, et cetera. I have a few things for you."

"Go."

"Georgia was a patient here."

"One of Cordelia's?"

"No. She was seeing Lindsey. She never saw Cordelia."

"What was she seeing Lindsey for? Do you know?"

"Family issues. She was very closeted and having a hard time with it." Georgia had been murdered. Her confidentiality was gone.

"Georgia was a lesbian?" The surprise in her voice told me she hadn't found that out yet.

"Yes, she was. Joanne, they're all lesbians."

She was silent for a moment. "Oh, shit. This is going to be a mess."

"I'm sorry. Yes, it is." It would mean exposing things that the murdered women's families would find painful to be so publicly and glaringly aired. Some, like Georgia's family, would find out things about their daughters in death that they hadn't known in life. If it was a woman murdering these women, that would be all some people would know of the lesbian community, lesbians kill people or get killed. It would be difficult to investigate. Many gays and lesbians are wary of the police and would see this as a witch hunt. And, of course, it presented a personal dilemma for Joanne. Except for a few people, she was in the closet at work. For a closeted lesbian, investigating the murder of lesbians would mean walking a very fine line. She was sure to run into comments about "dyke killers" and worse, and face the choice of coming out to gain the trust of the gay community and risk being outed publicly.

"Georgia didn't have a girlfriend, but she did tell an ex of hers that she'd recently gotten flowers from a weird former patient."

"And she worked as a psychiatric nurse. I guess we pick up Cordelia's stalker and ask her a few questions. Who's the ex?"

"Suzanna Forquet."

Joanne's silence told me she wasn't expecting that name. Finally, she said, "Not the society column Suzanna Forquet?"

"The same."

"But she's married. There was just some big picture in the society column about her and her husband."

"Perfect covers for each other."

"This is getting deeper and messier. Are you sure about her?"

"Short of actually doing the deed, yes."

"And I thought I had a headache earlier," was Joanne's comment.

"You might also want to consider that a number of lesbians come to the clinic because it's got a reputation as being a gay-friendly place."

"So it might be coincidence that three of the four women were patients there?"

"It's a consideration, but my money's on the woman who sends flowers."

"I hope you're right. I've got to go. Talk to you." She hung up.

I wandered into the hallway to see if Cordelia was out yet.

There was no sign of her, but on the reception desk was a big bouquet of flowers that hadn't been there when I'd walked in.

I quickly strode over to the desk. There was a small card hidden in the flowers. I grabbed it and tore open the envelope.

C.,
I just want to be your friend. Is that so bad? I won't hurt you.
F.

Maybe she wouldn't hurt Cordelia, but she might hurt some other people.

I ran out to the parking lot, still clutching her note in my hand. Only a few, familiar cars were there. I raced out to the street. A white Mercedes was turning the corner, driving away.

I almost started to run after the car, but did manage to realize that I couldn't catch it, and even if I did, then what? I wasn't the police. I couldn't arrest her. It might not even be her. It could just be a random car on the street.

My dashing out here had been more prompted by an insistent need to do something, anything, than some thought-out plan. I was very angry at whoever had killed Georgia Sherman. That person had invaded my life.

I headed back for the clinic. The police would pick her up. And they could probably question her much more effectively than I could.

Cordelia was in the waiting room, a bemused look on her face at the flowers.

"This is for you," I said, handing her note. "From your lady love."

"You're my lady love," she answered, then glanced at the note. She looked at me, exasperation on her face. "I would guess, since the note was in your hand as you came in, that you went out to the lot to catch her."

"I tried," I admitted. "But she was gone."

"Micky, goddamn it, if this woman is a threat, she's a bigger threat to you than to me! What did you think you were going to accomplish by chasing after her all by yourself?"

"I probably wasn't thinking as well as I should have been."

"Hold up on your lover's quarrel long enough for me to exit," Millie said as she came out of the back.

"We're not really quarreling. There's been another murder and Micky was attempting to talk to the flower woman alone," Cordelia said.

"I thought you were the one who was content to chase lost poodles and to leave the heavy stuff to Hutch and Joanne," Millie rejoined. "Well, I guess he's going to be working late tonight."

"He probably will," I agreed. "And I promise to do a better job of confining myself to lost bow-wows."

"Okay," Cordelia responded to my penitent tone. "Let me lock up and let's get out of here."

The three of us walked to the lot together, an unspoken agreement to leave no one alone. Cordelia and I let Millie pull out.

"I'm sorry. I was sharp with you earlier. I'm . . . worried. A killer targeting lesbians has me concerned," Cordelia said as we stood by her car.

"Me, too. I guess I overreacted. Saw the threat to you but not to me."

"I'll be careful until they catch this person, if you will."

"Careful's now my middle name, ma'am."

"Good. We're going to eat out tonight. We're going to spend the evening in a cheery restaurant surrounded by people."

"You get no argument from me."

And that's what we did, with no thoughts of murdered women and savage killers.

Chapter

17

The next morning, I decided that today was a good day to do something physical, boring, and safe. I heard a garage full of musty boxes in Chalmette calling my name.

I even left the garage door standing open so that if any knife-wielding maniacs came after me, everyone in Chalmette could watch the show.

I let myself mutter numerous curses under my breath at Bourbon St. Ann, but I knew if I really didn't want to be here, I could leave. The swearing and the physical labor were a good way to get rid of the agitation left over from yesterday's events.

By lunchtime, I had gotten rid of the agitation and acquired some sore shoulders.

As I drove around looking for a place to eat (Cordelia was worried enough about her weight to make me feel guilty for having a

burger and fries) I decided that today was it. I would keep looking all afternoon, but if I didn't find anything, Bourbon St. Ann's
case was going to be closed.

But he got lucky after I came back from lunch. On one side
the box said '68, but on the other it was labeled '74–'75. There
was a thick folder on a woman who had placed ten children for
adoption. The Hudsons of Ocean Springs, Mississippi, had been
the lucky recipients of child number eight.

I stopped at my office on the way home, to drop off the file.
This was work and I would look through it on work time. I also
gave my face and arms a good washing.

I ran my answering machine back. The first message was from
Hutch. They needed a statement from me. The next was from a
reporter wanting to interview me about finding Georgia. ("And
how did you feel, Ms. Knight, when you walked into that room
and saw all the blood and realized that she was dying right before
your very eyes?") I wouldn't return that one. Then there was a
message from Aunt Greta. All she said was for me to call her
back.

"Make me," I replied after the message finished playing. I
could think of no benign reason for her to call. Maybe one of the
neighbors had seen me throw that brick. Let her come after me.

I called the clinic, hoping to catch Cordelia, or at least leave a
message that as of four-forty-five, I was still alive and kicking and
I hoped she was, too.

I had to settle for the latter. Cordelia was on another line. I
considered heading over there, but she was fine, surrounded by
the staff, whereas there were probably some pretty hungry cats at
home.

That's where I went.

Torbin and Andy were out on their front porch, catching the
last rays of a fading sun.

"What time are we meeting tomorrow?" Andy asked.

"Meeting?" I inquired.

"I have two tickets for you for Art Against AIDS. You don't have to go, but you do have to pay for them," Torbin informed me.

"I think I'd like to go. But as Cordelia made the promise, she can fork over the bucks."

"Speaking of, here she comes now."

Cordelia's car pulled up. Then behind her was Elly, then Millie. Which probably meant that Hutch and Danny would be joining us.

"Ah, company tonight," Torbin said at seeing the entourage.

I gave Torbin and Andy a quick update of the murdered women and that they were lesbians.

"Micky, you know Torbin and I are around a lot. Except for a few trips to deliver a program or iron out a few bugs, I do most of my work here. So, if either you or Cordelia want a big, strong computer nerd to protect you . . ." Andy offered.

"Thanks, I will keep that in mind." I was comforted by his gallantry and the idea that people I trusted were around and watching.

"Well, if you promise to spare the graphic details, we're willing to break out a pitcher of mimosas and toddle over to your place," Torbin said.

"Grab your pitcher and let's toddle," I replied.

As we were crossing the street, Alex and Joanne arrived.

By the time we got through the front door, as predicted, two more cars arrived with Danny and Hutch in them.

We often have these impromptu get-togethers. Usually they're fun, letting loose at the end of the work week, but today there was an air of tension and seriousness.

The expected flow was taking place. Hutch, Millie, Danny, and Elly were deciding how many and what kind of pizzas to order. Torbin and Andy were raiding their larder to provide not only the mimosas, but beer and soda. Cordelia and I were doing a quick check of the house to make sure our lovely cats hadn't left any unlovely hairballs in conspicuous places and that the roll of toilet paper we'd meant to bring down from the upstairs bathroom to the downstairs one had actually made it.

After all these things were taken care of and the cats were fed (hungry cats and Hutch's taste for anchovies on his pizza didn't go well together), we settled into the living room.

"I don't like this," Joanne said, the first to broach the subject that was on all our minds. "Four women killed, all lesbians, and three are patients at the clinic."

"Do you think it's some psycho going after lesbians?" Alex asked.

"We can't rule out the possibility," Danny answered. "But these women are the 'invisible' lesbians—other than perhaps a trip to a gay bar or bookstore, they're not involved. You'd think someone targeting lesbians would go after the obvious ones, those whose names you see in the paper."

"Or can easily get," Hutch added, "like finding out the names of different organization's leaders."

"The killer could have gotten these women from hanging out at bars. Maybe a taxi driver who took them home," I suggested.

"We're looking into that," Hutch replied, "but we've only been able to place one of the women at a bar and even she wasn't a regular."

"What you're saying," I stated, "is that it's very possible that the killer is not an outsider to the lesbian community."

"I'm afraid that's a very real possibility," Joanne said.

"Lesbians killing lesbians?" Alex questioned. "But we don't do that sort of thing. Well, only in movies made by straight men in Hollywood."

"Do you have a reason to believe it is a woman?" Cordelia asked.

"We have no reason to believe it's not. What's done to these women is brutal, but it could be done by either a man or a woman,"

Joanne replied. "Also, there seems to be no sign of a break-in or struggle, which means either the victims knew the attacker or didn't feel threatened by him . . . or her," Joanne said.

"Oh, good Lord," Millie exclaimed. "Just last week a UPS driver dropped off a package. When I saw it was a woman, I let her come in while I signed for it. I never would have done that for a man."

"We should warn the lesbian community," Alex said.

"How?" Joanne questioned.

"An article in the paper, or on TV. Contact the gay rags, put flyers up."

"What do we warn them of? Someone is killing closeted lesbians. We have no idea whether it's a man or woman or how the killer finds his victims. Just be paranoid every minute of the day," Joanne responded. "What about the families of the women? Georgia Sherman's family still has no idea she's a lesbian. Do you know what kind of howl they're going to let loose if we publicly brand their daughters as lesbian?"

"Does it matter when you're trying to save lives?" Alex argued.

"Goddamn it, Alex!" Joanne exploded. "I've had to watch autopsies for these women. Do you think I want to witness another one?"

"It could matter if it sets up such a public relations fiasco that we alienate both the families and the gay community," Danny pointed out. "We'd do the right thing, if we knew what the right thing was. I don't think it would be out of place for the DA's office to issue a warning that single women are being targeted and that we can't rule out the killer being another woman. And if there are more killings and they're lesbians, we may have to revise that."

"I'm sorry," Joanne said both to Alex and the rest of us, "I'm afraid if we turn this into a media circus of 'shocking secrets' and blindsided, bereaved families of the victims who refuse to talk to us because they feel betrayed, and closeted lesbians scurrying for cover because they don't want their name in the paper, we'll lose our chance to find the killer."

"You have a point," Alex replied. "Things are always so damned complicated."

The doorbell rang. Our pizzas had arrived.

We didn't return to the subject of murdered women until the end of the evening, when people were leaving. Cordelia, Elly, and Millie were to watch out for each other. Joanne told me to carry my gun.

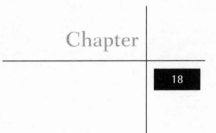

Chapter

18

Thank God for fall weather. It's hard to carry a gun in the summer when you look supremely foolish in a jacket. And I don't do purses well.

I have no illusions. I know there is no scriptwriter in my life who will guarantee that all my bullets find their targets while the bad guys can't hit me. The gun gave me a little bit of an advantage, that was all. But that little bit might be enough to save my life.

My first stop was to run by the police station and sign my statement like a good girl. Then I headed down to my office. I managed to make it there unscathed. So far, so good.

The dusty file was still sitting on my desk. I started to ignore it and go back to the envelope I had taken from Uncle Claude's office, but guilt, or actually something closer to if-I-got-it-over-with-I-wouldn't-have-it-hanging-over-my-head, prompted me to do my reluctant duty. I pulled out the papers that had the name Hudson on them.

There it was in faded type. Her name was Sindy Ponder. There was even a blurry copy of her birth certificate, and that's what was on it, Sindy with an S, not Cynthia (with or without an S). Her father's name was Ponder, her mother's wasn't. Sindy had been born out of wedlock and it looked like she had carried on the family tradition.

She'd had her tenth and last child when she was thirty-nine years old.

I did a quick count. She'd had ten children and placed them all up for adoption. Not placed, but sold. There had been an exchange of money for all the children, from one hundred dollars for the first to over ten thousand for the last.

This was the mother Bourbon St. Ann was looking for.

I had her address and I had her name. And an unpleasant task in front of me. To go talk to this woman and see if she wanted to be contacted by the baby she'd sold eighteen years ago.

I considered pretending that I'd never found this file. But I don't like to make decisions for people. It was also possible that Bourbon St. Ann would continue his search without me, hire someone else, spend a few more years and some money to again end here. I couldn't give him the kind of mother he wanted, but I could prevent him from wasting his time looking for her.

The address wasn't that far from Chester Prejean's office, according to the map.

My strong desire to put this off is what goaded me out the door. The less I wanted to do it, the more it would chafe at me until it was done.

The miles may not have been many, but the distance between Chester's office and the address I was stopped in front of was great. His neighborhood had been solid, comfortable middle class, the yards neat and the houses painted. This block had gone beyond poverty into squalor. One house had about six or seven cars cannibalized across its overgrown yard. The house next to it had mud for a yard, some boards thrown down to create a path to the door.

Sindy Ponder lived in a small shack, some of the boards drooping, none with more than a few scraps of paint. Her yard was full of scraggly, unkempt grass. Sitting in the middle of it was a couch. It had clearly been there through several rainstorms. That forlorn couch, ruined because no one could be bothered to throw a piece of plastic over it or corral a few neighborhood boys to cart it onto the porch, told me what I would find inside.

I got out of my car and went to bang on the broken screen door.

"Who the hell are you? You lost?" was her welcome as she opened the door.

"My name's Michele Knight. I'm looking for Sindy Ponder."

"You are, are you? Gonna award me some prize or somethin'?" she cackled.

Though I knew she was only forty-four, she looked like she was in her late fifties. Her teeth were tobacco-stained and several of them were missing. What may have been pouty slump as a teenager had turned into a round-shouldered slouch that wasn't going to go away. Her hair was a greasy bleached blond with lengthy dark roots. Her makeup had been put on by an unsteady hand in dim light, was garish and overdone. The children and years had caused everything to sag. Her chin, her breasts, her stomach all drooped.

"No, ma'am. I'm sorry, I'm not giving out prizes," I said in a neutral professional voice. "I'm a private detective."

"Yeah? Like on TV?"

"No, it's a lot different than on TV, a lot of boring, tedious work."

"So, what you want with me?"

"One of the children you gave up for adoption hired me to find you," I said. I waited for her reaction.

"One of 'em did, huh? 'Bout time someone thought to care for their old maw." She opened the screen door. "C'mon in, let's you and me talk."

I didn't really want to go in the house. Just don't sit down, I told myself as I entered.

"I'd offer you a beer, but I make it a rule to never give strangers a beer 'less they bring their own." She picked up the can she had been drinking and took a big gulp.

The room was a hodgepodge of furniture. Sindy sat in the best of it, a not too used recliner. My choice of seats were several rickety wooden chairs against the far wall or a couch that should have been sacrificed to the rain rather than the one out in the yard. It was a dirty yellow and had never recovered from some of the people who had sat on it. My decision to remain standing didn't change.

"That's all right. I'm not drinking."

"Oh, yeah, can't drink on duty, huh? Too bad or you coulda run down to the corner store to get some." Clearly she did hope I would run down to the store and bring back a six-pack.

"I don't want to take up too much of your time, so I'll be brief," I said, because I wanted to be brief and I wanted to excuse my not sitting down.

"Is it the rich one?" she interrupted me.

"I beg your pardon?"

"The rich one. The one I farmed out to Frannie Sue. That bitch took care of her, should take care of me, too."

"I was hired by one of your sons . . ." I said, trying to get control of the conversation back.

"She was my first. Didn't know I was even preggers until she was popped out."

"You didn't know you were pregnant until she was born?" I stupidly repeated before I could get my incredulity under control.

"Yeah, didn't know ol' Dick put his dick in me." She guffawed at her joke.

"What did you think was happening?" Too late I told myself, You didn't want to ask that question.

"We was out in the back seat of his car, doin' the usual things. He'd brought along a couple of six-packs and we was foolin' around and gettin' buzzed. I let him play with me down there 'cause he seemed to like it and, hell, it felt good. Guess I was too drunk to notice his fingers had gotten thicker."

"You didn't use any birth control?" Two stupid questions in a row. Good going, Micky.

"I didn't know he was gonna fuck me," she chided me.

I hurried on, "I'm here on behalf of the son you gave to the Hudsons from over in Ocean Springs, Mississippi."

"Don't make no never mind to me. I let old Chester handle that stuff. So you're not here for that rich girl that took care of Frannie Sue?"

"No, ma'am, I'm afraid I'm not." But I was curious about her. "She was your first child and you gave her to some friends of yours?" I inquired.

"Ol' Dick was the fuckin' kind, not the marryin' kind," she cackled. "I didn't want no kid. Frannie Sue wanted the girl. Told her I'd give the baby to her for a hundred dollars. She squawked big about that, but I figured a hundred for nine months of labor wasn't too bad."

"What happened to the girl?"

"I think old Chester paid the money, didn't think I'd be a good maw. I saw her every once in a while when she was living with Frannie and Hector. Grew up to be a pretty thing, almost as pretty as me when I was her age. She took off when she was out of school, didn't hear a word about her until one day I saw Frannie Sue and she was dressed up real nice, all new clothes, a fancy red coat. I knew it weren't old Hector, he'd broke his back and all he was good for was drinkin' and pissin'." She paused to take a drink of her beer. "So I says to Frannie, where'd you get all that stuff? And she says, 'My daughter, my daughter took me shopping,' like she forgot it wasn't really her kid, but mine. So I reminded her, told her, 'Oh, the one that come from me?' And she looked kind of shamefaced, like she knew she should be sharing the stuff my daughter bought her. Now, I don't mind sharin', Frannie brung her up and all, but seems only fair I get somethin' for having the child in the first place. Frannie just avoided me after that. Wouldn't talk to me none." She took another swallow of beer.

"Do you know if the girl still keeps in contact with . . . Frannie Sue?" Instead of Frannie Sue I almost said "her mother," for that was the truth of it, but not one Sindy Ponder would want to hear.

"Old Frannie, she stroked out about a year ago. Served her right, greedy bitch. And Hector, oh, Lord, his death was the funniest thing." She let out a loud laugh. "Old drunken pissant lived in his wheelchair, so one night he's rollin' around, and he goes right into this road work hole. It's got maybe three inches of water in it, but Hector's so drunk he can't keep his nose out. Drowns in three inches of water. Ain't that a pisser?"

"It's . . . an unusual way to die."

"Well, so that rich girl don't got to do nothin' for Frannie Sue, so I should get some. Could use some pretty clothes, a trip to a fancy beauty parlor. Say, if you can find me, could you find her?"

"I'm sorry," I said. "This is not what I usually do. I took this particular case as a favor for a friend."

"Shit, well, while back a gal pal of mine at the courthouse said someone was lookin' for me. Thought I might hurry her along. I need a new coat for the winter. Guess rich people are just busy, can't worry 'bout their poor maw with no winter coat."

"The reason I came here was to see if you would be willing to meet with your son." My curiosity was satisfied. It was time to finish my business here.

"He ain't rich, huh?"

"No, I'm afraid he isn't."

"Well, hell, tell him to bring by a six-pack and he can chat with his old maw."

"Thank you for your time," I said as I edged toward the door. "I've got to be going. I'll pass along the information."

"Yeah, tell him to bring a sixer or two and I'll chat with him."

I gave her a weak smile in acknowledgment, then was out the door.

I quickly got in my car and drove away. If the woman had a redeeming quality, I hadn't seen a glimmer of it.

I would pass on what I'd learned to Bourbon St. Ann, but I wasn't going to spare him what I thought of the woman. However, I wasn't going to do it today. The complication was the rich daughter of Frannie Sue.

Suzanna? Could she be Sindy Ponder's first child? The story Suzanna had told me when we met for lunch had too many common places with Sindy's narrative to be mere coincidence— Suzanna was adopted and Sindy had given up her daughter for adoption. The drunken father, disabled with a broken back. The location, both in St. Bernard Parish. Take away twenty years of rough living, and Sindy's blue eyes resembled Suzanna's to a remarkable degree. Why had Suzanna lied about any contact with her mother? Was her life so compartmentalized that she lied out of habit? Why tell me about the family she left behind, then? Perhaps Henri had insisted she sever all ties with her white-trash family and she had defied him to offer some assistance to her mother? It would make sense that she wouldn't want anyone to know she defied Henri. If it got back to him, it could have severe consequences for her. Wouldn't he just love to have his society wife revealed as the illegitimate daughter of a woman like Sindy Ponder?

What would Bourbon St. Ann do if he found out he had a wealthy half-sister? Would he be willing to aid and abet his slattern mother in hunting her down? It seemed unfair that if it was Suzanna, her kindness in buying her real mother—the one who had cared for her—a coat and some clothes should come back to haunt her. She had stood before Sindy Ponder's door and she had walked away. There should be some way to keep it like that.

I returned to my office and again looked through that dusty file. I wasn't going to take anything out—that would violate my agreement with Chester—but I had to know what was in there.

And it was in there. In the folder for the first adoption was a note to Chester. "Please accept this check in repayment for the money you advanced to my parents Hector and Frannie Bordeleon for fees associated with my adoption. I appreciate what you did for them and the difference it made in my life." It was signed by Suzanna Forquet. Below her signature was a note in Chester's writing, "One thousand, not bad on a one hundred I thought I'd never see again."

I tucked the note back into the file, making sure it was snugly in, to hide its newer edge from showing against the older yellowing paper.

Bourbon St. Ann didn't need to know about this file. Sindy knew that Chester had some paperwork and she might go after it to try to find her rich "daughter."

But I couldn't imagine that Chester had a high opinion of Sindy. He and I would have a talk about this file as soon as he got back. All he'd have to do is misplace the file or just lose Suzanna's note. Pragmatism alone might accomplish that. Sindy was unlikely to ever hire his lawyer daughters, but Suzanna Forquet might.

I put Chester's folder in my filing cabinet, so it would look like just one of my files—one of my old files. I didn't put it above Bourbon St. Ann to snoop if he could and I wasn't willing to chance anything lying around.

Then I again took out the envelope I had gotten from Uncle Claude. It was my turn now.

I spread its contents across my desk. I again looked at all the pictures, but still they told me nothing beyond the brief moment that they were taken.

I read the old letters from my father written while he was stationed in the South Pacific, to his younger brother, but they concentrated on the daily details, the weather, how bad the food was, what was the first thing he was going to do when he got home—every letter had a different first thing, like a running joke between them. First an oyster po boy, first a long fishing trip (they couldn't come back until they caught ten speckled trout), first a hot shower. Uncle Claude had been thirteen when my father had gone off to war.

Then tucked inside one of those old war letters was a note from my mother. It was dated just a few months before my father died.

> *Dear Lee,*
> *I will, of course, abide by your wishes—what choice have I—but when Micky is older I would like to be able to see her, perhaps spend some time with her. She should at least have the right to choose. I know you only want to be a good father, but you can't protect her from everything.*

What were his wishes that she alluded to? Was he the one who had ordered her out of my life? But if she had wanted custody, she had the upper hand, she was the mother, and if she had revealed that my father wasn't my biological father, it should have been easy for her to take me. The note didn't really tell me anything. It just deepened the puzzle of my mother's complete disappearance.

I picked up the old address book. These were the people who knew my father and me back then. Could they tell me anything? Of course, it was twenty years out of date. I eliminated all the businesses. Even if they were still around, I couldn't see my father pouring out his marital woes while purchasing barnacle remover. Then I eliminated those I knew to be dead or long gone.

Of course, there were the relatives, but I knew how to contact Aunt Greta, and Uncle Charlie and Uncle Claude were beyond reach.

Great-Aunt Eunice was still living at the same address. She was Maurice's younger sister, some fifteen years younger than he was. Would I dare call her up and ask her about my mother? She was old. Someday soon she wouldn't be here and I would never get a chance to ask.

I dialed her number.

"Hello?" she said, picking up the phone after six rings.

"Hi. Aunt Eunice, this is Michele . . . Robedeaux . . . Lee's daughter," I identified myself. "I hope I'm not disturbing you."

"Oh, no, not at all, just got up from my afternoon nap, so I'm feeling frisky, at least for a woman my age. How are you, girl? Seems we should have reasons besides funerals to get the family together."

"I'm fine, thank you. I hope you don't mind my asking, but the reason I'm calling is I'm trying to find out more about my mother. She left when I was so young and I thought . . . maybe you might know something," I faltered.

"Didn't know her real well. You should ask your Uncle Claude . . . oh, he's dead. So many of them gone, it's hard to keep track. My memory still works, it just works real slow."

"That's okay. I'm young and my memory is sometimes like that."

"I guess Claude died before he told you," she said.

"Told me what?"

"It's not really my place . . . guess there's no one in that place anymore."

I kept myself quiet. The impatience of youth wouldn't hurry Aunt Eunice.

The silence seemed to stretch before she finally said, "Your mama was in town."

Now I was silent, the words so unexpected that I could think of no reply.

"I don't know much more than that," Aunt Eunice added.

"My . . . mother was here?" I fumbled out.

"Was here, was going to be here. I'm just not sure, honey. Now, it wasn't Claude that told me, and I just heard that little bit."

"Who did tell you?"

"It was Cousin Rosemary, I think. She might of got it from Claude."

"Can you remember anything else? Anything at all?"

"No, honey, I'm sorry. Never thought I'd be the one to tell you. Sure wish I knew a little more."

"I didn't think we'd be having this conversation, either. You've . . . thank you for telling me. It does . . . give me something to go on."

"You go call Rosemary. Maybe she'll be able to help you."

"Thanks, thanks, I will do that."

Great-Aunt Eunice gave me Rosemary's number and we said good-bye.

I quickly dialed Rosemary, wondering if she would be at home at this time of day. I had no idea what she did.

Whatever it was, it allowed her to be home on a Friday afternoon. She answered the phone.

"Oh, little Micky," she said after I'd identified myself. "It's so good to hear from you. It was so sad the last time we saw each other. It wasn't sad seeing you, but it was sad Charlie being dead and then Claude dying like that. Yes, that was so sad."

"Great-Aunt Eunice told me that you knew something about my mother being here in the city. She said I should call you and ask about it," I said. I was guessing that the weight of Great-Aunt Eunice might prod Rosemary along.

"Oh! I thought Claude was going to tell you about that. Oh! But I guess he died before he got to it."

"What do you know about it?"

"Well, let me see. I was talking to Greta about it. She was upset. Well, not really upset, but a bit perturbed; well, maybe just concerned might be a better way to put it. Now, Claude wanted to tell you, but Greta thought it better to let sleeping dogs be dead. She just thought the past shouldn't be the present."

I interrupted to ask, "Did she tell you anything about when my mother might be coming to town? Or where she is now?"

"No, just that Claude was set on letting you know, and Greta . . . uh . . . wasn't comfortable with it. She had decided to go talk to one of the priests that she knew and ask his advice."

"When did you talk to her about it?"

"Oh, it was . . . it was . . . Oh, I'm not really sure. Maybe a week or two before all that sad stuff with your uncles."

That was all the information I could get out of Cousin Rosemary. It seemed the only focus of her conversation with Aunt Greta had been how upset Aunt Greta was over the whole matter.

When I put the phone down, my hand was shaking.

My mother was alive and she was coming here or had been here recently.

At times I cursed New Orleans for being such a small city where it seemed I couldn't walk down the street without running into people I didn't want to meet, but now it seemed vast and opaque. One women somewhere in this city. Perhaps she was getting on a plane to leave right now. Perhaps she had left last night.

Who would Uncle Claude talk to? Uncle Charlie. That was little help. Would Aunt Lottie know? I picked up the phone to call her but put it back down again. If she knew, she would have told me. Aunt Lottie would have no compunction about defying Aunt Greta, especially if she was aware that Uncle Claude had intended to tell me. And she would have enlisted Torbin to check up on me. I would call her, but it seemed a faint possibility that either Uncle Claude or Aunt Greta had confided in her.

"Why the hell didn't you write it down? Just a scrap of paper. Instead you bury it in the grave with you."

I could call Aunt Greta, let her scream at me for a few hours about the broken window. She wouldn't tell me, of course, but she might let something slip. I just looked at the phone, suddenly too enervated by the solid walls before me to tackle that hurdle.

I dejectedly stared at the pieces of my father's and mother's past spread out over my desk. "You should have left . . ." Something. That odd newspaper clipping.

I quickly flipped through the stack of newsprint to find it. Grabbing it up, I looked at the small ad about a gallery opening. Could my mother, who had always drawn and sketched, be an artist?

My dejection became agitation. That small clipping wouldn't reveal its secrets, the name or names torn off.

I quickly jotted down the address. It was in the warehouse district where a lot of the galleries were.

You could call, I thought as I got up to leave. But I wanted motion and action, and if this turned out to be a false quest, I didn't want to hear it over the dry lines of a telephone.

Early rush-hour traffic slowed me down as I made my way past the CBD, the Central Business District, the heart of commerce and tall buildings in New Orleans.

I found the gallery, but its doors were locked. I realized that I had left the newspaper ad sitting on my desk in my rush to get here. I had only taken the address, but not the date of the exhibit.

Peering through the front windows didn't help much. There were a few paintings still on the wall, but many had been taken down. It appeared to be in transition from one show to another. I didn't much like the few paintings I saw; they were abstract and the colors seemed heavy and depressing.

I stayed outside of the gallery for about half an hour, hoping someone might return and give me some information. But a meter maid was coming up the block and my lack of quarters was going to cost me a ticket.

I got in my car and drove away before she could see the expired meter.

I went back to my office. I had to know the date on that newspaper clipping.

Tomorrow night there was an opening reception from six to nine P.M. I just didn't know who the reception was for.

The gallery's number wasn't in the ad, so I looked it up in the phone book.

I got an answering machine.

"Hi, you've reached LA Gallery. Our usual hours are from one in the afternoon until eight in the evening unless we're changing exhibits or have real bad colds and feel miserable. Special showings can be arranged; either call us during regular hours or leave your name and number and we'll get back to you. Remember, in some parts of the world people are starving for art. You've got a whole gallery to go to," said a recorded woman's voice. Then came the beep. I hung up. I couldn't think of a message to leave.

I was hoping to find out who the artist or artists were.

Don't get your hopes up, I tried to warn myself. He could have kept that piece of paper for the crawfish bread recipe.

The phone rang. I grabbed it up as if it could be the gallery calling back or someone who knew where my mother was. For a split second I imagined a voice saying, "Micky, this is Mom."

It was Joanne.

"Just checking in with you. We haven't found Frances Gilmore yet." I thought of her as the stalker, so it took a moment for me to realize that that was her name. "We don't know whether she's just out—her neighbors say she keeps irregular hours—or if she's figured out that we're looking for her."

"Let me know when you get her. It's . . . nerve-wracking with her loose."

"I will. We also have a report of another missing person."

"A single woman, I suppose," I said bleakly.

"A lesbian. It was her lover who reported her missing. She's a professor at Tulane. She kept her morning office hours, but didn't show up to teach her two o'clock class." I heard the resignation in Joanne's voice, as if she knew she would be witnessing another autopsy soon.

"Maybe she ran off with a grad student," I said.

"Yeah, that'd be a nice change," was her comment.

"Thanks for letting me know. And thanks for checking up on me."

"You wearing your gun?"

"Yes, ma'am, you betcha."

"Don't leave home without it."

"I'm going to Art Against AIDS tonight. You really think I should be packing?"

"Within reason. You can leave it in your car. Alex might be there, but I'm not going to make it."

"Take care, Joanne."

"You too. Bye."

I put the phone down and it immediately rang again.

It was Cordelia.

"I just wanted to hear your voice, that's all," she said.

"Still alive and kicking," I reassured her.

"This has me spooked. We wouldn't even let Elly walk by herself down to the corner store to get a sandwich."

"Did you talk to Joanne?" She hadn't, so I passed on what Joanne had told me.

"Oh, God. Not another one."

"Maybe it'll be okay."

"Are you coming home soon? I'm about to leave. You need a cell phone. We're getting you a cellular phone this weekend."

I didn't argue or point out that I did have a car phone. Cordelia was upset.

"I'm going to lock my office and head out as soon as I put the phone down. If I'm not home by the time you get there, call the National Guard."

"I will, believe me."

Then I put the phone down, locked up, and was out the door. I realized that I hadn't told Cordelia about my mother. We'll see each other in ten minutes and we can talk then, I told myself.

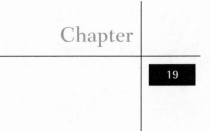

Chapter

19

I was attacked by two hungry cats when I entered the door.

"There are starving cats in India that don't get fed twice a day," I informed them as I scooped tuna surprise into their dishes.

Cordelia came in just in time to miss the ritual of the smelly tuna cans.

After we held each other for a long moment, I told her about my mother.

"What are you going to do?" she asked.

"Between now and tomorrow? Wait, go to the opening tomorrow. If that doesn't work, grit my teeth and call Aunt Greta. I don't know what else to do."

There was a knock on the door. "Oh, girls," Torbin called out for all the neighbors to hear. "I've come to give you sartorial advice, because I can't be seen with you wearing a black watch plaid evening gown with red sequined pumps like the last time we went out."

Torbin's visit was more for bedevilment than fashion tips.

Finally we shooed him off, turning down his offer of a "drag queen's guide to perfect panty hose placement."

We were going to meet in half an hour and go together.

"Well, at least I can wear my red dress to this," I said, it being my obvious wardrobe choice.

"I like you in that red dress. Should we take our car? We might want to leave before the boys do."

We met Torbin and Andy promptly half an hour later, me in my red dress and Cordelia in a midnight-blue silk ensemble with a plunging neckline that I enjoyed. Torbin and Andy were both in tuxedos. Torbin's cummerbund was a print of jungle animals with a matching leaf-pattern tie. Andy was in a more sedate royal blue.

"We should probably take two cars," Cordelia said. "I have to be at the clinic tomorrow morning, so we might have to leave before you." The clinic did have Saturday morning hours and the staff rotated who covered them. I thought it was a more decorous excuse than, "We're going to have wild, licentious sex tonight, so we're not staying long."

We followed them there.

Art Against AIDS is a big fund-raising event where all kinds of artists, from school kids making Christmas ornaments to big-name, big-buck artists, contribute their creations. It's set up in one of the tony shopping malls after the stores close.

I enjoyed the time with Cordelia, strolling from tree ornaments to candle holders. Torbin and Andy flitted back and forth between us and other friends and acquaintances. Cordelia was looking for some paintings for the clinic waiting room.

I was doing my significant-other duty, waiting patiently while Cordelia spent several minutes examining a trio of watercolors, when I heard someone call my name.

I turned to find Suzanna Forquet beside me. She was stunningly turned out, wearing a simple sheath dress in a shimmering white material. The dress let anyone within a hundred yards know that she had a perfect figure. She wore a few unostentatious but clearly expensive pieces of jewelry.

"Red is a good color on you," she said as she leaned to give me the standard social kiss on the check. Her lips lingered just a fraction of a second longer than strictly proper.

"How are you, Suzanna?"

"Fine. And you? Are you enjoying the evening?"

"Very much. Cordelia and I have been wandering around seeing what's to be seen."

At the sound of her name, Cordelia turned toward us. She did the polite thing, said hello to Suzanna and joined us.

Suzanna gave Cordelia a quick kiss on the cheek. Cordelia and I stood together. The message to Suzanna was, "This is the woman I love."

Henri came to claim his wife. He had the moves down, the hand cupped possessively and intimately around her bare shoulder, the stiff walk that kept her close to him. They were in public and she was on display. Bror was with them. A subtle but ironic smile played on his lips at the display of the happily married couple. Suzanna gave him a quick smile in return, as if he were her real companion, not Henri.

I shrugged at Cordelia as they made their way through the surrounding crowds. She shrugged back and returned to the paintings that interested her.

Another voice whispered from beside me, "Why don't you dump her and come have some fun with me?"

"Because I don't do men, even men in dresses." Bourbon St. Ann did have the face to look like a convincing woman. With a start, I realized that he and Suzanna resembled each other quite a bit. He had her cut, perfect cheekbones and strong jawline.

"How'd you know me?"

"Torbin's my cousin. I'm used to seeing behind the makeup.

Besides, I know your voice. Otherwise you might have fooled me," I added to mollify him.

"Who were those people you were just talking to?"

"One is my lover." I nodded my head toward Cordelia. "The other is Suzanna Forquet, an acquaintance."

"No, I meant the guy."

"That was her husband. Not your type."

"But I know him."

"Oh? You do? Well?" I skeptically asked.

"Intimately."

"He doesn't seem to remember you."

"It was a short intimacy. I was dressed in high school boy clothes. It was over in Biloxi, he picked me up. First man to bend me over. I think he infected me."

I stared at Bourbon St. Ann for a minute, trying to sort out the bizarre implications of what he just said. I decided I wanted to hear it again. "He did what?"

"I used to just blow guys, you know, quick on my knees and up. But this guy wanted more. Took me for a ride in his posh car, we went somewhere secluded, he made me drop my pants."

I thought to myself, I can't really be talking to a boy pretending to be a man pretending to be a woman who's discussing anal sex in street language at an elegant charity event.

"You're accusing him of infecting you with HIV? From your own account, you've been pretty active."

"Hey, why are you on his side? I've got two hundred and three T-cells. I was infected pretty early on."

"You can get infected from oral sex."

"Not near as easy."

"Besides, does it really matter?" I said gently. "Knowing doesn't change anything."

"No, but some rich straight guy might not like a little drag queen telling people where he puts it."

"That's blackmail and it's illegal."

"What's his name?"

"Get real." I cursed myself for letting him know that Suzanna was his wife. Bourbon St. Ann could easily be telling the truth, but telling me after he noticed that Henri had a wife with expensive jewelry, and not before, tainted his story.

"Oh, you're not fun. Have you found my mother yet?"

"Actually, I have."

"Really?" He did a half-jump, just like a little boy at Christmas. "Can I meet her?"

Cordelia would be working in the morning. "Tomorrow at ten A.M. If you're not ready to go then, the taxi leaves without you."

"Oh, great! Tomorrow at ten." He started to skip off.

"Hey, where do you live?"

"Kelerac Street. It's a little back apartment." He gave me the number, then did his gleeful skip away.

I would tell him tomorrow what to expect and see if he still wanted to meet her. I just hoped his euphoria could let in some reality.

"What do you think?" Cordelia asked me.

I thought I was in the middle of a great big mess. But she was asking about the paintings.

"I like the one with the purple pelican in it." We'd gone from blue dogs to red cats, and my nominee for the next animal of color to populate paintings was a purple pelican.

"I guess we keep looking." Cordelia had heard the joke before.

We never did find any purple pelicans—someone is missing a great trend here—but she did find some suitable paintings. Alex—who had joined us—Torbin, and Andy all approved of her choices.

"This is amazing," Alex said. "A lesbian biology major actually picking out decent artwork."

I let Alex blather on and excused myself. I saw someone I wanted to talk to.

"Hello, Karl," I said. Karl was a longtime French Quarter resi-

dent, knew everybody and everything, and could tell funnier stories than anyone I'd ever heard.

"Micky, darling, so good to see you."

"Can you spare a working girl detective a bit of gossip?"

"For you, anything. Let's go to my office." Karl led me to a
quiet place behind a table.

"Would it shock you if I said a client of mine alleges that, when
he was fifteen, Henri Forquet picked him up over in Biloxi, had
anal sex with him, and probably infected him with HIV?"

"My dear, nothing would shock me anymore. But what people
don't know about Mr. Henri, and what he doesn't want them to
know, so you didn't hear it from me, is that Henri was caught in
a bit of a scandal at a young age. Henri and the gardener's son
were found in a compromising position behind the rosebushes. I
think the sprinkler system came on. The boy claimed that Henri
made him do it, Henri claimed that the boy made him do it, and,
as we all know, money buys truth. Henri was sent away to college,
the gardener and his family had a job in California provided for
them, and the servants were paid too well to gossip.

"About five or six years ago, the gardener's son returned to New
Orleans, worked as a bartender, and died of AIDS a few years ago."

"Could he have been infected back then?"

"I think they were two young boys fooling around. I doubt they'd
done much before. Unless one of them had returned from a bath-
house in San Francisco, it was very early. The incident had to have
taken place in the late seventies, maybe '80 or '81, but no later."

"The person who told me this tale isn't the most upstanding of
citizens. I'm trying to gauge how likely it is that his story is true."

"When his parents were alive, they had Henri on a bit of a
leash. Now that they're gone, he does what he pleases. He's bel-
ligerently anti-gay, yet he still watches the boys. If I were to guess,
I'd say he's the kind of man who doesn't want to be so 'weak' as
to have sex with men, then finds himself in a situation where he

thinks he can get away with it and then does it without any real planning or foresight. He can't allow it to be real enough to think about except when he's doing it."

"Not real enough to think about things like condoms or safer sex?"

"I'm speculating, mind you. But that is the kind of man he strikes me as being. He is also a selfish bastard. Too much money, too much power at too young an age. People matter only if they're useful."

"What do you know about Bror, his assistant? What's the story there?"

"Very charming, very smooth. The one you talk to if you want to talk to Henri. Henri can be abrasive, but he has the money. Bror has the social skills to make things work. I suspect that Henri would love to get into his pants."

"He is a handsome man."

"Very. But also smart. I suspect that Henri needs him more than he needs Henri. It lets Bror say no to his advances and still have a tremendous amount of power."

"Thanks, that helps some."

"I give my all to help lady dicks."

"I've heard you're not too bad with the boy variety."

"You'll make me blush."

Karl was too popular for me to long claim his attention. He waved good-bye and hurried off to one of the several people calling his name.

Lindsey joined me in my table cul-de-sac.

"You look pensive," she said.

"Thinking."

"About?"

"Tomorrow morning I'm going to break a young man's heart. He hired me to find his biological mother and I did. She is not the mother he's desperately seeking."

"And tomorrow he's going to meet her?"

"Yes, in the morning I take him to her."

"A broken heart isn't such a bad thing."

"No?"

"I think perhaps it's the smaller breaks, the death of a pet, the first love that goes astray, that teach us how to survive the bigger breaks. Every heart gets broken someday."

"His adoptive parents found out he was gay and kicked him out, so she was his last chance at a mother."

"It's hard to not have a mother."

"I hate to be the one to do it to him."

"But Micky, save for those who die young, we all end up motherless someday. We all die, so all the mothers die, or sometimes before they die they become insane or alcoholic or abandon us. Our hearts will get broken many times. You're not the one who will break his heart," Lindsey said.

"No, life will. I'll just be a witness."

The ebb of people moved around us. Lindsey joined other friends. I found Cordelia.

After she and I thought we had seen everyone we wanted to see, and a few we didn't want to see, we went in search of Torbin and Andy to tell them to party hearty without us.

"Too bad you have to work," Torbin said to Cordelia.

"Sometimes a girl's just got to get to bed," I replied.

Cordelia took my hand to keep me with her as we navigated through the throng of people. Even after we were past the crowds, we still held hands.

We didn't say much as we walked to the parking garage.

I noticed Suzanna Forquet coming down the far end of the row we were parked in. That white dress made her stand out even in this shadowed garage. With no audience looking on, Henri was no longer glued to her. He trailed her by some ten yards, engrossed in a conversation with Bror.

I felt a moment of pity for Suzanna. Money can't buy it all, I almost said aloud to her approaching figure.

Suddenly I heard the sound of running feet. Appearing from between the parked cars, a man ran for Suzanna and grabbed her purse as he passed her. She held on for a moment, then he pushed her down and wrenched it out of her hand. He ran past us and then into the darkness behind a pillar.

I took half a step to chase him, but stopped. I wasn't going to catch him in the heels I was wearing, and there was nothing in that purse that was worth risking my life for.

It had happened in only a few seconds.

Bror left Henri behind and rushed to Suzanna. He scooped her up, cradling her to him. He held her as gently and protectively as a lover would.

Suzanna put her arms around his neck and let him carry her.

Several security guards appeared. Henri asserted his dominance long enough to tell them what had happened.

Cordelia went to where Bror was holding Suzanna.

"Are you all right?" she asked her.

Henri answered curtly, "She's fine. We're going home now."

"She's a doctor," I said, to explain her seeming interference.

At that, Bror turned to Cordelia, defying Henri's orders.

"Make sure she's okay," he said. He didn't put her down, but held her before Cordelia so she could examine her in his arms.

"Does anything hurt?" Cordelia asked her.

"My right ankle. I think I twisted it,"

Cordelia lifted the hem of Suzanna's gown to look at her ankles. "Tell me if anything is painful," Cordelia said, taking Suzanna's foot in one hand and placing her other hand on the lower part of the calf. She gently moved the ankle.

"It's not broken, is it?" Suzanna asked.

"No. If it were broken, you probably wouldn't even let me touch it. There might be a hairline fracture, but I doubt it."

Henri had been ignored and defied long enough. "You're letting a lesbian doctor put her hands all over you," he said. Henri
and Cordelia both came from the same small circle of old-
moneyed New Orleans families. Her decision to come out was
threatening to his choice to stay hidden.

"This isn't the most romantic of settings," I retorted.

"Who are you?" he demanded. I doubted he remembered me
from the party. He hadn't been looking at women.

"The lesbian doctor's lover. This is an ankle exam, not a seduction. Believe me, I know."

Cordelia let go of Suzanna's ankle. Not so much because of
Henri's outburst, but because she was finished. "When you get
home, put some ice on it, keep it elevated, and take some anti-
inflammatory like aspirin or ibuprofen. If it gets worse, you may
want to see a doctor. You've probably got some bruises, but other
than that, does anything else feel not right?"

"You're right about the bruises. But . . . I think I'm okay."

"You will excuse me, ladies," Henri sneered. "Like most men,
I don't like my wife manhandled by butch dykes."

"Not very perceptive of you, Henri," I said. "She's the femme,
I'm the butch."

"You think you're funny, don't you? We're going home. Bror,
take her to the car."

"No, I want to make sure she's all right," Bror said.

He didn't move until Suzanna said, "I'm okay, Bror. Let's go
now."

Henri strode away, with Bror, carefully cradling Suzanna, following.

The power triangle was now clear. Suzanna and Bror had
formed an alliance. If Henri took on the two of them, he didn't do
it often. Suzanna knew Bror was in love with her and she knew
he would protect her, even against Henri, if need be. Sometimes
it was hard not to like Suzanna and sometimes it was hard to like

her. It was difficult to believe that, as much as she needed the protection his love gave, she did nothing to encourage it. It's a dangerous game, I thought. Love that is casually taken, then not tended to or cared for, can easily turn to hate.

We had to walk past them to get to our car. Bror was gently lowering Suzanna into the back seat. Henri was standing back, waiting for them to get situated.

As we walked by, I softly called out, "Oh, Henri? Biloxi's not far enough away."

He spun to stare at me.

I ignored him and kept on walking. I had finally gotten my answer. Bourbon St. Ann was telling the truth.

Cordelia waited until we were in the car to ask what that was about.

I repeated a cleaned-up version of the tale Bourbon St. Ann had told me.

When I was done, she said, "I'm not really worried about Henri. I don't think he can do more to us than not invite us to parties we don't want to go to. But your friend would be a fool to try to blackmail him. And I'd feel better if you'd stay away from that."

"I'd feel better if I'd stay away from that." I told Cordelia about my planned trip tomorrow, all the gory details. "After I've gotten him as prepared as I can for his un-mother mother, I'll try to hammer a few pounds of sense into his head about taking on Henri Forquet." The one thing I didn't tell Cordelia was that Henri's wife might be Bourbon St. Ann's half-sister. Not that she would betray the secret, but it felt like something that was hidden and should stay hidden. "But that's tomorrow," I said. "Let's get home before we both get too tired."

For an answer, Cordelia put her hand on my knee, then slowly ran it up my thigh until she was under my skirt with her hand on my garter. She worked a finger under the elastic strap and went farther up my thigh until . . . until she could go no farther. I felt the warmth of her fingers through my panties. That was all she did, just let her hand rest there.

"Why don't we go home and continue this?" she said, and then took her hand away.

"Tease," I muttered to her retreating hand.

"I need two hands to drive, otherwise we won't get home."

"Drive. Now. Let's go."

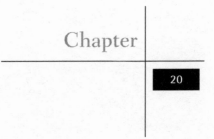

Chapter

20

Saturday hours at the clinic start at the reasonable hour of nine A.M. I joined Cordelia for coffee before she left, then, after she was gone, took my shower and made myself presentable to face the day.

Just as I got out of the shower, the phone rang.

It was Joanne. She sounded very tired.

"I just wanted to update you," she said, "before I crash for a few hours."

"What's been happening?"

"Laurie Silverman's body was found early this morning in an abandoned lot over in Algiers."

"Same killer?"

"Looks a hell of a lot like it. About one hour ago we picked up

Frances Gilmore. She's not talking without a lawyer. That's all she said, 'I want my lawyer, I want my lawyer,' except once she slipped and said, 'I want my mama.'"

"You think she might break?"

"I think she'll either break or go crazy. She was on the edge of hysteria when we brought her in. We've got a team with a search warrant going over her apartment."

"I'm glad to know she's off the street."

"Yeah, I just hope we find enough evidence in her place to keep her off the street."

"Me, too. Thanks for calling."

"Keep wearing your gun. Just in case."

"I will if it makes you happy."

"Sleep will make me happy."

"Joanne? The murdered woman? What was her name again?"

"Laurie Silverman. Why?"

"Sounds a bit familiar." Joanne gave me a moment to think, but I had to admit, "I can't place it."

"It's a small community here. You many have met her in passing."

"Yeah, maybe. I'll think on it. You get some sleep."

We hung up.

In the hopes that Bourbon St. Ann would be laggardly and give me an excuse to avoid this treacherous reunion, I was at his doorstep at a very prompt ten A.M.

The gate immediately swung open and he came out. He had been waiting for me.

"You think I should bring something? Like a gift or flowers?" he asked as he slid in.

All traces of last night's makeup were gone. His shirt and even his jeans were pressed. His hair was neatly combed. He looked like he was auditioning for the role of clean-cut, all-American boy.

"She said if you brought her a six-pack, she'd talk to you," I replied. I saw no point in sugar-coating this. He'd find out soon enough.

"Oh, okay. Is there a place that's close to where she is? That way it'll be cold."

"I'm sorry, but I don't think this woman is the mother you're hoping for."

"You met my adoptive mother. You know I'm not expecting perfection."

"Forget perfection, don't even expect minimally adequate. I'm going to take you to see her because I don't want you to waste any more of your life looking for her. This isn't going to be a happy, loving reunion."

"Okay, okay. I hear what you're saying. You know, I don't really think I want an honest-to-God-apple-pie-baking mom. I think I just want some frumpy thing to sit in the Mom slot. Someone I can send a Mother's Day card if I'm feeling sloppy and sentimental. A lousy mother is better than no mother at all."

I pulled away and headed downriver. "There's another thing. Remember that guy you pointed out last night?"

"Henri Forquet, who lives in a mansion on St. Charles Avenue." Bourbon St. Ann had done his gossip homework after he'd left me.

"He's powerful, he's ruthless, and he's really fucked up and angry about wanting to have sex with men. A person blackmailing him about being queer might end up taking a long swim in the river."

"What if I took him to court and sued?"

"Think about it. The man probably has more lawyers around him than Tulane spits out every year. You'd have to testify and they'd rip you apart on the witness stand. Also, if you admit to having anal sex with him you will have admitted in the record of the court that you have committed a felony."

"What ever happened to doing the right thing?"

"There is also something called, forget about doing the right thing if you don't have a chance in hell of succeeding."

"But . . . but he shouldn't be able to get away with it," Bourbon St. Ann let out, his voice that of a boy on the verge of manhood who has just found out that some wrongs will go unavenged.

When we stopped to get the beer offering, I found a phone book and looked up Sindy's number. It seemed only fair that she get a little bit of warning. I told her we'd be there in about fifteen minutes.

When I turned onto Sindy's block, I drove slowly, letting Bourbon St. Ann take it in.

I stopped in front of her house. "That's it."

"You know, you're going to think I'm crazy, but this is better than that tacky, sterile, middle-crass place I grew up in."

I sighed and shook my head. If he had really grown up here, I doubted he'd find it quaint.

We walked across Sindy's overgrown lawn. I knocked on the door, Bourbon St. Ann hanging shyly behind me, holding the two six-packs he had bought.

She opened the door. I stood aside so they could see each other.

After a quick glance at the beer, she said, "Sonny boy, come to your maw!" and opened her arms wide.

Bourbon St. Ann looked surprised, then pleased, then he was in her arms, murmuring something that sounded like, "Mom, I'm so glad I finally found you."

After a suitable embrace, Sindy invited us in. She took charge of the beer, helping herself to one, graciously offering one to Bourbon St. Ann and me, then putting the remaining ones in the refrigerator.

I glanced around the room. She had cleaned it. It wasn't much more than fifteen minutes' worth, all the warning she had had, but she had made some attempt to put on a good show.

"What's your name, honey? I know I bore you, but they didn't let me name you."

"Uh . . . Stone, but I hate it. They named me Stone Zachary Hudson."

"Well, why don't I call you Zack? That's a good name. So, Zack, what kind of work you do?"

The newly christened Zack fumbled for a moment before he came up with, "I work in a bar in the French Quarter."

"You do? That's good work. The French Quarter is so posh. We do 'bout the same thing. I wait tables over at Ernie's Grill. Gotta take care of myself. Ain't married. Just had no luck with men."

"Yeah, me, too," Bourbon St. Ann/Zack said.

"You go after boys?" Sindy asked, then reached over and patted him on the knee. "Oh, honey, gotta live and let live." She took a swig of the beer he'd bought her. "Just you don't go after any fellow I'm set on and we'll do fine."

The panic was chased off his face by an almost beatific smile. This mother had no problem with his being gay. Bourbon St. Ann relaxed enough to say, "Don't worry, you probably go after much younger ones than I do."

Sindy slapped his thigh in laughter, then her own. "Oh, what a funny boy. Takes right after me."

I smiled, commented that he was funny, then excused myself, saying I'd give them some time alone.

Not wanting to just sit in my car, I took a walk. So I had been wrong about this reunion. Or rather, I had judged by my standards. I found nothing redeeming in Sindy Ponder, so I had assumed that Bourbon St. Ann wouldn't. But he'd found what he was looking for, someone to accept him.

I gave them half an hour, then returned. "I'm sorry to interrupt, but I've got to get back to the city," I said.

With great reluctance, they said their farewells, exchanged phone numbers, and again belabored how happy they were to find each other, before I got Bourbon St. Ann out the door.

"She's not perfect, but I like her," he pronounced the minute we got in the car. "Did you see how cool she was about my being gay? Didn't bat an eyelash."

"Nope, she just sat there contentedly drinking her beer."

"Get off it, don't be one of those moralistic tofu dykes. She's funny and she's earthy and lives life the way she wants to live it. You've got to credit her for that."

I suspected that Sindy had been blown through life sideways because she couldn't think or plan for anything other than the next beer, the next party, or the next boyfriend. Not quite a philosophy of living life the way you want to live it, but there was no use in trying to burst his bubble. "I'm glad things have worked out this well, and that you and she have a lot in common. Since I fulfilled my part of the bargain, why don't we talk about the fee for this?"

"Well, things are tight. . . . I would really like to get a car to visit Mom and—"

"To visit the mother I found for you?" I pointed out. I suspected it would be more of a fight than it was worth to get money out of Bourbon St. Ann, but I wasn't going to just let it go. I could at least make him squirm a bit.

"Give me a little time, okay? Mom tells me I have a rich half-sister somewhere. If we find her, that might take care of a few things."

"If you can find her and if she wants to be found. Get real, Zack, do you think a high-society lady is going to want you and Sindy hanging around the mansion?" With Sindy egging him on, I doubted I'd talk him out of looking for this fairy godmother of a rich sister. But Suzanna had stood in front of that house and turned and walked away. And if I could, I would influence events to keep it that way. "Maybe we can work out an installment plan. You know, ten dollars a week for the next five years."

"For five years?"

"Interest. It adds up."

I dropped him off at his place without having come up with a better payment plan than "Give me a couple of weeks. Something should work out by then."

I gave him a skeptical look, waved good-bye, and headed off. Except for a word with Chester when he got back from his vacation, this case was closed.

With Bourbon St. Ann out of my car and out of my life, I found myself trying to think where I'd heard the name Laurie Silverman before.

I drove by my house, but Cordelia's car wasn't there, so I decided to make a quick trip to my office. I felt I had seen Laurie Silverman's name written down somewhere. Maybe that somewhere was in my office. I glanced at my watch. It was a little past noon.

Of course, I checked my mailbox on the way in. Every few years I get something besides bills or junk mail. And today was one of those days.

My address correction request letter from Lorraine Drummond had come back. I now had her current address. Another case almost closed. It was going to be a busy day for mother-child reunions. With a start, I realized that I might be including myself in that category. My stomach lurched at the thought. All the what-ifs came rushing in. What if the gallery opening has nothing to do with her? What if it does? What if she's there, what do I do? What if she wants nothing to do with me? What if she's cold or distant? What if she abandoned me because she didn't want to be bothered with a kid? What if she says, "Too bad your aunt wasn't understanding and you got abused by your cousin, but I had a boyfriend who wasn't interested in women with children. He's gone, so I'm ready to have you back in my life," what would I do? Would I take a bad mother rather than no mother at all? Or would I walk away?

I didn't know.

I busied myself looking at papers, flipping through files,

searching for names or something that would remind me of where I saw some names.

Then it came to me. Silverman. Sherman. An address book. I had seen Laurie Silverman's name in Suzanna Forquet's address book when I had glanced at the names on the page beside Georgia Sherman's name.

Reuniting Lorraine Drummond with her mother would have to wait. I needed to talk to Suzanna. If two of her ex-lovers had been murdered, it could be some bizarre coincidence or it could mean that somehow she was the link.

I wouldn't swear that Suzanna would never murder anyone, but I couldn't see her being this kind of killer, one who sexually mutilates the victims.

How did she meet this woman? If she had a place or person that she had used, that might be the answer.

I didn't like the implications of this. At best, it meant that I had to again tell Suzanna that someone she'd been involved with—however briefly—had been murdered. It also meant that it would be almost impossible to keep Suzanna's name out of this.

I debated calling Joanne, then decided not to just yet. I would let her sleep for a bit more, and call her after I talked to Suzanna. I called home and left a message for Cordelia on the machine, telling her that I was busy doing detective work and would probably be home mid- to late afternoon.

Then I drove uptown to Suzanna's mansion, hoping that the gods of ugly encounters would keep Henri safely tucked away.

Bror opened the door.

"Is Suzanna in?" I asked. "It's important I speak to her for just a few minutes." I was betting that her twisted ankle would keep her close to home.

"Hi, Micky," he greeted me. A charming man who remembered people's names. "Good of you to come and check up on Suzanna. Henri's got some overseas investments that are making roller coasters look sedate and he can be a bit of a bear when his money is dizzy." Bror gave me one of his ironic grins to let me know he was apologizing for Henri's behavior last night without really saying the words. "So he's not much good company for a woman with a hurting ankle."

"Is she doing all right?" I asked.

"She'll be fine, a few days of rest and ice. But resting is not what Suzanna does well. Let me make sure she's up to company, but I'll bet that she'd like to see you."

He gave me the usual ten minutes to study the ever-changing flower arrangements before returning. "Come on back, but first please give me your gun," he continued in his same friendly voice. "It will be returned when you leave." He held out his hand for it. "You do understand why I have to do this."

Well-trained bodyguard that he was, of course he could spot the bulge under my jacket. I handed my gun over. It was a reasonable request under the circumstances. Unless I wanted to assassinate Suzanna, I had no need of my gun.

He then led me back to Suzanna. She was in her private office, on the couch with her foot propped up.

"Micky," she said. "It's good of you to come by and see how I am."

That wasn't why I'd come, but I wasn't going to disabuse her of the notion. "How are you? How's your ankle?"

"My ankle's sore, but I can hobble around on it. I'm a bit bruised and I've got a scrape on my elbow, but I suspect I'll survive."

"Good. Glad to hear that. It's scary to be attacked like that."

"I didn't get scared until it was all over. It happened so quickly."

After a brief pause, I said, "There's another reason for my coming here. Laurie Silverman."

"I know. I heard it on the news."

"That must have been a shock for you."

"Why?"

"You don't remember her? She was one of your lovers."

"How do you know that?" Suzanna demanded. "Who told you?"

"No one. I saw her name in your address book."

"Are you sure? You only got a brief glimpse of it. What are you accusing me of?"

Suzanna's defenses had gone on full alert. I couldn't tell if she really had no memory of Laurie Silverman and was trying to cover how casual some of her affairs had been, or if she was trying to bluff her way out of being any more involved in this murder investigation.

"I'm not accusing you of anything. But if someone is killing women close to you, you may be in danger."

"The news said the police had a suspect in custody. Besides, I don't remember that name."

"There's a quick way to find out," I said as I crossed to her desk.

"Keep your hands off my address book," Suzanna ordered.

I ignored her, opened the desk drawer, and took the book out.

She was right, she could hobble. But she didn't get to me before I had flipped it open to the S's.

Georgia Sherman.

Laurie Silverman.

Suzanna grabbed for the book, but I spun out of her reach.

"Laurie Silverman. She's here," I informed her.

"Give me that. It's private. You have no right—"

"Were you lying or do you just forget your lovers so easily?"

"I was doing you a favor when I let you see that. Now you're using it against me."

"I'm not trying to use it against you. Where did the killer find these women? Most of them were closeted. The police need evidence to hold their suspect and this might lead them to that evidence. Can't you see beyond your narrow self-interest?"

"These women are dead. There's nothing altruistic that I can do to bring them back. Why drag my name through the mud to lead the police on a wild goose chase?"

She again lunged for the address book, but her twisted ankle slowed her enough for me to easily step away.

I suddenly wondered why she was still so desperate to get the book back. "Who else is in here, Suzanna? What else are you hiding?" I quickly flipped through the pages to B. Though I was looking for it, I was startled to actually see Tasha Billings's name there.

"How many others?" I said, staring at her.

"No! Give me that." This time she ignored her ankle to jump at me and grab my arm.

I backed away, but she wrapped her other arm around my shoulder. I tried to pull away from her, but she held on.

I didn't really want to get into a physical fight with Suzanna. And if she really wanted to hurt me, she could scratch or bite. Instead we staggered in our awkward embrace until she abruptly swung her weight to pull me off balance. I tripped and fell backward onto the couch. Suzanna went with me, landing on top, as I'm sure she'd planned. The address book was caught between us.

"Is that how you silence your lovers? Kill them?" I said.

"No. Oh, no," she answered, her eyes suddenly wide at the implication of what I was saying. "No. You've got to believe that. I'm not a killer."

"Suzanna," I said gently. "You've got to see what's at stake here. Of the five women murdered, three of them have had affairs with you. That can't be coincidence. You're involved. You may be innocently involved, but you are. The police have a suspect. What if it's not that person? You may know a murderer."

"No, no," she repeated softly. "It can't be. It can't be . . . him. There are too many consequences."

"Where's Henri?"

"New York. He flew there this morning."

"When is he coming back?"

"Monday or Tuesday. I'm not sure. Oh, God, what am I going to do?"

"You need to go to the police and tell them everything you know."

"I can't do that. I can't."

"You've got to. I'm sorry, there's no choice."

"Will you help?" Her hand moved to my neck, a caress.

"I'll do what I can."

I felt some of the stiffness leave her, her body relaxing into mine.

"Why don't we go ahead and go? Get it over with?" I suggested.

"No, not yet. Not . . . just yet. I'll do this for you. But I need . . ." She put her other hand between my legs. "I need you to hold me."

"I'm sorry, Suzanna—"

"Please. I need this. I am . . . so lonely," she said, the last a bare whisper.

I gently put my arm around her shoulder, not because I was going to make love to her, but because for the first time she was completely guileless.

"I'm sorry. Even if I made love to you, it wouldn't take away your loneliness."

"Yes, yes, it would. At least . . . for a while." She started to unfasten my jeans.

I put my hand on hers to stop her. "I'm not a quick, temporary fix to your loneliness. There isn't an easy way out. And there's no way out if you choose to live here, as Henri's fake wife." I said it as gently as I could, but still my words stung.

"Damn you!" She jerked her hand away from mine, then heaved herself off me, grabbing the address book as she stood up. "I don't need your pious morality."

I sat up.

"I don't need you at all!" she finished.

"No, you don't," I told her.

"And I'm not going to the police. They'll catch the murderer without my help."

"Think about it, Suzanna. Don't let your anger at me blind you to your self-interest. If Henri's the murderer and you don't go to the police, you become an accessory after the fact. Even if you escape all criminal liability, you'll still get dragged through something unpleasant by the media. If he's not guilty, his having sex with men will likely be discovered during the investigation and at least you'll be even in that."

"But it's not true. He told me he stopped all that before we were married."

"Suzanna," I said, a sudden sick feeling in my stomach. "Do you have sex with Henri?"

"Well . . . we are married."

"You have sex?"

"Don't be so shocked. He wants children. Someone to carry on the family name."

"And he told you he hasn't had sex with any men since you married?"

"Yes. Why do you care?"

I liked Suzanna and I didn't like her. She may have used people, but she had been used in turn.

"There's an eighteen-year-old gay man who claims that when he was fifteen, Henri picked him up and had sex with him."

"I don't know that I believe that and even if it's true, so what? I don't expect him to be faithful to me. Does it matter if he cheats on me with men or women?"

"He claims that Henri was the first person he ever had anal sex with and that that was how he became infected with HIV."

A look of shocked horror spread across Suzanna's face. She burst out, "No! No, he couldn't be . . ." Then a mask slipped over her face, the one she had worked so hard on, the mask that let her live so many lies. "Nice try, Micky. Get me to hate him and run to the police. I think it's time for you to go."

"For God's sake, Suzanna, I'm not making this up! I don't know if it's true. It may not be. But if it is . . . don't you see, I had to tell you. I like you, Suzanna. On some level, I think you use people, but I don't think you'd use someone like this. Think about going to the police. Think very hard about it."

She stared at me for a moment before saying, "All right, I will. Do you plan to call them the minute you walk out of here?"

"I'll call the police if I feel I have no other choice."

"Give me a few hours. I need to think things through. Will you do that?"

I didn't know if her seeming cooperation was manipulation or if it was real. There was no way for me to know.

"I'll give you a few hours. Call me around five and let me know what you've decided."

"Thank you. This isn't easy for me. I appreciate your understanding."

"Consider this: It's easier than being murdered the way those women were."

"Bror will see you out." She opened the door to the hallway and called for him. He almost immediately appeared.

"I've got a headache," she said to him. "Please escort Ms. Knight out."

He nodded, then turned on his heel, demanding that I follow. Suzanna closed the door as soon as I was beyond it.

I've got long legs, but his are longer. He made no attempt to moderate his pace. I had been discarded, and friendliness wasn't wasted on the discarded.

"What do you get out of it, Bror?" I said as we entered the foyer. "Do you get off standing outside the door and listening?"

For an answer, he opened a drawer in the flower arrangement table and took out my gun. He slowly took the bullets out of it, then handed me the unloaded gun. "You were a fool to think she cared for you. You'll do well to forget that you ever knew Suzanna. She doesn't like gossip about her life. And what she doesn't like, I don't like."

He opened the door for me to leave. He would protect Suzanna from me. I walked out.

The door slammed behind me.

I got in my car, drove a few blocks, and then pulled over. It was starting to rain. I needed to think, and I couldn't do that and drive in New Orleans in the rain.

I was sure that the address book was destroyed by now. What did I really even know, let alone could prove? Suzanna had had affairs with three of the murdered women. My instincts said she wasn't the murderer; her surprise and shock were too real for that. I'd seen no hint of the kind of viciousness and fury that it would take to commit those murders. Maybe Cordelia's stalker really was the killer and they all belonged to the "Closet Club," and if Suzanna got most of her lovers there, and the stalker got most of her victims there, there might be that kind of overlap.

If Henri was capable of risking infecting his wife with HIV, he probably wouldn't have scruples about killing her ex-affairs. And he did have the right level of viciousness and anger. If it was him, would Suzanna protect him or sink him?

I would give her the few hours she requested. If he was the killer, her cooperation might be essential in trapping him.

Henri was in New York anyway. Then I realized that with the stalker in custody and him gone, the two most likely suspects were out of the way. For the first time in what felt like days, the tension went out of my shoulders.

I picked up the car phone to call Cordelia. However, I only got my voice on the answering machine. I glanced at my watch. It was a little after two. She should be finished at the clinic by now. I called home again and this time punched in the code that let me listen to the messages.

First I had to hear the message I had left, then Cordelia came on. "Hi, Micky. I'm with Alex over at her mom's. Mrs. Sayers has a touch of the flu, so I'm giving her doctor-approved chicken soup. If you need, you can call me there or page me."

That explained her absence. She and Alex had known each other since high school, so Cordelia was also friends with Alex's parents. Much as I wanted to see her, I wasn't interested in playing nurse to her doctor (well, not with anyone watching).

On the seat beside me was the envelope with Lorraine Drummond's address. Maybe I could reunite a daughter with a mother who wanted her.

Lorraine had moved only two blocks up and four blocks over from her old address.

That's where I headed. It was back downtown in the Bywater area. The rain increased to a downpour with its usual accompaniment of thunder and lightning. I hoped its intensity meant that it would soon be over.

That seemed to be the case. It was already beginning to slow up when I reached Lorraine's address.

I sat in my car, hoping the rain would lighten even more. But it was clearly waiting for me to get out and get wet.

I got out of my car and made a quick dash to Lorraine's porch.

As I rang her doorbell, I hoped I didn't look too wet and bedraggled. Even more, I hoped that Lorraine wanted to be reunited with her mother.

"Who is it?" a voice called from inside.

"My name is Michele Knight and I'm looking for Lorraine Drummond."

She opened the door and peered at me. "Yes?"

"Are you Lorraine Drummond?"

"Yes, I am. What can I do for you?"

Lorraine was a handsome woman. Maturity hadn't taken away the hint of mischieviousness and independence evident in her high school pictures, but in her face was grace, and the composure that comes with surviving loss and knowing you can survive it.

"I'm a private detective. Your mother hired me to locate you. I don't know if you know this, but your father died a few months ago. Your mother told me that life was too short to live it without her daughter."

Lorraine just stared at me for some time. Finally she stammered out, "My mother hired you . . . to look for me? My mother wants . . . me . . . wants me . . . ?"

"Wants you back."

"Oh, my God," Lorraine said. "I thought she'd go to the grave without wanting to see me." Her eyes glistened. She quickly wiped the tears away. "This is . . . this is unexpected. And . . . this is . . . wonderful. Oh, hell, my car's in the shop and Abby won't be home until this evening . . ."

"Abby's your lover?"

"Yes, she is," Lorraine answered easily, then she realized that she had told a stranger that she was a lesbian.

"I'm gay," I said. "I didn't ask, but I think that's one of the reasons your mother hired me."

Lorraine again smiled. "She wanted me enough to hire a lesbian detective to find me."

"If you want to go now, I'll be glad to take you," I offered.

"Are you sure? That's very generous of you."

"One of the perks of the job. Watching happy reunions."

"I'll take you up on it," she said, her grin growing wider. "Come on in, I've got to throw on some shoes. Can't go meet Mama without having socks and shoes." She turned and led the way in.

I followed, shutting the door to keep the rain-chilled air out.

"I'll be just a second," Lorraine called as she went down the hallway.

I stayed by the door. I could see only the living room and part of the kitchen. They both seemed comfortable and inviting. A cat was spread across a magazine on the coffee table, contentedly licking herself. Suzanna is a fool, I thought, to take Henri and his marble and perfect flower arrangements instead of the comfort and love evident in this house.

Lorraine reappeared. "I should leave Abby a note . . . no, I've got a better idea. I'll bring Mama home for dinner. We'll have a big sit-down Saturday dinner and Mama and Abby can meet. She'll like Abby, I know she will."

"She'll like the woman her daughter's grown up to be, too," I said.

"Let's go," she said, grabbing her keys.

We went out the door. I watched Lorraine as she locked it, then we both turned around.

And stopped.

We were staring at a gun that was pointed at us.

I looked at the man holding the gun. I had assumed that Suzanna had meant Henri when she said he couldn't be the murderer, there were too many consequences.

But she hadn't. She had meant Bror.

"Does Suzanna know you're here?" I asked.

"Suzanna knows exactly what I want her to know. Both of you, get in your car," he said.

I glanced desperately up and down the street, hoping someone was around to witness this. But the rain had driven everybody indoors.

"And if we don't?" The official advice is, if at all possible, not to let yourself be taken to a different location.

Bror strode onto the porch, grabbed Loraine, and put the gun to her temple. Despite the gun, she struggled for a moment, but he tightened his grip around her neck, lifting her so her feet were barely on the ground. He was strangling her. "Any other questions?" he asked. His voice still held the ease and confidence that had caused me to like him. I had only seen the charm, the monster beneath it carefully hidden.

"Let her go. We'll get in the car," I bargained. As long as we were alive, we had a chance to stay alive.

He loosened his grip, but didn't completely let go of her. He kept the gun pointing at her head.

I reluctantly turned my back to them and went down the stairs to my car.

Bror let me unlock my door, then took the keys from me. Still holding Lorraine, he led her to the passenger's side. He opened both the front door and the back door, shoved Lorraine in front, then very quickly got in back, keeping the gun pointed at her the entire time.

"Why should I chauffeur us to the place where you're going to kill us?" I said. I was trying to buy time, hoping for the miracle of a cop car or a noisy neighbor.

He was holding the gun between the two front seats. He could shoot either one of us from there, but the gun wasn't easily visible from outside.

Switching the gun to his left hand, he put his right arm around the seat. He placed his hand over Lorraine's breast. She gasped.

"Because if you don't drive exactly where I tell you, I will rip it off. Then I will rip off the other one." He delivered this macabre threat in the voice that he had used when asking me to wait while he checked if Suzanna was in. The calmness in his tone was all the more chilling. "You will drive carefully and you will do what I say or I will hurt her and I will keep on hurting her."

He handed me the keys back.

I started the car.

Bror gave me instructions to cross the Crescent City Connection, the bridge over the Mississippi that connects downtown New Orleans with the Westbank.

As I merged into traffic for the bridge, I asked again, "Did Suzanna get you to do this?"

"Suzanna? I do what I want to do. Just drive."

He had taken his hand off Lorraine's breast, but it remained draped over the seat, like a coiled snake at her shoulder, ready to strike.

There were tollbooths from the Westbank to the east bank, but nothing slowed us down as we came off the bridge. Given New Orleans and the rain, I was hoping for an accident—one in which no one was hurt—but one that would stop us while waiting for the police to come and clear it up.

No such luck. Traffic was light on this rainy Saturday afternoon. Light and safe.

We quickly left the well-traveled roads, Bror giving me directions that led to streets I was unfamiliar with.

Finally he told me to pull the car over. I wasn't quite sure where we were; my best guess was an industrial area near the Harvey Canal. But I didn't have to guess why he'd brought us here. It was a deserted area, the buildings abandoned and in disrepair. The few other cars around looked like they'd been here for a long time. The road was rutted and there had been no street signs at the last two intersections.

I had considered grabbing my car phone and punching in 911, but cellular doesn't give location and I knew Bror would never give me a chance to say anything useful.

But we were here and I knew if I ever wanted to leave this desolate area, I would have to do something.

In some of the busier parts of town, I could have jumped out of the car at a red light, but with his hand on her right shoulder, Lorraine wouldn't have a chance. I had led Bror to her and I couldn't abandon her.

"You're going to destroy Suzanna by doing this," I said. "The police already know she and one of the murdered women were lovers. Soon they'll find out that she had affairs with all of them. They might arrest her, they'll question her for days. Every sordid detail of her life will be on the front page. Henri will divorce her and leave her without a dime."

"Oh, please, do you really think that the cops are smart enough to put the pieces together? Henri might guess, but he'll need me more than ever. Enough to give me Suzanna," he said, an eerie gloating in his voice.

"You really think she'll turn to you after you've caused her to lose everything that matters to her?"

"She needs me. She knows how much she needs me. She's not as smart as she thinks she is."

"So she didn't ask you to do this? She has no idea you're killing the women she loved?"

"She didn't love them," he retorted. "They were nothing to her. Just physical. Nothing else. It's me she really wants."

"If it was nothing, why kill us?" I said.

"Because I want to," and his voice was again tinged with that eerie gloating. "Get out of the car."

"No," Lorraine said. She mouthed, "Run," to me and her eyes flicked on the phone.

The snake struck. Bror grabbed her, pulling her back between the seats and with him as he got out of the car.

I quickly stuffed the phone in my jacket, then got out, half-torn between running and staying to try to prevent what I knew he was going to do to Lorraine.

One glance at them told me that I couldn't just run away, particularly given how quickly one bullet could stop me.

He had her head bent back, the hand with the gun yanking her hair. With the other hand, he had her arm twisted up her back. A second more and he would break it. She was biting her lip, desperately trying not to scream.

"Stop!" I shouted. "Stop it!"

"Get over here," he growled, not letting her go.

I came around the car to his side. Only then did he relax his grip on her.

Without warning, he threw her down into the weeds beside the road, then grabbed me, and slammed me against the car with his body.

Just because they hadn't found any semen didn't mean that the other women weren't raped, I thought, as he pressed his weight into me. I was surprised and relieved to notice that he didn't have an erection. Or maybe it was just a very small one.

"The phone, you bitch. I'm not stupid," he snarled. He backed away a couple of inches then thrust his hand into my jacket. He took the phone and my useless gun, then stepped away from me.

Lorraine was starting to get up, and for a moment he seemed confused as to what to do.

He's never killed two women at one time before, I reminded myself. Maybe that can work to our advantage. The problem was that I wasn't going to use his being preoccupied with Lorraine to get away and it looked like she was also a bit too altruistic for her own good.

He thrust the barrel of his gun under my chin. "If you try anything again, I will hurt both of you for a long time."

"Aren't you going to do that anyway?"

"Cooperate and I kill her quickly. One painless bullet. Fight and you will watch her die very slowly. Is that what you want? Would you like to watch?" he taunted me.

I did notice that he wasn't offering me any mercy. "All right, we'll give in," I said, because at the moment I couldn't think of anything else to do.

He backed away from me so he could keep both of us in sight. Then he threw the phone and unloaded gun down beside the car, leaving them in plain sight, as if mocking me.

I went to help Lorraine to her feet, aware that the gun was pointed at both of us.

"Walk across the lot. To that building," he ordered.

It was a half-abandoned construction site, more a skeleton of a building than a building. It was about four stories tall. Some of the floors had walls, others didn't. The only access that I could see was an outside metal staircase. Our derelict tomb.

"Go up the stairs," he ordered.

"Will they hold us?" I asked, stopping. Once we were inside the building, the last chance that anyone would see us was lost.

"Why do you care?" he taunted, a defiant admission that he was going to kill us. "Come on, girls, keep going." He kept enough distance between us so that if we tried at attack him, we'd be dead before we reached him.

At the foot of the stairs, I motioned for Lorraine to go before me. "You're the lightest," I told her. But the real reason was that I planned to use the slight advantage the stairs gave me to attack him. He would be behind and below me. I could launch myself at him with a chance that I might actually be on him before he could fire.

Lorraine started up the stairs. I followed. Bror let us get about five steps ahead before I heard his boots scrape the metal of the stairs.

"How high do we go?" I said, slowing just a bit, trying to close the gap between us.

"I'll tell you when to stop."

"How are you going to protect Suzanna while you're sitting on death row?" I said, slowing a little bit more. I was trying to rile him. Anger might distract him enough so he wouldn't notice my slowing.

The banister under my hand wobbled, one end rusted free. I exaggerated my loss of balance, to stop and pretend to right myself.

"You're boring me with your prattle. Keep going," Bror ordered. He had also stopped.

Lorraine, partially hidden from Bror's view by my body, gave the other end of the metal railing a good yank. The section was about six feet long, with the ends screwed in place. This entire stair had never been intended to remain in place this long. I was guessing that construction had started during the oil boom in the mid-eighties. These temporary screws had been exposed to ten years of rain and humidity.

Lorraine had freed her end, the metal piece just resting on its supports.

"Turn around," Bror suddenly ordered.

Reluctantly, I did as I was told, trying to keep one hand on my potential weapon so it wouldn't fall off.

Bror raised his gun. He had a problem with two of us. In the building with its shadowed spaces and debris, he would have a hard time controlling two desperate women. It looked like he was going to solve his problem here on this outside staircase.

He stepped slightly to the side, so he could shoot past me to Lorraine.

I heaved the metal railing at him, throwing it like a javelin.

The gun went off.

The railing hit him squarely in the chest, knocking him back down the stairs.

I quickly turned to Lorraine. She was all right. Hurling the banister at him had been enough to throw his aim off.

Both of us ran quickly up the stairs and into the building. We were on the top floor. I was hoping there would be some other exit, an interior stairway that would let us escape to the car.

We were in a big open space with a concrete floor. There was nowhere to hide and no way to get out except the way we came in.

From the outside came a howl of pain and outrage. Then the sound of Bror's heavy boots coming up the stairs.

Without needing to say anything, Lorraine and I both ran across the open space. The floor continued beyond that open area, but it was shadowed and partly closed off by a wall and I couldn't make out clearly what was there. Whatever it was, it was better than waiting in the open for Bror to come get us.

But beyond the partial wall that separated this part of the building from the open space was nothing. Only haphazard boards crossed the spaces between the girders. There was no running room and, save for the two-foot ledge we were on behind the wall, nowhere to hide.

Lorraine looked at the gaping empty spaces, then at me, and said softly, "Well, it was nice knowing you."

No! I thought. It can't end like this. Mrs. Drummond wasn't going to finally be reunited with her daughter at her funeral. A split-second cascade of images ran though my head—Mrs. Drummond in my office, Lorraine and the single tear as she heard that her mother was looking for her, the torn newspaper clipping that teased me with the possibility of finding my mother. Two daughters looking for their mothers. At least Lorraine's mother was also looking for her. If any daughter survived today, it should be her.

"I'm going to lead him across that," I said, nodding at the boards and the hazardous path they made across the building.

"It won't hold you," she said. "And if it does, he'll notice I'm not with you."

"You're light; you'll have already made it across and you're going to be hidden on the far side—I'll make him think you're there," I said quickly. We had little time. "You'll really stay here. When you can, sneak down those stairs and get to my car phone. He doesn't want to just kill me, he wants to play with me for a while. Help might get here by then."

"Why don't I lead him across and let you get the phone? I'm lighter. I've got a better chance on the boards."

"Because he really wants me."

Lorraine had no argument for that. Bror had only used her to keep me in his power. That she was going to be killed first meant she wasn't the one he really wanted.

"Be safe," I said, and gave her hand a squeeze.

She slid as far as she could into the protective cover of the wall. If he looked directly at her, he would see her.

The sound of his feet on the reverberating metal stairs ceased. He was now in the open space.

The boards, three six-by-twos nailed together, were laid out like narrow catwalks so workers could get across the girders. Like the stairs, they had been intended only to be used for a few months, not left out for ten years in the weather.

I hurriedly crossed the closest one. The wall still blocked me from Bror's view. The second set of boards swayed under me, barely holding my weight. Safely on the girder, I walked across it to move more into the center of the building. I caught a glimpse of Bror, then ducked behind one of the upright supports so he couldn't see me. He was slowly and carefully crossing the open area. He could afford to be careful. He knew we had no place to run.

I cautiously peered from behind the upright. He had disappeared from my view. Obviously he was going to completely check out that area before coming to this part of the building.

I could only use the solid girders to travel parallel with the opening. I had to use the boards to travel farther into the building. The other beams were X's and they skipped floors. Taking advantage of Bror's thoroughness, I crossed farther back in. I was trying to balance haste and stealth. I wanted to be close to halfway before I let him know where I was. But this set of boards made me abandon furtiveness for haste. Up close I could see the bore of termites in it and felt it giving way.

What if he doesn't follow me out here? I wondered. If he stayed in the area by the wall, Lorraine wouldn't be able to get by him. He could just stand there and take potshots at me.

I saw Bror again. My haste had made enough noise for him to hear. He was cautiously coming toward the opening that led to this part of the building. He was probably twenty feet from Lorraine.

I quickly skittered across another length of board, making no attempt to be quiet. This time I wanted Bror to hear.

Using an upright as a bit of cover, I called out in a harsh whisper, "Keep going! I see him. You're almost there. There has to be another way out."

Bror came through the opening, quickly scanning the area

before him. But he stopped looking back and forth and I knew he had spotted me.

I felt a jolt of dread, then reminded myself he was supposed to see me—but that did little to quell my fear. I thought of Cordelia. That brief message I had left on the answering machine might be my farewell to her.

Bror bent down, grabbed the board catwalk nearest to him, and upended it. I listened to it crash as it fell the three stories.

Run, run now, I silently told Lorraine. Use the noise to cover your steps. I glanced once in her direction. She was still there.

Bror strode to the next set of boards and did the same thing.

When he reached to upend the next catwalk, I used the seconds during which he couldn't fire at me to cross to the next girder and then behind the closest upright.

This time, when I looked for Lorraine, I couldn't see her.

Bror left only one set of boards remaining. He was going to make sure I couldn't backtrack around behind him.

Suddenly Bror cocked his head back to the staircase as if he heard something there.

"You don't think she loves you, do you?" I yelled at him. "She told me she can't stand touching you." Then, using the same stage whisper as I had before, "Hide, hide, back there. I don't know if I can go any farther."

"Shut up!" Bror shouted at me. "She had me walk you out the door. I got rid of you."

"Too bad you weren't around when they were passing out brains, Bror, old buddy. Her getting rid of me doesn't mean she wants anything to do with you. It's called a gap in logic."

But Bror wasn't as stupid a man as I wanted him to be. He was already walking back to the stairs to check out the noise he thought he'd heard.

"How many times have you made love to her? Ever seen her breasts? I have," I taunted him.

"She's mine in a way you can't understand. She needs me," he shouted back.

"She uses you," I retorted. "She lets Henri fuck her because he gives her money. But she won't let you touch her."

"Liar!" He stopped. "You don't know her. I know what a woman like her needs, and it's not Henri's faggot dick."

"She doesn't want any man. I've never been her servant, but I know her in ways you don't. She at least liked me enough to have sex with me. She's got really nice breasts, very pale, small pink nipples." Of course, I was making that up, but I was betting that Bror hadn't seen her breasts, either. I was also betting that, given the way he had mutilated his victims, he had a bit of a fetish about them. "She let me put my hands all over them. Has she ever let you even touch one?"

"Shut up!" he screamed at me. "She just plays with girls. It's a game to her. She belongs to me, not to you. You'll never have her the way I will." He forgot about any noise on the stairs. I had won my bet.

He ran toward me, not even pausing as he crossed the first boards.

Placing another dangerous bet, I skittered from behind the safety of the upright, made it to the catwalk, and put another set of boards between me and Bror. I was betting that he would not be content with merely shooting me. He wanted to make me suffer.

In an attempt to make it harder for him to get to where I was, I shoved at the end of the boards, attempting to dislodge them. Rotten and worn as they were, the boards were still heavy. I did manage to get these displaced, but my hopes of knocking out an entire swath between me and Bror was clearly hopeless.

He started to cross another catwalk, but quickly backed away as he realized that they would not hold him. He cursed at the useless wood, then walked the girder to get to the next set of catwalks.

I crossed another section, trying to keep distance between us. But I was running out of room. There were only two more sections before I came to the outer wall of the building.

Bror was a big man. He couldn't move as quickly as I could along the beams and catwalks. If I could get him to come after me instead of upending the catwalks, I might be able to get around him.

"You can kill as many of us as you want, but she won't let you touch her," I shouted at him. "She hasn't yet, has she? You just get to stand outside the door and listen."

Bror wasn't worried about hiding behind the uprights. He came in a straight line across two sections of boards.

I retreated back across another section, but I realized that I could go no farther. The back wall had no exposed girders. If I took the catwalk back there, I would be stuck in that one place.

Lorraine had gotten away. All I had to do now was play hide and seek (and not get killed) with Bror until the cavalry arrived.

Bror came closer. Now there were only three spaces of catwalk between us. I could see the glisten of sweat on his upper lip.

"Where is she?" He was close enough to realize that Lorraine wasn't anywhere around me.

"She's hidden over in that corner. What's the matter? Can't you see her? Are you some stupid white man who can't see her unless she smiles?" Might as well throw a little race-baiting into the mix.

For a moment he fell for it, peering into the far corner, trying to make her out. Then he shouted, "Bitch! She's not there!" He quickly backtracked across the catwalks. When he got to the open space, he ran to the end of the building facing the road, where he could see my car and phone in the grass.

I heard a shot, then a second shot. He didn't fire again. I gathered he didn't need to.

I felt a hollow queasiness in my stomach. For a moment, I considered just letting go and falling. I could take away the pleasure of the hunt. But I knew that I might survive the fall, and have no choice but to lie broken and battered, waiting for him to slowly finish me off.

Maybe someone heard the gunshots. He was a big man; not all the boards would hold his weight. He might get careless and I might get lucky. If I survived, I could tell Mrs. Drummond that her daughter had wanted to see her again.

Bror appeared in the opening, the late afternoon sun throwing his shadow a long distance. He moved easily, as if he intended to take his time and enjoy himself.

That was okay by me. I saw no reason to hurry.

Bror started crossing the catwalks to get to me. If I wanted to be able to get behind him, I would have to let him come fairly close.

I took a long look at the vertical beam I was standing next to, wondering if I could shimmy down it. It was smooth, no easy handholds. There was also a lot of debris between here and the ground. I could probably do it, but it would be slow, much slower than a bullet.

Bror was making his way to me, no hurry, an easy (and careful) saunter.

I couldn't afford to be careful. To be able to keep him guessing about what I was doing and to have any chance at all of getting behind him, I had to move quickly.

I waited until he was in the middle of a catwalk to make my move.

As quickly as I could, I ran the length of the girder to the other side of the building. From there I managed to cross one catwalk back to him before he realized what I was trying to do.

As I started to step out onto the next catwalk, he fired a warning shot, shooting into the board beneath my feet.

I quickly stepped back, the impact of the bullet sending a

shudder through the board. He'd made his point, nothing as easy as a simple bullet for me, he would shoot the catwalk out from under me first.

I wasn't going to make it easy for him. To put more distance between us, I started to cross back to the wall.

He fired again, shooting into the boards I was walking across. They shook under my feet, a touch of earthquake on this tiny path that kept me suspended in air.

Again he fired. I felt the bile of panic rising in my throat. This time a slow cracking sound followed the bullet's impact.

I scrambled to reach the safety of the steel girder, diving for it as the catwalk collapsed from under me.

I couldn't stop a loud groan as I crashed into the steel. My arms were wrapped around the girder and I had managed to get one leg over it, but my other leg and lower torso were still dangling.

As I struggled to right myself, I could hear his laughter. He was enjoying this, the hunter toying with his prey.

My ankle hurt, but I couldn't pay any attention to it. Slowly I hauled myself up, getting my weight centered on the steel beam. I wondered if I could chance standing or if that would just make me an easier target for him.

Then I had an idea.

I slowly tried to stand, but fell back on my knees as I attempted to put weight on my left leg. My accompanying moan was answered by a guttural chortle from Bror.

I crawled on my hands and knees to the supporting beam, so I could use my arms to pull myself up. I did it slowly and painfully, letting my useless leg dangle.

Bror was getting closer, so confident that I was helpless, he even put his gun in his waistband. He was close enough that I could see the glittering delight in his eyes. The hunter and his wounded quarry.

He was crossing the last catwalk, the one that would bring him to the girder that I was standing on. He walked slowly, savoring the climax of the hunt.

Then he was twenty feet away from me, standing on the same steel beam as I was. All that was between us was the supporting upright that I was using to keep myself standing.

That's when I turned and ran back on the girder to the nearest catwalk. I sprinted across it, then across the next one.

"What? You were hurt," he bellowed in surprise.

"Fear, the miracle cure," I shouted back. But I didn't pause. Other than a few bruises, my leg still worked. The ankle would probably be swollen tomorrow, if I had a tomorrow, but I would worry about that then. A confident hunter is an easily fooled hunter.

I heard the crack of a pistol shot, but I was a moving target and he was trying to shoot me through the upright supports. I'm not as easy to get as Lorraine, you bastard, I thought.

He probably realized that, because I heard the sound of his heavy footsteps echoing across the catwalks.

I was on the catwalks spanning the far side of the building. Bror was more in the center. Because he had left only the one center catwalk in the first section, I would have to cut back to the middle to be able to get out. I had a good lead on him, but I didn't know if I had that good a lead. Not to mention that it would give him an easier shot at me. The devil is always in the details.

The sound of our running feet filled the building. That and my ragged breath.

One more section. When I crossed that, I would have to turn and head for the center.

As I cornered from the catwalk onto the girder that would take me there, I chanced a hurried glance back at him. My lead and his slowness had put me several sections in front of him. I couldn't move as quickly on the girder—it was narrower and I had to swing around the upright beams—but I was still going to beat Bror to the finish line.

I had one big advantage over him. I didn't really want to fall, but considering that risking a tumble or facing a much worse fate were my only choices, I had dispensed with caution as I ran across the narrow walkways.

Bror was bigger, heavier, and he didn't want to fall.

As I stepped onto the final catwalk, he fired.

I don't know if he intended it or not, but the bullet missed me and instead hit the wood in front of me.

The next bullet told me that that was his intent. It slammed into the far end of the catwalk, causing it to shudder and shimmy and move just enough so that my next step slid off the edge of the board.

I went down, landing hard on my knee and grabbing with my hands to keep myself from falling.

"You thought you could get away from me," he sneered. "You stupid bitch."

I looked back over my shoulder at him. He was still a few sections back, but his gun made the distance irrelevant.

I only had one plan left. If he wanted me, he was going to have to come out onto this board and get me. Already weakened by his bullets, it might not hold our combined weight. If I threw myself to one side, I could probably flip it. Beyond that I could only hope fate would let me survive the fall and damage him enough that he couldn't come after me.

He fired again, sending up a shower of splinters in front of me.

He's too focused on getting me and not thinking clearly, I realized. If he destroys this catwalk, he's going to be stuck back there. He might be able to move one of the other ones, but even as big and strong as he was, it would be hard to balance that much heaviness from one end to get the other end across the space.

The board he had just shot gave a groaning crack, then sagged under me.

I carefully shifted my weight onto the two remaining boards, but the heft of the broken third was pulling them down.

I again glanced back at Bror. He was standing two sections

behind me, a cruel smile on his face. His grin widened when he saw me looking at him. I couldn't move forward and I couldn't move backward, and one bullet from his gun could stop me from ever moving again.

"They all opened their doors to me," he said, unable to resist boasting before he killed his quarry. "They thought I was from Suzanna. Then it was easy, a choke hold until they blacked out, then a tight gag because I knew they would scream. I bound their hands and feet and waited until they were aware.

"Then I touched them in all the places she had touched them. I took back all the pleasure they had stolen from her."

"You're sick," I spat back at him. I had no interest in his confession, in the twisted reasoning that allowed him to make the choices he had. It wasn't really a confession, but gloating in his prowess and an attempt to add to my fear. "This is how you protect Suzanna? With murder and torture? I thought you said she needed you to protect her like your mother. Would you give your mother murder and torture for a present?"

"As long as Suzanna doesn't act like my mother, she's safe. I'll protect her. Women who behave are protected. My father protected my mother as long as she behaved. And when she didn't . . . he taught her a lesson she never forgot."

"A lesson you'll teach Suzanna?"

"She knows. She knows what my mother did and what happened to her. The women didn't bother my father, he liked to watch. They don't bother me. Women don't count. But when she threw herself at other men, she had to be punished."

"Your mother?" I wasn't sure what he was referring to. Perhaps he wasn't, either. "Punished? Punished how?"

"In the way she deserved. She wore tight dresses, low-cut, she thought I was sleeping, but I saw the way she let other men touch her. Yes, she thought I was sleeping, but I snuck to the telephone and called my father, told him to come home. He did. He saw them. He made sure no man would ever touch her breasts again."

"He mutilated her?"

"She deserved it. She never reported him. Lied in the hospital. Said some strangers attacked her. Her left breast was almost cut off, but she never said he did it to her. She knew she deserved what happened. She became the kind of wife she should have been all along. She never argued with him after that."

"She was terrified of him. That's what shut her up."

"Then the terror was good for her," Bror shouted at me. "She learned her place. Women that behave are protected. Women that don't, get what they deserve. It's their choice."

Bror had chosen to bring us here. What he did next would be his choice. I hoped it was a bad one.

"You don't protect Suzanna. You just terrorize her. She knows she has to get away from you," I taunted him. "The police will find out you're the killer, and that will expose everything she wants hidden. She'll be more than happy to see you get locked up, to put all the blame on you. She told me she has to get rid of you."

"Liar! You fool," he shouted. "I use her. I've been toying with her. Killing her lovers. Bringing her the papers with their names in it. Telling her I talked to the police about it, so I knew exactly how they were killed. The cutting of the breasts."

"She's not going to want a demented killer near her. Soon she's going to get rid of you."

"No! You're stupid. She has no choice. She's mine and she knows it. She's played the game with me. Teasing me, letting me know she wants a real man."

"She laughs at you. The only way you touch women is with knives. She's pretty kinky, but I don't think she finds that a turn-on."

"Shut up! You have to listen to me, but I'm not listening to you. You don't matter. Suzanna belongs to me."

"She'll never let you touch her. And after today, she'll want nothing to do with you," I threw back at him.

"You don't know what you're talking about! You're wrong. Stupid and wrong!"

"She's never let you touch her," I hammered at him. "I didn't even have to ask her to take off her shirt. She just did it for me. She was so ready, she wasn't wearing a bra. She ever not worn a bra for you? Protect her? If she really wanted you, don't you think she'd at least let you touch her?"

Then he made the wrong choice. Goaded by my taunts, he came toward me.

But the catwalk he stepped out on was the one he had backed off earlier. Then, he had been slow and deliberate, taking his time. Now his focus was on me, on avenging my mocking him that I had so easily touched Suzanna's breasts and he would never even see them. In his anger, he had forgotten his caution. He strode onto the boards before he realized that they were rotten and crumbling and would not hold him.

Even as the catwalk buckled beneath him, he made one more attempt to revenge himself on me, aiming and firing as he was falling.

But the collapsing boards were too unstable for him to aim with any accuracy and the bullet went wide. The recoil from the shot only hastened his fall.

He disappeared from my view. On my stomach even with my head angled uncomfortably back, I couldn't look to see where he had fallen or how far.

The rotten catwalk hit something and a cloud of dust rose under me.

It hadn't ended yet and there was no guarantee that it would end well. My position was still very precarious. It would not be hard for me to join Bror in his free fall.

I slowly started to inch myself to the safety of the solid floor. But the two boards with their dangling third and my weight had a chancy balance. The far end of the catwalk was only a few inches over the girder supporting it. As I tried to shimmy toward that end, my movement caused the boards to slip.

I stopped. Maybe I should go back, I thought, and try to push the catwalk more firmly in place. But I was a little over halfway across, and going the other direction was no guarantee that the boards wouldn't slide off the edge and fall.

I finally realized that I had no choice but to keep going. Again I started to move forward, but the boards gave an ominous groan under me.

"Don't move."

I looked up at the voice. "Lorraine!" I yelled, causing the catwalk to groan again.

"Don't move," she again cautioned.

She started taking off her clothes. I stared at her in amazement until she knotted the leg of her pants with the sleeve of her jacket.

Good thing this is autumn and not summer, I thought, as she pulled off her sweater and added it to the rope of clothes.

Then she sat down on the lip of the solid floor, bracing her feet on the girder in front of her.

"I'm going to toss one end to you. Don't take it or do anything until I get set," Lorraine instructed.

She threw the sweater end to me. It was, I was pleased to note, solid cotton, not some fake synthetic. Then she wrapped the pants leg end around her wrist and lay back so that the pivot point for my weight would be directly in line with her braced legs, not above them as it would be if she had remained sitting.

"I'm ready," she called.

I grabbed the sweater. The boards shuddered under me. Half-crawling, half-pulling myself with her clothes, I headed for the safety of the floor.

The boards groaned and started to twist, the mass of the broken board pulling them askew.

I reached the jacket.

Suddenly the middle board gave way. It had been weakened by a bullet and when my weight hit that unsound spot, it cracked.

"Keep going," Lorraine encouraged.

I wasn't planning on doing anything else.

The remaining board trembled, as if deciding whether to hold to its solitary post or join its broken brothers.

It wasn't wide enough for me to crawl. I was pulling myself along it, hoping that Lorraine could hold on.

I made it to the leg of the pants.

The board twisted off the lip that had been holding it. In the penultimate moment before it fell, I gave myself one final push, thrusting forward and trying not to get caught in the buckling debris.

For a moment, I was dangling in air. Then my hand came in contact with the girder that Lorraine was braced against. I realized that she was pulling me up as I was climbing her jeans.

My shoulders were above the edge. My torso and hips, then I had a knee on the girder and I was crawling over Lorraine.

I was safe.

I rolled off of her, reveling in the feel of rough, dirty concrete under me.

"I am so glad that I got those dumbbells for my last birthday," Lorraine said.

"Me and you both," I agreed as we sat up. "I've been a lesbian since I was fifteen, but I don't think I've ever been so happy to see a woman take off her clothes."

"Glad to assist. But I'm freezing."

I took one knot and she undid the other, then Lorraine put her pants, sweater, and jacket back on.

"I thought he shot you," I said as she was dressing.

"He shot at me. Inner-city girl like me knows that when bullets fly, you go down and you stay down. I clutched my chest, hit the car, rolled down the trunk, flopped around enough to get my head and upper body under the car, then didn't move."

"And he thought he'd killed you or at least put you out of action until he finished with me."

"Yeah, good thing you kept him busy up here and he didn't have a chance to check the body." She finished tying her shoes and straightened up.

"Let's get out of here," I suggested.

She started to nod, then gasped, staring at something behind me.

I spun around to look.

Bror hadn't fallen very far. The dust had finally cleared enough for us to see him.

He was alive. His hands were flailing, reaching for something to grasp on to. But there was nothing. He was suspended in mid-air, held in place only by the rusted pipe that he was impaled on.

"Oh, my God," Lorraine whispered.

I took her by the shoulders and turned her away from him.

"Did you call anyone?" I asked.

"Yeah . . . yeah. Nine-one-one, but I couldn't give them an exact location."

"Let's get away from here," I said, leading her back to the stair-case.

There was nothing we could do for Bror. We had no way even to get to where he was suspended.

"He's going to die there, isn't he?" Lorraine asked as we went down the stairs.

"I don't know," I answered. "It's likely. I don't know if it's possible to get him down before blood loss and shock take his life."

She didn't reply.

As we made our way across the empty lot to the road, Lorraine kept her eyes resolutely focused on the grass under her feet.

Will I turn to salt if I look back? I wondered. But I did, half-hoping I couldn't see him.

He was there, like some giant insect, the flailing of his arms and legs noticeably weaker. No, he would not survive this.

When we got to my car, I asked, "Did you call for the police or an ambulance?"

"Actually, I got out that there was an emergency and that I wasn't quite sure where we were, when he started shooting. I lost the phone in my fake death scene."

"Where is it?"

"I don't know. I lost it."

"Oh."

We searched for the phone. Lorraine never looked up, never chanced that she might see the building.

The phone was hidden in the shadow of the front tire.

Just as I picked it up, I saw an ambulance on the road that intersected with this one. I stepped away from my car, waving my hands over my head to get their attention.

It worked. They turned this way and pulled in behind my car. A man and a woman got out.

"What's the problem?" the man asked.

I pointed to the building. "He fell."

The woman saw him first. "Oh, sweet Jesus, God Almighty," she exclaimed.

"Oh, fucking hell," he added as soon as he caught sight of Bror. "Call the fire department. We gotta get a ladder in there. Oh, that poor bastard ain't gonna make it."

"You related?" the woman asked us, a subtle chastisement of her partner's assessing his chances.

"No," I said for both of us. "Don't really know him at all."

The man loped across the lot to get a better look at what they were facing. The woman got on the radio to call for the needed backup. Then she went to join her partner at the building.

I looked at Lorraine and said, "I'm a great believer in doing my civic duty . . . but I don't think we need to stay here."

"Won't the police need to question us?"

"Yes, they will. We won't get out of that. But we don't need to do it right this minute."

"If I get arrested, I'm blaming it all on you," she said as she got in the car.

I gave the derelict building one final glance. Bror was still feebly moving, as if he knew that it was futile, his hands would never touch anything again, but even that useless motion was better than nothing at all.

I turned away. Off in the distance I heard sirens coming this way.

As I started the car, I dialed Joanne's number. Nobody noticed us leaving.

No, I didn't plan on getting out of talking to the cops. But I decided it would be better to talk to her directly than to some beat cop, who would tell his sergeant, who would tell a few other people, until they finally figured out that we should be talking to Joanne and Hutch. Actually, by leaving the scene I was saving the taxpayers a fair bit of police overtime.

"You heard?" she said when she picked up her phone. She had caller ID.

"Heard?" I repeated.

"We had to let Frances Gilmore go. No evidence, good lawyer."

"She didn't do it. Bror, Suzanna Forquet's personal servant, is the killer."

Joanne was silent for just a second, then asked, "Where is he? Is he still free?"

"No, he's not free. He'll never be free again." And I told her the whole story.

"I'm glad it was him killed and not you," was her comment when I finished. "I'm going to get a search warrant for his quarters and Ms. Forquet is coming in for questioning. Do you think she set him up?"

I paused for a moment before answering. "Not directly. I don't think she knew that he was killing her ex-lovers. But she used him."

"That's not a crime under the Louisiana penal code," Joanne said. "But she's going to have to answer a lot of questions."

"Just a crime of the heart. How does love go so far awry?"

"I leave that to the philosophers. I just arrest criminals when I get the chance."

We said good-bye and I put the phone back in its charger.

"How are you doing?" I asked Lorraine.

"I'm alive and that bastard's dead. Better than the reverse." She paused for a second, then asked, "He killed Georgia, didn't he?"

"Yes, he did."

"That fucking bastard. You know, Georgia introduced me to Abby."

We were both silent until we got back across the river.

"Do you want me to take you home?" I asked.

She looked at her watch. "Damn, Abby's still at work. She's a nurse midwife, so she keeps odd hours. She once told me that when people die they clutch their genitals and ask for their mother. Why don't you take me to see my mother? It's been ten years already."

Lorraine gave me directions. The address I had for her mother was still the same address where Lorraine grew up.

When we got there, we spent a few minutes dusting ourselves off and combing our hair before climbing up the steps to the porch.

She stopped a foot away from the front door. She wiped the back of her hand across her eyes, trying to fight back the torrent of emotions she was feeling.

"I'm scared," she whispered to me.

"It's okay," I said.

"You do it."

I stepped around her and knocked on the door.

"Who's there?" Mrs. Drummond called from inside.

"Mrs. Drummond?" I answered. "It's Michele Knight, the detective you hired."

"Just a moment," she replied. I heard locks being unlocked.

I stood aside, so she could see her daughter as she opened the door.

"Mama?" Lorraine said in a high, thin voice, the most scared tone I'd heard from her all afternoon.

Tears and a smile spread across Mrs. Drummond's face. "Oh, honey! Oh, my baby! You're home! You've come home!"

And Lorraine Drummond had come home. They stood on the porch hugging and crying for several minutes before Mrs. Drummond thought to go inside out of the cold.

I took my leave then. They had ten years to catch up on. Another case closed.

Mine was the only one left to solve.

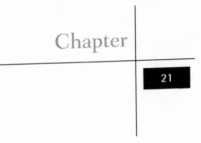

Chapter

21

As I left the Drummonds, the day was slipping into evening. I glanced at my watch. It was only six P.M.

I went home. There were no lights on, so I knew Cordelia wasn't here. "Goddamn it, Alex," I muttered as I let myself in. "House calls are one thing, but house marathons are a bit much." I wanted Cordelia here and her arms around me and I was peevishly cursing Alex for dragging her away.

I knew I was being a bit unreasonable, I-want-what-I-want-and-I-want-it-now, but only the cats were here to listen to my churlish grumblings and the cans of cat food I was dumping in their food bowls would bribe them into silence. Don't tell on the one who feeds you the most.

Then I went in the living room and was about to call Alex and demand the return of my lover when the phone rang.

It was Cordelia. "Micky. You're home."

"You're at the hospital," I said as I noticed the background noise. The Sayers residence did not sound like a hospital cafeteria.

"I think the only way to silence my beeper is to dump it in the toilet. I've had to get three people admitted today, including a friend's brother who went off the deep end. We can't figure out if he had a psychotic break or if it's drugs. She was so upset, I had to give her a tranquilizer. And . . . it goes on. The bottom line is, I'm stuck here for at least another hour or so."

"I'm sorry. I've had a . . . somewhat interesting day, too." I heard a beeper go off on her end of the line. It was either hers or that of someone standing right next to her.

"Oh, hell," she said, confirming that it was hers. The beeping stopped. "What about tonight? And meeting your mother? I'll try to get out of here as fast as I can."

"I don't know. I don't know about tonight. I need to take a quick shower and change. Then I guess head over to the gallery."

"Don't wait for me."

"No, I won't. Why don't we just plan on that? Don't kill yourself trying to get away."

"Give me the address. I'll go by when I'm done."

"It's okay if you don't," I said. "This may have nothing to do with my mother and I'll only stay two minutes. Or . . . or she may want nothing to do with me and I'll only stay a minute and a half."

"If it's not too late, I'll drive by, and if I see your car, I'll go in. And Micky? I hope it works out. I love you very much."

"I know. I do know that. And I love you." I gave her the address and said good-bye.

As I was taking my shower, I realized that maybe it was just as well that I was going by myself. Cordelia could pick up the pieces afterward, if need be. Did I really want to meet my mother and introduce her to my lesbian lover all in one night?

I got out of the shower.

I remembered all too well the years when I felt an aching loneliness that I desperately tried to fill with alcohol and sex that was merely physical. Anything to dispel that I was solitary and adrift. I had friends, but no parents or lover or children, none of the bonds that can only be broken with great force. How desperately we look for love. Sometimes we never find it. Bourbon St. Ann settling for a semblance of a mother. Suzanna and her quick love affairs.

Cordelia couldn't meet my every need. We argued, struggled, but we forgave each other and loved each other. Sometimes I think it's an astonishing miracle when we love someone who loves us.

I put on a pair of pants, then rejected them, agonized over earrings, worrying about the impression I would make.

I finally decided on my best black pants, a light gray V-neck sweater and small silver earrings. I didn't want my mother to think I was a flashy dresser.

Then there was nothing more to do, no change of clothes that would make me more acceptable, I was as showered and deodorized as I could get. I was either good enough or I wasn't.

As a last-minute thought, I took the picture of my mother holding me and the final card she had sent me, the one I found in the garage room, talismans to prove that I had once been deeply connected to this woman.

I glanced at my watch. It was a little after eight. What if she leaves early? I suddenly panicked. Then I reminded myself she may not even be there. Cousin Rosemary might have been mixed up, and maybe the newspaper clipping meant nothing.

I drove up to Rampart Street to avoid the French Quarter—it would be clogged and slow on a Saturday night—then headed for the Warehouse District, where the gallery was located.

I parked about half a block away, in the first open spot I saw. I sat in my car for several minutes, trying to think of what I might say to her. But there were so many things I wanted to say to her, I couldn't pull anything useful out of the jumble. I could see myself saying anything from "Fuck you, you left me," to "I love you."

I couldn't sit here all night. I looked at my watch. It was eight-thirty. For a moment I considered leaving. Then I took the picture out of my jacket pocket. I looked at the woman who looked so much like me. I put the picture back in my jacket and got out of the car.

The LA Gallery was brightly lit up, its sign a hot pink neon LA over a green neon outline of the state of Louisiana (abbreviated LA).

The formerly empty windows now had paintings in them.

I stopped in front of the first one and stared. It was large, taking up most of the window.

It was a vast expanse of marsh, the picture defying the flatness of the canvas to give the feeling of great depth. At the edge of that horizon, standing tall and stark against it, was the skeleton tree. I felt like I was looking at a memory.

I forced myself to turn away from the picture, wondering if I was reading things into it that weren't there. It was the view from my father's shipyard looking off into the bayous.

I turned back to the painting, determined to see only what was there. But it still held that feeling of both possibility and loss, as if the people who had lived in this place had left some piece of their soul on that landscape.

On the door was a big placard with the name of the artist, HELEN NIKATOS, my mother's maiden name.

Several people left the gallery, but she wasn't one of them. Though all I had was a picture of her from about thirty years ago, I knew I would recognize her when I saw her. She'd look like me, only sixteen years older.

I wondered if she would know it was me. She had last seen me as a little girl with long hair in pigtails. Could she see the child inside the adult I had become?

I again thought of turning away, running from the risk that she might reject me one last time, but I wanted to see her other paintings.

I took one last glance at the painting, then went up the stairs into the gallery.

It was a large space, built on two levels. A number of columns broke up the area. The upper level was about four steps up; on its walls were some smaller paintings, a desk to conduct the business of selling paintings, and a table holding wine and soft drinks for the opening.

I didn't immediately look for my mother. There were still a fair number of people about. Instead I took my time and looked at the paintings. Some were city scenes, others of the bayous. They all seemed to possess that luminous quality of space and depth that indicated these were places where people had lived and loved and passed on.

There was another one of the skeleton tree, this time painted with lowering thunderclouds overhead. But over the tree, a shaft of sunlight had broken through the clouds, bathing the bare branches in golden light.

I remembered that same scene. The wind whipping my hair in my face and the close crack of thunder. I was running from where I had been playing on the dock for the shelter of the house when my mother had turned me back to face the marsh. "Look," she said, "the tree is pulling light from the sky." We stood for a moment, watching that golden glow against a dark day, then the sheets of rain let loose, catching us before we made it to the sheltering porch.

As we stood shivering and soaking wet, my father had commented on us not having enough sense to come in out of the rain. My mother tried to explain that singular moment that had kept us in the rain, that perfect alignment of cloud and light. But he hadn't been able to understand why anyone would get drenched just to see a shaft of sunlight.

"I can't decide, Gerald," a woman said to the man beside her. "I rather like this one," she continued, pointing at the painting that I was standing in front of (trying to stand in front of; they were doing a good job of edging me out). "It goes well with the colors in our living room. But I also like that city one."

"Whichever you want, Martha," he said.

This one's mine, I felt like saying. A few days ago, Cordelia had asked me what I wanted for Christmas. I had just found it. And I knew I couldn't let the supercilious couple take the painting of my memory just because it matched their living room.

Cordelia can afford this, I reminded myself. And this will be the first time I've ever asked her to spend a large amount of money on me.

As I turned away from the picture, I saw her. She was tall. We had the same hair, though hers was shot through with silver. She was standing in the upper section, talking to several people. They moved on and another group took their place. In the brief interval, she started to glance around the gallery.

I turned away, not wanting her to see me staring at her. I looked again at the painting, afraid that Gerald and Martha would decide to buy this one.

"It's one of my favorites, too," said a woman who came up beside me.

"It is . . . powerful," I replied. "Are you going to purchase it?"

She shook her head. "No, I'm Nina, Helen's manager. I already have a few of her paintings. And limited wall space."

"Who would I see about buying it?"

"Me, for one."

"Uh . . . I don't have the cash on hand . . . but I want this painting."

"That's okay. We'll give you a few days to cough it up." She put a SOLD sticker on the price tag. "Have you met the artist yet?"

"I did . . . but it was a long time ago."

"Are you related?" she asked.

"Why? Do we look alike?" I played dumb.

"You could just about be her sister."

I gave a nervous laugh and shook my head, then said, "Maybe. I grew up in a place that looked like that." I gave a nod toward the painting.

"I've never been out to the bayou. She keeps promising to take me."

Only a few people were still here: Gerald and Martha, not realizing that a decision had been made for them; a few other people on the upper lever who were talking to the artist; her manager; and me.

"Why don't you go on up and introduce yourself?" she said before heading over to the beckoning Gerald. "I'm sure Helen would like to know who purchased this painting." She left to tell Gerald that he was buying Martha the city scene.

I turned back to look at the painting I had just bought. I could bring Cordelia tomorrow to take care of the money end of it. It would be stunning over the mantel in our living room. Then I wondered what it would be like to stare each day at this moment from my childhood.

Now only Martha and Gerald, Nina, and a woman I guessed to be the gallery owner were still here. The two of them were dickering with Martha and Gerald.

My mother was alone, pouring herself a glass of wine.

I had to decide now. Either to leave or to talk to her.

She looked tired. I wondered if the loss and solitude that so many of her paintings evoked was something that she carried deep within herself. Was I a part of it?

Was it possible it was her lost daughter that she mourned?

It seemed such a long distance to cross the floor, my steps slow and hesitant.

I mounted the steps to where she stood.

She looked up as she heard my approaching footsteps. A slightly puzzled look crossed her face, as if she recognized that we looked alike, but knew we couldn't be related. It's a shock to see yourself in a stranger's eyes.

I felt disjointed for a moment at seeing her eyes level with mine. As a child I had always looked up to her. Now I was staring directly at her.

"Hello," she said. "I'm Helen Nikatos." It was the voice I'd heard read my bedtime stories and point me to the light in the sky.

She held out her hand to shake. "And you are?"

Who was I? Her daughter? That was over twenty years ago. A distant memory? A woman you don't know—your daughter grown up?

I reached to take her hand, and said, "Michele Robedeaux."

We both stopped, our hands outstretched but not touching, the power of that name and what it meant riveting us both in place.

Suddenly she said, "No!" a look of shock and anger spreading across her features.

"I don't want—" I started to say.

"No! Why are you doing this to me?" she cut me off.

"Helen?" her manager came up the stairs.

"I just wanted to see you, that's all," I said. "I don't want anything—"

"Who are you really?" she demanded, her hand no longer outstretched, but crossed across her chest like a barricade.

"Your . . . daughter. I am . . . your daughter," I said softly, shaken by her anger.

"No," she repeated harshly. "My daughter was killed in a traffic accident when she was ten years old."

Now it was my turn to feel shock and anger. "No! I survived!" I turned to the desk and grabbed one of the phones that was on it. I dialed the number that I still couldn't forget.

It rang several times before Aunt Greta picked it up.

"Hello?" she said, her voice suspicious of anyone who would call after nine P.M.

"Aunt Greta, it's Michele."

"Michele?" she was surprised to hear my voice. "What do you want?"

"Did you tell my mother that I was killed in the accident?"

"Michele, it's late for you to be calling about—"

I cut in and asked again, "Did you tell her that I was killed?"

"I was getting ready for bed and I don't appreciate—"

"Answer me!" I demanded, beginning to lose control.

"Don't use that tone with me, young lady."

Aunt Greta wasn't going to reply. But I knew the answer.

Suddenly another voice cut in. My mother had picked up one of the other phones. "Greta. This is Helen. Did my daughter survive the wreck?"

"Helen!" Aunt Greta exclaimed, clearly shocked to hear her voice again.

"Did she survive?" she repeated.

"You have to understand," Aunt Greta sputtered. "We thought it better for everyone—"

Helen cut her off. "You thought it was better for me to believe my daughter was dead?"

"For everyone, not just you," Aunt Greta retorted. "We didn't want you coming back. We knew you couldn't raise the child, not a suitable mother. It was better this way."

"You goddamn bitch!" I screamed at her, so angry my hands were shaking.

"Michele!" Aunt Greta scolded.

I cursed myself for giving her the chance to berate me instead of trying to defend the indefensible.

"It is late," she continued. "I do need to go to bed."

"And when you wake in the morning, look in the mirror, Greta, and you will see evil. For only evil could leave a mother in grief for so long and feel no remorse. Not even your God will leave that unpunished."

Aunt Greta had enough of a sense of fear to gasp at Helen's curse.

I slammed down the receiver. I wanted to hurl the phone as far as I could, but I held it in check by telling myself that it would have no effect on Aunt Greta. Or Uncle Claude, or any of the others who had created the lie and held it in place. Twenty years ago, to have heard my mother curse Aunt Greta as she just had would have saved my soul. Today? Did it matter?

It did, I realized, but it was a bitter hammering-in of what I had lost. My mother would have stood up to Aunt Greta; what I desperately needed had been possible.

I stood with my eyes closed, gripping the edge of the desk with my hands to keep them still. They had told her that I was dead, that I had died in the wreck that had killed my father. That was why her letters stopped abruptly and why Aunt Greta tried to prevent me from writing her.

I felt a hand on my shoulder. I turned to face my mother. Her face was a mask of anguish. Tears streamed down her cheeks. Twenty years, twenty years of thinking her child was dead, when I was alive. From pictures of a girl of ten to a woman of thirty-three. Everything between that was gone.

My mother embraced me. We said nothing. When I had last held her, I could barely reach all the way about her, my fingers just touching. Now I easily encircled her with my arms.

Her hair was shot through with gray, and mine had the first beginnings of its coming gray. The years were gone.

"Oh, my daughter," she said, brushing the hair off my face with a motherly gesture. "Nina, I have my daughter back." Her voice started to crack.

We loosened our clasp. I quickly wiped my eyes. She looked at the grown woman who was her daughter. And I looked at the woman I hadn't seen since I was five years old.

"You survived the wreck?" she asked. "And went to live with Greta and Claude?"

I nodded. "Yeah, when I was ten. I so much wanted you to come . . ." And save me.

"If I had known . . ." her voice trailed off. "If. . ."

"I have some questions . . . a lot of questions," I stumbled out. Could I ask this stranger? I wanted twenty years of knowing her.

"Of course you must have questions. I will answer as best I can."

"Is it okay . . . here?" Gerald and Martha were still trying to decide and they had the gallery owner in tow, but they were at the far side of the building and oblivious to our saga.

"I don't hide anything from Nina," she said, who was the only person to overhear us.

"Who was my father?"

"They never told you?"

"No. Was it Lee?"

"No. It was Claude."

I stared at her.

She continued, "He was, of course, already married to Greta. I used to baby-sit when they would come to the shipyard to visit Lee. One night Claude drove me home. . . ."

"He raped you?"

"I didn't fight . . . there were no bruises. He cried the rest of the way home, apologized for what he'd done. He was drunk."

"Uncle Claude raped you?" I still couldn't quite come to terms with it. "I never knew he was . . . that kind of man."

"He offered to divorce Greta and marry me. But they already had two children and she would have fought the divorce. I think he would have welcomed an excuse to get out of that marriage. Since Claude couldn't do the right thing, Lee stepped in and did it."

"Did you want to marry him?" I asked.

"I . . . it was different then. I was pregnant and sixteen. My father threatened to throw me out unless I got married. Lee was the only one . . . who could offer."

"Did . . . did you care for him at all? He always treated me like his child and loved me. I guess I want to know if there was ever love between you."

"Lee was a kind, gentle man. I respected him. And cared for him. But there was no passion between us. I . . . endured his touch."

"Is that why you left?"

She didn't answer immediately. She and Nina exchanged a look that told me that Nina knew the answer to this. Finally she said, "I fell in love with someone else. I thought we were being discreet, but . . . Lee noticed. And we both knew that our marriage would collapse, so we agreed to separate. He would not let me take you with me and he didn't want me visiting you until you were much older."

"Because you found love outside your forced marriage? His brother raped you, but he wouldn't let me see you because you dared love someone else?" I again felt anger at all the adult decisions that had ripped apart my life.

"Remember this was twenty-eight years ago. Things were very different back then."

"Yeah, rape is okay, but adultery gets you banished."

"You need to tell her," Nina said softly.

She and Nina again exchanged another look. Helen slowly took a sip of wine. I heard the sound of the door opening and Gerald and Martha making a noisy exit.

Finally she said, "Lee would not let me see you because the person I fell in love with . . . was a woman."

Until she said it, the idea had never entered my head. Then it made perfect sense. It was the only thing that would. A custody battle would have been impossible for her to win. My father—Lee, not Claude; I would never think of Claude as my father—could have cut her off completely and she would have had no recourse. It also explained why no one had told Helen that I was alive. They weren't about to let me go off and live with my lesbian mother. It also explained, in part, why Aunt Greta hated me so much. I was her husband's bastard child and he had been willing to divorce her to marry my mother, who turned out to be lesbian.

I must have sat in a stunned silence for a full minute.

"Nina and I are lovers," she said quietly, as if afraid to let the silence stretch too far.

"We've been together for seventeen years," Nina added.

We were interrupted by the sound of footsteps coming up the stairs.

I glanced up to see Cordelia.

"Micky?" she said. "I saw your car."

She must have come in when Gerald and Martha were leaving.

"Hey, guess what?" I said to her.

"Yes?"

"My mother's a dyke." Okay, it was over the top, but I was beyond polite and genteel at this point.

"What?" Cordelia said, though she had clearly heard me. She was somewhat surprised at both the information and my delivery of it. But she recovered enough to say—and this is one of the reasons I love her, because she is capable of this kind of thing— "Don't worry. Her daughter's a dyke, too."

They got their minute of stunned silence.

Then I introduced Cordelia.

As they were shaking hands, the abandoned child in me returned. Where the hell were you when I was eighteen? I wanted to demand. When I was struggling with being queer—perverted? And fucking away my loneliness. When a mother . . . a mother who was a lesbian . . . could have made such a difference. But she hadn't been there.

Those years were gone.

My mother and I looked at each other. She took my hand in hers, as if feeling the size and weight of it, the startling difference between the hand of the child she had last held and this foreign, adult grasp.

"Michele," she said, as if trying to fit her child's name onto the woman in front of her. "My daughter . . . I want your childhood back, I want . . . all those years . . ." She trailed off.

But those years were gone.

Chapter

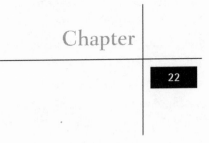

22

I was doing some last-minute errands, getting enough cat food for a cat-sitter to survive a week of finicky eating. Cordelia and I were going to spend Christmas in New York with my mother and Nina. Cordelia had insisted on it, saying that I had missed too many Christmases with my mother to let another one go by. I was both scared and happy. My mother and I were still struggling with knowing each other. Sometimes I wanted the woman I remembered back, and was angry when I couldn't find her. And, I suspected, at times she wanted the daughter back, not this thirty-three-year-old woman I had become in her absence.

Cordelia loved the painting and decreed that it was a joint present to both of us, rather than a gift from her to me.

As I was waiting in the grocery checkout line, I saw the tabloid. Suzanna and Henri were national news. She, of course, had expressed horror and shock when learning that Bror had been murdering her passing affairs. I wondered if they were real, those tears she cried so copiously for the TV cameras. The murders were grisly enough, but the divorce added a frothy icing to the scandal cake. She was suing him, claiming that he had been having affairs with men and had deliberately exposed her to HIV. If Bourbon St. Ann hadn't already offered himself up as a witness for her side, I was sure he would soon. I wondered how long it would take for them to notice their resemblance. Henri had barricaded himself behind lawyers, but he was losing the media battle. It was hard not to like Suzanna, and the cameras and reporters certainly did. If Henri tested HIV negative, he might win, but Danny, legal eagle that she was, said that that was his only chance.

I had put the file back in Chester's storage garage and decided not to talk to him about it. I didn't think that Suzanna had directed Bror to kill any of the women, but I couldn't call her innocent. When she saw the names of the victims, she had to know that she was involved, that the murderer was either Bror or Henri. Yet she had done nothing. I could not forgive her that. If Sindy and Bourbon St. Ann found the file and discovered that Suzanna was the "rich one" they were looking for, Suzanna would have her own version of the furies—not harpies or flies. They would be the life she had left behind, coming back to claim her.

After leaving the grocery store, there was one more place I wanted to go, before going home to pack.

I drove out to Metairie, to the cemetery.

I placed flowers at Uncle Claude's grave. He would always be an uncle to me, not a father.

Aunt Lottie had told me a few more things—not everything; some of the past was lost and I would never find it. No one thought that Claude, the youngest of the brothers, a bit indulged as the baby in the family, would make a good marriage with the pious and prim Greta Jenkins. But Bayard had shown up within seven months of the wedding date, answering the question of why he went through with marrying her. "They said she trapped him," Aunt Lottie said, "but looks to me that she may have laid the trap but he walked in."

When I was ten, the bastard child of the woman that Uncle Claude had really loved came to live in Aunt Greta's house. So, of course, she had hated me, particularly given how much I looked like my mother.

The decision to lie to me and to my mother had been made, and after enough years had passed, it couldn't be unmade.

"As time when by, I think Claude regretted it more and more, but he didn't know where your mother was or how to find her. I think he lived a life of lost dreams, and he died a broken man with a broken heart," Aunt Lottie said.

It was how I thought of him, a broken man with a broken heart. It was why I put flowers on his grave. Some broken hearts never mend. Even the ones that do mend still carry their scars.